DOWN
FOR THE
COUNT

DOWN
FOR THE
COUNT

BRANDY PELLETIER

Developmental editor: Melanie Yu at Made Me Blush Books

Copy/line editor: Beth Lawton at VB Edits

Cover design: Sarah Hansen, Okay Creations

For the chronically single late bloomers.
I see you. I am you.
Never stop believing in happily ever after.
Our stories are not over.

And to the cougars of the world—get it, babes.

Also by Brandy Pelletier

Between the Lines
Keeping the Score

<u>Lacey Bros:</u>
The Check Down

Author's Note

Dear reader,

Down for the Count is intended for adult readers, ages 18 and up. It contains adult language and explicit sexual scenes, plus a few content warnings I'd like you to be aware of before you read.

This book features a main character with PCOS (polycystic ovary syndrome), a hormonal disorder that affects women of reproductive age. I recognize that PCOS is different for everyone diagnosed with the condition, but some symptoms that are discussed in the story include depression, irregular periods, and possible infertility. I share this condition with Natalie, and I've based her experiences with the disorder on some of my own.

Also, a character suffers an on-page panic attack after receiving shocking news. This is in response to the major plot twist toward the end of the book. I'm going to spoil that plot twist in the next paragraph, so if you'd like to keep it an actual "twist," then skip the next paragraph in italics.

LAST WARNING: spoiler ahead!

[Spoiler: Toward the end of the book, Tucker learns that a one night stand in his past resulted in a pregnancy. Together he and Natalie must navigate this life-changing surprise.]

I hope you love Tucker and Natalie's journey to forever. Happy reading!

Down for the Count Playlist

"Fat Bottomed Girls" | Queen
"The Prophecy" | Taylor Swift
"Wonder" | Shawn Mendes
"Crush" | Billianne
"When I Get My Hands on You" | The New Basement Tapes
"State of Grace" | Taylor Swift
"That Feeling When" | Dagney
"Love the Lonely Out of You" | Brothers Osborne
"Cool Rider" | Michelle Pfeiffer
"Call It What You Want" | Taylor Swift
"#Beautiful" | Mariah Carey, Miguel
"(You Make Me Feel Like) A Natural Woman" | Aretha Franklin
"Fly" | Anna Graves
"Man of Me" | Gary Allan
"Take Me Away" | Morgan Wade
"Alone" | David Pugh
"Banks" | NEEDTOBREATHE
"Queen of the Night" | Hey Violet
"Make You Feel My Love" | JJ Heller
"Heartache Tonight" | Eagles
"Oh, What a World" | Kacey Musgraves
"Your Bones" | Chelsea Cutler

Chapter One

Tucker

“Why are you staring at my sister’s ass?”

My best friend’s voice barely registers as I take in the perfect heart-shaped backside. My mouth has gone dry, making it hard to swallow. The denim hugging this woman’s curves looks like it was painted on by a Renaissance master.

Camden clears his throat next to me.

Still glued to the window overlooking the parking lot, I spare him a glance.

I take in his stance—hands on hips, eyes narrowed—but like a siren calling a wayward sailor, the *Mona Lisa* of asses lures me back in.

The woman stands from where she’s been bent into the trunk of a sedan, hefting a black bag, an action that finally allows his words to penetrate my distracted brain.

“Sister?” My stomach sinks like a boulder as I turn to him again.

He’s still glaring at me, his hazel eyes sparking with annoyance.

“That’s Natalie?”

“Yeah, that’s Natalie.” His voice is a fortress. A stronghold. An impassable mountain.

He crosses his arms, but his eyes soften when he twists back to the window.

I can't help but follow his line of sight.

In addition to the da Vinci-brushed jeans, she's wearing a short-sleeved black shirt and black Adidas. She sweeps her thick brown hair to one side as she settles the bag's strap on her shoulder. When she reaches back into the trunk, I mentally curse the bag that's now resting on one hip, covering half of her denim-covered masterpiece.

Most women would bargain with the devil for an ass like hers. No number of squats or lunges or deadlifts could create an asset so magnificent. I've seen my fair share of great asses, right here in my own gym, high and tight and Spandexed, but hers is the kind of shapely perfection only nature could produce.

Camden huffs a breath heavy enough to fog up the window, once again pulling me out of my stupor. He's watching me now, his eyebrows practically touching the dark blond strands that graze his forehead, his head tilt screaming *Are you effing serious right now?*

Right. I'm a grade-A perv for staring at *this* particular ass.

The one attached to my best friend's sister.

His *older* sister.

I clear my throat and dig deep for a response that will help me save face, but the best I can come up with is "What's she doing back in town?"

He smooths a hand along his stubble-free jaw, his stare burning holes in my face. The look sends a clear message: his sister is off limits.

But he has nothing to worry about. Sure, I might have been *ass-notized* for a moment, but there's no way I'd go there. Cam and I have been best friends since the third day of kindergarten, thanks to what my family has affectionately dubbed the Green Crayon Incident, and apart from my four years at college and the few I spent fighting in Memphis, we've lived in the same zip code since birth.

So yeah, I wouldn't jeopardize my friendship with him over a woman. Especially one he's related to.

He crosses his arms over the Holly Holler Fire Department crest on his navy T-shirt and widens his stance. Although he's a few inches shorter than me and a good thirty pounds lighter, he wouldn't hesitate to kick my ass to defend his sister's honor. Even though they're not particularly close, that's the kind of guy he is.

I roll my eyes at his drawn-out dramatics. "Dude, I didn't know it was Natalie." His answering scowl has me fighting a smile. "I swear."

Shoulders relaxing, he punches my arm. "She's taking over for Wayne for the next couple months." He turns back to the window, and when his sister pulls a second heavy bag from the trunk, he springs into action, smacking my arm on his way to the door.

He calls her name the moment he steps off the curb, and when she spins, the smile that lights up her face hits me square in the solar plexus. It's genuine and joyful and fucking contagious. So much so that I can't stop my lips from stretching into one just as wide.

Cam snags one of her bags and stoops to hug her, and when she tousles his hair, I'm hit with a memory of her doing the exact thing when we were kids. She'd always greet him this way. He'd bunch his shoulders and his cheeks would turn pink, but he secretly loved every scrap of attention she gave him.

The two of us were gearing up for fourth grade when Natalie left Holly Holler to attend college, so he's done a lot of growing up since. She's come back to town here and there for holidays and brief visits over the years, but she and her brother haven't lived in the same place in a while.

I bet Cam's thrilled as hell to get to spend the next few months with her.

No longer under his scrutiny, I study the woman Natalie has become. Perfect ass aside, she's beautiful. But she's always been beautiful to me. Hell yeah, I had a crush on her when I was a kid, and that was way before I even knew what it meant to truly crush on a girl.

Of course, I'd never ever admit that to Cam.

It may be the only secret I've ever kept from the guy who's been like a brother to me since our bikes still had training wheels. Confessing that I used to sweat profusely when she entered the room, back before puberty turned her brother and me into mindless hormone-addled, girl-crazy adolescents, would do me no good.

When the mid-morning sun disappears behind a cloud, a spring breeze glides through the parking lot, and Natalie tucks a wayward strand of hair behind her ear. The shoulder-length toffee-colored locks are several shades darker than her brother's and frame her oval face. She's got a pert button nose, thick, dark eyebrows, and rosy pink lips. Lips that break into a laugh as her brother yammers on. As she swats his arm, I give in and assess her from head to toe once more. She's curvy in all the right places.

And damn it, I wish like hell I hadn't noticed.

Or made this effing appointment.

Cam's deep chuckle grows in volume as he holds the door open and ushers her in.

"She's probably at the pet store right now, splurging on gourmet treats or one of those bougie dog beds, like he doesn't sleep with me every night. He'll be spoiled rotten in a week."

"Let her spoil him," he says, his voice softer than I've heard it in years. "And you. She's missed you."

Natalie bumps him with her shoulder and peers up at him with an affectionate look. "Just her, huh?" There's a vulnerability in her words, like she's worried her younger brother hasn't spared a thought for her absence.

His face falls like he caught that same hint in her tone. His Adam's apple bobs in a hard swallow. "Not just her, Nat."

Her eyes mist over, and she gives him a soft, close-lipped smile.

Watching their interaction makes me feel like a nosy interloper, but it also makes me hella thankful for the bond I share with both of my brothers. Sure, Shaw can be a standoffish grump, but my oldest brother would drop everything in a heartbeat if I needed him. Even when Griff was hours and hours from home, dominating the NFL, he rarely missed a phone call, and when his schedule permitted, catching up with us was a priority. Now that he's playing for our hometown team and has a place an hour away, we see him often, and no one in our family takes that for granted.

After a beat, Natalie sighs. "When my dog becomes too high-class for regular kibble, we know who to blame."

Cam hugs her to his side. "Noted."

Grinning, I cross my arms. "A dog-spoiling mom, huh? I've got one of those, too."

Both siblings swivel my way, and Natalie's hazel eyes narrow before widening in recognition.

"Tucker Lacey?"

Warmth blooms in my chest. "In the flesh."

Cam huffs an annoyed breath.

His sister smiles at me. It's genuine but it doesn't quite reach her eyes. It's not a full-fledged smile like the one she gave Cam in the parking lot.

It's a gauntlet thrown at my feet.

Challenge accepted. I'll coax a real one from her before she leaves.

"You're all grown up," she says, her gaze lingering on the ink on my arms for a beat too long before returning to my face.

Unbidden, inappropriate responses bubble through my brain, but I lock them down. "Happens to the best of us."

She presses her lips together, twisting them like she's holding back, and my grin stretches wider.

Cam, who's still got an arm draped over Natalie's shoulders, takes a step back and checks his smartwatch. "Shoot. I've gotta get over to the square for parade prep. Are you meeting Mom and Dad there after this?"

"Wouldn't miss my first Founders' Day parade in over two decades," she answers, her lips curving up a fraction.

With a nod, he squeezes her shoulder. Then he turns my way. "Just…" His eyes narrow, like he's running through possible directives. Finally, he settles on "Best behavior, Tucker."

"When am I not on my best behavior?" I goad. If he's going to use my full name, then he's earned a ribbing. I can count on both hands the number of times he's used it in the past twenty-six years. It's always *Tuck*. Or *dumbass* when I'm exceptionally brilliant.

"You know what I mean," he grits out.

Natalie darts a look at me, then her brother. "What—"

"Here's this." He sets the second bag at her feet, cutting her off. "See you in a few." With a smirk, he tousles her brown waves and strides out of the gym.

When the door has shut behind him, I give the woman before me my full attention.

"So," I say, as she smooths a hand over her hair. "You're Shutterbug."

One side of her mouth tilts up. "In the flesh." She reaches across the space between us, confident and professional.

I slide my hand into hers, ignoring how her soft, warm skin heats me the way the bright May sunshine streaming through the windows behind her does.

When Ms. Nancy called a few days ago to inform me that Shutterbug Photography would be taking over while Mr. Wayne recovers from surgery, she failed to mention that Cam's sister owns the company. Her home base is Austin, hundreds of miles from Holly Holler, Arkansas, so there's no way I would have made the connection.

As I release my hold, I resist the urge to flex my hand. Can't stop the shiver that trails down my spine, though.

"I'm sure Mr. Wayne and Ms. Nancy are happy you're here."

She ducks her chin and places a hand on her chest. "I'm the one who's happy to help them out. They mean a lot to me."

That's right. High school Natalie worked as an assistant for Mr. Wayne. With that realization comes one memory after another of her carrying a camera everywhere she went.

She surveys the space, taking in the rows of machines under the gleaming lights and the words painted on the concrete floor by the entrance. "Club Lacey Fitness." When she brings her focus back to me again, I stand a little taller. "This is all yours. It's incredible, Tucker."

My cheeks heat, but I paste on a smile. "It's been my dream for a while."

I squash down the doubt and worry that have become my ever-present partners in this venture. Even more than a year after opening, nerves still churn in my gut just as fiercely as they did the night I showed Griff the business proposal slides I'd created. I sat next to my older brother at our parents' kitchen table, silently praying he would see the value in investing in a small-town gym.

In investing in *me*. The least responsible Lacey in the bunch.

"Why don't we get started?" With a half smile, Natalie pulls an expensive-looking camera from her bag. She fiddles with the buttons on the back, then examines the facility again. "I'll take some preliminaries to get an idea of what kind of lighting I'll need for the actual shoot. Do you know what kind of photos you want for the website?"

As I tell her about the gym and my vision, professional, no-nonsense Natalie aims her camera and takes shot after shot of the main gym space. One lone treadmill is occupied; this place is a ghost town today.

"Saturday mornings are usually a lot busier," I explain as she crouches to get a better angle.

"Cardio can't compete with a parade and funnel cakes." She spares me a glance but quickly returns to her camera. Though her comments are quippy and succinct, there's a layer of sadness in her tone, like a hidden passageway she hopes no one discovers.

Naturally, it piques my interest.

Before I can ruminate on it too much, she returns to her full height and places her bag next to the one at her feet. "Okay, I have what I need from this space. You mentioned training rooms?"

"Uh, yeah. They're this way." I lead her through the main area and down the hallway, past a couple of offices, the staff breakroom, and the locker rooms. On our trek, I search my memories for evidence that Natalie was this quiet when she was younger but come up empty. Truth is, anyone would probably seem quiet when compared to Cam and me back then. Our volume was always fixed on high.

As I step into the dimly lit cavernous space we've set up as a training room, I sweep an arm to the side. "This is my favorite place in the gym."

She snaps a couple shots, then studies the images she's captured, eyes narrowed at the camera with her lips pinched to the side.

God, the urge to make this woman smile, laugh, or, hell, even smirk needles me, like an itch I can't satisfy no matter how much I scratch.

While she works her photographer mojo, I take a deep breath and inhale the rubber and sweat and antiseptic cleaner fumes that permeate the air. This windowless room holds two rings—a traditional square for boxing, and an octagonal cage for mixed martial arts practice. Bags hang in a row from a ceiling beam along the back wall, and a rubber mat covers the concrete floor in the front corner, the teal, gray, and black design coordinating with the gym's color scheme.

The colors I wore every time I stepped into a cage to fight.

Just being near that eight-sided enclosure gets my adrenaline pumping. Eight sides and vertices that hold some of my best *and* worst memories. That ring was a second home to me. Much like rows of soybeans and soil still are for Shaw and green turf is for Griff.

Natalie peers over her shoulder. "Any way to make these lights brighter?"

With a nod, I step back and adjust the dial on the wall, turning it all the way up. "Better?"

"Better." She moves through the space, pausing here and there, methodical and measured and mesmerizing.

The words escape before I can stop them. "I like watching you work. I can tell you're good."

She freezes, then lowers the camera from her face and turns to me, her cheeks pink. I like that, too.

I like that I'm the one who brought that bit of color to her face. Maybe a little too much.

"You might want to wait until you see the pictures before you make that declaration."

Amusement winds through me. "Nah. I'm old enough to recognize a genius at work."

Old enough. Those two words hang heavy in the space between us. I refuse to acknowledge why the hell my brain snuck them into that statement.

Natalie's rosy lips part but then snap closed. Then, with an exhale, she rolls her shoulders. "I think I've got what I need today. It's almost time for the parade, and I promised Mom and James that I'd meet them."

I nod, a tightness constricting my ribs. "Yeah, sure. I'll, uh, walk you out."

On our way to the front, I replay every word we've exchanged today, analyzing each comment for missed opportunities to make her laugh. Or at least smile the way she did when she saw her brother earlier.

I hate leaving behind unfinished business when I step out of the ring.

The good news? She'll be back for the real photo shoot. I've got time to plan, and I'll make damn sure I'm successful then.

At the doors, I snag the bags she left on the floor and ignore her attempt to take them from me. Without checking to see if she's following, I rap my knuckles on the front desk to get Bethany's attention.

When she looks up from her phone, I say, "You're good here until I get back?"

The college freshman blinks her heavily lined eyes and nods once before returning to her screen. I hired her two days ago. My mother sweet-talked me into it. Apparently, Bethany's mom is her hairdresser.

Gotta love a small town and all the connections that come with it.

I hold open the front door, and when Natalie tries to take the bags from my arms again, I smile. "I got you."

Her greenish-brown eyes lock on mine, and that gut-punch sensation returns. I'm nine years old again, struck dumb by my best friend's older sister.

She's forced to draw close to me as she passes, and when we almost touch, her sharp intake of breath sends a thrill through me.

Only once she opens the trunk of the maroon Camry do I hand over the bags.

She secures the lid and waves a hand at the car. "Wayne insisted I use his car when I'm out for his sessions. Doesn't want me putting miles on mine."

"Wayne is good people."

That earns me a slight lift of her lips, but not full-fledged. *Damn it.*

"He is." She runs a hand up and down her thigh, like maybe she's nervous, then reaches into her back pocket. "Here's my card. Call me when you're ready to schedule the shoot."

I take the thick white card and run my finger over the embossed logo, printed in black. *Shutterbug Photography* in a classy font, a simple doodle of a camera. And her name.

Natalie Torres.

I swallow thickly, trying like hell to ignore the swooping sensation in my gut. "And you're here for the summer, Natalie?" It's the first time I've said her name in her presence today. Pretty sure I could become addicted to the satisfaction I get from her reaction.

She licks her lips, their rosy stain a few shades darker than the pink that's glowing on her cheeks. "For the summer."

"Good. Welcome home, shutterbug."

Chapter Two

Natalie

Every soul who lives within a twenty-mile radius of Holly Holler is crammed into the town square today.

I luck out when a family of five loads up their minivan early, leaving a parking spot not too far from where the crowds have gathered. Dodging revelers and baby strollers and panting dogs on leashes, I make my way past the fire station where my brother spends many of his hours. I pause at the corner before turning onto East Street, taking in the chaos of my hometown on Founders' Day. The four streets that form the perimeter of the square are blocked by barricades, ready for the parade that will roll through at any moment. But every other available inch of concrete or grass is covered with folks lounging in camp chairs, sprawled on quilts, or milling around. At every corner, carts selling funnel cakes, cotton candy, and hot dogs have been set up, and a small stage has been erected near the oft photographed gazebo. The white structure stands proud in the middle of the square, a quaint centerpiece that's served as the setting for many marriage proposals over the years as well as a few wedding ceremonies.

Just the sight brings with it the phantom pinching sensation I endured because of the new white patent leather Mary Janes I wore when Mom married James under the gazebo's haint blue ceiling.

The annual celebration commemorating the founding of Holly Holler takes place the third Saturday in May. Though I haven't attended a Founders' Day since my senior year of high school, and though this little town hasn't been home to me in over two decades, I can't deny its whimsical charm.

Its inhabitants will use any excuse to plan a gathering.

I'm jostled by a vaguely familiar short redhead dressed in period garb as she pushes through the crowd. "Sorry! Sorry!" she shouts over her shoulder as she darts under an outstretched arm to dash across the street to the square.

"Nat!" James's voice rings above the din of the crowd. "Over here."

My mom and my stepfather are exactly where they said they'd be, standing in front of the business that sits at the corner of East and South Streets. A place as familiar to me as my childhood bedroom or my condo in Austin. I smile at the gold letters neatly painted on the window.

Wayne Gann Photography.

"You made it." Mom links her arm through mine and drags me closer. "Parade's about to start."

I squint across the street. "What's with the roped-off area?"

James smiles fondly at Mom. "They're adding to the Heart Path this year."

The urge to roll my eyes is strong, but I manage to resist it.

The Holly Holler Heart Path. A concrete walk-of-fame where the loved-up citizens here leave their coupled handprints as a declaration to the world. One that screams *We've found our person, so we're gonna stick our hands in cold, wet cement to make sure everyone knows it.*

I wasn't always this cynical, but living a perpetually single existence will do that to a girl. With each passing year, the bitterness has crept in, and now that I'm forty, it's nearly impossible to keep it at bay.

"It's been a couple years since they've added a new section." Mom sighs and rests her head on James's shoulder. Despite my disillusion, she's starry eyed as she surveys the Heart Path, where their handprints have been memorialized in the section of sidewalk labeled 1993. The town will only jackhammer a perfectly fine segment of concrete and prepare new wood forms when the requisite number of couples have put in requests.

James bounces up on his toes, peering past a couple who've paused on the curb in front of us. "The reenactment starts right after the handprint ceremony."

Ah, yes. The reenactment. One more evergreen component of Founders' Day. The reason for that redhead's enormous bustle and frilly bonnet suddenly slides into focus.

Thank God women don't dress like that these days. I've got enough junk in my trunk without having to wear an extended cab under my dress.

Not that I'm unhappy with my body. I've come to appreciate the thick thighs and round butt that I definitely did *not* get from my mama.

"Which version is it this year? The tree one or the yelling one?" I ask my stepdad. He's a member of the town council and keeps up with this stuff.

"Tree this year." He smirks.

That expression makes me smile. The tree one is good, but the yelling story is our personal favorite. We've been Team Yelling for as long as I can remember. James and I bonded over it early on, in fact. Back when I was a shy first grader meeting the first man Mom let into our little bubble.

The origin of our town's name is a hotly debated topic around here. There are two camps, and each is so steadfast in their beliefs that the council alternates years for the historical reenactments in order to satisfy both.

Sirens blare as a Holly Holler police vehicle (one of four, by the way) slowly crawls around the corner, followed by the town's lone fire engine.

"There's Cam!" Mom hops up and down, waving wildly.

My little brother is hanging out the passenger window, grinning, waving, and tossing candy at the kids along the route. When he spots us in the crowd, we're pelted with Tootsie Rolls and Jolly Ranchers. As we're surrounded by tiny humans scrambling for the sugary bounty at our feet, I discreetly flash him the bird.

His resulting guffaw can be heard over shouts and cries of "Over here!" and "This way!"

My heart pangs at the sound of his laugh. I've missed so many little moments with my younger brother over the years. He's the only reason I've ever second-guessed escaping my hometown and never looking back. Regardless of how often we talk, the distance has affected my relationship with Camden. I've come back for most of his big milestones—the day he got his license and insisted he take me for a spin in his beloved used truck, the night during his junior year when he started as pitcher in the quarterfinal game, his high school graduation, his first solo flight in one of James's planes—but the everyday moments I've missed sometimes feel just as big.

There are so many things I don't know about him. He was unexpectedly tidy when he was a kid. Is he still that way, or has adulthood loosened him up? Is he an every morning cup of coffee kind of adult, and if so, how does he take it? Does he even drink coffee?

"Does Cam drink coffee?" The words are out before I can stop them.

Mom and James, who've been watching the high school marching band as it passes, turn and stare at me like I've grown an extra head.

After a beat, Mom dips her chin. "Yes, he drinks coffee."

I bob my head, a rapid motion that I hope hides the sheen of emotion in my eyes. "Okay. Good to know. Is Loblolly still the best in town?"

James turns back to the parade, but Mom's attention lingers, her gaze softening. Gentle as a whisper, she smooths a strand of hair behind my ear. "Loblolly is great."

The diner on the square has been popular for generations. It's good to hear that hasn't changed.

"And," she goes on, "there's a newer little coffee shop on the corner across from the fire station. Holler Haven. Cam loves their muffins."

"Cool." Blinking, I force myself to focus on the parade rather than the doubts that creep up on me here and there.

The Hornets' cheerleading squad, wearing my alma mater's colors—yellow and black, of course—performs a stunt that makes the entire block applaud. When they realign in marching formation, Mom links her arm through mine and squeezes.

"I'm glad you're home."

"Me too."

My relationship with my mother is another that needs tending. She and I were thick as thieves when I was little. From the age of two, when my parents divorced, up until James came along when I was seven, it was the two of us against the world. But her last name wasn't the only thing that changed when she and James got married. Our relationship shifted too. How could it not? Our family of two grew to three, then four, and we moved from a two-bedroom apartment into James's four-bedroom house on the outskirts of town.

I was no longer the sole recipient of her attention, so the close bond we'd shared for years loosened and shifted. James is incredible. I'd never blame him for the distance that developed between Mom and me. He accepted me and took care of me from the start, and I adore him. He's been a fantastic partner for my mom, her missing piece. And their relationship gave me Cam, the younger sibling I begged Santa for every Christmas until he was born.

But since I moved to Austin at eighteen to live with my dad and attend college, the small divide between us has widened into a sizable canyon. One I hope to bridge during my time here.

Keeping with tradition, the last float in the parade holds the town's proud military veterans. They inspire respect and awe each time I see them like this, though the way their numbers have dwindled since the last time I attended is heartbreaking.

The last time I watched this float drift down the street, my mom's father, my poppy, was one of the stoic men nodding subtly to the crowd. We lost him ten years ago. That's another regret that weighs on me. I wish I'd visited more before he passed.

Mom squeezes my arm again, no doubt thinking of the man who raised her and spoiled me like any good grandfather would. "Let's go watch the handprints." She links her other arm through James's, and we step off the curb, winding through the throng of people who've filled the streets now that the parade has moved past.

As we cross over to the square, I roll my shoulders back, lift my chin, and imagine a full suit of armor snapping into place from my head to my toes, like a Marvel-esque superhero preparing for battle. The armor shielding my heart is extra thick. Multi-layered and reinforced and impenetrable. The organ there guarded and untouchable. Protected above all else.

This mental exercise has become a necessity since I resigned myself to the truth. That romance and a happily-ever-after *probably* weren't going to happen for me. Even though I've trained my brain to include the word *probably*—only to appease my best friend, who often reminds me that I'm not dead yet and it could still happen—in my heart of hearts, I've recognized that it's highly unlikely. The magic eight-ball of my life will forever be stuck on *outlook not so good.*

The absence of romantic love has left a gaping hole in my heart. A physical ache I can't soothe away. In the privacy of my home, in my darkened bedroom, I let myself wallow and cry and shake a fist at the moon like it will make a difference.

But in public? Especially at an event like this, when I'll be assaulted with living, breathing examples of what I'll never have, when I'm surrounded by loved-up couples and precious little families with look-alike stairstep children? Full. Fucking. Armor.

There's a smattering of applause as we approach the edge of the crowd. The mayor, my former high school principal, stands behind a small podium near the gazebo, giving a speech about the history of the Heart Path, explaining its origin to the crowd.

"But Constance was persistent, and she convinced the town council to create this permanent walk-of-love..."

I tune out Mayor Staley's nasally voice and scan the crowd.

Five couples stand opposite the empty wooden sidewalk frame. The youngest couple looks as if they might still be in high school, the rest of them in early adulthood or middle-aged.

The man and woman at the end only have eyes for each other. She's lovely, a smitten brunette with ivory skin and a brilliant smile, wearing an army green romper that shows off long legs. Her beau towers over the other four men who are here to "cement" their love for eternity. And he's gorgeous. He's fit and muscular, his build promising he's a force to be reckoned with. His dark hair is shorn into a classic fade, and his beard is short and neatly trimmed. He's...wait, he's *so* familiar.

I'm trying to place him when his face splits into a joyful smile.

Instantly, his identity hits me. His smile is a near-replica of the one directed my way several times this morning.

And you're here for the summer, Natalie?

For the summer.

Good. Welcome home, shutterbug.

I blink to clear the memory of our parking lot goodbye from my mind.

He's got to be Tucker's older brother, Griffin. NFL superstar and Holly Holler hero. He's kneeling in the grass now, his lady love at his side, preparing to press his hand into wet concrete. As they lean forward to squish their hands into the gray sludge, they share a kiss that causes the whole crowd to erupt in cheers and whistles. The sight makes my heart pang, even with the added layers of protection. While every phone in the vicinity is pointed at the happy couple, I tear my attention away, seeking out the rest of the Laceys in the crowd as a distraction.

They're off to the right, all beaming faces and, in the case of Mrs. Lacey, tearstained cheeks. The cute redhead from earlier, dressed like she's just time-traveled from the 1890s, elbows Tucker, who's murmuring in her ear. In my memory, she's a scrappy ten-year-old with braided pigtails and scraped knees. The girl lived to boss Tucker and Cam around like a tiny dictator, though she was prone to getting her feelings hurt when they refused to grant her access to the treehouse that James surprised my brother with for his fifth birthday.

Clearly, Trixie McNeill has left her tomboy days in the past.

She's the first girl my brother asked me for advice about, and one he still mentions on our catch-up calls.

As if summoned by my thoughts, Cam throws his arms around me and Mom, startling us both.

"Goodness," Mom says with a hand to her chest. "My heart can't handle a jump scare, and you know it."

His response to her half-hearted complaint? An obnoxious smacking kiss to her temple.

"Did I miss Griff and Brynn?" He peers over the rows of townsfolk standing between us and the now-drying sidewalk.

"Sorry, but yes. They're so cute together." Mom cranes her neck to catch my eye. "Don't you think so, Nat?"

"Sure." I work to keep my tone upbeat, but her question is a pelt to that reinforced patch of armor. It may be soft-lobbed ammo, but it stings, nonetheless.

Cam watches me, his scrutiny a little too palpable, for a beat. When he changes the subject rather than calling me out, I'm tempted to give him my own version of an obnoxious smooch. "Are we taking this one out tonight? Her first official night back in the nest?"

Technically, I've been here since last night, but it was so late that Mom and James spent mere minutes hugging us and fawning over us before they sent Goose and me off to bed.

Mom's grayish-brown locks sway as she shakes her head, a glimmer of pride shining in her hazel eyes. "I have a roast in the crock pot. Dinner's at home tonight."

My brother and I trade glances. When we were kids, Mom and James both worked long hours, so family dinners were rare. And as far as I know, neither of them has become any more adept in the kitchen in the two decades since I left. Sure, we'd eat together at Loblolly here and there or enjoy a "home cooked" Hamburger Helper meal or pizza at the round four-top in the kitchen, but Cam spent more time at the Laceys' table than ours. And I often had dinner with Nancy and Wayne or made myself a sandwich.

It warms my heart, really, that they're making an effort now.

"Cool." My brother squeezes our necks once and releases us. "I'm gonna go say hey to Tuck and the Laceys. I'll catch up with y'all after. Nat owes me a sno-cone for flipping me the bird during the parade."

A scoff escapes me as he saunters across the grass toward his best friend.

"Narc!" I yell after him.

His shoulders bounce, but he doesn't fire back.

Before my mother can chide me, an older couple stops to chat with her and James, leaving me free to people watch. Inexplicably, my gaze is drawn back to the Laceys. Their oldest son, Shaw, is nowhere in sight, but Donna and Fred haven't left their position. Mrs. Lacey's sister, Dottie McNeill, is there, talking to her daughter Trixie.

The youngest Lacey is still in attendance as well, and he's the one who holds most of my attention.

He's beside my brother, his head thrown back in laughter, clad in the same gray T-shirt and black gym shorts he had on at the gym. As he talks, waving his hands animatedly, the colorful tattoos on his forearms flex in a way that's nearly hypnotic. His dark hair is long enough to curl up at the edge of his backward ball cap. He's taller than Cam, but not quite the height of his giant of a brother, with wide shoulders and well-defined muscles his T-shirt can't hide.

I swallow and spin on my toes, putting him at my back, lest I be tempted to continue to drool over my brother's best friend.

What in the actual hell, Natalie?

This fascination with Tucker has nothing to do with how gorgeous he is. No, it's just that I can't reconcile the man he's grown into with the little troublemaker who engaged in a years-long prank war with my brother. It has to be. Because this is the boy who ate popsicles on our swing set and drank from our water hose in the heat of the summer and taught Cam how to backflip off lawn chairs into the pool. The boy who's practically a decade younger than I am.

I like watching you work. I can tell you're good.

Those words, and the confident way he spoke them?

I give my head the tiniest of shakes. I refuse to acknowledge how that comment not only sent an undeniable shiver coasting down my spine but awakened a part of my soul that's been dormant. Like a piece of me has suddenly stirred to life after being asleep for years.

Nope, definitely not going to acknowledge those words now. Instead, I'll store them away for later. Much later. Like when I'm back in Austin. Once Holly Holler and its intriguing residents are firmly in my rearview mirror.

Chapter Three

Natalie

The moment I open the back door to Wayne's studio, I'm greeted by a nostalgic scent combination of Pine-sol, dust, and peppermint, mixed with that slight chemical smell leftover from the days of developing film in the tiny closet of a darkroom. Now that everything's digital, Wayne uses that room to store backdrops and umbrella lights.

Goose trots ahead of me as I switch on all the lights, the faint tapping of his toenails on the tile giving away his location as he explores the place. In the small kitchenette across from Wayne's cluttered office, I unpack the food and water bowls I brought and fill them. Then I find the perfect spot for them by the door.

My next stop? The small office stuffed with photography relics, sports memorabilia, model vintage cars, and boxes and boxes of paperwork. Needless to say, Wayne is a pack rat.

He'd call himself a collector, I suppose. A collector of *things*, yes. But also a collector of *memories*. It's why he's so brilliant at this job. He has the patience to wait for that perfect shot. He's great at getting those polished, staged, smiley moments that fill frames in most of the homes in this town. But he's even better at catching those one-of-a-kind moments, those unexpected blink-and-you'll-miss-them shots that capture the soul of an individual, or a couple, or a family.

He taught me everything I know about being a photographer.

From the moment I marched into his studio at the age of fifteen, determined to make photography my whole personality, Wayne Gann has been my champion. He put up with my teenage know-it-all mentality and emotional mood swings, and with infinite patience and understanding, he shaped me into a genuine moment-collector.

So when Nancy called last week, voice watery and breathless, and recounted how Wayne's fall from their roof resulted in a compound fracture that required immediate surgery, my offer to move home for a few months to make sure his clients weren't forced to find someone else to capture their special moments came easily.

Though I'd never wish a broken femur on anyone, especially Wayne, the timing couldn't be better for me. Months ago, I was chosen by the Arkansas Department of Parks, Heritage, and Tourism for their campaign to feature photos of Arkansas's natural resources and attractions shot by natives to the state, so my calendar has been blocked off. I had a few bookings in June and August to shuffle around, but most of those clients were flexible, and I only had one cancelation.

I sigh as I plop into the worn, creaky leather chair behind Wayne's desk and boot up my laptop. While I wait, I scan the appointments jotted down in the planner left out for me. Though my mentor has reluctantly embraced the digital side of photography, he's still clinging to his ever-present paper calendar, I see.

Two warm paws land gently on my thigh as Goose peeks his head over the edge of the chair.

"Hey, buddy." I lavish him with ear scratches as I add Wayne's bookings into my digital calendar. When I get to the two weddings in June, I roll my shoulders and inhale deeply.

It's fine, Natalie. You've done this hundreds of times before.

I've photographed hundreds of weddings over the years. In the early years of Shutterbug Photography, weddings were my bread and butter. And when those couples started their families, my days were filled with baby bump bookings and newborn photography and first birthday cake smash shoots. At first, those events filled me with joy. I was honored to document such monumental moments for my clients.

But as my twenties bled into my thirties, and the patience I clung to, the hope that soon, it'd be my turn to experience those milestones, morphed into a deep, aching fear that it never would be, those photo shoots became an albatross around my neck. For my mental health, I pivoted and took on more commercial clients.

Now, the only family pictures I take are for my best friend.

But filling in for Wayne, this community's go-to guy for documenting those big life moments, means I'll need to don my full mental armor more often.

As I'm adding the last of the August bookings, Goose whines at the front of the studio. Ready for a break myself, I attach his leash and stuff a poop bag into my back pocket. Then we step out onto the sidewalk and greet the small-town day.

Holly Holler is subdued this morning, like the whole town partied a little too hard over the weekend. Somber gray clouds blanket the sky, and the colors of the square are muted in comparison to the bold, festive hues that filled it two days ago. Even the grass Goose sniffs is dull.

The Holler has a hangover, it seems.

We meander down the sidewalk along South Street, past the businesses that share the block with Wayne. Next to the studio, there's a law office, followed by the town's beloved bookshop, the Nook. On the corner of South and West is this community's favorite spot to eat and gossip. Loblolly Diner was named after Arkansas's state tree, the loblolly pine.

Scents of coffee and bacon waft through the air, making my mouth water. As I survey the diner's morning faithful, who fill the booths along the front windows and the stools at the counter, I decide I can spare a few minutes to pick up a coffee.

I step off the curb to cross the street, but as my foot hits the asphalt, a hot pink and tan blur whizzes around the corner, almost colliding with me.

"Sorry!" a masculine voice shouts as the bicycle speeds down the street.

Goose, always ready for a chase, dashes after it. When he reaches the end of the leash, he pulls up short. But the lack of freedom doesn't deter his enthusiasm. He pulls and pulls, throwing every ounce of his twenty-two pounds into dragging me toward the rider, tail wagging like crazy, barking like mad.

"Goose, stop." One handed, I wrangle him back to my side. Only when I've securely tightened the slack of his leash do I realize my heart is racing.

A near-collision with an enthusiastic bicycle rider was *not* on my agenda for today.

I shake off the adrenaline surge and take a step toward the diner, but rather than follow, Goose resumes his frenzied barking, pulling and running circles around me.

At the dull buzzing sound behind me, I turn and discover the cyclist has returned, this time cruising at a much slower speed.

He slows and stops at the corner, and as he unhooks his sleek black helmet, my would-be collider is revealed.

Tucker Lacey tilts his head back and runs a broad hand through his dark hair, the ghost of a smile lifting his lips. "Almost clipped you, shutterbug."

My hackles rise. How dare he be so nonchalant about practically bowling me over? "*Clipped* me? That's what we're calling it?" I huff a breath. "You almost flattened me like a damn pancake."

His mouth twists like he's trying not to laugh at my bluster, but when his eyes trail a leisurely path down to my feet, his expression sobers. Gray-blue irises meet mine again, and his throat bobs. "Wouldn't want to flatten any part of you."

What. The. Hell?

My cheeks, which were ablaze with anger, now flame for an entirely different reason.

Squinting, I search his face, looking for evidence that he's fucking with me. But his features remain serious. And contrite.

I don't know how to handle grown-up Tucker.

"Who's your friend?" He dips his chin, gesturing to Goose, who's peeking up at him from between my knees.

Looking down, I sigh at the tangled web of leash wrapped around my lower limbs.

"This," I explain as I turn in a circle to extricate my legs from the blue nylon trap, "is Goose." Still tangled up, I lift and twist my left leg to pull it free, only to find myself tipping sideways.

"Whoa. I got you."

Strong hands clasp my arms, saving me from tumbling into the grass that divides the sidewalk from the street.

Only once I've escaped Goose's web does he release me. And only then do I take the time to really look at him.

And it's a terrible, terrible idea.

He's shirtless, for one, tanned, inked skin and taut muscles on full display. And the hot pink that whooshed by earlier? His shorts.

Hot pink *short* shorts.

Short shorts that expose inches and inches of his thick, muscly thighs and a glimpse of an intricate tattoo. The design, though only half visible, is unmistakable. It's a black line rendering of Van Gogh's *The Starry Night*, with the words *makes me dream* swirled along the bottom.

Still out of sorts, I force my focus back to his face, only to find he's watching me with a satisfied smirk. I open my mouth to speak, to distract him, to stop him from staring at me like *that*, with that smug *caught ya* written all over his expression. But before I can find my voice, he clears his throat and tilts his chin down.

"Goose, huh?" He cocks a brow. "You a big *Top Gun* fan?"

Now it's my turn to smirk. "Nope."

Brows raised, he scans my face, waiting for me to elaborate. When I don't, he leans forward, still straddling his bike, and cautiously offers his hand for Goose to sniff. "Hey, little one."

I almost warn him not to bother. Goose doesn't spend much time around men, thanks to his mom's chronic singleness, so he's mistrustful of most males. He's tolerant of James and Cam when we visit, but it takes a few days, and he still tends to stick close to Mom or me when we're all together.

Rather than shy away, my dog surprises the hell out of me by not only sniffing Tucker's hand with zero hesitation but by braving a few steps in the man's direction and even allowing him to scratch his ears.

When Goose rears up and rests his front paws on Tucker's tattooed thigh? My mouth drops open.

"What a good boy," the man croons. "Aren't you the goodest boy ever?" The words of praise and attention make Goose's fluffy tail swish. "What breed is he?"

Still in shock, it takes me a moment to answer. "He's—he's a schneagle."

"A what?" Tucker peers up at me but continues to love on Goose.

"A schneagle. Half schnauzer. Half beagle."

Goose gives Tucker's leg a thank-you lick, then drops back to all fours. After a full-body shake, he returns to my side and sits.

"He might be the cutest dog I've ever seen."

The confession makes me grin at my companion. He *is* freaking cute, and I'm filled with undeniable pride every time someone notices.

When I zero in on Tucker again, his eyes shine with something like wonder, and his slightly parted lips melt into a smile so dazzling, it would almost outshine the sun if it weren't hidden behind the clouds.

Baffled by the joy in his expression, I blurt the first thing I think of to hide my confusion.

"You have a dog, too, right?"

He tilts his head, giving me a puzzled frown.

"Er, on Saturday, at the gym, you said—" I take a deep breath to rein in my thoughts and try again. "You said you know all about having a dog-spoiling mom."

His eyes brighten. "Ah, right. No, Shaw has a dog. Delta. She's a golden retriever. Mom calls her their granddog. Spoils her rotten, which drives Shaw nuts."

I chuckle. "Sounds like my mom with Goose."

"How'd you become Goose's mom?"

A man exits the diner and yells, "Hey, Tuck!"

He lifts a hand in greeting but keeps his focus on me and my furry companion.

It's unnerving, being the object of another's undivided attention like this. So, pulse fluttering, I switch Goose's leash to my left hand, then tuck a chunk of hair behind my ear. "I volunteered to do a photo shoot for an animal shelter a couple of years ago. They wanted eye-catching pictures of the dogs and cats for their website. This guy was still a puppy. I snapped one picture of his furry face and I was a goner."

"Love at first sight." Tucker's voice is low, yet full of emotion.

Tears prickle at the backs of my eyes as I survey my dog.

Sure, I may have saved Goose's life three years ago, but he saves mine right back every single day. He depends on me, and that knowledge helps to keep my dark thoughts at bay. He gives me a reason to get up every morning, even when the heaviness threatens to pull me under.

Tucker's quiet as I wrangle my emotions back in line, as if he can sense that I need a moment. But then he clears his throat, and his next words are upbeat, teasing. "And you're sure his need for speed didn't play a part when you named this little guy?" He smiles at my dog with fondness.

I roll my eyes, despite how grateful I am that he's lightened the mood. "I promise, he's not named after Goose from *Top Gun*. But he is named after a movie character."

"Oh yeah? Which one?"

"Un-uh," I say, my voice far flirtier than I intend. "Can't spill all my secrets at once. A girl's gotta maintain a bit of mystery, right?"

A slow grin stretches across his face, and his grayish-blue eyes twinkle. The gold hoop in his left ear twinkles, too, as the sun barely peeks out from behind a cloud.

The sight of it makes my insides flutter in the most ridiculous way.

"Fair enough. But I will get to the bottom of this one, shutter-bug." His tone is confident, determined. And hell if that doesn't intensify that internal fluttering.

What the hell is going on? Am I flirting with Cam's best friend? Who's almost a whole damn decade younger than I am?

My cheeks heat at the thought and also at my sudden, uncharacteristic brazenness. To deflect, I fake a laugh. "Try not to run over any other old ladies on that thing."

Tucker settles back on the seat of his bike and grips the handlebars tight enough to make his knuckles turn white. He rolls his lips together, one side tipping up. "Natalie, *old* doesn't appear on the list of words I would use to describe you."

My breath stalls out. What do I say to *that*?

Undeterred by my speechlessness, he goes on. "I'm calling you this week so we can get our next meetup on the books."

Faster than I can formulate a response, he snaps on his helmet and takes off down South Street.

The *meetup* he's referring to is the photo shoot for his gym. And I can't figure out whether that makes me giddy or sad.

Probably a combo of the two, which is confusing as hell.

Sadness is ridiculous. I have plans to take photos for him. Nothing more. What other type of meetup would I expect?

The whole interaction with Tucker was confusing, honestly.

I pinch the fabric of my shirt and pull on it, fanning my overheated skin. The brutal heat of a southern summer hasn't reached us yet, so I can only assume this is my already out-of-whack hormones staging an uprising. Or perhaps caffeine withdrawal is to blame. Whatever the reason for my sudden hot flash, I choose not to dwell on it.

Chapter Four

Tucker

"'**T**uck.'"

I peek over my shoulder and find my roommate standing next to the open refrigerator, an empty juice carton in his hand.

"You did it again."

I turn off the blender and pour the frothy green concoction into my tumbler, then snag the carton. With an easy hook shot, I toss the cardboard container at the trash can. It bounces off the heaping pile bursting over the rim and lands on the floor in the corner of our tiny kitchen.

Damn. That would've been two points. Seems I forgot to take out the trash, too.

With a shake of his head, he picks it up. When he smashes it onto the top of the trash heap and ties up the plastic bag, guilt spears through me.

Have my religiously tidy bestie and I experienced some growing pains in the two years we've lived together? For sure.

But we were aware of each other's housekeeping habits long before we signed the lease on this place. I was introduced to Cam's orderly tendencies the summer after sixth grade, when we bunked together at camp. He made his cot every morning and folded his clothes and stored them neatly in his suitcase, while my T-shirts, gym shorts, and socks were strewn all over the cabin, as if they'd exploded from my duffel.

Every time I recall the look of horror on my mom's face when I told her we were going to live together, I chuckle. My folks probably thought we'd ruin our friendship if we became roommates. But Cam and I are solid; it would take a hell of a lot more than a few dirty dishes and overflowing trash cans to wreck what we've built.

Like a swift kick to my gut, a vision of Natalie's guarded hazel eyes invades my thoughts.

It's both an admonition and an inevitability, and the image brings with it a sense of discomfort in my chest.

Cam prepares his breakfast, his movements as predictable and precise as he is. As he splashes milk into his bowl of plain Cheerios, he says, "It's your turn to pick up the groceries."

"I'm on it."

He sets the milk jug down and gives me a look of scrutiny.

I prop myself up against the counter and chug the last of my smoothie. "I'm on it," I repeat, firmer.

This kind of unintentional flicker of doubt weighs on me. And Cam isn't the only one who looks at me that way. My brothers' questioning looks are subtle—a press of their lips or a slightly cocked brow—but I catch them, nonetheless.

Yeah, I've demonstrated my fair share of irresponsibility and fuckery over the years, but damn, what I wouldn't give to erase every ounce of their skepticism. For good.

With any luck, nurturing my gym into a successful business will go a long way. The chance to plant my own roots next to those of my family was one of the factors that motivated me to step away from the ring, away from the brutal training and travel that MMA requires. Holly Holler is my home, it's the place that made us Lacey boys who we are, and I'll devote everything I have—money, time, sweat—to helping it thrive.

I rinse the green residue from the tumbler and load the dishwasher, then clap Cam on his shoulder.

"Semper Paratus."

It's my traditional farewell for him. A phrase that perfectly describes my best friend, whether he's responding to an emergency or piloting an aircraft: Always ready.

Cheeks puffed out, he salutes me with his cereal spoon and a closed-mouth smile.

On my way to the door, I snag my phone and keys from the counter, and outside, I stride to my Jeep with an extra bounce in my step.

As I open the door to my black Wrangler—a surprise from Griff for my thirtieth birthday—a feminine voice trills from across the street.

"Have the day you have, neighbor."

Trixie gives me a quick wave as she bounds down her front steps, a large canvas tote bag slung over one shoulder.

"Right back atcha, Ms. Frizzle."

Even with the street as a buffer, the daggers shooting from my cousin's narrowed eyes land.

Riling up Beatrice "Trixie" McNeill is a beloved pastime for Cam and me, but we enjoy it for entirely different reasons. For me, it's a familial privilege; she was raised alongside me and my brothers, almost like a sister. My roommate's intentions are a whole other story.

But she gives as good as she gets, so living across the street from her is hella fun.

Trixie's dark skirt swishes around her legs as she stomps over to her SUV and heaves her bag onto the passenger seat. When she slams the door, I get a better look at what Griff would call her *teacher fit*; she's layered a jean jacket over a NASA T-shirt, and yep, those are tiny stars and planets on the fabric of her skirt.

Ms. Frizzle, indeed.

Arms crossed, she pops a shoulder. "It's the last day of our space unit."

"You look adorable, Trix. The kids are gonna love it."

Her scowl softens to a smile. "Yeah, it'll be a fun day."

My cousin is devoted to her job, so her second graders will live their best lives today.

After waving goodbye, we slide into our vehicles and head in opposite directions.

As I near downtown Holly Holler, a fizzy anticipation hits me. It's the same sensation I've experienced the past few mornings.

When I turn the corner and spy an empty spot in front of the little coffee shop on the end of the block, I do a mental fist pump. Holler Haven has been open for a couple years, but I hadn't stepped through its doors until three days ago.

On my way to the gym on Tuesday morning, the day after the near collision with Natalie and her dog, I spotted familiar brown hair ducking into this shop. Convinced I should apologize again for almost running her over, I parked my bike and joined the line of folks seeking their morning caffeine fix.

I've been back every morning since.

Like the residents of this town who can't get their days started without their lattes and espressos and Americanos, I, too, have become addicted.

I'm addicted to making Natalie Torres smile.

The sight is magnificent. Like a spring sunrise lighting up the world after months of darkness, promising warmth and vitality.

Thoughts like that may be dangerous, not to mention cheesy as fuck, but I can't convince my brain to quit having them.

I drum on the steering wheel as I peer into the shop, looking for my target. There are three patrons waiting in line at the counter, but none have the shapely figure I'm searching for.

The clock on the dash changes to 7:50, and for a moment, I panic, thinking she's changed her routine, whether to avoid me or for other reasons.

I've straightened in my seat and put my hand on the gearshift, readying to give up and head to the gym, when those bouncy waves enter my periphery.

Natalie sets a brisk pace down the sidewalk, head lowered as she scrolls on her phone. I follow her path to the door of the shop, noting her jeans, faded gray Eagles T-shirt, and the black Adidas she's worn every day this week.

I wait until she's in the short line, then run a hand through my hair and give myself a cursory glance in the rearview. When I've confirmed I'm presentable, I make my way to the door. The strong coffee aroma hits the instant I step onto the welcome mat.

Still engrossed in her phone, she's oblivious to my presence as I take my place behind her. She stands half a foot shorter than me, her hair sleek and smooth in varying shades of brown.

For a moment, I remain silent, considering my opening line. I've won a genuine smile from her every morning this week, and I'm determined to finish five-for-five. The topic most likely to earn a full-wattage beam? Her dog, Goose.

I angle toward her ear and catch a whiff of either her perfume or shampoo, a floral, spicy scent that I want to hold in my lungs. It knocks me off-kilter, but only for a moment. Before she can turn, I've gathered my wits again.

"I think I've discovered Goose's name origin."

She startles, slamming one hand to her chest and peeking over her shoulder. "Tucker?"

This close, the wild fluttering of her pulse at the base of her neck catches my attention and makes my own kick up a notch.

"This is becoming a pattern, shutterbug."

She steps back and spins around, almost bumping into Mrs. Jenkins, who's asking a hundred questions about her coffee order.

Mrs. Jenkins can continue her interrogation all day for all I care. Her indecisiveness gives me more time with the woman before me. The woman who visibly swallows, then closes her eyes as she takes a calming breath. Is she nervous, or is she still rattled from my sneaky approach?

Why has the need to figure her out consumed me this week?

When she focuses her cautious eyes on me, I give her a broad smile, and when her shoulders relax a fraction, my chest expands in triumph.

Her lips twitch just a little. "We should've planned better. I could've gotten your coffee and brought it with me."

She could have, I suppose, since I get to spend several hours with this woman for the photoshoot for the gym today. The reminder sends my heart rate racing further. It's like those first moments after I rev my bike down an empty highway.

I almost confess that I wouldn't want to give up *any* chance to run into her. To hell with how inappropriate it would be to say that to my best friend's sister. Instead, I spin my key ring around a finger and say, "Next time."

Because, damn, I want there to be a next time.

As Mrs. Jenkins collects her change and moves aside to wait for her order, I panic. Damn it, I'm running out of time to earn that smile.

Natalie steps up to the counter and quickly orders a skinny vanilla latte with extra cinnamon like she has every day this week.

"Oh, Tucker, I thought I heard your voice." Mrs. Jenkins clutches her cup in one hand as she fights the straps of her massive purse with the other. "Tell Donna and Fred we missed them at this month's potluck."

I give her a polite smile. "Yes, ma'am."

She absentmindedly pats my arm and squints at the front window. "Shoot, there's Lisa Marie. I gotta go call Randall." She scurries out the door before I can ask her to categorize the Lisa Marie sighting.

At the sound of a throat clearing, I turn back to the counter. Suzie Hightower smiles at me as I step up. When I order the simplest item on the menu, a small black coffee, she slips her long blond ponytail over a shoulder and rings me up. "Tucker, you're becoming a regular, huh?"

Heat licks down my spine. Damn it. With my luck, she'll keep going with this line of questioning and give away my secret.

"Uh." I stall for time. Natalie has moved down to the pickup counter, but the weight of her stare is heavy. "Uh, yeah, got tired of the line at Loblolly." As the lie escapes me, I silently thank every star hidden in the bright morning sky that Donna Lacey and her lie-detecting rock are nowhere near. It's been over two decades since I believed that nondescript rock held any magical aim, but my mother would no doubt still chuck it my way for being dishonest.

Suzie beams, the pride shining in her blue eyes making me feel like an enormous ass. Her parents own this coffee shop, and if anyone knows how difficult it is to get a new business up and running in a small community, it's me. Yet until this week, I'd never so much as stepped inside the place. Swallowing down the guilt, I shove a five into the tip jar. Then I shift over to where Natalie waits for her latte, studying the handwritten chalkboard menu above the counter.

I prop an elbow on the glass display case full of muffins, cookies, and bagels and survey her. "Eagles fan, huh?"

She tips her chin down to study her shirt.

"What's your favorite song?"

She glances at me, though she quickly averts her attention back to the menu, her lips quirking. "You know the Eagles?"

I scoff. "Of course I know the Eagles." I lean in close, my voice low. "'Hotel California,' 'Witchy Woman.' 'Take It Easy.' 'Tequila Sunrise.' And my personal favorite, 'Life in the Fast Lane.'"

One dark brow lifts in a way I hope means she's impressed. "I'm surprised."

When I tilt my head, she raises a hand in surrender.

"Just thought they were a little before your time. Cam always makes fun of my taste in music."

An undeniable urgency to rid her of any thought that compares me with her brother washes over me. "They're a little before *your* time, too, wouldn't you say? And Cam has no room to judge anyone's taste in music. He still thinks Creed is the greatest band of all time."

She huffs a small laugh, her mouth curving up at the corners. Hmm, closer. But we're not in full-smile territory yet.

Time to pull out the big guns.

"So back to Goose."

Two lines form between her brows. "You've figured out where I got his name?"

Before I can answer, Suzie sets Natalie's latte and my coffee on the counter and grins. "Thank y'all for comin' in this morning."

As we take our cups, I panic. Our morning interaction is nearing its end, but I've yet to complete my mission.

"I gotta say, naming a dog after a movie cat is hella creative."

Boom. There it is.

Her perfect, rosy lips stretch so wide that a slight indentation pops in one cheek—almost a dimple, but not quite. Her flawless white teeth gleam, while tiny crinkles form around her vibrant hazel-green eyes.

In response, adrenaline rushes through me, lighting up my nerve endings.

Her smile dims a tad, but her eyes remain bright as she shakes her head. "I didn't name my dog after Captain Marvel's cat."

I gape. Seventies rock *and* Marvel? Damn, this woman continues to surprise me.

"Yes, I know Marvel," she says as if reading my mind. "And not just *movie* Marvel. My best friend's husband co-owns a comic book store in Austin." She points at her chest as we make our way to the door. "Fully indoctrinated, I'm afraid."

Outside the shop, we pause on the sidewalk. When a tendril of hair blows into her face, I'm tempted to tuck it behind her ear.

Instead, I clear my throat and fight the heat creeping into my cheeks. "So, not Captain Marvel's Goose, then. Am I going to have to keep digging, shutterbug?"

Now she's the one blushing. "Keep digging," she confirms.

As I hold her gaze, I'd give anything to know what she's thinking. Does she feel as drawn to me as I am to her?

She takes a sip of her latte, like she wants to hide behind her cup, her attention drifting past me.

Eyes widening, she tilts her head. "Is that a…" She squints. "A goat?"

I turn toward the square, where a brown and white goat munches on the grass beside the small playground. "Yep." Looks like I can put my curiosity regarding Mrs. Jenkins's Lisa Marie sighting to rest.

With a hum, Natalie pulls her phone from her back pocket. She opens her camera app, and with ease, she zooms in and captures an image of the munching goat. "I guess I'll see you in…two hours?"

I nod, twirling my keys around my finger, stalling for time. "Need any help loading or hauling equipment to the gym?"

"No, thanks." She takes a step back, then another. "See you in a bit."

With a long exhale, I raise a hand in farewell and turn away, heading for my Jeep. Because watching her walk away would be too damn creepy. But as I reach for the handle, she calls out.

"Hey, Tucker."

When I turn around, she's grinning, holding her Holly Haven cup in one hand while returning the phone to her back pocket. In this moment, she's carefree and unguarded and beautiful. This image of her is one I want to store in my memory bank for the rest of my days.

"It's 'Heartache Tonight.'"

I tilt my head, confused.

She lifts her chin, her eyes dancing. "My favorite Eagles song." With that, she spins back and continues down the street.

When I get to the gym, Bethany, who's perched at the front desk, greets me with her customary half-glare, half-smirk, the look accentuating the electric-blue makeup lining her eyes. Like I've done for the past three mornings, I extend the still-warm cup in her direction. Sticking with the routine, she gives me a wrinkled-nose head shake.

"You remember we have the photographer coming today?"

By some miracle, she's wearing the new Club Lacey Fitness shirt I asked all my employees to don today, even after the way she grimaced when I handed it to her yesterday.

With a nod, she hops off her stool and follows me down the hallway to the break room.

"You need something?" I ask as I pour the entire container of black liquid into the sink.

Hands on hips, she glares at the empty cup in my hand. "You know you can order something different or at least doctor that up, right?"

When my only response is a simple "yep," she huffs an impatient sigh and whips her dark hair over her shoulder, then whirls back into the hall.

I rub a hand over my day-old stubble and run through the tasks I need to accomplish before Natalie arrives. Knowing damn well I have to get on with my day and not linger on this morning's interaction, I stuff the empty cup into the break room trash can, where three other identical cups are nestled among paper towels and sports drink bottles.

Oops. Looks like I forgot to take out the trash here, too.

Chapter Five

Tucker

"She's good."

Chris, the gym's manager and one of two personal trainers I've hired since opening, props his forearms on the counter, watching Natalie as she charms a reluctant smile out of the elderly gentleman shuffle-stepping on a treadmill.

"I didn't know his face was capable of *that*," he says, his tone full of appreciation.

Jaw clenched, I stack the membership applications that Bethany printed this morning a little too aggressively. The ire building inside me only grows when I pull my attention from the row of treadmills along the front windows and notice that same appreciation in his gaze.

I roll my neck left to right, trying to dispel the tension in my shoulders. It does little good.

Before I can kindly ask him to return to monitoring the floor, he says, "And that's Cam's sister, huh?"

His question makes me pause. It's easy to forget not everyone in town knows who Natalie is. Chris graduated the same year as Griff, but his family probably didn't move to town until after she'd already left.

With a clipped "yep," I nod at the college-age guys at the bench press. "Keep an eye on those two." They signed up for a summer membership and have been coming in every morning for the last couple of weeks. "They got a little carried away with the weights yesterday."

"On it." With a tap to the counter, Chris saunters over to the weights area. Though every so often, his eyes return to the pretty photographer.

I force my jaw to relax and will the possessiveness flaring hot in my veins to temper.

Why should I care if Chris is interested in Natalie? He's a good guy. We lucked out when he moved home after his divorce. His personal training experience and solid work ethic have helped grow this business tremendously. He's closer to her age, too. And he doesn't come with the complication of being her brother's best friend.

Except...I do care. I care a fucking lot.

Sighing, I focus on the administrative tasks I've been distracting myself with while Natalie finishes up on the main floor. She's already taken group photos of the staff and several artsy shots of empty machines. Now she's getting action shots for a testimonials page on the website. Her suggestion about showcasing how the gym caters to folks of all ages and fitness levels was brilliant. Every member I approached heartily agreed to sign a release form. Even cantankerous Mr. Abernathy, the elderly curmudgeon dressed in sweatpants and *World's Best Grandpa* T-shirt, has broken into a face-splitting grin in Natalie's presence. Arm in arm, they wander to the front of the building. All the way, she matches his pace and listens intently to the yarn he's spinning.

"And that, my dear, is why Mrs. A would only allow me to play golf on Tuesdays back in my younger days."

Natalie gives him an indulgent smile. "You're still in your younger days, Mr. A."

He nudges his glasses, shifting them on the bridge of his nose, and taps his chest. "Eh, this ole ticker ain't what it used to be. But thanks to this young man," he pats the counter in front of me, "I've got a place to get my steps in, even when it's hot as blazes or raining like the dickens outside."

Like clockwork, Mrs. Abernathy pulls up to the curb in their well-loved Town Car.

"My chariot awaits." He gives Natalie a jaunty wink and shuffles to the door. Despite his advanced age and stooped posture, he's surprisingly spry as he slips into the tank of a car out front.

"That's the last of the member testimonials." Natalie rests her elbows on the counter. "I've gotten some really great shots for that section of your website."

I click out of the membership spreadsheet and give her my full attention. "I never doubted you would, shutterbug. Some kinda mystical mojo happens when you point that camera."

Her cheeks pinken a bit, but she tilts her head, doubt written all over her features. "Mystical mojo?"

"Yep." I wiggle my fingers like a magician about to show off his greatest trick. "It's obvious to anyone who witnesses you in the zone."

Her hazel eyes narrow, full of disbelief.

"I told you, I like watching you work."

The slight pink tinge deepens to a rich rose, making it hard to resist the instinct to smooth a knuckle over the rounded curve of her cheek.

Every time I'm near her, I fight like hell to smother the temptation, but it's damn near impossible. All I want to do is flirt with this woman. Relentlessly.

To hell with the age difference. Or the best friend complication.

I clear my throat, forcing myself past the fixation once again. "Your ability to make Roscoe Abernathy smile like that is proof of that mojo. The only other person who makes him smile like that these days is his granddaughter."

"Mabel, right? What's she up to now?"

I dip my chin. "Teaching art at the high school. She and Trixie are tight."

"And the Abernathys still own the DB?"

"They do." The Dusty Britches Mercantile takes up the majority of one downtown block and offers everything from clothing to home decor to personal hygiene products.

She loosens a soft sigh. "I loved going there as a kid. Back then, Mr. Abernathy wasn't so crotchety. He always made sure I didn't leave without a—"

"Candy stick," I finish for her. "And he remembered which flavor every kid liked best. What was yours?"

Her eyes sparkle. "Watermelon."

"That was Shaw's favorite, too. I always asked for blueberry."

A throaty laugh escapes her. "Because you liked that it turned your lips and tongue blue."

I shrug. "Of course."

When her slight smirk widens into one of her full-wattage smiles, my chest expands and I can't help but grin back.

That's how Luca finds us, standing across from each other, grinning like a pair of Cheshire cats.

"Hey, are y'all ready for me?" He waits in the hallway that leads to the training rooms, shifting his weight from one leg to the other.

"Oh, sure." Natalie ducks her head like she's been caught doing something naughty, and when she pulls away from the counter, I follow like there's an invisible tether connecting us.

"Let me grab the equipment," she calls over her shoulder as she pads to her camera and bag.

While she collects her things, Luca and I snag the pair of silver umbrella lights and head for the training room.

I blocked off this area for the afternoon to give Natalie an hour to get action shots in the octagon. Since Luca's been training with us for some time, I asked him to spar with me today. Even though he falls into the cruiserweight class while I'm a heavyweight, I've only got about twenty pounds on him.

While Natalie sets up the umbrella lights and Luca bounces on his bare feet inside the cage, getting his muscles warmed up, I hustle to my office to change. Quickly, I strip out of the polo, ironed shorts, and pristine sneakers I wore for the staff photo and pull on black compression shorts, making sure the athletic cup is firmly in place to protect my Lacey legacy. When I pad back into the training room, Natalie is studying the height of the cage and my opponent has moved on to warming up with a series of jabs and undercuts.

"You'll have to stand on this ledge, shutterbug." Gently, I clasp her elbow, pulling a soft "oh" from her. With a tilt of my head, I lead her to the other side of the cage. And even though the attached metal ledge is only about a foot off the ground, I offer my hand to help her step onto it.

She hesitates. For a moment, all she does is stare at my open palm, but with a series of blinks, she looks me over, perusing the ink that covers my skin. The journey begins at the designs at my wrist. She lingers on the details on my forearm for a beat, then continues higher, her attention skating over my biceps. The entire process takes seconds, but each one will be seared into my memory like the ink engraved on my body. When she reaches my shoulder, she pinches her lids tight. I'd like to think it's because she's also filing the moment away like a precious keepsake, but I'd wager it's to stave off embarrassment.

It kills me to think she's embarrassed, though. I'd love for her to study and memorize every inch of me.

With a thick swallow, her throat bobbing, she focuses on my hand again and tucks her camera under her right arm. With it clutched tight to her body, she takes my waiting hand.

The touch of her skin isn't a lightning strike from the heavens or an explosion of fireworks lighting up my brain like a bat signal. It's more understated but no less powerful. A solid grounding sensation that expands from my chest and flows outward through my extremities, down through the concrete slab under our feet. It's as undeniable as gravity and as certain as day following night.

As the sensation registers, I know without a doubt that I'll do whatever it takes to spend more time with this woman while she's here.

Her eyes widen and slice to mine, as if she felt the shift too, wonder and confusion evident in her parted lips and raised brows.

"I got you." My words are low and gruff. So much so that I almost don't recognize my own voice. But I clasp her soft hand and relish the way she grips me as she steps up onto the metal platform.

When she's steady on the ledge, I pat her hip and cross behind her to enter the cage.

As I put on my sparring gloves, Luca eyes her, then smirks at me.

When our mouthguards are secure, we take up our stances and begin.

Luca and I spar as though there's not a photographer capturing our every move, but I remain aware of Natalie's presence, nevertheless. She takes several shots over the fencing, her face a mask of concentration each time she stops and studies our movement. Eventually, as we punch, kick, and grapple our way around the enclosure, she hops down and moves along the cage. Halfway through the session, she switches lenses and climbs back up on the platform to shoot from a higher angle again.

We focus on proper form rather than heavy contact, and every few minutes, we stop so I can coach or correct Luca. He's in his mid-twenties, but he started training later than most young fighters do, so he's putting in extra hours to fine-tune his fundamentals.

Twenty minutes in, he's winded and not following through with his punches, so I call it.

I pull out my mouth guard and circle him as he rests his gloved hands on his knees and catches his breath. "You've been hitting that jump rope hard like we talked about?" He's got to build up his endurance or he'll never last in a real match.

He straightens and nods, still breathless.

"Good. I'll see you on Monday."

We bump gloves, and as he heads toward the locker room, he gives Natalie a weak salute.

"You're a good teacher." Head bowed, she packs her camera and equipment into her bag.

I unstrap my gloves and tuck them into the gaps of the chain link. "Yeah? You ready to spar with me, Nat?"

She whips her head my way, her shoulder-length waves fanning her face, her expression admonishing. Like she's ready to lecture me, to tell me that I shouldn't say things like that to her. Because I'm her brother's best friend. Because I was learning how to talk when she was learning how to write in cursive.

In the end, she doesn't scold. And she doesn't try to hide like she has before. Instead, she rises, squaring her shoulders, and approaches the cage. She laces her fingers through the gaps of the fence, one link below where mine rest.

When she locks eyes with me and finds me grinning like a fool down at her, her breath hitches.

That small response speaks volumes. She's not unfazed. She feels this too.

I hold my breath, ready for whatever she wants to throw my way.

But nothing could've prepared me for the one-two punch that hits me.

Lashes fluttering, she licks her lips. Then, in a breathy voice, she says, "I want to photograph you. At the studio. Alone."

CHAPTER SIX

NATALIE

My best friend answers on the fifth ring, and I'm greeted by a cacophony of little girl shrieks, shrill baby wails, and even the gruff bark of a dog.

"Hello? Nat? Hang on a second."

The tingling in my fingers intensifies as the noise on the other end of the line continues to assault my ears. Thank the technology gods for voice control capabilities. The barked command to "Call Olivia" slipped from my lips as soon as I closed myself in my SUV.

Static crackles over the line, then Liv shouts, her voice muffled. "Jordan! Come get this baby."

The scene playing out in their living room is one I can imagine easily. Liv's good-natured husband is probably tripping over the baby activity mats and discarded dolls that litter the blue geometric rug in the living room. When the low murmur of his voice is audible, he's no doubt wrangling sweet ten-month-old Sophie from his wife's arms.

Thoughts of their loud, happy chaos calm my pounding heart.

There's no need for me to don my mental suit of armor around Liv's little family. They've always made me feel like I belong, like I'm theirs. And when I'm with them, the empty corners of my heart fill, leaving no space for sadness to creep in.

But those moments of happiness and security are just that. Moments during which I forget how fucking lonely the rest of my life is. And inevitably, they fade, like temporary bouts of amnesia, and the pain returns.

A door shuts on Liv's end, and then my friend heaves a relieved sigh. "Still there?"

"I just made a colossal, dumbass mistake."

"Ooh, my favorite kind." She grunts slightly, like she's making herself comfortable. "Tell me everything."

So I do. I recount every interaction with Tucker over the past week: Our initial appointment at the gym. The almost-bike crash. Each one of our coffee shop run-ins. And today's photography session, which ended a mere ten minutes ago, after I abruptly requested a private photo shoot. I couldn't make eye contact after that, even as he and his manager helped me load up my equipment.

What in the actual hell was I thinking, asking him to come to the studio? It's like all his muscles and tattoos and testosterone hijacked my common sense.

I may have left the gym in a solid, human-shaped form, but my insides were minutes away from melting into liquid. That would've been preferable, actually, because then I could've disappeared through the cracks in the flooring.

When I finish telling Liv all the mortifying details, she's quiet for a moment. I assume she's choosing her words carefully to spare my feelings, so when her enthusiastic reply blares through the car speakers, I almost swerve off the road.

"Natalie! *Yes*. I love this journey for you."

"Wait...what?" My stomach tumbles.

Thank heavens the next stop light switches and I'm forced to stop, otherwise I'd be liable to careen off into a ditch. While my car is immobile, I hold out one arm, then the other so the vents send cold air up the short sleeves of my dark gray T-shirt.

"I don't see the problem, my friend. The man is *flirting* with you."

Liv's confirmation and the subsequent realization that Tucker's flirting hasn't been a figment of my imagination only provoke a new, more confusing question: *Why?* Why the hell has he been flirting with *me*? I'm not a woman who gets flirted with. I'm not the kind who garners attention from random men. And on the rare occasions I do? I'm horrible at reciprocating. I'm awkward and tongue-tied, or I spew the most bizarre, random facts.

Over the years, my mother has told me I should flirt more far too many times to count, as if that's the magical remedy for my chronic singleness. But my flirting game remains nonexistent.

"What did you say after he agreed to the photo shoot?"

Oh God. He agreed to the photo shoot. Despite the AC I've turned all the way up, a new layer of sweat coats my back and underarms. "I-I tried to explain why it was necessary. The private shoot."

My request that he come in for a beefcake playdate at Wayne's studio went something like *"Y-you could use the pictures for the website, like a 'meet the owner' kind of thing. You're the heart of this place. Including your backstory would help future members connect with you, with the gym."*

"Because his muscles are very photogenic and you think it'd be fun for the two of you to peep each other's pixels?"

"No," I sputter. "Oh my gosh, he's way younger than me." My cheeks flame, the heat of them raising the temperature in the car.

"He's the same age as Cam?" she asks, and when I hum in the affirmative, she says, "It's a less than ten-year age gap, ma'am. Next."

"He's my brother's *best friend* and roommate."

"Pfft." I can imagine the stubborn jut of her chin as she argues. "You're both single, consenting adults. Cam can deal. This guy is single, right?"

The light turns green, and as I ease through downtown Holly Holler, the thought of Tucker being someone's person makes me irrationally ill.

"Nat?"

"Uh, yeah, I think so." I pull into the space behind Wayne's studio and let my car idle while I convince myself that Tucker wouldn't act this way if he had a girlfriend.

"Hmm, surely he wouldn't be so forward if he was dating someone," she muses, corroborating my theory that she and I sometimes share a brain. "Just confirm that Hottie McGym-Bro is single when he flexes those muscles for your camera this afternoon."

"He's not really a gym bro," I mumble. "He owns a gym, yeah, and he's definitely fit. But I don't think he's one of those annoying *my life revolves around working out* fanatics."

"Score another point for the hottie. I haven't heard a single valid reason why y'all can't participate in some grown-up extra-curriculars while you're there."

"Because." I swallow to keep a barrage of emotions in check. "I don't have grown-up extra-curriculars."

And I don't just mean that my sex life is nonexistent. It's so much more than that. I've been deprived of everything that comes along with being in a relationship, and the truth of that threatens to bury me under metric tons of sadness, disappointment, and failure. The weight of it piles up until my lungs struggle for breath and my muscles ache.

I have dated, though most were blind dates set up by friends that didn't lead anywhere. And I had two romantic relationships in my twenties, but both of those men broke it off with me after a few months and then went on to marry the next women they dated.

The world is full of adults who are single by choice and damn happy about it. But I've never been content in my singleness. Like a vital part of me is missing. Like my journey through life has been taken in half-measured steps.

Loneliness has etched itself into my soul and covered me like a second skin.

Liv's sad sigh makes me homesick for her. "Just because you aren't right now doesn't mean you never will, Nat. Your story isn't over yet."

She tells me this often, and I love her all the more for it, even if I don't always believe it. If we were sharing the same air right now, she'd wrap me in a hug.

I push the depressing thoughts down. Though they'll linger in the periphery of my mind like shadows, just like they always do, I don't have time for them at present. I have to deal with the fallout of my earlier idiocy.

I clear my throat and sit taller in the driver's seat. "I'm going to text him and cancel the shoot. I'll tell him I forgot I had another session booked, or that I need an emergency surgery this afternoon and will be out of pocket for the next ten weeks."

"Don't. You. Dare." The fierce warning in her voice is undeniable and not the least bit surprising. "I will pack up my two children and all eighty-seven bags of crap they require and drive ten hours to tie that camera to your body and supervise the whole shoot."

I huff a disbelieving laugh, but she's not having it.

"I mean it, Natalie Torres. I'm damn sure you'd prefer Tucker be the one to tie you up, but I'll do it. You know I will."

Half scared she'll follow through, I sigh deeply. "Fine. I'll do the shoot."

Rather than respond, she's silent. Like she knows I'll feel forced to fill the quiet space. "He has a motorcycle," I whisper.

Images of him on his bike, effortlessly cool and sexy as he parked in front of the coffee shop on Tuesday morning, flash through my brain and light me up inside.

"*Natalie.*"

"I know," I wail.

I've harbored a thing for men on bikes since puberty, and my best friend knows it.

"Have a summer fling with a younger guy, Nat. Chase a little happiness. You deserve it."

Terror floods me. A fling? I wouldn't even know how.

Yes, I know *how*. Though my current dry spell falls into the Saharan Desert category, I remember the mechanics. Surely sex is like riding a bike. But I'm not sure I have the skill set required to be a participant in a fling.

A *fling* implies furtive meetups and rules like *no feelings allowed*.

And a fling with my younger brother's best friend? It sounds messy and complicated and scandalous.

Liv interrupts my thoughts, correctly interpreting my silence again. "You are a badass with a good ass. Embrace your cougar era for the summer. Go take a bite out of that man."

A squeak of protest escapes my lips. It's the only response I can manage.

"Was my pep talk sufficient, or do you need more?"

I refuse to acknowledge the *cougar* comment. "It was adequate."

She chuckles. "Good. I better go check on my family. Gotta make sure Jordan still has what remains of his hair. Have fun with the hottie. And don't forget the condoms—"

She's interrupted by three sharp knocking sounds. Then the sweet high-pitched voice of four-year-old Chloe comes over the line. "Mommy? What's a condom, and why are you hiding in your closet?"

Over the next few hours, I force myself to sit at my computer and edit the gym photos from this morning. Though I typically don't have trouble losing myself in the process, today, I'm constantly distracted by thoughts of Tucker. Every twenty minutes, I pick up my phone, determined to send him a text to cancel the shoot, only to set it down again, convincing myself to let him be the one to cancel instead.

Surely he will. He'll realize that he doesn't want to follow through with it, right?

If not for the decisiveness of his tone when he answered my out-of-nowhere request, I'd believe it. But every word he spoke in response was clear and confident, and each one lives rent-free in my mind, playing on a loop.

"I want to photograph you. At the studio. Alone."

"Today? Name the time, shutterbug."

With every replay, a flush of heat rushes to the surface of my skin.

There's no denying that I'm attracted to Tucker. I can't imagine any woman could be immune to those blue-gray eyes, the dark let-me-run-my-hands-through-it hair, and his tall, powerful body. Even memories of him as a seven-year-old kid in Spiderman pajamas don't temper the unfamiliar giddy thrill that courses through me when he smiles at me. Or drinks me in like he's memorizing every dip and curve of my body.

My skin still carries the brand of that hip pat he gave me after he helped me onto the metal ledge, and I'm half certain I'll find a handprint there when I peel my jeans off later.

At three, I'm still editing, my knee bouncing under Wayne's cluttered desk. It takes effort to ignore every little sound from the front of the studio, but I keep my focus locked on the computer.

When the clock rolls over to 3:05, I press my lips together to hold in a dejected sigh. But at 3:07, the deep rumble of an engine pricks my ears, and my heart stutters in my chest.

When it cuts off outside the front door, I eye my ratty old jeans and Eagles band tee with a curse, questioning my decision to not change.

When the bell on the studio's door jingles, I spring up from the rickety chair. From here, I can't see him, which is for the best, because my armor has slipped.

Is it possible that my full-armor ritual will keep my libido under control and temper my nerves long enough for me to conduct this session in a professional manner?

Only one way to find out.

Eyes closed, I square my shoulders and exhale a slow, deep breath. Then I slip my hands into my back pockets. I can do this; I can be cool and collected.

But when I round the corner and find Tucker Lacey running his hand through his dark hair with a helmet tucked under an inked arm?

Danger: system malfunction signs light up my brain like billboards in Times Square.

"Sorry I'm late. I promised Cam I'd get the grocery pickup, and it took longer than I thought it would." He scans me from head to toe and back up, taking his sweet time. When his eyes return to my face, they're starry and confident. "Then I had to unload the Jeep and wash the gym off me."

Don't do it, Natalie. Absolutely do not *think about him in the shower.*

"You ready to do this, shutterbug?" He sets the black helmet on the reception counter, then lifts both hands. "I'm at your mercy."

As my heart beats a frantic rhythm in my chest, I keep my hands locked in my pockets so their trembling won't give me away.

But Tucker's sly smirk tells me he knows exactly how affected I am.

"I, uh, wasn't sure about clothing."

I scan his boots and dark jeans, and when I take in his black T-shirt, it takes willpower not to linger on the way the cotton of the shirt stretches over his broad chest and shoulders. With one booted foot, he nudges a small black duffel on the tile floor in front of him. "Brought a pair of gym shorts and sneakers if you need me to change."

I swallow past the lump in my throat, and when I speak, my voice is huskier than is appropriate. "Um, that works. Let's get a few like this and go from there."

"Sounds good."

"I've got us all set up in here." I spin, and the moment Tucker is out of sight, a fraction of my confidence returns. As I lead him through the door to the high-ceilinged room where the sets are located, I take slow, even breaths, centering myself. This man has praised my ability as a photographer more than once. I refuse to let jitters taint his opinion of me or my professionalism. So I dig deep to calm myself, letting his words bolster my confidence.

I like watching you work. I can tell you're good.

He might be a master of the octagon, but this is my domain.

I direct him to take a seat on the stool in front of a stark white backdrop and floordrop. I want the colors of Tucker's tattoos to pop, so I chose a minimalist set. While he gets comfortable, I flip on the small radio on a side table, leaving it tuned to the yacht rock station Wayne's been listening to for years.

I step behind the tripod and my trusty Canon and snap a few shots to get my bearings, then use the rear monitor to assess the images. Tucker's just as attractive on camera as he is in person, but his charm and personality are missing.

I need him to loosen up, so I do what Wayne taught me many moons ago: I ask him to tell his story.

Chapter Seven

Natalie

"How did you find yourself on the path to becoming a fighter-slash-gym owner?"

Tucker shifts on the stool and breaks into a slow smile, revealing dazzling white teeth. "You remember me as a kid."

I roll my lips to keep them from twitching. Young Tucker was a force of nature, perpetually running on a set of fully charged batteries. All the Lacey boys were, really, which is probably why they were all so active in sports from an early age. Their parents likely appreciated the outlet. And like my brother, they played every team sport available.

But I want to hear his version, so I stay silent.

He shrugs and stares past my shoulder, as if lost in a memory. *Click.*

When he crosses his arms and leans back on the stool, his biceps cause his cotton T-shirt to stretch dangerously, and I fight like hell to pretend I don't notice.

Click. Click. Click.

"Even with football and baseball and soccer, I needed an additional outlet for my," he clears his throat, "overabundance of energy. So my parents signed me up for jiu-jitsu classes over in Jonesboro." A fond smile lights up his face. *Click.* "Mom and Dad were pulled in all directions back then, getting the three of us to one practice or another, so my granny would drive me. She'd sit in the foyer reading her Harlequin romances while I trained."

I can't help but smile at the memory of Mrs. Lacey's mom. The woman was barely over five feet, but she was all vim and vigor. She had every one of those boys, Cam included, toeing the line. My brother was devastated when she passed away several years ago.

"My brothers eventually focused on one sport each. For Griff, it was football. For Shaw—and Cam—baseball. But me?" He shakes his head. "I didn't have a natural talent or love for a singular sport the way they did. Yeah, I played football in college, but it was never my passion the way it is for Griff." He shifts, propping one foot on a rung. "In high school, I was on the wrestling team, and while I played football for Oklahoma, I kept up jiu-jitsu in the offseason and started boxing lessons, too. A couple of guys from the gym approached me about training for MMA, but I couldn't with my commitment to football. But as soon as I graduated and moved home, I started training."

"And you fell in love with it?"

His bluish-gray eyes cut to me. "I did."

Click.

"Because it's a mash-up of multiple sports?"

"Mmm." He tilts his head one way, then the other, thinking. "That's part of it. It means the training never gets boring. It held my attention. If I didn't feel like boxing, I could focus on grappling or takedowns. But more than anything, I fell in love with it because it was mine."

At the sincerity in his voice, I stand to my full height, my finger hovering over the shutter release.

"I didn't have to share MMA with my brothers. Or with Cam."

I can't help but smile. "Not so good at the sharing thing, huh?"

"I'm the youngest of three." His eyes darken as they hold mine captive. "Of course I don't like to share."

Click.

With a heavy swallow, I force my focus to the display and scroll through the last few shots. They're a hell of a lot better than those first few. These are fluid, like each frame has been infused with a drop of Tucker's vitality. He's in constant motion; even when talking, his hands highlight his words like a conductor directing a symphony. He's magnetic.

And even though a part of me is still mortified that I asked him to do this, a bigger part of me—the artistic, creative, always-looking-for-inspiration side—doesn't regret it one bit. The camera loves him, and any good photographer would jump at the chance to capture an essence like his.

He's watching me intently when I focus on him again, his expression thoughtful. I'm dying to know what he's thinking while he studies me like that, but I don't have the nerve to ask.

"What about the gym? How'd that come about?"

He swivels on the stool and rolls his shoulders back. "A few years ago, training and traveling for fights started to feel like a grind. I still loved stepping into the cage, but it was taking a toll on my body. I lived in Memphis while I was pro, and I missed home. And carbs." He brushes a thumb along the stubble under his lower lip, a move that makes my fingertips itch to do the same. *Click.* "I hated not having a place to train when I was home visiting. Figured the town could support a gym. I socked away as much money as I could while I was fighting, and when I stepped away two years ago, I made plans in earnest. Can't tell you how thrilled my mother was when I finally put my business degree to use."

"Enter Club Lacey Fitness. A small-town success story?"

"Eh, I don't know that I'd call us a success yet." His expression is a little reticent. "But we're definitely getting there. Growth has been slow. Steady but slow. As our membership builds, we've added more offerings. Started a senior jazzercise class last month."

The reserved smile turns into one full of pride, and in turn, my lips quirk up.

"Senior jazzercise? Does Mr. Abernathy know about this?"

He chuckles. "Mr. Abernathy is a devoted treadmill user. Same machine every single morning. If someone else is on it when he gets there, he'll wait them out."

I check the time on Wayne's beloved vintage Kit-Cat wall clock, noting the way its tail wags in sync with the thump-thump of my heart. "I think we've got plenty of shots to choose from." I tuck a lock of hair behind my ear as Liv's advice replays in my mind. "Don't want to keep you from any big Friday night plans."

His body locks up and his eyes narrow for a beat, but just as quickly, his posture relaxes. Arms crossed loosely over his chest, he lifts his chin, like he's figured me out. "I don't have any big Friday night plans, shutterbug."

Will I ask the question? Or will I play it safe?

When his lips curl up in a smug smile, the decision is made for me.

"No girlfriend to take out?"

"No girlfriend." His response comes without hesitation, accompanied by a satisfied gleam in his eye that douses the flames of embarrassment that scorch my insides.

"Right. Well—"

He stands, his boots thudding heavily. "I'm going to change real quick. We can take a few like that." He rubs the back of his neck, his smile sheepish and his cheeks tinged pink.

We can take a few like that—meaning muscles and tattoos on full display.

Damn it. My breathing picks up at just the thought.

"Uh, sure." I cling to my professionalism like it's the lone twig keeping me from being swept away in a flood. "The bathroom's down the hall behind the front desk. First door on the right."

Tucker sweeps up his duffel and bolts from the room like he's afraid I'll change my mind.

It's what I should do. I should reiterate that I have more than enough photos for him to choose from. And I should remind myself that this is a bad idea. This wanting to be near him. Wanting to talk to him. Wanting to touch him.

Instead, I use the brief respite from the lure of Tucker Lacey to pinch the fabric of my shirt and tug, fanning my overheated skin.

When he reenters the studio, wearing only a pair of black gym shorts, all those *should*s vanish like footprints erased by the tide.

Gone is the bashful, endearing Tucker from moments ago. This Tucker is bold and determined, sauntering into the space with sure, unhurried steps. Shoulders back, chest puffed out, arms loose by his sides.

This is the Tucker who faced down opponents in a fighting cage.

My brain and eyes battle over where to look first while my core muscles clench. This man is hotter than fish grease, and the sight of him shirtless literally makes my mouth water.

By some miracle, I shake myself from my hot-man stupor. "Let's get a few without the stool."

I step closer, arm outstretched to move it, but he beats me to it, snagging it with ease and pulling it off the floordrop.

"You want me here?" he asks as he steps, barefoot, onto the white neoprene spread out on the floor. "Left the shoes off since we fight this way." He props his hands on his hips. "I can get them if you—"

My heart stumbles. "No, this is fine." *Click.*

I examined the ink on one of his arms at the gym, but behind the lens, I take my time cataloging the rest of his tattoos. His arms are covered from wrists to shoulders with colorful designs woven between grayscale swirls. The bunches of flowers stand out to me first. There are several along both arms, each grouping unique, but the sunflowers on his left bicep are instantly recognizable. Van

Gogh. Upon further inspection, I notice the artist's famous blue irises on his right forearm.

He smirks when I ask him to turn around—*click*—but he complies, facing the backdrop, hands still resting on the waistband of his shorts. The upper portion of his back is inked with various patterns and pictures nestled between and along his shoulder blades. On his left shoulder, a trio of swallows takes flight, the wing of one bird wrapped over his trapezius muscle.

Click. Click. Click.

"Does the gym have an Instagram page?"

"It does."

With his back to me like this, a boldness takes over. "You should post some of these pics there. Every woman under the age of thirty in a fifty-mile radius will flock to the gym after seeing these thirst traps."

His shoulders bounce with silent laughter. "That would be a smart business move." With a sigh, he twists to face me. "But personally, I'm not interested in any woman under the age of thirty."

It's foolish to pretend the camera and tripod can hide me from the smolder in his eyes, but I try anyway.

Tucker runs a hand through his hair, then holds it out to one side. "Stool again?"

"Uh, sure." I'm unmoored, my body a riot of sensations too overwhelming to even name. Thank heavens the dark gray cotton of my T-shirt hides the flop sweat.

He settles on the edge of the stool, knee bent and foot propped on that rung again. This position exposes more of the black line rendering of *The Starry Night* on his muscular thigh.

I zoom in and capture a few close-ups, my heart hammering the whole time. "Do your brothers have tattoos?"

He inspects his forearm, twisting it over as he inspects the artwork. "They don't."

I nod. Makes sense. Yet another way he's set himself apart from Shaw and Griffin.

"Why Van Gogh?"

"He's my favorite. The quintessential tortured artist."

Tortured? What the hell does this man have to feel tortured about? I lick my lips, gearing up to ask that very question, but the hint of pain swimming in his irises stops me.

My heart thrums as I find myself locked in his gaze. In this moment, something passes between us, like a piece of his soul whispers to mine, saying, *We're alike, you and me.*

After several heartbeats, he blinks and shakes his head, like he's clearing a haze. "The subjects of his paintings are easily identifiable and ordinary. A chair. A building. A woman or a man. A nighttime sky." He pats his thigh. "But they're not painted in ordinary, flat brush strokes. They're layered and exaggerated and bold." He leans back, not breaking eye contact. "That's how I strive to live. To find the extraordinary in the ordinary. To infuse everyday moments with joy and excitement. Essentially, to live life out loud."

My chest tightens in response to his statement. God, what a privilege to live that way, to grab life by the horns and hold on for the ride. His outlook is different from my quiet, lonely existence in every way. He lives with a wild abandon, happy and unfettered.

I blink away the watery sheen in my eyes, thankful he doesn't point it out, and remind myself why we're here.

Right. *Take the damn pictures, Natalie.*

With a deep inhale, I force myself to concentrate on the camera's settings.

"Van Gogh is my favorite," he says, pulling my attention back to him, "but he's not the only artist here." He points to a pair of clocks melting over the curve of his arm.

"Dali."

With a nod, he touches the dreamy green water lilies floating among the designs close to the bend of his left arm.

"Monet," I say.

Another nod. With one finger, he traces the single white lily near his right shoulder. "O'Keeffe."

The angular black lines and bold shapes near his wrist are similar to works by Kandinsky. The loopy minimalist doodles are no doubt inspired by Picasso. Every piece is seamlessly joined to the next by swirling gray and black ribbons and lines.

He's a living, breathing work of art.

And I'm not only referring to the works inked on his skin. The cut of his muscles, the lines of his body, the strength in his frame all make this man a beautiful masterpiece.

"They're incredible," I say. "Who did them?"

"A buddy. Met him at a gym in Memphis. He's an amazing artist. Has his own shop downtown." He surveys me, his attention sweeping down my body, causing goose bumps to prickle my skin. "You have any tats, shutterbug?"

I shake my head. "I've always wanted one," I say before I think better of it.

His slow smile is a little wicked. "You should get one. I'll take you to Lux's."

Ignoring his offer, the flush it brings to my cheeks, and the challenge in his stare, I ask, "How did a football-playing, MMA-fighting boy from Arkansas become such an appreciator of fine art?"

The smirk he gives me in answer makes my stomach swoop. *Click.*

"I was eleven. Granny promised Cam and me a Saturday at the Little Rock Zoo, but halfway there, it started storming. Instead of driving home, she insisted we could use a little culture and dragged us to the Museum of Fine Arts. The two of us bellyached the rest of the way there, but drawings and sculptures of half-naked ladies kept our attention well enough." He wags his brows.

I laugh at the thought of the two of them at that age, elbowing each other, unable to contain their shocked amusement.

"I kept coming back to this one painting. Every time I stood in front of it, it spoke to me. Like it held the secret of life or something. When I close my eyes, I can still see every detail. An abstract painting on canvas, full of bright lines and shapes and scribbled curves." He moves his hands as though he's sketching the painting in the air. "It was just some piece by a local artist, but for the first time in my life, I found something that both captured and quieted the chaos in my brain." He pops a shoulder. "Like the artist had cracked open my skull and studied the clutter he found inside, then replicated it on that canvas."

"Tucker." It's all I get out. He's baring another piece of his soul to me, and I don't know how to respond. Every layer peeled back reveals another facet of this man that draws me in. Each time, I want more. I want to study each one until he's no longer a mystery. Until he's as familiar as my own reflection.

"Granny noticed my interest," he says, "and for Christmas that year, she gave me a book of famous artists and their best-known works. I flipped through that thing so often, the cover detached from the pages." He cocks his head at the memory. "I minored in art history, even though my parents argued it was useless."

Damn. Of course he took art classes just for the sake of it. For the knowledge and enjoyment.

I've already taken more pictures than he'll ever need or want. It's time to wrap this up. But I can't seem to quit.

"Can you shift your left shoulder forward a bit? Yeah, like that, but down a little? Now tilt your chin."

He runs a hand through his hair and makes the adjustments, but the move causes a piece to stick up on top. Rather than try to direct him to fix it, I leave the safety zone behind the camera and approach.

As his gray-blue irises track my every move, he widens his stance, like he's making room for me between his thighs.

This close, I'm enveloped in his scent. The fresh water and citrusy hints of his soap or body wash mix with subtle notes that remind me of the training room in the gym.

"Can I..." I raise my hand to his head, but I don't touch, not without his permission. "Can I fix this?"

He dips his chin.

When I brush through the soft waves to smooth the hair back into place, his eyelids drift closed. When I pull my hand away, he watches me again, his clenched fists resting on his thighs, like he's restraining himself. Like he's tempted to reach for me.

Oh, how I want him to.

We stay this way, suspended between wondering and wanting, for several moments. I trace a path over his features, from the dark brows and thick lashes that frame his slate blue eyes, to the slight bump on the bridge of his nose to the dark stubble that covers his lower cheeks, chin, and upper lip. It's there my journey pauses, on the perfect shape and shade of those lips.

When he swallows, the column of his throat rippling, I suck in a breath and spin back to the tripod. If I don't put space between us, I worry I'll do something I'll regret.

I take a few more pictures, and when I'm finished, he silently slips into his T-shirt and toes on his sneakers.

To keep from staring, I fiddle with the camera and move the umbrella lights away from the set.

He lingers at the door, watching me instead. After I've run out of legitimate ways to avoid him, I clear my throat. "I'll let you know when I'm finished editing these, and I'll have a disc with all the pictures ready for you sometime next week."

"Sounds good."

Rather than turn and exit like I expect, he remains planted to the spot.

Heat creeps up the back of my neck. "Is there something else you need?"

"Yeah." His lips twitch slightly. "I need to give you a hug."

"Wh-what?"

"A hug." He smirks, but it's not cocky. "It's this thing where humans show care and affection for each other by—"

"No," I say, cutting him off, "I mean *why*?"

He shrugs. "Just thought maybe you could use one."

My stomach sinks. Can he tell? Is it glaringly obvious that, deep down, I'm so starved for affection, its absence is a physical ache?

I open my mouth to respond, but the best I can do is sputter out a couple embarrassing sounds.

Unbothered, Tucker ambles over, ducking his head. "Or maybe I'm the one who needs it. Either way, can I hug you, Natalie?"

And here come those pesky *should*s again. I should laugh it off. I should say no thanks. I should offer him a handshake or a high five or a fist bump instead.

But God, I want to be hugged by this man. So I let myself have this.

"Sure." The word is barely a whisper.

But he doesn't miss it. And he doesn't give me a chance to change my mind.

He grasps my forearms and guides them around his middle, then settles his around me, like he doubted that I'd hug him back. He cocoons me, his hold firm, buffering me from the negative thoughts that try to attack.

I soak it up, this sense of peace and safety, wishing I could bottle it up for later. When he makes the first soothing pass up and down my back, I fist his T-shirt, willing the moment to continue.

When I find my voice and speak into the soft cotton of his shirt, his hand stills. "I read an online article that claims a person's mood can be boosted and their stress can be reduced if they receive eight hugs a day."

He squeezes me tighter. "Then this is..." He breathes out and drags his hand over my back again. "Twelve and a half percent of your daily hug requirement, shutterbug."

Of course he's good at math, too.

I ease back and give him a shy smile. "Thank you."

"Anytime." His grin is intoxicating, making my knees weak.

After another heartbeat, he drops his arms. Quickly, I step away, needing to put some distance between us before I really show my hand and beg him for another hug. But the absence of his warmth leaves me bereft.

I tuck my hands into my back pockets and tilt my head. "Drive safe."

He shoulders his bag and rubs his hands together. "Yeah. See you soon, Nat."

With those parting words, he turns to leave.

I remain a statue in the middle of the studio, cataloging each sound of his departure, from his footsteps across the tile in the foyer to the tinkle of the bell above the door as he exits.

As the rumble of his motorcycles fades into the distance, I'm left wondering what the hell I'm going to do about my crush on my younger brother's best friend.

CHAPTER EIGHT

TUCKER

"Ooh, don't you two look so tan and rested."

"Mom, let them get in the door."

"Here, I'll take y'all's bags upstairs."

"Delta, down girl."

"I've got 'em, Dad."

The house breaks into chaos, as it always does in the midst of a Lacey family homecoming, as Griffin and his girlfriend Brynn cross the threshold.

I savor every second of it with a wide grin on my face. There's nothing I love more than being with my favorite people.

I hang back while Mom and Dad hug the happy couple. They're fresh off a ten-day trip to the tropics to attend the wedding of one of Griff's teammates. As Mom *ooh*s and *aah*s over them, I sneak a peek at Brynn's left hand and bite back a curse.

Shaw catches my eye across the entryway and raises a satisfied brow.

Griff reaches for the handle of the suitcase Dad's gotten ahold of, but when Dad backs away, he gives up with a good-natured shrug and picks up the second one. As the two of them make their way upstairs, Delta follows and Mom steers Brynn farther into the living room.

When it's just the two of us, Shaw wordlessly sticks out his hand.

Damn, I was sure I'd win. Griff's had the ring for over two weeks.

With a roll of my eyes, I slap a crisp one-hundred-dollar bill into his hand. "Double or nothing, he does it before training camp starts."

Adjusting the brim of his faded Lacey Farms ball cap, my oldest brother peers into the living room, ensuring Brynn and Mom aren't listening to our scheming. "Done."

We shake on it, and as he steps away, I plot to get Griff alone sometime during their weekend visit to offer grand gesture suggestions.

While Dad grills steaks on the back porch and Mom brings side dishes to the table, Griff and Brynn regale us with details of their vacation and their friends' wedding.

My brother is so ridiculously in love. The way he smiles at the woman next to him like she's the best thing in the world brings me intense happiness along with a slight pinch of jealousy. It also conjures visions of the woman who's staked a claim on my thoughts lately.

We shared a handful of Capital-M Moments last Friday. Moments that replay like a montage in my brain several times a day. Moments that've made me crave more time with her. It felt right, having her in my arms when she let me hug her, and her openness to accepting that gesture from me lit me up inside. A one-time hug could be just that, of course. There's no guarantee it will lead to something bigger. And damn, is the woman guarded. If I had to guess, she's erected those walls to protect herself from disappointment, and I have zero intention of disappointing—

"Earth to Tuck." Griffin's voice pulls me out of my reverie.

As I blink out of my daze, I find every member of my family staring at me expectantly. Like they're waiting for a response I can't give.

This kind of moment has happened so many times at this table, it's become a staple of the Lacey family dinnertime.

Brynn, sitting directly across from me, takes pity on me and gives me an encouraging smile. "Where's Cam tonight?"

"He's finishing up at the hangar. I think we're gonna hit up the Hoot later on if y'all want to join."

She pins a hopeful look on my brother. "You want to go? Just for a little while?"

He tucks a chunk of her hair behind her ear. "Whatever you want, baby."

"I want to see Trixie. And Dottie."

With a nod, Griff wraps an arm around Brynn's shoulders. "We're in."

I smirk at my soon-to-be sister-in-law. "Fair warning: yesterday was the last day of school, so Trix and Mabel will no doubt be tying one on." I nudge my eldest brother with an elbow. "What about you?"

He stalls, head bowed, a sure sign he's about to decline.

"Yes, Shaw," Brynn pleads. "Come with us."

If sighs carried weight, the one my brother exhales would be heavier than a boulder. But when he peers at her from under the brim of his cap, no doubt noting the warmth of a blush on her cheeks and the hope sparkling in her eyes, he's as good as committed.

He gives a gruff dip of his chin, and she snuggles deeper into Griff's side, a look of triumph on her face.

My parents watch on, both beaming at her. Damn, this whole fam is ready for Brynn's last name to become Lacey.

"I'll need to drop Delta off first." My eldest brother twists to where his faithful golden retriever is working on the bone Mom slipped her earlier.

"Let her stay," Mom offers. "She loves to cuddle with your father while he dozes on the couch after dinner."

Shaw sighs again, this one about as weighty as the lying rock that rests on the fireplace mantel. "She's not supposed to get on the furniture. That's what the bed is for." He gestures to the giant plush dog pillow in the corner of the living room.

Our mother's eyes narrow on him. Shit. That look means she's about to middle-name somebody. And if she barks out the triple name? We're in big trouble.

It's surprising, really, that I've yet to hear her middle-name Brynn. She might not know it yet, but it's coming.

Sure enough, her next words are spoken in that mom tone we all know so well. "I'll spoil that girl if I want to, Shaw Morgan. Until these two," she flaps a hand at Brynn and Griffin, "give me a grandbaby, Delta's all I have."

I roll my lips to keep from laughing at the wide-eyed shock on the happy couple's faces.

She pivots quickly, redirecting her displeasure, and my glee quickly evaporates. "And if my other thirty-something year-old sons would get busy finding themselves nice girls to settle down with, that would be lovely."

Now it's Griffin's turn to smirk. "Mama Lacey is not playing tonight."

At the same time, Shaw mumbles "goddamn it" under his breath.

Dad jumps into the fray with a barked "language" as Mom narrows her eyes at her oldest son and says, "Shaw Morgan Lacey, you know better than to say that word at my table."

"Lacey family rules," the three of us mutter in unison. It's a routine we've kept up since we were old enough to understand that this is Donna and Fred's world, and we're just living in it.

Damn, I love my family.

Mom's fury dissipates like early morning fog in the sun, and a heartbeat later, she's smiling sweetly at Shaw. "It's settled, then. Delta will stay here. Go out, have fun. You can pick her up in the morning."

Griff and I eye each other across the table. He knows as well as I do that this is Mom's way of denying Shaw the chance to back out of joining us at the bar. If he were to stop off at his cabin to drop her off on the way, chances are he wouldn't leave again.

He's not a fan of people-y places. Or of most people, honestly. He has a heart of gold hidden under all his grumpiness, though not many are privileged enough to witness it. My heart aches for him today as much as it did when his world collapsed and this grumpy persona really took over.

What I wouldn't give for him to find a slice of happiness and claim it for himself. To see him as settled and content as Griffin.

Those thoughts immediately lead me back to Natalie.

Maybe I can put a bug in Cam's ear. Get him to invite his sister tonight. I want to see her again. Our brief morning interactions at the coffee shop this week have only driven my interest in her higher.

After dinner, the four of us shoo Mom and Dad into the living room to relax so we can tag-team the clean-up. After, Griffin and Brynn take off in his truck. I try to convince Shaw to let me ride with him, but he won't give up his opportunity to leave early, so as he rolls down the long driveway, I hop on my bike and head downtown.

The sight of the full parking lot outside the saloon-style building my aunt and uncle built over twenty years ago makes my chest swell with pride. Not only is every spot taken, but most of the spaces that line North Street and the town square are as well.

In situations like this, riding a bike has its perks. Slowly, I cruise toward the dumpster, and sure enough, the patch of concrete near it is open. It's too small for a car, but it's the perfect size to park my Gold Wing.

Music and voices spill out into the warm evening. While this corner of the square is alive, the rest is dark. Loblolly is still open, but this late on a Friday night, it's a ghost town.

As I round the building and head for the swinging doors that knocked Trixie on her ass many, many times when we were kids, I admire the violets and pinks and oranges in the dusk sky. I'm too busy marveling at how the colors layer and swirl like broad, textured brush strokes on a canvas to notice the body paused in my path until I almost collide with the person.

"Tucker Lacey, always with your head in the clouds."

I tuck my helmet under my arm and give Mabel a side hug. "Happy first day of summer, Mabes."

Trixie's best friend grins up at me, her crystal blue eyes twinkling in the glow of the neon lights. "We've got quite the crew at our favorite table." She holds out a hand, gesturing to the front door, a blond brow arched. "Including one reclusive Lacey brother. How'd y'all manage to get Shaw out tonight?"

I smile at the woman who claimed several of my adolescent firsts, including first kiss, first girlfriend, first fumbling trip to second base, and first heartache. We long ago moved beyond the throes of teenage puppy love, and these days, we maintain a friendship I'm proud of. It was awkward the first couple years after we broke up, but we decided long ago that remaining friends was in our best interest. In a town like this, we cross paths often, and neither of us had any interest in constantly finding ourselves uncomfortable in one another's presence.

Plus, Trixie would've kicked my ass if we didn't find a way to get along.

"That was all Brynn."

"Ah." She bobs her head. "So she's not just Griffin's saving grace. She makes all three of you look good."

"Without question." I palm the brim of the cap I pulled out of my saddlebag. "What are you doing out here? I thought you and Trix would be well past buzzed by now."

"Oh, she's not far from it." With a smirk, she holds up her cell phone. "I was halfway through my second round when I realized I left this in Cam's truck."

"Y'all rode with Cam?"

She huffs a laugh. "He was leaving when I pulled up at Trixie's. Insisted on being our DD tonight."

"Of course he did." We break into matching snickers. "Who else is here?"

A zip of excitement courses through me at the possibility that Cam invited Natalie, but I tamp down on the sensation.

Humming, she tilts her head toward the crowd gathered near the entrance.

Ah. Standing room only tonight, then.

I follow her lead, pushing through the throng of bodies until the warmth of the waning sun is replaced by the crisp coolness of the Hoot's air conditioning. She winds through the crowded space easily, waving at people as she goes.

It takes my eyes a moment to adjust to the dimness of the bar, but all the way, I greet acquaintances as well.

When we reach the table on the edge of the dance floor where our crew normally holds court, I scan the faces around it. When I don't see the one I'm looking for, my gut bottoms. She's not here.

"Tucker!" A tipsy Trixie flounders when she stands to greet me, but Cam steadies her quickly with a hand on her hip. She flings her arms wide, grinning like a loon. "It's summer."

I can't help but get caught up in her joy. Nevertheless, I have to tease her. "Take it easy there, Ms. Frizzle."

She scowls, but as Mabel slides into the empty chair beside her, the expression morphs into another giant grin. "Mabes! You're back. Let's get shots."

"Uh, let's not." Cam frowns at a phone covered with a glittery purple case.

I take the seat next to him and peer at the device. Sure enough, he's examining the peaks and troughs on the app that connects with Trixie's continuous glucose monitor. Since her type-1 diagnosis a few months shy of her fourth birthday, we've all become vigilant experts. My brothers and I all have the app on our phones so we can monitor her blood sugar when necessary. Pretty sure it's on Mabel's, too. It would be on Cam's if Trixie would give in and give him the login information.

"Camden Little, you're not in charge here." Trixie snatches her phone from his grip with a huff. "I've only had two."

"You're tipsy after one, silly rabbit."

She rolls her eyes at the nickname he's taunted her with since we were kids. "Let's go program some tunes." Snagging Mabel's hand, she heads to the TouchTunes jukebox along the wall closest to the stage. Though the Hoot typically brings in a live band on Friday and Saturday nights—often with Trixie up on stage with them—it appears that we'll have to make do with recorded music blaring from the speakers.

Griffin ducks in close to Brynn, and when she nods, he points to our end of the table. "Cam, you good?"

My friend holds up the lone beer he'll nurse all night.

"Tuck, Shaw, the usual?" Once he has our confirmation, he grasps Brynn's left hand and lifts the third finger. He gives it a wiggle and presses a quick kiss to it. "Soon, Brynn Nelson." With that, he disappears into the crush of bodies blocking the path to the bar.

Even in the low lighting, Brynn glows as she grins at Shaw and me. She leans in, a conspiratorial lift to her brows, so my brother and I angle closer to the table. "I know he has a ring."

Neither of us moves a muscle, and I'm pretty sure my heart stops.

"He's beginning to think I know about it, so he keeps teasing me to see if I'll fess up." She jabs her pointer at me and then at Shaw. "Don't tell him."

I mime zipping my lips, and Shaw sits upright, giving me major side-eye. Yeah, he's going to owe me cash soon. There's no way Griff will delay a proposal once he discovers Brynn's on to him. Hell, if I tattled on her right now, he'd be on one knee in the middle of our family's bar.

Cam's phone buzzes on the table, pulling his attention away from Trixie and Mabel, who are talking to a group of guys by the jukebox. He glances at it, does a double take, then snatches it up. Thumbs flying over the screen, he pushes his chair back with a screech. He stands and lifts up on his toes, and with a huge smile, he throws his arm up and waves. "My sister's here."

I swivel around fast enough to give myself whiplash.

The instant I see her, adrenaline surges and my pulse picks up.

I don't care that her brother's here. Or that she's only in town for a few weeks. The age difference doesn't deter me either.

And as Natalie Torres approaches and I drink her in, cataloging her enticing curves, I know I'm making my move tonight.

Chapter Nine

Natalie

"After you set the dial to the correct wash cycle and choose the temperature, you add the detergent."

Goose, the goodest boy in all the land, sits on the laundry room rug, tracking my every move with his dark eyes. He's rapt, soaking up my instructions like he understands every word, just as he's done with each lesson I've given him over the past three years.

Last month, I walked him through how to make the perfect omelet. He loved the bacon bonus he earned for being a perfect pupil.

"Be sure not to overfill the washer. If you do, they may not get as clean as they should, and it's hard on the machine." With a flourish, I flip the last of the jeans and T-shirts into the drum and close the lid. When the rhythmic whirring of the wash cycle begins, I lean a hip against the machine, an action that prompts my dog to stand and give me a friendly bark.

"I know. It will probably take you longer to load since you can only fit one or two pieces in your mouth at a time."

He tilts his head, ears perked.

"But laundry is a necessary part of being a grown-up, Goosey boy."

His tail twitches back and forth, matching the *swish-swish* sound emanating from the washer.

"When this load is done, we'll go over the difference between permanent press and normal drying cycles." Crouching, I ruffle his ears. "Task complete. Time for a treat."

In the kitchen, I snag a gourmet peanut butter-flavored biscuit from the almost-empty package—proof of Mom's incessant spoiling—then one of the homemade chocolate chip cookies Nancy sent home with me tonight.

The Ganns invited me over for a home-cooked dinner, and during the meal, I debriefed Wayne on how things are going at the studio. He and I discussed the upcoming Ketchum wedding while Nancy fussed over us, refilling our sweet teas and coaxing us into second helpings of beef tips and rice. The meal was delicious, but I regretted that second plate the entire car ride home. The moment I walked in the door of my mother's home, I made a beeline for my childhood bedroom and the stretchy pants inside.

Mom and James are out, both working late tonight, so I figured I'd catch up on my neglected basket of laundry.

With Goose hot on my heels, I pad across the cool tile floors of the sprawling ranch-style home. They've remodeled over the years, so it no longer looks like the house Mom and I moved into after James proposed, but Cam and I still have bedrooms down the long hallway to the right of the spacious living room. The frames that line the walls serve as a pictorial timeline of our childhood and adolescence, culminating with images of us each wearing our senior cap and gown—taken by Wayne, of course.

While I settle under the plush sage green comforter and use a spare pillow to prop up my laptop, Goose spins in circles, creating a nest at the end of the bed using the crocheted blanket he's laid claim to.

The second bowling alley scene has just begun when Mom calls my name from the end of the hall.

"We're down here."

She pokes her head into the open doorway. "Have you had dinner?"

"Yeah, at Wayne and Nancy's. She sent a container of chocolate chip cookies."

"That was nice of her. Wayne's getting along all right?" She ventures to the foot of the bed on stockinged feet and plants a kiss on Goose's furry head.

I nod once. "As good as he can manage in a full leg cast and wheelchair."

She gives Goose a good ear-scratching, then sidles up and kisses my head.

"Don't think I didn't notice that you kissed the dog before your firstborn," I tease. With my hands planted on the mattress, I slide over so she can prop against the headboard.

The familiar light rose petal-scent of her beloved perfume washes over me, comforting me as she twirls chunks of my hair like she did when I'd lay my head in her lap as a girl.

Ignoring my comment, she squints at my laptop screen and bunches her lips. "This one? Still?"

"What?" I press pause, leaving Stephanie and the gang frozen as they scramble outside to watch the Cool Rider take on the Cycle Lords. "This is my comfort movie."

I tuck the blanket under my chin and sigh. I'll never in my life be as cool as Stephanie Zinone.

"It's your fault, really. You let me watch it at a very formative age. Long before I had any clue what Mr. Stuart was teaching in that biology class."

She playfully pinches my side. "You've had every line memorized since you were ten. I'll never forget when James had to rescue you from the top of the ladder when you attempted to act out 'Cool Rider.'"

I bark a laugh that makes Goose lift his head. "Ugh, don't remind me."

Mom's silent laughter jostles the bed. When she sobers, she says, "Cam and his friends are hanging out down at the Hoot 'n' Holler. Why don't you meet up with them? It's still early."

According to the tiny digital clock in the corner of my computer screen, it's 8:32. "Going out would mean hard pants." I groan. "And a bra."

And if Cam's there, then Tucker will be, too. And the thought of seeing him causes all sorts of confusing feelings to bubble up inside me.

I've run into him at the coffee shop every morning this week. And for the past couple of days, as we've parted ways on the sidewalk, he's initiated a hug. It may be a tiny molehill of an act, but it provides a whole mountain of comfort to start my day.

"I have a load in the washer."

"I'll switch it over for you." She gives my side another pinch. "You're way too young to be an old fuddy-duddy like me. Go hang out with your brother. He's so excited to have you home."

My stomach sinks. Ugh. Mom-guilt. It never fails.

But she's right. One of the biggest perks of working here this summer is the opportunity the time gives me to bond with Cam.

"Fine. I'll go for a little bit." I close the laptop and sit up.

Goose stands, too, stretching, and gives me his best *what now?* face.

"You good hanging out with Grammie for a while?"

Mom smiles at the scruffy dog who's stolen both of our hearts. And my stepfather's. "He'll keep me company until James gets home." She checks her watch. "He should be here any minute now. I'm going to throw together some sandwiches." She pecks my cheek, then stands. "Have fun. Flirt with a man. Call us if you or Cam needs a ride. And you have permission to break curfew."

I give her a wry look. Not once in my teenage years did I break curfew. My brother, on the other hand...

Goose follows Mom to the kitchen, and she chats with him the whole way.

Begrudgingly, I strip out of my comfy clothing. Luckily, my favorite jeans are clean, and the fitted tank I find is printed with an abstract black-and-gray pattern that reminds me of the swirls and ribbons of Tucker's tattoos. My boobs look amazing in it, and it highlights the nip of my waist perfectly, but I rarely wear it. Honestly, I can't remember why I even packed it. But tonight, I'm glad I did. As I scrutinize my reflection, I consider changing into a comfier band T-shirt, but a boldness I don't often experience threads through me, and I decide to go for broke.

My erratic period should be making an appearance next week, so I might as well save my coziest, roomiest clothes for then. If it even shows up at all. PCOS is a fickle bitch.

Downtown, I'm forced to park a couple of blocks away. Rather than let annoyance creep in, I think about how happy Cam will be when he sees me. That alone is enough to have me hoisting up my metaphorical big girl panties and trudging to the bar. Small groups of folks cluster outside, laughing and enjoying the cooler temps of nightfall. Settings like this—where I'm certain my awkward introversion stands out like a sore thumb among crowds of revelers—have always intimidated the hell out of me.

But for my brother—and maybe for the chance to be in Tucker's proximity—I push through the throng and maneuver my way to the entrance.

Inside, the cacophony of music and voices overwhelms me. I freeze next to the swinging doors and wrestle my phone from my crossbody, all the while fighting the instinct to flee. As I'm jostled to-and-fro by passers-by, I type out a message to my brother.

I'm at the Hoot. Are you still here?

As I'm clutching my phone, keeping it from being knocked out of my hands, Cam's reply buzzes through.

Cam:

We've got a table by the dance floor! Back right corner!

His familiar overuse of exclamations calms me, allowing me to fill my lungs completely for the first time since I stepped out of my car.

I follow his directions, and when I spy him, one arm up, waving wildly, my breath releases in a rush. His welcoming grin makes me quicken my pace, though I can't ignore the intensity in Tucker's gaze as he watches me approach.

"Nat!" Camden greets me with a hug and slings his arm over my shoulder. "Y'all remember my sister Natalie?"

I'm met with a chorus of *heys* and several friendly smiles, along with a clipped nod from Shaw. Tucker offers me his seat next to Cam, and when his arm brushes me as he moves to take the empty spot at the head of the table, a tingle zips down my spine.

As I settle on the wooden seat, the pretty brunette I saw with Griffin at the handprint ceremony extends her hand across the table, beaming. "Hey, I'm Brynn."

The kindness glittering in her brown eyes would put me at ease if not for the blue-gray irises searing into me from my side. This type of scrutiny usually makes me want to hide, to shield my face with my hair or shift away. But with Tucker?

I covet his attention.

For most of my adulthood, my self-confidence has remained hidden below the surface, an untapped resource. I've started addressing this with my therapist back home. But Tucker's unexpected interest has helped chisel away my doubts and insecurities.

I lift my chin and smile at the couple across from me. "It's nice to meet you, Brynn. I'm Natalie."

Griffin takes a pull from his bottle and drapes his arm along the back of his girlfriend's chair. "Tuck said you're home for the summer?"

I give him a small smile. "Yeah, I'm filling in for Wayne the next couple months. I was already scheduled to be here in July to shoot a few places for the state tourism department, so extending the trip was pretty simple."

"You should have Cam take you up to get some aerial shots." Tucker's jean-clad leg brushes mine under the table, but his face remains innocent as he twirls his bottle on the tabletop.

"Ooh, have you ever flown with him?" Brynn asks, her attention darting from me to my brother.

Cam smirks. "She's been up with Dad, but not with me."

A sudden surge of pride in my little brother threatens to overwhelm me.

He has plans to follow in his father's footsteps and one day take over the family ag piloting business. Little Aviation provides crop dusting and seeding services to farms in the region.

I nudge Cam with my elbow. "I'd love to go flying with you."

His brows climb. "Really?"

"Sure. I've never attempted aerial photography, so the pictures might be shit, but I'd love to try. And there's no one I trust more than you to take me up."

Shoulders pulled back, he nods, unmistakable pride gleaming in his eyes.

When I dare to look his way, Tucker lifts his chin subtly, genuine appreciation in his expression. And when he raises his bottle to his lips, warmth flushes my skin.

Thank God it's dark in here.

He bumps my leg again. This time, though, he doesn't retreat. Instead, a warm weight settles against my calf, firm and unyielding.

Banter and inside jokes flit around the table, and even though I'm not involved in most of the conversation, I enjoy the company.

Cam flags down a harried waitress and orders a cocktail for me. To my surprise, the woman who approaches the table is the same woman who's taken my coffee order every morning this week. Her T-shirt is dark, with *Hootin' Leads to Hollerin'* printed across the chest, and her long blond hair is tied back in a low ponytail. After she's taken my order, she lingers at Shaw's end of the table for a beat. When he doesn't look her way, she flounces off with her tray tucked under her arm.

"Don't start," the eldest Lacey grumbles when she's out of earshot.

Cam raises his hands and laughs. "We know how one-sided that is. But she asks about you every time I stop in the coffee shop. And I'm not even related to you."

Shaw's eyes narrow as he drains his beer. "Not interested."

"Oh, we know." Griffin's tone is light, though the way he eyes his brother hints to deeper meaning.

Shaw pivots, glaring at the middle Lacey brother, but Griffin's too caught up in Brynn to notice.

Ever the peacemaker, Cam slaps a palm to the table, drawing the attention of the entire group. "Almost ran over Lisa Marie when she was crossing West Street earlier." He leans in, one brow cocked, like he's waiting for a response.

Griffin takes the bait. "Two-legged or four?"

Everyone except Brynn chuckles. Even Shaw snickers.

Damn, I haven't thought about this town's abundance of Lisa Maries in years, though the four-legged component of Griffin's question is surprising.

This bit of town lore feels like sinking into a warm bath after a long day. Comforting and familiar.

"Believe it or not, two," Cam answers.

Brynn scans the table, frowning. "Wait, I don't get it."

Tucker quells his laughter. "Holly Holler is home to *four* Lisa Maries." He cups the bill of his cap and squeezes it, curling it further.

The move is simple, a habit a lot of guys possess, but it instantly causes my body temperature to spike. Blessedly, the waitress returns, and the second she sets my rum and pineapple concoction in front of me, I pick it up and take a long sip.

"Three of them are human. And the fourth..."

Brynn frowns, her dark brows furrowed. "Don't leave me hanging, Tuck."

"Belongs to the bovid family." Arms crossed, he settles against the back of his chair.

I take another gulp of my drink to distract myself from his forearms.

Brynn purses her lips. "The Bovids? They're a family here in Holly Holler?"

Shaw expels a put-upon sigh. "It's a damn goat." He glowers at his youngest brother, then tilts his head toward Brynn, his expression softening. "A bovid is a mammal with hooves, like cows and sheep. And goats."

"Wait," I interject. "There's a *goat* named Lisa Marie, too?"

Tucker nods.

"The one we saw in the square that morning?"

He straightens, his mouth opening to answer, but before he can, my brother lurches forward.

"When were you two together in the—"

Trixie glides up to the table, the sight of her causing Cam to snap his mouth shut. A woman with thick, beachy waves appears as well, and the two of them sink into the lone vacant chair, squishing in close.

In the dark, it takes a moment to recognize Mabel Abernathy, Trixie's friend. Her family has owned the Dusty Britches Mercantile on the town square for generations. Both women regard me with curious expressions, though Trixie's quickly morphs into one of recognition. She tips her empty bottle my way and smiles. "Hey, Natalie. Good to see you again."

"You too." I return the smile, then turn it on the blonde perched next to her. "Mabel, right?"

Beaming, she bobs her head. "And you're the photographer who charmed the pants off Grandpa. He's telling everyone that he's going to be a cover model for Tuck's gym." She raises a brow and directs the look at the man by my side. "I tried to convince him it's poor form for him to model for my ex-boyfriend's business, but he wasn't having it."

While the group breaks into laughter, my heart sinks.

Of course he dated her. She's gorgeous and effervescent. Literal sunshine in human form.

While I'm a gray cluster of sad and lonely.

Tucker nudges my leg with his. "Ancient history, Mabes. We were practically babies."

She winks at him and raises her glass. "Friends forever?"

"Forever." He salutes her with his bottle.

As he sets it down, I can feel his attention on me, but I stare at my half-empty glass, afraid I'll reveal too much if I make eye contact.

"Speaking of your exes," Trixie drawls, "I ran into Sydney Peterson at the DB this afternoon."

My stomach drops, joining my battered heart on the floor beneath me. Fucking fabulous. The parade of Tucker's exes continues.

"Would we call her an ex?" Mabel asks. "We were never officially official."

We? Frowning, I survey the blonde.

Trixie slings her arm around her bestie and leans forward, zeroing in on me like she's caught on to my confusion. "Mabel here has boyfriends *and* girlfriends."

The blonde pops a shoulder and smiles. "I'm ambisextrous." Brows pinched, she surveys the table. "And right now, I wanna dance with the most handsome man at this table." She side-eyes her friend, then springs to her feet. "Cam Little, I hope you're wearing your dancing shoes."

My brother's dragged from his seat by an enthusiastic Mabel as Randy Travis's voice blares from the speakers.

Griffin pushes his chair back and stands, extending a hand. "What do you say, professor? Dance with me?"

With a small smile, Brynn clasps his hand. The two are swallowed by the crowd the moment they step onto the shiny hardwood.

Trixie rests her chin on a fist and taps the fingers of her other hand to the beat as she surveys the dancing couples with interest. Before long, she expels a heavy breath and latches on to Shaw's arm. "You owe me a dance, favorite cousin."

Shaw doesn't budge. "Trix…"

"*Please*? We're the best dancers in this dang family," she cajoles. "You're gonna let Griffin show you up?"

Tucker huffs a laugh, and Shaw scowls. He holds her stare, his brows pulled low, but after an agonizing moment, he groans. When he reluctantly rises from his chair, Trixie bounces on her toes and drags him to the dance floor.

"And then there were two." Tucker angles closer, his masculine scent engulfing me. "What do you say, Nat?" He wags his brows. "Let me take you for a spin."

Butterflies take flight in my belly, but I swallow, fighting the sensation. God, I want to say yes. I'd love to slide close to him, our bodies aligning from head to toe, and let him lead. Let him cage me inside the strength of his arms and shut out the rest of the world.

But I shake my head, propriety and unrelenting self-doubt taking over, and offer him a weak smile. "That's all right."

What would Cam think of us dancing together? What would the people of this town think?

Tucker clenches his jaw, his irises nearly a gunmetal color. "We're dancing, shutterbug."

With a scoff, I wave at the couples sashaying to the beat. "But Cam—"

"Wants you to have fun." He tilts his head toward the dancers, the gold of his tiny hoop earring shimmering in the neon lights. "So let's have some."

Before I can protest further, he seizes my hand.

Chapter Ten

Natalie

I tug against his hold weakly, though my sputtered excuses get swallowed by the music. With a firm yet gentle grip, he leads me to the shiny wooden planks where dozens of boots and tennis shoes and sandals keep time. As he slides into a space among the two-stepping couples, Tucker swings me around and holds me close.

Muscle memory kicks in without my permission, and my legs and feet follow his lead.

With a hand at the small of my back, he guides me even closer. Much closer than necessary for this dance. Instead of putting proper distance between us like I should, I shuffle in tighter and curve my left hand around his shoulder.

"How long's it been since you two-stepped?" His warm, hoppy breath ghosts over my ear, sending a shiver coasting down my spine.

Though his eyes are shadowed by the brim of his cap, I don't miss the way they dart to my lips.

Heart in my throat, I force myself to answer. "It's like riding a bike, isn't it?"

He chuckles, and when a smug smile stretches his stubble-covered cheeks, I can't help but wonder how that growth would feel beneath my fingertips.

That thought is followed quickly by a wave of embarrassment that has me jerking my gaze to the couples on the other side of the floor, certain my thoughts are being broadcast to the entire bar.

I spot Cam and Mabel first, and my stomach plummets. But when my brother tips his head back in laughter, not paying me a lick of attention, I relax my shoulders.

It's not like I'm doing anything wrong, right?

Liv's words from our last conversation float through my mind: *Cam can deal.*

A low rumble works its way up his chest. "I'm a better bike rider than dancer, so..."

I raise a snarky brow. "I've seen your bike riding skills, sir. If that's the case, then let's hope that my feet make it out of this unscathed."

His responding grin makes my knees weak.

It takes approximately five seconds to determine that he's downplaying his dancing skills. He slides his right hand lower on my back, the warmth of his palm radiating through the fabric of my shirt and causing my breath to hitch.

I revel in the strength and power in his muscles, the quickness of his feet despite his size.

"Ready for a spin?" He wags his brows, a mischievous glint in his eyes.

"What?" My heart rate accelerates. "Tucker—"

Before I can voice my refusal, he raises our arms and spins me out, then twirls me back into form without missing a step.

"Not bad."

A thrill courses through me. "Not bad yourself."

"Aunt Dottie would disown me if I couldn't keep up."

"She taught y'all, right? Pretty sure my brother owes his dancing skills to her. He didn't inherit them from Mom or James."

"Yeah, one summer she forced the four of us to spend two afternoons a week here. Poor Trixie was forced to be our partner as she and Aunt Dottie taught us the basics." He nods to where his cousin and his brother are dancing, showing off impressive twists and spins. "She had to dodge the clumsy feet of all four of us idiots, so she got really good."

Before I can think better of it, I ask, "Have she and my brother ever—" I squeeze my lips together, catching myself. Even voicing the question I've been curious about for years feels like a betrayal to Cam. I should be asking him, not his best friend.

He blows out a breath. "They have not. Much to Cam's torment."

My heart pangs for him. He's dated and had girlfriends here and there over the years, but none of those relationships ever went anywhere, and I suspect it's because of the sassy redhead.

"Hey." The word is a warm caress sweeping across my cheek, pulling my attention from Trixie. "I have a feeling they'll figure it out one day."

I tilt my head, my chest tightening. "Are you a romantic, Mr. Lacey?"

A vivid beam of neon from a sign illuminates his face as he says, "You bet your fine ass I am."

"I don't think you should be talking about my ass," I declare with a boldness that only seems to surface when I'm in Tucker's presence.

His voice is pure gravel in my ear. "Been thinking about it an awful lot, shutterbug."

I rear back, my heart hammering. He absolutely did not say what I think he did.

Right?

The confident wink he gives before he spins me out again tells me my ears aren't deceiving me.

Tucker Lacey just confessed to thinking about my ass.

Speechless, I study him for a beat. How's it possible that he looks just as at home in a honky-tonk as he does in a gym? That he's equally confident and comfortable in this navy short-sleeve pearl-snap and jeans as he is in gym shorts and a T-shirt?

Tucker is unapologetically himself no matter the setting. No matter the company.

But his is a quiet, grounded self-confidence rather than the overtly macho, cocky bravado that so many younger men possess.

It's attractive as hell.

Shit. Not only am I attracted to him physically—how could I not be? He's the perfect mix of *tall, dark, and tattooed*—I'm also insanely attracted to him as a person. To the way he carries himself. How he loves his family and his job.

When he shines his brilliant light my way, the dark clouds don't stand a chance.

He's exactly the kind of man I've longed for in the depths of my heart. Like I designed him in a metaphorical Build-A-Man workshop, carefully curating every last detail until he became my perfect match.

Except...he's almost a decade younger. And he lives here, while my life is in Austin.

Then there's Cam to consider. I obviously don't need his approval to date anyone, but Tucker is his best friend. How would he feel if the two of us gave in to this pull between us?

Date? What the hell are you thinking, Natalie?

"Nat?" Tucker's voice drags me from my mental merry-go-round.

Rather than acknowledge his confession about my *ass*, I opt for a subject change, jutting my chin toward the faded Memphis Blues cap covering his dark hair. "Your hat is missing a few gallons."

Most of the hats in here are of the cowboy variety, with a few approaching ten-gallon status.

"I have one. It's a requirement for anyone whose family owns a honky-tonk. Pretty sure it's still in my closet at Mom and Dad's. I haven't worn it in ages, though." He angles closer and rests his large palm on my crown, a conspiratorial gleam in his eye. "If I'd donned it tonight, it would look right at home here."

As the final twangy notes of the song fade out, movement on the dance floor pauses. I attempt to pull away, but Tucker keeps hold of my hand.

"Go again?" he asks as a new tune blares from the jukebox.

"I, uh—"

Cam appears at our side, robbing me of the chance to answer. "Cutting in."

Tucker opens his mouth, but before he can protest, my brother slaps his bicep, sweeps me into his hold, and guides me into the flow. A glance over Cam's shoulder reveals that Mabel has replaced me as Tuck's partner.

Feeling like a kid caught cheating on a spelling test, I blurt, "We were the last two at the table."

A wrinkle forms between his brows but disappears in a blink. Rather than commenting about my dance with his best friend, he surprises me by saying, "We haven't danced since your quinceañera."

I shake my head, studying his earnest expression. That can't be right. Cam was only six the summer we road-tripped to Austin to spend a week celebrating my fifteenth birthday with my father and the Guatemalan side of my family.

A memory of boogying to "Smooth" by Carlos Santana and Rob Thomas flits through my mind, me, in my sparkly turquoise dress, little Cam in a matching vest. But surely we've had occasions to dance since then?

"Aunt Janet's wedding?" As the words leave my mouth, I distinctly recall a sullen teenage Cam sitting with arms crossed in an untucked dress shirt, refusing to dance with me at James's sister's reception. "Oh, that's right. You were pouting because you had to miss baseball."

He barks a laugh. "It was a *playoff* game. And I was not pouting."

I grin. "Definitely pouting."

When he breaks into a matching expression, genuine amusement and affection wash over me. Damn, it feels good to be in his company.

Because of our significant age gap, the relationship I had with Cam when we were kids looked little like those my peers had with their siblings. We didn't fight over toys or get into arguments about hogging a shared bathroom or team up to prank our parents. Instead, I was fiercely protective of him. My role as backup mother-hen didn't allow much opportunity for a friendship to blossom while we lived under the same roof. Now my brother is a man, with adult worries and responsibilities, I find myself longing to be a true friend to him.

His grin morphs into a tight smile as his attention drifts over my shoulder. "You'd, uh, really let me take you up in one of the planes while you're here?"

I squeeze his bicep. "I'd love to go flying with you."

His hazel eyes shine, his throat bobbing. "Cool. We'll get you some sweet shots of the river."

"Do you love what you do?" I ask.

I've often worried that Cam's followed in James's ag pilot footsteps out of obligation. He's been fascinated with planes since he could say the word, but that passion could've led him down many different paths.

He purses his lips, considering his answer. "Do you feel like your camera is an extension of your body? Like it's an extra limb you didn't know you were missing until you held one for the first time?"

My throat burns unexpectedly as I nod. I don't think I could have put the sensation into words so eloquently, but yes, that's exactly how it felt the moment I unboxed my first camera—when

I held the weight of it in my hands, brushed my fingers over the smooth buttons, marveled at the zoom capability. Even at ten, I understood on a fundamental level that my future would include capturing images.

"That's how flying is for me," he says. "I love working with Dad, and I love what I do at the station, too. Helping people, saving lives when necessary. Flying satisfies the part of me that craves freedom, while firefighting keeps me grounded—literally. I get the best of both worlds. So...yeah, Nat, I love what I do."

A warm affection blooms in my chest. "I'm proud of you."

Even in the dim lighting, there's no mistaking the pink staining his cheeks. "Love you."

"Love you, too."

He folds me in a hug as the song ends. When the beginning notes of a slow ballad play, we skirt our way back to the table, where everyone, minus Griffin and Brynn, is sitting.

As soon as I'm settled in my chair, Tucker's leg again finds mine under the table.

Heart thumping, I desperately search for our waitress, to no avail. I need a ten-gallon hat of ice water to cool me down from his constant contact.

"The lovebirds called it a night?" Cam asks as he swipes up his half-finished beer.

The other women in the group appear to be on the downhill slope. With a yawn, Trixie props her chin in her palm. "Yep. Said their long day of travel caught up with them, but we really know why they left early." She wags her brows, though in her sleepy state, the expression looks more like an odd grimace.

"We're getting too old to hang," Mabel wails as she rests her head on her bestie's shoulder.

Trixie's auburn bob swishes as she shakes her head. "No. I refuse to accept this. If Yeehaw is still going strong, then we've got to rally." She raises a hand, probably to flag down a server, but Mabel lowers it to the table.

"Don't bring me into this." Shaw's gruff voice startles me. Five words. That's the second-longest sentence he's uttered tonight.

I sneak a peek at the oldest Lacey brother. His eyes are hidden under the brim of a well-worn Lacey Farms cap, but if memory serves, they're a vibrant blue color. Much bluer than Griffin's or Tucker's. His face is shaped like theirs, but his expression is more haunted. There's a loneliness there my soul recognizes instantly.

Like calls to like, after all.

This man is lonely, even surrounded by a loving, boisterous family. And he's weighed down by a bone-deep heaviness. When he presses his lips together at a comment my brother makes, it hits me: Shaw Lacey wears grief like a favorite shirt.

The realization makes my heart squeeze. What on earth caused this man to carry such weariness?

He catches me observing him. But rather than look away, I hold his gaze, hoping to convey a message: *I acknowledge your sadness, and you are not alone.*

Shaw breaks the connection first, downing the rest of his beer in one gulp. "I'm out." He stands and digs a key fob from his front pocket, ignoring protests from Trixie and Mabel, then gives my brother a pointed look. "You good to get the girls home?"

Cam salutes him and gestures to the drink he's been nursing since I arrived. "Affirmative."

With a nod, Shaw squeezes Trixie's shoulder. When he reaches our end of the table, he gives his brother a subtle tip of his chin. "Tuck."

"Glad you came out tonight, Yeehaw."

Shaw's jaw ticks, but as it relaxes again, there's nothing but affection in his expression. "Good to see you again, Natalie," he says, his soft tone warming my heart. "Keep these boys in line."

After a quick adjustment of his cap, he disappears into the crowd.

Tucker angles in a fraction, his voice low. "My brother is a man of few words."

"Definitely economical with the language, that one," Cam confirms.

Trixie smacks his arm. "Don't make fun."

Cam raises his hands and barks a laugh. "I would never. Shaw could kick my ass."

"*I* could kick your ass," Trixie brags.

My brother breaks into a shit-eating grin. "Name the time and place, silly rabbit."

"Ugh, I'm too sober for this." Scowling now, she flags down the blonde who helped us earlier.

She and Mabel order another round, while I request an extra-large ice water.

Over the next hour, the group catches me up on the juiciest Holly Holler gossip from the past decade, filling me in on what my favorite elementary teacher has been up to since she retired and whispering about the couple locked in an argument two tables down from us. Trixie and Mabel both regale us with stories from the teaching trenches, and Cam shares a few of the funniest calls he's been on, without naming names, of course.

Every few seconds, Tucker looks at me, his gaze as visceral as the weight of his leg against mine. Each time I allow myself a glance his way, the intensity in his stare fans flames that threaten to scorch me from the inside out.

Fortunately, Cam's too focused on Trixie to notice the way his best friend is eye-fucking me.

How the hell did we end up here? And what the hell am I going to do about it?

Before they've finished this round of drinks, Trixie's increasing tipsiness and Mabel's decreasing alertness bring their fun to a close.

"I'm *so* sleepy," Mabel drawls, resting her head on the table.

"Ugh, same." Trixie pats my brother's cheek, nearly poking his eye out in the process. "Cam, let's go."

He grasps her wrist before she can blind him. "Sure thing. Let me walk Nat to her car and then I'll pull the truck up out front."

Before I can argue that I am perfectly capable of walking to my car, Tucker straightens and intervenes. "I'll walk Natalie out."

Cam squints at his friend, then me, suspicion evident in his features.

"Perfect." Trixie stands on newborn foal legs and links arms with Mabel.

The two of them wave goodbye to Tuck and me and stagger toward the door.

Cam stands, too, though he doesn't move, as if he's conflicted about leaving me.

"It's fine." I wave him off. "I can see myself—"

"I'll walk her out," Tucker repeats, his tone unyielding.

With a sigh, my brother looks to me for approval.

"It's fine. I won't be long anyway. Just want to finish my drink." I hold up said drink. Only then do I remember it's just water, but I stick with the bit, unwilling to back down.

With a sigh, he tousles my hair. He plants a kiss on my crown, and with a fist bump to his friend, he takes off after the girls.

Then Tucker and I are alone. Alone in a teeming bar. With so much unspoken between us.

His chair legs screech as he slides closer to the table, the sound causing goose bumps to erupt along my skin. "Finish your water, Natalie."

Though my initial instinct should be to rebel at the bossiness of his demand, I'm instead hit with a strange craving for it. For someone who makes endless decisions on her own, it's refreshing to be told what to do.

As I tip the glass up and swallow the last dregs of water, he tracks my movements. Once I've drained it, he snags it from my grasp and forcefully sets it on the table, causing the leftover ice to clink. Without a word, he takes my hand and tugs, a gentle request for me to follow.

So I do. I follow him through the crowd and out the door, not once trying to extract my hand from his.

Tucker slows his strides once we exit the bar. "Where are you parked?"

I clear my throat, panicked that the spectrum of emotions I'm experiencing may inhibit my ability to speak. "Um, it's down this street."

We're silent as we trek the two blocks to my car, and the farther we traverse, the quieter the music and merriment from the Hoot get. When the only sounds are our footsteps on the concrete, my brain shuffles through possible comments, only to reject them as quickly as they form.

Tucker squeezes my hand, and as it hits me that his fingers have somehow ended up laced with mine, my breath falters. What's even more shocking is how natural the hold is, like our hands were always meant to join like this.

"This is mine," I say, my voice reedy, as we approach my car.

He swings me around to face him, and like our cores contain magnetic poles, we draw closer.

This feels dangerous. But I don't give a damn right now.

He rakes his teeth across his bottom lip, assessing me. "I'm giving you a good night hug, if that's all right."

My heart trips over itself at the gravel in his tone. "Y-yeah, okay."

When he has me wrapped snug in his arms, he releases a satisfied sigh that makes me squeeze him tighter. I inhale against his collarbone as he rubs soothing circles on my shoulder blade.

"Now we're up to 25 percent of your daily hug requirement." His chest vibrates as he speaks, a rumbly sensation that makes goose bumps dot my skin. "My goal is 100 percent."

As we pull apart, he tilts my chin up with his knuckle and makes a proclamation that leaves no room for doubt. "In case my actions haven't done the job, let me make this clear for you, shutterbug: I'm pursuing you. And I'm gonna be persistent."

Chapter Eleven

Tucker

"I now pronounce you husband and wife." The officiant steps to the side. "You may kiss the bride."

As the bride and groom authenticate their newly hitched status with a kiss, cheers and whoops and whistles erupt, filling the muggy twilight air.

Rather than watch Jeremy and Amanda lock lips, I'm homed in on the photographer, just like I've been all afternoon.

When I arrived at the wedding venue four hours ago, the last person I expected to bump into in the converted warehouse that serves as a reception hall was the woman I'm crushing on like a lovesick teenager.

She sputtered and blushed and stared in disbelief when she saw me with my garment bag slung over my shoulder. Me? Couldn't wipe the grin from my face.

That *persistent pursuing* I promised her a couple weeks ago outside the Hoot? Yeah, it's taken more finesse and patience than I expected.

She feels this thing between us, this chemistry that's as undeniable as water is wet. She has to. But she's hesitant. And shy.

Rather than make me reconsider, those traits have drawn me farther into her orbit.

This may be the biggest challenge I've faced, but that's not why I'm into her. She's not a conquest to be won. She's a gift to be earned.

So far, though, she's guarded, and she's damn good at acting immune to my charms.

Though serendipitous run-ins have been few and far between for the last two weeks, we continue to "bump into" one another at the coffee shop each morning. This, at least, has allowed me to provide 25 percent of her daily hug requirement—an embrace when we greet one another, and another when we say goodbye. But any time I hint at wanting to hang out with her, she changes the subject or finds an excuse to rush off.

Natalie's currently in professional mode, standing in the center of the aisle, her beautiful face hidden behind the camera as she captures memories for the newlyweds. She looks amazing in a simple, swingy black dress with a scalloped V neckline that shows the barest hint of cleavage. The dress is modest, its hem falling below her knees, showing off tan, shapely calves. In true Natalie-style, she's paired it with her beloved black-and-white Adidas. Her brown waves are pinned back on the sides, and her makeup is minimal yet perfect.

She's gorgeous, and I have an overwhelming desire to tell her so.

After the kiss and announcement of Mr. and Mrs. Ketchum, she lowers the camera for a beat and catches my eye, a brief slip of her professionalism. The enticing flush that saturates her cheeks as she realizes I'm watching her makes my chest inflate.

Not so immune after all, huh?

I haven't had a chance to speak to her alone, but I'm determined to get some one-on-one time during the reception. She's gotta get a few minutes to herself, right?

As instrumental music plays, each of us pairs up with a bridesmaid and follows the happy couple down the petal-strewn grass between the rows of white chairs.

Beads of sweat roll down my spine as the raven-haired woman beside me (Addison? Adalyn?) clutches my bicep. When we reach the last row, we pause, like each couple ahead of us has, so Natalie can snap a picture.

She remains professional, but there's no denying the smile she tosses at the woman I'm escorting after she's captured our pose is fake as hell.

"See you inside, shutterbug."

"Not yet." Addison/Adalyn squeezes my arm. "We still have to do the wedding party photos."

Mother effer. What's a guy gotta do to get a cold beer and some damn AC?

After an eternity spent posing and sweating our asses off, we're released to the cool confines of the reception building. The space is open and inviting, the only evidence of its former life as a warehouse the exposed brick walls and metal support beams. The industrial facets are softened by the large chandeliers hanging overhead and the cream and blush flower arrangements and flameless candles dotted around the space.

While Amanda and Jeremy begin their first dance, the other groomsmen and I head to the buffet—whose line is blessedly short, since most of the guests have already been through it—and pile our plates with fried catfish, pulled pork sliders, and au gratin potatoes.

Once we've found our assigned table, I set my plate down and drape my tux jacket over the back of a chair and roll up my sleeves. Besides Jeremy's older brother, who's serving as best man, I didn't know the other three guys before last night's rehearsal dinner. Guess that's to be expected when one agrees to be in the wedding party of a high school teammate he hasn't seen in years.

Shaw's always telling me I need to learn how to say no.

Should probably start working on that.

But as I observe Natalie, who's capturing the big and little moments this couple will show their grandkids one day, I'm certain I'll never say no to *her*.

She's only in town for the summer. I've reminded myself of that fact many times. And she's got family and a whole life in Austin. Is it foolish to start something with her, knowing it has an expiration date? Probably. But will it stop me? Hell no.

She hasn't agreed to a date yet, and I'm already dreading having to say goodbye.

I can't squander the opportunity to spend time with her, even if there's a chance I'll be wrecked in the end.

I'm biting into my second slider when one of the guys pipes up, his tone incredulous. "So you're Racy Lacey's brother?"

Napkin in hand, I take my time swallowing and wiping my mouth. Already, I know this will go one of two ways. This guy is either a fan or a hater. Fans, I can handle. The haters, however? Let's just say I've gotten into my fair share of scrapes with bozos who've had the audacity to bash my brother to my face. "Yeah, I am."

He gapes. "Wow. What's that like?"

As relief weaves its way through me, I chuckle. "Like being related to a world-famous athlete. It has its pros and cons."

As the guys discuss the Blues' playoff chances next season, I keep half of my focus on the conversation, and the other half on Natalie's movements. If there's a chance I can talk to her, I refuse to let it pass me by.

My shot comes when the bride and groom finally sit down to eat.

As Natalie retreats to a corner, I excuse myself from the table and hit up the bartender, then head her way.

The closer I get, the more palpable the fizzy sensation in my stomach becomes. Like every one of my cells bounces with unrestrained excitement.

As I step up close, I extend a dripping bottle of water. "Thirsty?"

Hazel eyes widening, she straightens. "Oh, God, you have no idea." She downs half the bottle, then says, "I forgot how daunting a wedding shoot can be. I don't know how Wayne still does this."

"You don't shoot weddings in Austin?"

She takes another long pull from the bottle and holds it up between us. "Thank you for this. And no, I haven't shot a wedding in years. But once upon a time, they were my bread and butter." She scans the room, wearing a wistful expression, then shakes her head. "I still can't believe you're here."

I palm the back of my neck and take a step closer. "Yeah, I'm pretty sure I was a last-minute replacement. I haven't seen Jeremy since high school other than on social media and here and there around town."

She visibly swallows, clearly affected by my proximity. "Do you, um, know many people here?"

I hum. "Just Jeremy's family. And Lisa Marie number two." I tip my head to where Holly Holler's lone cake decorator sits with her husband, Randall. "She made the cakes, though I think she's related, too. Jeremy's mom's cousin, maybe?"

"I thought she looked familiar. She made my graduation cake when she was just starting her business."

"Oh, I want to show you something." I pull out my phone and navigate to the gym's brand-new website. "It went live yesterday. And my web designer had a hell of time choosing the best pictures. I can understand the dilemma, since they're all amazing."

She scrolls through the mobile version of the website and pauses on each section. "Tucker, this is phenomenal, like the perfect mix of badass and professional. I love it."

As pride swells my chest, I pocket my phone. "How long is your break?"

Brow furrowed, she peers around me. "I've got until they finish eating. There's still the cake cutting and the bouquet and garter tosses. And the big exit. Like I said...daunting."

As she views the festivities, she balls her hands into fists and releases them again. When she repeats the motion, I swipe up her right hand and massage the muscles there, relishing the smoothness of her skin. Her body locks for an instant, but the tension melts away as I gently dig my thumb and fingers into her palm.

Though I can feel her eyes on my face, I can't stop staring at our hands. Because, damn, they look good like this. Our skin tones complement one another perfectly, and her softness is the perfect contrast to my rougher, more callused skin. Her fingers are shorter and more delicate than mine, tempting me to measure our hands palm to palm. I resist. And I also manage to resist the urge to nip the pads of her fingers to see if her eyes darken or she tips her head back in laughter.

God, I want my life's mission to be making this woman laugh. Need it listed on my résumé under *achievements*.

It takes an overwhelming amount of self-control to not kiss her knuckles once I've finished the massage. Or when I repeat the ministrations on her other hand.

Finally, I find the strength to force my gaze away, only to find it immediately drifting to her face.

Her cheeks are flushed and her stare is soft but intense. But then her mouth moves, and I'm captivated. "Tucker..."

Fuck, I want to memorize the shape of her lips when she says my name.

A loud burst of laughter from behind me breaks the spell, and Natalie slips her hand from mine and steps back.

"Thank you," she says, her voice barely above a whisper.

"Sure thing, shutterbug." I run my thumb along my lower lip, stalling. I'm not ready to give up this connection. "Would it be unprofessional for the gorgeous photographer to dance with one of the handsome groomsmen?"

She arranges her mouth in a flirty smirk that heats my blood. "Oh, which one of them asked about me?" Shoulders back, she whips around, as if she plans to stride for the table.

I snag her wrist before she can take off and pull her in, the scent of her perfume engulfing me, the warmth of her body soaking into mine. Trying, and failing, to not sound like a possessive caveman, I bring my lips to her ear. "Un-uh. I've got dibs."

She rears back like she's affronted, but her eyes sparkle with humor. "Dibs? Like I'm the shotgun seat in a car or the last piece of cake? Sir, you cannot call dibs on a person."

"Fuck that," I grit out. "I'm calling dibs. On you."

A laugh escapes her, open and unfettered, as she smooths her palm down the buttons of my shirt.

I soak up the sound, resisting the urge to pump my fist. Not only did I get a pure, genuine laugh out of her, but *she* initiated contact.

She pats my chest, her smile making me dizzy. "I'm sorry to disappoint, but dancing with handsome groomsmen is not proper wedding photographer etiquette."

"Damn it." I fake-scoff.

She glances over my shoulder. "I've got to get back..."

"Of course."

With a close-lipped smile, she hoists her camera, then she skirts around me.

"Hey, Nat."

Spinning, she assesses me with lifted brows.

"Don't leave without a hug."

She dips her chin, then gets back to work.

Me? I politely decline when Adalyn/Addison asks me for a dance, then fulfill the rest of my groomsman obligations. But my eyes don't stray from Natalie for long.

And when I catch the garter and give the photographer a saucy wink, earning myself a blush the most delectable shade of pink? I might as well be house hunting on cloud nine.

As the new Mr. and Mrs. Ketchum exit, shrouded in a swarm of bubbles, I lose sight of Natalie in the hubbub. And when I fetch my jacket from inside and still haven't found her, a sharp sting of disappointment hits me in the gut.

After helping the bride's and groom's families gather the floral arrangements, cake, and presents, I give Jeremy's mom a hug, shake his brother's hand, and head to the mostly deserted parking lot.

The chirp of crickets and the crunch of my footsteps on the gravel are my only companions until I near my car. When the unmistakable clicking of an engine not turning adds to the nighttime symphony, I slow, and when a muffled "damn it" floats by on the night air, I pivot toward the car at the back of the lot.

Wayne's elderly Camry sits immobile, facing the woods that surround the property. The driver's side door is open, and one perfect calf sticks out.

"Nat?"

She gasps and smacks her chest. "Oh shit. I didn't hear you."

I stride straight for her. "Won't start?"

She pushes off the seat with a heavy sigh. "Wayne insisted that I drive his car out here, but I think the battery's dead."

Silently, I send up a quick prayer that Mr. Wayne isn't a well-prepared motorist. "Pop the trunk."

Once she's found the button inside the dark car, I sift through the photography equipment, but I emerge empty-handed. "No cables."

"Damn it." She closes her eyes and takes a deep breath. "Maybe someone inside has a set?"

I peer over my shoulder quickly. "They're busy cleaning up. Just ride with me."

She bites her lower lip, her focus flitting away. "But the car…"

"It'll be fine here overnight. I'll drive you back tomorrow and we'll jump it."

With a sigh, she fetches her camera bag from the trunk. "But it's almost an hour away." She waves a hand. "Cam can bring me—"

"Nat." I take the heavy bag from her and heft it onto my shoulder. "I got you."

Her shoulders slump. Not in defeat, but in relief.

Damn, why is it so difficult for her to accept help? Because she's lived independently for so long? Or does she struggle admitting that she can't always do everything on her own?

I may not know the reason behind her reticence, but the more time I spend with Natalie Torres, the more I want to be the man she relies on. The man who takes care of her, who shows up for her. Who will remind her that though she can do it for herself, she doesn't always have to.

"You owe me a hug, by the way," I tell her as we stroll to my Jeep.

She falters, sending several chunks of gravel skittering ahead, and when she speaks, her voice is soft, a whispered confession. "I looked for you. After."

I nudge her with my elbow. "Me too, shutterbug."

We're silent for several steps, but then she asks, "How about now?"

Before she changes her mind, I slip the bag off my shoulder and extend my arms.

Without hesitation, she slides her arms around my torso. And when she squeezes me as tightly as I'm holding her?

Damn, I've never felt like more of a champion.

CHAPTER TWELVE

TUCKER

"It's not as much as last time, at least." I shrug. Sure, I could have done without waking up to discover our yard has been TP-ed overnight, but it'd take a helluva lot more than a little dew-soaked toilet paper dangling from the bushes and our lone crepe myrtle to ruin my day.

Cam is not so buoyant. He eyes the Tudor-style cottage across the street, then huffs a heavy sigh. "Mabel's car was there when I left for my shift last night."

"But when I got home around midnight, it wasn't. And this"—I snatch a long white strip off the ground and hold it up—"wasn't either."

Jaw clenched, he turns in a slow circle, assessing the mess. "We know they did it, Tuck. Just like the last three times, regardless of their Oscar-worthy declarations of innocence." He tosses me the box of trash bags and peels a strip of soggy paper from the branches. "I'm catching them in the act next time. I'm gonna order one of those doorbells with a camera. Should've done that already, damn it." He mumbles to himself as he shoves another handful of wet tissue into a bag, using phrases like *red-haired menace* and *get them back for this* as he works his way down the hedge.

I refrain from reminding my best friend that the TP-ing pranks are retaliatory after he put a *For Sale by Owner* sign in her front yard, complete with her cell number. She fielded calls from interested buyers for hours before she could leave school during her planning period to remove it. Only for him to replace it with a new sign the next day.

As I step into the yard, the still-wet grass soaks the leather of my flip-flops. It's another reminder that it's my turn to mow the yard. Fortunately, Cam's early morning freak-out leaves me plenty of time to cut the grass and shower before I have to pick up Natalie.

Natalie. Thoughts of her consume me. I fell asleep thinking of her beautiful smile and woke up hard, imagining how perfect her hips would feel in my hands.

I'll get an hour alone with her this afternoon. It's not enough. I discovered that when I drove her home last night. Today's objective: get her to agree to a date.

I've never had to work this hard for a date, but I'm not complaining. I love that she's making me work for it. When she says yes eventually, I imagine I'll have an inkling of how Griff felt after winning two Super Bowls.

When we're done with the clean-up, Cam drags our trash can out to the curb for tomorrow's pickup. As he closes the lid, he eyes me. "How's your day look?"

My stomach twists itself into a knot. If I tell him that I'm driving Natalie to get Wayne's car, he'll insist on being the one to take her. Plus, he might be upset with her for not asking him in the first place. The guy is a fixer at his core. I don't want to cause a rift between them, but I don't want to keep secrets from him either. I need to man up and tell him how I feel about his sister. Sure, he'll be pissed at first, but he'll get over it. He's not one to hold a grudge.

Unless someone TPs his yard, I guess.

I'll tell him. Eventually. For now, I'll deal with the slimy sensation in my gut that comes with not being entirely truthful with my best friend.

"I've gotta drive a buddy out to the wedding venue to jump off a dead car." God, it feels wrong calling her a buddy, like someone calling *The Starry Night* just a painting. *Please don't ask which buddy.* "But first I'm gonna tackle this grass. Are you heading to bed?"

"Yeah, gonna get some shut-eye, then I've gotta meet Dad out at the hangar."

Cam's gentle snores are just audible outside his closed door when I leave to pick up his sister five hours later.

Natalie was quiet on our drive home last night, the day's hustle catching up with her. But I'm determined to keep her talking this afternoon. I want to learn everything I can. I want to know her likes and dislikes. Her favorite memories. Her future plans.

I spent an embarrassing amount of time choosing my clothing for this errand-that's-way-more-than-an-errand. Even now, as I make the turns to get to the Ganns' house, I debate going back to change. But a glance at the clock tells me I'll have to be satisfied with the cream joggers, white sneakers, and T-shirt that's the same orangey tan as the pots on Mom's back patio.

When I turn into the driveway and spot Natalie's SUV parked behind Nancy's car, I'm hit with a rush of endorphins, like I've just finished an intense workout.

I put the Jeep in park, and as I'm hopping out, Natalie exits her vehicle. She's cozy-casual in a pair of worn-in ankle-length jeans and a soft-looking blue shirt.

Her smile is small but genuine. "Hey."

"Hey yourself." I open my arms. "Twelve and a half percent."

She lets me hold her longer than usual, so I take advantage of the closeness and breathe in the combination of her shampoo and perfume while rubbing circles on her back. "This shirt feels like a cloud," I mumble into her hair.

Her body quivers in silent laughter.

"Let's head out." I release her and peer up at the sky. "Speaking of clouds, those look legit."

Once she's settled, I ease the passenger door closed and round the hood. When I climb behind the wheel, she's adjusting the rubber ducks that line my dash.

"My duck pond."

"Hmm. Looks like the whole gang's here." She points to the duck wearing a helmet and jersey. "Griffin." Then the duck in overalls and a ball cap. "Shaw." Next are the firefighter duck and the one holding a chalkboard and an apple. "Cam and Trixie." The last duck in the row, the one holding a book, is the newest to my collection. "And I'm guessing that one is Brynn?"

"Correct. She'll be an official professor soon. Plus, she's writing a book."

"Don't Jeep owners randomly leave them for each other? Were these very specific-to-you ducks left by strangers?"

I huff a laugh. Pretty sure Trixie and Cam are responsible for most of them, but I swear I saw Mom hovering in the gym parking lot the day I found the firefighter duck on the bumper. But I keep my family's probable participation to myself. "Believe it or not, every single one was left on my door handle or bumper. I leave most of the ones I receive on other Wranglers. These are permanent."

We ride in silence for a few minutes. If I had to guess, she's just as unsure about how to navigate the conversation as I am. Though maybe that's not true, because I'm fighting the urge to dive in and ask her to dinner right out of the gate. While the temptation tries to overwhelm me, I mentally shuffle through acceptable topics until I land on a safe one.

"I never would've taken you for an eighties post-apocalyptic movie aficionado, shutterbug."

Her dark brows furrow. "Sorry, what?"

"Your dog. You named him after the guy in *Mad Max*. The main character's buddy."

She tips her head back in laughter, the sight nearly impossible to look away from. "I've never seen that movie."

I smack the steering wheel in mock-outrage. "Just tell me already. How many more movies have a character named Goose?"

"At least one more."

"And that movie is..."

Her lips twitch. "My favorite movie ever."

A half-hearted growl escapes me. "Natalie Torres, tell me the damn movie." Despite my demand, I secretly hope she won't divulge it. I love when she's relaxed and unguarded like this. Playful. Mere inches from dipping her toes into a sea of flirtation.

"Hmm." She tilts her head, pretending to consider. "I don't think I will. Kinda can't wait to hear your next guess."

The tease sends a thrill through me. "Oh, I'll figure it out," I assure her. I'm not above asking Cam, even if it triggers his brotherly protectiveness.

I glance her way, noting the pink that stains her cheeks, then focus on the highway again.

"Have you recovered from last night?" I ask, recalling her comment about how long it had been since she photographed a wedding.

"Slept like a baby." She sighs.

Without my permission, my brain sparks with one image after another, each of her dressed in sleepwear. What does she wear to bed? Satiny lingerie? Tiny shorts and a cozy, soft T-shirt? Nothing at all?

Damn, the thought blots out all good sense and sends all my blood straight to my groin. And I'm definitely not wearing the kind of pants that can hide *that*. Still, I bargain with the universe for a chance to find out if she sleeps in pajamas or her birthday suit.

My kingdom for one night with Natalie, please.

The request is ridiculous, really. One night would never be enough.

I clear my throat, but when I speak again, my voice still grates like I raked sixty-grit sandpaper over my vocal cords. "H-how long has it been since you shot a wedding?"

"Nine years. The last one was my best friend's wedding."

I latch on to this detail, hungry for every morsel she offers. "Tell me about your best friend."

"Liv is a nurse in Austin," she says, her smile evident in her words. "Married, with two precious girls who call me Aunt Nat. Chloe is four, going on fourteen. And baby Sophie turns one next month. Her birthday is a week after mine."

Vague memories of birthday parties with hot dogs and fireworks and Bomb Pops and giggling teenage girls flood my mind. "Your birthday is…"

"July fifth." She shifts in her seat. "Liv and I met when she was shopping around for a wedding photographer. I defended her style choices to her future mother-in-law at our initial meeting, and Liv swears that from that moment, she was determined to make me her friend. Neither of the other photographers she'd met with had stuck up for her, probably because they assumed Jordan's mom was the one holding the purse strings. She called me that afternoon to book me for the wedding, then convinced me to meet her for a chips-and-salsa date. The rest is history."

"So, chips and salsa are the way to your heart? Noted."

Her laugh lights up the gloomy Sunday sky. "That's definitely one way."

"I want to know all the ways." I lift the lid to the center console and take a quick peek inside before turning my attention back to the road. "Damn, no paper to take notes."

She laughs again, a sound I'm becoming addicted to.

All too soon, we arrive at the wedding venue, and I curse myself for not driving slower to drag out our time together. I still haven't asked for a date, and as I come to a stop, a desperate ache blooms in my gut.

Just as I've connected the jumper cables I borrowed from Cam's truck to Wayne's car, a light drizzle starts. With a frown up at the sky, Natalie slides behind the wheel of the Camry to try the ignition. After a couple of tries, the car finally turns over, and she steps out.

The drizzle has morphed into larger droplets by now, glistening in her dark hair and spotting our clothes.

As the engine purrs, drowning out the pitter-patter of the rain, I pull her in for another hug, my heartbeat racing in a sped-up tempo like the music at the end of a video game. I'm running out of time to work up my nerve.

"Thank you so much for doing this." Her words are puffs of heat that sear my skin through my shirt.

"I told you, Nat. I got you." I hold her tighter, memorizing the way our bodies fit together.

We pull apart, but I keep my hands on her shoulders while she grips my waist, blinking up at me, raindrops clinging to her dark lashes.

The desire to kiss her soft, pink lips hits me like a sucker punch. "Have dinner with me."

Her forehead wrinkles, and her lips part, but before she can turn me down, I repeat my request, punctuated with a squeeze to her shoulders.

"Have dinner with me."

"Tucker—"

As if Mother Nature has set a countdown clock, the sky opens up and the steady rain turns into a downpour. With a yelp, Natalie loosens her hold on me and twists toward the Camry's open door.

I can't let her go without securing this date. So, giving zero fucks about the rain and being drenched, I pull her hand to my mouth. As I practically beg, my lips brush her skin and my eyes remain locked on hers. "Say yes, Nat."

With the tree line as a backdrop, her hazel irises look more green. They swim with uncertainty as she searches my face for a beat. When her lids flutter shut and her chest deflates, my heart sinks into my stomach.

She's going to say no.

Instead, a soft "yes" breaks through the deluge. It takes my brain a moment to catch up, but when it does, elation floods me.

"Yes?" I'm almost scared to confirm, but she nods, and I wrap her in another hug. "Thirty-seven and a half percent," I say into her wet hair.

The sweet smile she gives me when she pulls away is accompanied by a playful eye roll. "You're scarily good at math."

"I'm scarily good at lots of things, shutterbug."

She breaks free then, darting to the car with a wave.

"I'll follow you back," I call, "to make sure there's no trouble with the car."

Through the rain-soaked window, she nods and swipes at the strands of hair that stick to her cheeks.

As soon as I've closed myself inside my Jeep, I swipe at my phone's screen and navigate to Natalie's contact. No way am I letting another second pass without locking down the details.

> Friday night. Six o'clock. My house. I'll cook for you.

> And before you worry, that's Father's Day weekend. Cam and James will be gone on their annual fishing trip.

I glance over at Wayne's car. Through the rain, I can just make out her figure. Her head's bent over her phone, and a quick check of my screen reveals those three dots teasing me.

Natalie:

> **You cook? Is that another thing you're scarily good at?**

> It is. But I can't wait to show you the thing I'm best at.

She sends me the thinking face emoji, and a moment later, she backs out of the parking spot.

I follow, watching the glow of her taillights as the car bumps over the gravel, already planning what I'll make for her on Friday.

One thing that will for sure be on the menu? Our first kiss.

CHAPTER THIRTEEN

NATALIE

"Cam doesn't know about any of this?"

I assess my reflection in the full-length mirror, contemplating both my clothing choice and Liv's question.

With a grunt, I whip off the blouse and toss it onto the mountain of cast-offs teetering at the end of my bed. What does one wear to a secret dinner with her little brother's best friend?

"He doesn't. I was going to fess up when we met for lunch today, but I chickened out."

"Nat."

"I know." I hang my head as if she can see me. "I'm the worst sister ever."

Liv's sigh crackles over the speaker. "You know that's not true. You're allowed to have some privacy, especially where your love life is concerned. But you don't want to find yourself in a predicament that might lead to Cam discovering his bestie and sister doing the deed on his couch."

"Olivia." I jerk another shirt off the hanger and wrangle it over my head. "We're not doing the deed."

"*Yet,*" she emphasizes. "God, please have hot, sweaty, not-vanilla sex with that man. The kind that makes it hard to even look each other in the eye after."

I swallow hard. The thought of being intimate with Tucker is both thrilling and terrifying in equal measure. "It's been so long," I whisper, once again scrutinizing my reflection. "What if I'm awful?" Before Liv can reassure me, I shake my head. "Nope. Doesn't matter, because we're not having sex. This isn't going to become a thing. I'm only here for a few weeks, and he doesn't want a forty-year-old woman in his bed. We're not having sex because this..." I wave a hand, grappling for a suitable term to downplay the big, scary emotions swamping me. "This *flirtation* isn't going beyond tonight. God, why'd I even agree to dinner?"

"Nat." Liv's tone is gentle. "Are you spiraling?"

I drop my hands to my sides and force a deep breath, pinching the bridge of my nose. "Little bit."

"Have you talked to Regina about it?"

"Yeah. A little." I've been meeting with my therapist virtually since leaving Austin. "She reminded me that it's okay to let happiness in."

Happiness has clung to me this week in a way I haven't experienced in a long, long time. If I'm honest, it's chafed a bit, like a new pair of shoes. Every day this week, I've wandered around wearing a ridiculous grin. Because each morning, I've discovered a little surprise at the back door to the studio. A bundle of watermelon candy sticks. A nosegay of wildflowers. A jar of homemade salsa. The gifts are simple, but they're sweet and thoughtful.

"Good. Let's just see where this *flirtation* goes, okay?" my best friend says. "The only opinions and expectations that matter are yours and Tucker's. Whether that means a summer fling or a long, passionate affair or a just-for-tonight is entirely up to y'all."

I dig a fuchsia-painted toe into the rug, giving myself permission to focus on the good, and inhale deeply. "You're right."

"Of course I am." Her tone is pure confidence. "Jordan's picking up the girls from his parents, so I have a little time before chaos descends. Let's FaceTime and I'll help you pick out what to wear.

And for the love of God, humor me and wear a matching set of undergarments, please. Just in case."

———◆———

Tucker and Cam rent a house in my favorite Holly Holler neighborhood. It's close to town square, the street lined with squat bungalows with wide, welcoming porches and charming cottages with gabled roofs. The yards are picturesque and the sidewalks are perfect for bike rides or Sunday strolls. Even the street names are quaint and whimsical: Storybook Lane and Everafter Circle and Starlight Court. My best friend in elementary school lived on Dragonfly Drive, and every time I played at her house, I'd beg to borrow her sister's bike so we could ride up and down the quiet streets. All the while, I'd imagine which house I'd claim as my own one day.

On the drive over, Tucker's request from last Sunday flitted through my mind on repeat.

Have dinner with me.

It wasn't so much a question as it was a command. An impossible-to-refuse order that's replayed on a loop all week, like it's been copied and pasted into my subconscious.

Goose barks from the back seat as I turn left onto Storybook. The fourth house on the right is a slate gray Craftsman with bright white trim. When I discover Cam's truck in the driveway, a bolt of panic hits me. It subsides, mostly, when I remember that they usually take James's Suburban on their fishing weekends.

My stomach is a bundle of nerves as I park behind Tucker's Jeep. Behind me, Goose whines, anxious to get out and explore, but I'm frozen to the spot, staring at the front porch, wondering for the hundredth time whether I'm making a mistake. The last time I went on a date, McDreamy was alive and well on *Grey's Anatomy*. What the hell am I doing? And why am I doing it with *this* man? This hot, charming-as-hell, out-of-my-league man who lives hours away and is my little brother's best friend.

On cue, that man opens the front door and leans against the jamb, arms crossed, with a flirty smile on his lips.

I'm done for.

It's all the motivation I need to cut the ignition and step out into the humid evening air. The moment I free Goose from his back seat prison, he makes a beeline for the porch, greeting Tucker like a long-lost buddy.

When I reach the top step, Tucker's crouched and scratching Goose's ears, grinning. "Be a pal and tell me where your mom got your name."

My dog simply cocks his head and savors the attention.

"Good boy," I croon. "He's been trained to keep all my secrets."

Tucker peers up at me, taking me in from head to toe, the look so heated I swear it'll leave scorch marks. "You look good, shutterbug."

I fidget under his blatant assessment, but in a good way. Liv and I finally settled on a pair of distressed boyfriend jeans and a three-quarter length semi-sheer cheetah-print top layered over a low-cut, lacy black tank. From the appreciation in his gaze, I'd say we knocked it out of the park.

When he stands, I get my own opportunity to ogle him. The dark hair curling from beneath the edge of his Club Lacey Fitness cap appears damp, like he's fresh out of the shower. The image my brain conjures of him naked and wet makes my face go hot and my mouth go dry. With a thick swallow, I banish the thought. His faded gray Memphis Blues T-shirt stretches across his broad chest perfectly, and his navy track pants showcase his muscular thighs and calves. Last but certainly not least, the man is barefoot. And the sight, ridiculously, makes me blush.

"What do I have to do to get you to call me 'good boy'?" he asks, his voice a deep rumble.

I force my attention from his feet, blinking, and fight the urge to look over my shoulder to confirm that those words were truly meant for *me*. The woman who's rarely been a man's first choice. Who's never been on the receiving end of such attention.

I'm pursuing you. And I'm gonna be persistent.

Tucker's eyes twinkle with mischief and what I swear is hunger.

Once my brain comes back online, I square my shoulders, determined to step into the ring with him. Maybe if I can successfully fake confidence, I'll eventually believe it.

I tilt my head. "Maybe you'll earn yourself a 'good boy' or two before the night is over."

Smirking, he hooks his fingers through my belt loops and pulls me into a hug. "Challenge accepted."

I inhale a lungful of his freshly showered masculine scent, hoping like hell the move isn't too obvious. "Thanks for letting me bring Goose."

"Of course. C'mon in." He releases me and gestures to the open doorway.

Instantly, I miss the comforting warmth of his embrace, but I lift my chin and feign nonchalance.

The tags on Goose's collar jangle as he trots inside, and as I follow, I refuse to dwell on the doubts that rode shotgun on the way here. Instead, I vow to soak up every morsel of this man's attentiveness and reciprocate it.

I've gotten glimpses of the living room during video calls with Cam, but this is the first time I've been here in person. As expected, it's clean and uncluttered—definitive proof that my brother resides here.

Once I've slipped my mules off by the door, I pad onto the plush tan rug that still bears evidence of a recent vacuuming. The walls—typical bachelor-pad bare, save for a couple large framed black-and-white prints—are painted a neutral off-white. A large coffee-colored leather sofa takes up most of the space, a huge flat-screen TV and entertainment console set up directly across from it. A plain black coffee table is centered on the rug, and the matching end table holds a lamp and a framed photo. In it, two eight-year-old boys beam up at the camera with their sun-kissed arms propped on the edge of a swimming pool.

It's a Natalie Torres original.

Seeing it is jarring, like the universe is hellbent on reminding me of the years between us.

"You took that at your seventeenth birthday party." The closeness of his voice and the heat of his body make me shiver. "After swimming, you and a couple friends got dressed up and headed to a movie in Jonesboro, but you snapped that picture of us before you left. I was just a dumb kid, but I thought you were the prettiest girl I'd ever seen." The warmth at my back intensifies as he slides a hand around my waist and pulls me flush to his chest. "Still think that, by the way."

"Tucker." I rest my hand over his, and when the tickle of his stubble grazes my cheek, I take a shuddering breath.

"Come keep me company while I finish dinner." He pats my hip and steps back. With a click of his tongue, he beckons Goose to follow him through the wide archway that leads to the kitchen.

I'm frozen in place for a moment, trying to anchor myself and shake off my reservations.

"Nat."

I follow Tucker's voice into a cozy little kitchen, relishing the coolness of the beige tile under my feet. The room is a perfect square, with white cabinets and butcher block counters between the fridge, stove, and sink. Centered in the small space is a vintage kitchen table with chrome edges and white Formica top, complete with four red vinyl chairs.

As a Fleetwood Mac song softly plays from Tucker's phone on the counter, he stands with his back to me, a red-and-white checkered dish towel slung over his shoulder, chopping away at something I can't see from here.

The sight prompts me to pull my phone from my back pocket. After adjusting the settings in the camera app, I snap a few pictures.

As he works, Goose pads over and slurps from a bowl of water next to the fridge.

The simple sight melts my heart. Such a thoughtful gesture, him making sure my dog feels at home.

Tucker spins from the counter and places two bowls on the table, one empty and one full of steaming edamame. "A little appetizer. It doesn't really go with what we're having, but Shaw keeps us flush with beans, so they're kinda a staple around here." He shrugs, his smile reminiscent of the one the eight-year-old in that picture wore. I tense up in response, all my promises to enjoy the evening gone in a blink.

What the hell are you doing here, Natalie?

I receive yet another reminder of our age difference when I pull out a chair and discover a wayward Nerf dart in the seat. The bright orange and blue foam brings memory after memory to mind. For years, I dodged battles Cam and Tucker waged. I hold up the tiny projectile and raise a brow.

Tucker's boyish grin turns sheepish as he rubs the back of his neck, a slight blush staining his cheeks. "Yeah, we still ambush each other occasionally. Missed that one." He plucks the dart from my fingers and pockets it.

I grasp the back of the chair, my knuckles turning white, wrestling with the urge to call it a night. To thank him for dinner, scoop up my dog, and flee to the comfort of my childhood bedroom, where I'll wallow and curse the universe for sending me a man I shouldn't want.

He studies me, brows furrowed, clearly sensing the indecision. "Lower your shoulders, Natalie."

Goose bumps erupt at his use of my full name.

"It's just dinner. Relax."

I lift my chin. "Most women hate being told to relax."

Lips twitching, he takes half a step closer to the table. "You'll like it when I tell you that."

His confidence disarms me. Like a dutiful soldier, I lower my shoulders and release my muscles, the tension clearing like water down a drain.

"Good girl."

With a playful glare, I sink onto the sparkly red vinyl.

He laughs, and with a wink, he resumes his chopping at the counter.

As I watch him work his magic, I snag a pod from the bowl and savor its salty flavor before chewing the warm beans.

"Do you, um, need any help?" I ask after I place the empty pod in the extra bowl.

He glances over his shoulder. "Just talk to me. I'm almost done with the pesto, and all that's left is to cook the noodles." He nods at the counter on the other side of the kitchen.

On the surface, rolled-out dough and a pasta cutter rest on a floured cookie sheet. "Homemade pasta?"

He shrugs casually. "Yeah. Gotta impress my date."

I gape at him. "You didn't have to go to all this trouble—"

"Let me stop you right there." He wipes his hands on the towel still draped over his shoulder, the move causing the muscles in his forearms to ripple, and props himself up on the back of the chair across from me. The move makes my mouth go dry. "You are worth all this and more." Bluish-gray eyes narrowed, he ducks, surveying me under the brim of his cap. "I don't know if it was a man who made you doubt your self-worth, but I'm sure as hell gonna do my damnedest to rid you of it. You. Are. Worth. It."

My lips part, but no words come out. Because what the hell am I supposed to say to *that*?

In one fluid motion, he straightens. "Now, tell me about your day, shutterbug. I'll pour you a glass of wine."

Chapter Fourteen

Natalie

"This looks delicious."

He's arranged the dish artfully, the bright green of the pesto and deep red of sun-ripened tomatoes the perfect contrast to the creamy noodles and sauce.

As I breathe in the enticing aroma, I twirl my fork and scoop up a bite.

He holds the wine bottle aloft, observing my reaction.

The flavors come alive on my tongue, the basil of the pesto the perfect balance to the tartness of the tomatoes and the richness of the sauce. I close my eyes and savor it. I savor this moment. This man made this meal from scratch. For me.

When I open my eyes, he's still watching, his brows raised in anticipation.

"It's fantastic," I gush. "How'd you learn to do all this?"

He leans back, his lips kicked up in a satisfied smirk. "Remember how I told you I spent a lot of time with Granny?"

Nodding, I stab a chunk of chicken. "Jiu-jitsu lessons."

"Right. With Mom and Dad off with my brothers or dealing with farm stuff, she cooked for us on most weeknights. She'd prep meals while we were at school, but she'd let me help with the cooking. Shaw and Griff usually handled clean up since their practices and games ran later, but they learned a thing or two over the years as well." He waves his fork in the air. "Though I'm the best, of course."

"Of course." I snort.

He shovels a huge bite into his mouth, unabashedly moaning at the taste.

"Do you do all the cooking around here?"

He wipes his mouth with a napkin and swipes up his glass of pinot grigio. "Nah, we trade weeks. Cam's decent, since he cooks at the firehouse too."

I take another bite and allow myself to examine his arms as he enjoys his dinner. Though I've studied his tattoos more than once already, I find new details every time. "Your friend who did your tattoos, he's in Memphis?"

"Lux? Yeah. He rents the shop below Griff and Brynn's place." He sips his wine, eyeing me over the rim. "You finally decide to commit to some ink? I'll take you to see him."

He offered during our photo shoot, too. But I was too timid to acknowledge the invitation. Now, though?

"I've wanted one for years, but I've always talked myself out of it. Maybe now's the time."

"Now's definitely the time. What design are you considering?"

"Something simple." My cheeks heat with embarrassment, but I force myself to share my idea anyway. "A dandelion. They represent hope and resilience. Plus, my dad and I made wishes on them during the summers I spent in Austin as a kid."

Tucker's lips lift in a soft smile. "How's he doing?"

Now, it's my turn to smile. "He's great. Keeps threatening to retire, but he still loves teaching too much to walk away."

My father's taught Spanish at the same high school for the past twenty-five years. He's constantly complaining about all the gray hairs his students have given him, but from what I've witnessed at football games and such, Señor Torres is well-liked and respected.

"I remember when he'd come get you for the summer. He'd always bring Cam these watermelon candies—"

"Sandillitas."

He dips his chin. "That's it. And when he caught me begging Cam to share, he started bringing me my own bag."

At the memory, nostalgia flickers its usual bittersweet warmth in my core. My parents married, had a child, and divorced before either of them had celebrated their twenty-fifth birthday. I was a toddler when they split, so I don't remember those first few tense years after the divorce. Dad moved back to Austin, but he'd drive up to get me for a whole month every summer until I graduated from high school, and I'd spend some of my longer school breaks with him and my Guatemalan aunts, uncles, and cousins.

It didn't take terribly long for my parents to figure out how to co-parent well, and as a result, they've developed a friendly rapport over the years. Dad attended Mom's wedding to James, and the five of us even braved a couple of blended family vacations when I was a teenager.

Spending time in Austin was always an adventure for me. The city's quirky vibes fed my creative, artistic side. And surrounded by my father's joyful, close-knit family, I soaked up every ounce of Guatemalan culture I could.

When the time came for me to choose a college, UT was a no-brainer. It meant I could live with Dad while getting my degree and get to know that side of my family even better. Putting down roots there after graduation felt like a natural progression.

Tucker takes another gulp of wine, and after he sets his glass down, he scoots forward and rests his forearms on either side of his plate, his demeanor turning serious. "Now, you want to tell me what made you freeze up tighter than a bowstring earlier?"

I hate myself a little for it, but I play dumb and push a tomato around with my fork. "I don't know what you mean."

"Nat."

That single word hangs between us until I find the courage to make eye contact. When I do, there's no judgment, only concern.

"I had you all soft and pliable in the living room, but by the time you came in here, you were tense. Was it—" His throat bobs. "Was it because I touched you? Was I too forward?"

I shake my head, my heart aching. He's so damn sincere, so concerned. "No, Tucker. I promise." My confession comes out in a near whisper. Being vulnerable like this is difficult, but he needs to know the truth. "I like when you touch me."

"Yeah?" He breaks into a slow, sexy grin. "Good, because I like it, too." He slides his arm closer, fingers splayed in invitation.

I accept, lacing my digits through his.

He drags his thumb along my skin in a soothing pattern. "Tell me what spooked you, please."

I study our joined hands, relishing the way they fit together. I could so easily become addicted to his touch. My first instinct is to blow off his question and convince him that I'm fine. But I don't want to hide from Tucker.

In our last phone call, Regina referred to me as a late bloomer. I laughed off the term at the time. Now, as I sit across from a man who swears I'm worthy of homemade romantic dinners and eight hugs a day and intimate touches, I've never felt like more of a baby bird perched on the edge of my nest, looking out on a wide wonderful world ripe for exploring. I've never wanted to spread my wings so badly and just fucking fly.

Tucker's patient as I collect my thoughts, and it makes me like him even more.

So with a deep breath in, I spill my worries. "I don't know what this is or why it's happening or where it's leading. And you're...Cam's best friend. Plus, there's our age difference."

I don't mention my other concerns, like my temporary status in town or that I'm relationship challenged.

Still swiping his thumb over the back of my hand, he leans in a fraction. "Let's squash all of your doubts tonight. This," with his free hand, he gestures between us, "is a legit attraction between two consenting adults who have ridiculous chemistry. Yes, your brother is my best friend. But who you're related to shouldn't impact how we feel about each other." He arches a brow. "Are we good so far?"

I nod, though I'm not totally convinced the Cam thing can be brushed under the rug so easily.

"Now, the age thing." He squares his shoulders. "Why is that an issue?"

My heart lurches. "Why *isn't* it an issue? You know I'm forty, right?"

"Yep. And you'll be forty-one in a couple weeks."

"And that doesn't bother you?"

"Nope."

"Tucker—"

"Natalie," he counters, a challenging glint in his eyes. "Climate change. Letting my family down. Not knowing where Goose's name came from." The tags on my dog's collar jingle when he hears his name. "Those things bother me. The years between us definitely do not."

I pull my hand from his and cross my arms.

His brows disappear beneath the brim of his cap. "So it's up to you to figure out if it bothers *you* too much to get past."

With my jaw locked tight, I let his comment marinate. Why am I so concerned about our age difference? Sure, people can be judgy about this type of thing, especially if the woman is older. But when I turned forty last year, I discovered I have far fewer fucks to give than I used to. I no longer care about what strangers think of me. What does concern me is that the distance is too much to overcome. He's in the prime of his adulthood, whereas I'm on the fast track to middle age.

But does it really matter? There's no denying the chemistry he mentioned. And it's not like this can be permanent. He breezed right over the *where it's leading* part of my mini freak-out. Since I came to town, one thing has become clear: Tucker is a live-in-the-moment guy. He doesn't stress about the future, and he's likely only interested in a Ms. Right Now.

Maybe I can be that for him.

Liv's encouragement to have a summer fling clangs like a mental gong, right along with Regina's reminder to choose happiness. Even though it's way out of my comfort zone, maybe I should leap onto this moving train, let it carry me away for a little while, and enjoy the ride.

But can I have a dalliance with this man knowing full well I'm not equipped to handle a casual, just-for-the-summer romance? Knowing my heart will likely be shattered when it's time to say goodbye?

Exhausted from all the mental gymnastics, I gather what little strength I have left and pull my shoulders back. The disappointed puppy eyes he'll give me when I tell him that, yes, the age thing is too much for me, might just be too much to take. It's a lie, of course, but it's the path of least resistance. A closed door he won't knock on again, I hope.

Before I can force the words out, he takes my hand, pulls it to his mouth, and playfully bites the pads of my fingers.

And all my resolve evaporates.

"That was some mighty heavy thinking you did just now," he says, his irises alight with unwavering certainty. "What's it gonna be, shutterbug?" He plants a lingering kiss on the back of my hand and breaks into his signature sexy smile.

The words escape me without my permission. "It's not too much to get past."

Releasing my hand, he leans back and exhales a satisfied breath. "Good. I say we make a pact: After tonight, we won't mention the age thing again. Deal?"

My heart stutters. Fuck it. I'm already in too deep.

With a deep breath in, I nod once. "Deal."

He rises from his chair, reaching for my hand. "C'mere."

"Wh-what's happening?" I frown down at my half-eaten plate of pasta.

"We're gonna hug it out." He pulls me to my feet for an embrace.

We stand like that for several seconds, letting the quiet settle around us, the only sound the tippy-tap of Goose's toenails on the tile as he explores every nook and cranny of the kitchen. The thump-thump of Tucker's heartbeat lulls me, and when I gently scrape my nails up and down his cotton-covered back, I marvel at the way the patch of his skin visible at his throat pebbles with goose bumps.

God, I could get used to being held like this. His arms are starting to feel like home, and he's been healing my touch-starved soul, one hug at a time.

I'm unsure of what the future holds, but I make a vow to myself in the middle of Tucker's kitchen: I'll cling to the promise of Liv's words, repeat them like a mantra until they're etched into my subconscious.

My story isn't over yet.

And the plot twist I never saw coming? The man who's holding me like I'm a precious possession.

Tucker smooths his hands down my back and slides them into my back pockets, cupping my ass through the denim. Just like that, the temperature in this kitchen ratchets up ten degrees.

"For the record," he starts, kneading my curves, "we're now up to 50 percent of your daily hug requirement. And the night's not over yet."

Amusement mixed with desire threads through me. "Still aiming for a 'good boy'?"

"You bet this sweet ass I am." He angles his head back to regard me but doesn't break our connection. Sincerity and affection shine from his gaze. "I can't believe someone hasn't snatched you up. You're gorgeous and kind and smart and funny. But I'm fucking ecstatic that you're still available. It means I get the chance to make you mine. And I'm not going to fumble you."

An effervescent weightlessness overtakes me. I'm a cheery yellow balloon, floating through the fluffiest clouds.

Thank goodness he's still gripping my ass, tethering me to the earth. To him.

But I'm still me, so the sensation is fleeting. In a matter of seconds, a menacing gray cloud creeps in, threatening and persistent.

This is going to hurt like a bitch when it ends.

Soft eyes bounce between mine, then dip to my lips. "I want to kiss you so fucking bad."

Moment of truth: Do I linger at the edge of the nest, or do I take a leap and spread my wings?

Time to fly, Nat.

When I find my voice, it's surprisingly steady and sultry. "Guess you better do it, then."

He flips his cap backward. Then he cups my cheeks, his hold gentle but firm. He inches forward and a ragged "finally" leaves him an instant before he seals his mouth to mine in a soft kiss that goes on long enough to quicken my breath.

I grasp his forearms, greedy for more, and in response, he deepens the next kiss. When he uses his lips to coax mine open, the hot, wet warmth of his mouth is my undoing.

Without a second to overthink it, I knock his hat to the floor and delve my fingers into his soft locks.

Tucker tilts my head and sweeps in, his tongue flirting with mine. I can't hold back the soft whimper that escapes as we duel in a sensual give-and-take, setting a rhythm that muddles my brain and makes my knees forget their job.

When my legs weaken, he hugs me to his body, his mouth continuing to claim mine. I arch my back, pressing into him, and he moans into the kiss, the sound guttural.

I may be inexperienced in relationships, but I have been kissed plenty of times.

Though it's never been like this.

This connection is all-consuming. The kind poets pen odes about and artists attempt to capture on canvas.

I'll remember this kiss for the rest of my life.

Way too soon, he slows and backs away a fraction. With his bluish-gray irises trained on me, their color darker than I've ever seen it, I'm certain that being up close and personal with Tucker is my new favorite place.

Gently, still entranced, I smooth a wayward lock of hair from his forehead.

He's just as fixated on me. After another glance at my lips, he presses several firm pecks to my mouth, like he can't get enough of it, then gives me a smug, satisfied smirk.

"Well?"

The man already knows the answer to that simple question. I consider teasing him. Instead, I dive in and give him what he wants.

I rake my teeth over my swollen lips. "Good boy."

Then I crush my mouth to his once more. And it feels like flying.

Chapter Fifteen

Tucker

Natalie and I are tangled up in each other, limbs intertwined, hips rocking, bodies sweaty and fighting for breath when an incessant buzzing breaks through the haze of need engulfing me.

As the fantasy dissipates, reality crashes in, pulling an exasperated groan from deep in my chest.

Fuck. Another dream. I'm alone in bed again, my only companion the painful hard-on tenting the sheet like a white flag.

I scrub a hand down my face, then squint at my alarm clock as I snatch my vibrating phone from the bedside table.

At the sight of Griff's name on the screen, panic washes over me. He never calls this early, especially on a Saturday. Heart racing, I sit up and swipe to answer his call, doing my best to ignore the situation in my lap.

"What is it?" My voice is raspy and unused.

Griffin, however, sounds chipper as a damn lark. "Tuck. You still sleeping, bro?"

I drop my head back against the headboard. "Not anymore, jackass."

He chuckles, unbothered. "Sorry 'bout that. I was calling to see if you were up for a Shaw ambush and workout."

Still half asleep, I rub an eye with the heel of my palm. "It's been a while, huh?"

During his offseason, the two of us occasionally team up to do weekend proof-of-life checks at our oldest brother's cabin. If Shaw wasn't running the family farm or required to put in face time with our parents, I swear he'd live like a hermit.

Five years ago, he custom-built a swanky log cabin on a secluded wooded section of our family's land. He added a couple of outbuildings, too, one of which he's turned into a workshop and makeshift gym. Griffin and I love to do what we call farmer circuit training there. Real manly lumberjack shit.

An intense workout is exactly what I need to take my mind off how badly I want to get Natalie naked.

First, I have to take care of the erection caused by visions of her tangled in my bedsheets.

I shake my head to pause those visions long enough to focus. "Yep, I'm in."

"Cool. See you in thirty. Bring Cam if he's game."

Yeah, I will definitely *not* be doing that.

I've avoided my best friend as much as possible since his sister and I started making out on our couch like a pair of hormone-addled teenagers every night. It's been days, and already, keeping this secret from him is eating at me. We need to fess up soon.

After I end the call, I go through my morning routine, one that takes longer than normal lately because of the fantasies that plague me night after night. When I finally wander into the kitchen, I'm surprised to find Cam guzzling a cup of coffee at the table.

"You're off nights." *Good job, Captain Obvious.*

He wouldn't drink coffee at this time of the morning unless his schedule had changed. Which means Natalie and I will need an alternative location for our make-out sessions.

Gah, I'm a shitty friend.

"Yep." The single word is clipped, his expression cool.

"Uh, cool." Ignoring the dread in the pit of my stomach, I pull out the blender and gather ingredients for a smoothie.

"When were you going to tell me you're seeing someone?"

I fumble a handful of blueberries and they scatter across the counter and onto the floor. When I turn his way, willing my face to remain its usual shade, he's holding up a sparkly, dangly earring.

"Found it between the couch cushions."

My breath stutters in my lungs. Natalie's earring. *Fuck.*

"Uh..." I crouch and collect the runaway berries, silently praying he doesn't recognize the jewelry. As I work to collect my thoughts, I fetch the last couple of blueberries, then stand to face him. "Yeah, uh, it's new. I wasn't sure it was going to turn into anything."

Pain lances my chest as his eyes widen in interest. Damn it. I am the actual worst.

"Oh shit, for real? I was totally messing with you. I assumed it was Trixie's." He breaks into a grin. "So it's turning into something?"

Trixie's. Of course. Why didn't I think to say that?

I rub the back of my neck. "Yeah, I-I think so."

He sets his mug on the counter. "Well? Spill the deets."

His request slices me to the bone. We've always shared details of our romantic pursuits with each other. We long ago agreed we'd keep the private details to ourselves, but neither of us has ever held back on topics including the excitement of meeting someone and first-date jitters or even the mundane arguments and heartbreak. Neither of us could ever be considered a playboy, so romantic interests aren't common, and the topic is usually one we're eager to discuss.

I can count on one hand the number of girls Cam has been with, and he can say the same of me. It would crush me if he ever kept a woman a secret.

Which is why that pain in my chest turns into more of a stabbing sensation when I say, "Like I said, it's new, so...I'm just gonna see how it goes for a minute, if that's okay."

The set of his jaw and the disappointment in his eyes almost make me confess every damn thing. But I can't. Not without talking to Natalie first. We've kept our mouths busy and our hands full every evening since our dinner, so we haven't exactly had the chance to talk about her brother.

Cam rinses his cup in the sink and sets it in the dishwasher. Then he leans back against the counter and crosses his legs at the ankles, regarding me. The stance is rigid, his expression closed off. When his eyes narrow, I start to sweat.

Please don't ask who it is. Please don't ask who it is. Please don't—

"Do I know her?"

Shit.

I go with the vaguest answer I can formulate. "Uh, maybe?"

Tucker Lacey: the dumbest of all the dumbasses.

Brows cinched together, he hands me the earring. "Fine. Keep your secrets. I'll be here to listen when you're done figuring it out."

I quickly tuck it in the pocket of my shorts. "Cam—"

He waves me off. "It's fine, Tuck." The frustration in his tone belies the sentiment, but he doesn't give me time to smooth things out between us. "You headed to the gym?"

I turn the blender on, then pull a tumbler from the cabinet. Once the consistency of the smoothie looks about right, I hit the off button, and when the whirring stops, I say, "Griff and I are meeting at Shaw's to get in a workout."

I nearly cave and invite him to join us, an olive branch of sorts, but I choke back the offer before it can escape me. I need my brothers' advice about this situation ASAP.

"Speaking of Shaw," he says, straightening. "I was thinking. Maybe we should set him up with Nat while she's in town."

My gut plummets to the floor. "What?"

"Tuck." He tosses a dish towel at me.

Only then do I realize that I've sloshed a healthy amount of my smoothie on the floor.

While I wipe at the puddle of green liquid, he elaborates. "It's not so far-fetched. She's older than him, but only by a few years. And Shaw—"

I cut him off. "Shaw doesn't date. Period."

"He and Whitney divorced like five years ago. And it's been, what, fifteen, since—"

"Cam." The single syllable is sharp. I'd prefer not to start my day with a reminder of the most painful time in my brother's life. Or with this asinine idea of playing matchmaker with him and the woman I'm having nightly wet dreams about.

He sighs, his shoulders drooping. "Sorry. I just think they'd be a good match. They're both lonely introverts. Home bodies. And God knows they each deserve to find their person. Plus..." he says, his tone softening. "If she had a reason to, then maybe Nat would want to stay. Permanently."

My breath stumbles, though I quickly school my expression to hide the hope bubbling in my chest. "You think she wants to move back?"

Cam shrugs. "She hasn't said anything about it. But when I take her up for aerial shots next week, I plan on campaigning to convince her. I know Holly Holler can't compete with Austin, but I'm selfish. I want my sister back."

The two of us have been friends nearly our entire lives, so I've cataloged the many faces of Cam. The goofy expression he wears when he's laughing at his own jokes. The sly, mischievous look he adopts when he's planning a prank. The calm stoicism he exhibits at work, whether at the fire station or with his dad. His gaze of quiet longing when he stares at my cousin. And every variant in between. But I've never witnessed this despondence.

Maybe Natalie isn't the only sibling in the Torres-Little fam who needs a hug. Or eight.

I have my own set of selfish reasons for wanting his sister to stay, so I'm more than happy to assist my friend. Though I'll have to do it from behind the scenes for now.

If only that could assuage my guilt for keeping our mutual attraction a secret.

The panic that swamped me when Cam mentioned setting Natalie up with Shaw still lingers, so I circle back to the topic. "Like I said, Shaw isn't interested in dating. Anyone who mentions a single daughter or granddaughter gets shot down."

He shrugs again, looking sadder than when his beloved bulldog had to be euthanized. We were twelve, and he's sworn off the idea of ever owning another dog. The sigh he loosens physically hurts me. "Yeah. Forget I even mentioned it."

Not likely. I pinch the bridge of my nose in an attempt to slow the whirlwind in my brain. Time to focus and get out of here. If I don't, I'm liable to fuck up further.

"It's cool. How does this week look for you?" I tie a bandanna around my head, then wander to the front door in search of my shoes. "And do you have any dinner requests? It's my turn to cook."

While I tie my shoelaces, Cam goes over his work schedule. I take note of when it will be safe to have Natalie over, then I consider which of his favorites to cook on the nights he'll be home.

I gulp down my smoothie on the drive to Shaw's, ensuring I finish it before navigating my Jeep up the bumpy gravel road that winds through towering loblollies and aged oaks and hearty hickories. When I park next to Griffin's truck, he's leaning against its side, workout ready in gym shorts and a muscle tee.

At Shaw's absence, I peer at the clock on the dash. Ah, it's still early. This wake-up call is gonna suck.

For him. Griff and I will enjoy every damn second.

I slam the door to my Jeep and round the hood. "Signs of life?"

My brother pushes off his truck and starts for the cabin's front porch. "That door slam should about do it."

Sure enough, the heavy front door swings wide before we reach the steps.

"What. The. Fuck?" Shaw crosses his arms over his bare chest. From his mussed hair and sleep-wrinkled—not to mention, pissed off—face, he's just rolled out of bed.

"Rise and shine, Yeehaw." Griff taunts him with the high school nickname he earned as a local tie-down roping badass.

He loathes that moniker to the depths of his soul.

His hatred only makes it that much more fun to use.

I hang my head to hide the grin that wants to break free.

"What the fuck time is it and why the fuck are you two fuckers here?"

"Griff," I say, amusement rushing through me, "based on all the fucks he's throwing around, he's really happy to see us."

If looks could kill, we'd be seconds from wearing concrete shoes at the bottom of the pond that separates Shaw's property from the clearing where Griff and Brynn's new house is being built.

With a laugh, Griff trudges up the wooden steps.

As I follow, the aroma of fresh coffee and something sweet waft from Shaw's open door. Delta appears as I hit the top step, nosing the door wider and pushing past her owner, a stuffed squirrel in her mouth. Her entire rump wags with happiness as she greets us.

Gah, I love this dog. She's sunshine in dog-form, the perfect counterbalance to grumpy-ass Shaw. She's without a doubt the most beloved Lacey family member, though Brynn is unwittingly making a case for herself.

Our eldest brother props his fists on his hips and glares at Griffin, his plaid pajama pants making it hard to take him too seriously. "What are you doing here, fucker?"

"Brynn and I are here for a week before our extended stay in Florida. She's gonna visit with her parents and work on her book while I'm at training camp."

Brynn grew up in Cocoa Beach, and she and Griff recently closed on a condo a few streets over from her quirky folks. The Laceys haven't met the Nelsons in person yet, but the families have already been introduced via video call and family group chats have been established.

Shaw scrubs a hand over his neatly trimmed beard and sighs. "No, dumbass. Why are you *here* at my home at this ungodly hour on a fucking Saturday?"

"Isn't it obvious?" Griff clamps a hand on my shoulder. "We're here for a workout."

"You do remember that he," Shaw gestures my way, "owns a fucking gym, right?"

Our middle brother pokes out his bottom lip. "But you won't come to the gym."

"Why do I need to be involved at all?"

With a laugh, he aims a soft punch at Shaw's shirtless torso. "Getting kinda soft in the middle there, old man. We're here to whip you into shape."

Shaw growls. "Get fucked."

Griff's smirk is smug as he smooths a hand over his abdomen. "Already did. This morning."

I punch his bicep. "No wonder you were so damn perky when you called."

"Shit, Tuck. That hurt." Grimacing, he massages his muscle.

"Serves you right, you braggart."

Shaw takes a step back. "I'm going back to bed. Don't kill each other in my shop." With that, he spins and steps inside.

"No!" I call out, as Griff yells, "Wait!"

To my surprise, our grumpy brother actually pauses and turns back to us.

"Come work out with us. Please," Griff says.

What he doesn't add? *We want to spend time with you. We love you and care about you. We worry about you.* He doesn't have to say it. We all know it's implied.

I clear my throat and give him the expression I perfected as the baby of the family. The one that always wears Mom down. "Yeah, bro. Let's hang out for a bit. We promise not to talk your ear off." I adjust my hat, curling the brim. "After I get some advice from y'all, that is."

Shaw's hardened gaze softens, a sure sign he's going to cave, and he huffs the most put-upon sigh in history. "Fine. But keep the goddamn yapping to a minimum, please." This comment he directs at Griff specifically.

Twenty minutes later, the three of us are sweating in Shaw's workshop. The wooden barn is stained to match the cabin and holds worktables laden with tools and pieces of farm equipment. On the left wall, he's got a side-by-side parked in a row with a couple four-wheelers. The far right corner next to a back entrance is penned off and filled with hay. He uses the area to hold animals from Lacey Farms that need nursing or rehab.

The workout area in the center is equipped with heavy ropes and tractor tires that we upend or drag with a rope tied around our waists, along with pull-up bars, kettlebells, sacks of feed we heft during squats, and a lone punching bag.

Griff drops the pair of heavy battle ropes and wipes his forehead with the hem of his tee. "How's the gym doing?"

I eye the pull-up bar that's bolted into a ceiling beam and drag my sweaty hands down my shorts. "It's good. We've had an uptick in memberships, but that's to be expected during the summer. The website's gotten decent traffic since its launch, and we've added a section to the membership questionnaire to get data on how people are hearing about us."

"That's great." He nods once, his expression sincere. " Sounds like you've got a good handle on that place. I'm proud to be a part of it."

Those words, especially coming from one of my personal heroes, make me feel like I can conquer anything. My belief in myself has progressed along with the gym's growth, and it's satisfying as hell when my family validates the path I've chosen and acknowledges that I've matured beyond the irresponsible days of my youth.

After my third set of pull-ups, I'm still riding high on Griffin's praise. So I drop to the ground, deciding it's the perfect time to confess my secret. "So, um, I'm kinda seeing someone. A woman."

In unison, my brothers stop their workouts. They share a glance, then both sets of eyes land on me.

"Before I tell you who it is, I want you to know that I really like her. Like, a helluva lot. This..." I scratch at the back of my neck. "This feels different."

A slow smile streams across Griff's face. "Different, huh?"

I bob my head. "Yeah. But there are a couple..." I swallow thickly, searching for the best way to describe the situation. "A couple of obstacles in the way."

Shaw lowers a kettlebell and swipes a hand across his brow, waiting. My brain can get messy from time to time, but for all his gruffness, he's always shown me the utmost patience.

"She doesn't live here, for one. And I don't mean like she's forty-five minutes from town. It's more like nine hours." I raise the hem of my T-shirt to wipe my mouth, stalling. Shit, here goes nothing. "And the other obstacle is...she's Cam's sister."

"Natalie?" Griff gawks, his eyes going ridiculously wide.

Shaw, always the silent one, only gives me a questioning look.

Rather than dive into a lecture like I feared they would, my brothers simply eye each other, communicating silently. Being only a year apart in age, they've always shared a bond no one else could penetrate, not even me.

"And you haven't told Cam." Shaw's response isn't a question.

"You gotta do it," Griff says before I can respond. "Full transparency."

My pulse kicks up, defensiveness rising inside me. "Yeah, I get that. I will. Soon. I just need…" Frustration joins the party, bubbling in my veins. I squeeze my eyes shut and blurt, "I just need y'all to tell me what to say to him. How do I tell my best friend that I'm falling in love with his sister?"

When I force myself to look at my brothers again, expecting to find pity or censure, all I find is compassion and understanding.

"Tuck." Griff's tone is gentle. "If you're serious about her, you just gotta be honest. Let him know that this isn't about a quick fuck."

I tip my head back, the relief of finally opening up washing over me.

"He'll be pissed at first," he continues. "Shocked, no doubt. But Cam knows you're a stand-up guy. He'll come around."

"Falling in love, huh?" Shaw asks after a quiet moment.

"Seems soon to be making that declaration," Griff chimes in. "She's been back in town, what, a few weeks?"

I scoff. "Says the man who asked Brynn to move in two weeks after meeting her."

He cocks a brow. "As a roommate."

"It might seem too soon to throw around the L-word, but I don't know how else to describe it." I rub my chest as if I can massage away the tightness. "I think about her from the moment I wake until I close my eyes at night. She's in my dreams, the sweet ones and the naughty ones."

Griff wags his brows. Shaw is once again watching me with a scrutinizing expression.

"When we're together," I continue, "it's like my brain unwinds, rearranges. It feels *right*. Like when I study a painting for the first time. Colors are richer, the details are sharper. And when we're apart? I feel like a raw nerve, exposed and blistered. It fucking *hurts.*"

Shaw's sigh weighs a ton. "Yep. That tracks."

Griff's shit-eating grin is obnoxious. "Look at our boy, all grown up."

"Does she feel the same?" The protectiveness in Shaw's tone makes my throat burn.

It's my turn to sigh. "Yeah, I think she could. But she's hesitant. The age thing bothered her at first, but I think we've moved past that. But I don't know that I can convince her to move back."

"Try my method. It works with Brynn every time." Griffin rolls his sneaker over the coils of rope at his feet. "Hold her on your lap and don't let her get up until she agrees with you."

With a groan, Shaw points at him. "You're an idiot."

Our middle brother waves a dismissive hand. "Whatever. It works."

Before they can take their bickering up a notch, I cut in. "When are you gonna wife her up?"

"I'm not telling you fuckers a damn thing." Griff pins us with a mock-glare. "Like I don't know about your little wager."

Shaw and I lock eyes. "Trixie," we say in unison. She's the most likely snitch.

"Never could keep a secret." Snorting, Griffin retrieves his bottle of water. He downs it in three gulps, then wipes his mouth with the back of his hand. "Let's recap," he says, setting the bottle down again. "You're gonna tell Cam ASAP. Then you're gonna pull out all the stops to bring your woman round to the idea of making Holly Holler home again. Anything else we need to cover before this one has a coronary?"

I shake my head.

"Good." He dodges the weights and equipment scattered on the concrete floor between us and pulls me in for a sweaty, bone-crushing hug. "Proud of you, little brother." The weight and warmth of his hand as he cups the back of my head and jostles it is a comfort.

I pound his back in an effort to quell the emotions surging inside me. "Thanks."

"Glad that's sorted." Shaw ambles to the sacks of feed stacked in the corner. "Now that the talking portion of this goddamn workout is over, let's get on with it so you fuckers can get out of here and let me enjoy the peace of a Saturday alone."

CHAPTER SIXTEEN

TUCKER

Sweat rolls down my neck and back as I turn onto West Street and slow my pace. The sun inches higher, the sky clear and blue and cloudless. The temperature this early is creeping toward uncomfortable, but in a couple hours, the heat rising off the concrete will be unbearable.

I jog past a shuttered Hoot 'n' Holler, and as I approach the town square, the scent of bacon floats on the air, making my mouth water. Our town's beloved diner, Loblolly, is bustling, even this early. The townsfolk are out already, fueling up for the day with fresh coffee and heaping piles of scrambled eggs and hash-browns. The parking spots close to the diner are all occupied, but most of the spaces that line the square or face the businesses are empty.

Save for one.

A lone white SUV sits in front of Wayne Gann Photography already. Natalie must be finishing up some editing this morning, taking advantage of the quiet, barren downtown.

When I reach the diner, I slow to a walk, a smile overtaking my face. We didn't meet up yesterday. She spent the afternoon and evening photographing a wedding while I joined Griff and Brynn for a Marvel marathon at Mom and Dad's, followed by tacos and a heated game of progressive rummy.

After shuffling through the small crowd waiting for a table outside the diner, I bound down the sidewalk toward the photography studio. The entry is dark, the light of the sun mostly blocked by the wide hunter green awning that covers the sidewalk. Though as I step closer and shield my eyes, I note the light from Wayne's office bleeding into the hallway.

I rap my knuckles against the window and step back. While I wait, I pinch the damp material of my shirt and fan myself, surveying my reflection. I wish like hell I wasn't a drenched, sweaty mess right now, but there's no way I'll miss out on a chance to see Nat. When my first knocks go unanswered, I do it again, harder this time.

When she sticks her head out of the office, her brows lifted, I break into a smitten grin that makes my reflection look a little unhinged. She shyly tucks a chunk of hair behind an ear as she crosses to the door.

"I'm sweaty," I warn her when she ushers me in.

"I don't care." She loops her arms around my torso and steps into my hold.

A pleasant warmth rushes through me. Yeah. This is what coming home feels like.

When she leans back, I plant a soft kiss on her lips.

"What are you doing?" She takes me in from head to sneakers and back up.

I clear my throat and adjust the bandana covering my hair. "Just getting in some cardio," I say. A rush of boldness overtakes me, so I roll with it. "Because the cardio I *want* to be doing hasn't invited me into her bed yet."

The lovely blush that colors her cheeks makes my pulse hammer harder than it did while I pushed through the last couple of miles of my run.

"Tucker." Her lips twitch as she toys with the material of my T-shirt.

"It's the truth, shutterbug." I drag the backs of my fingers up and down her arm. "But I promise, there's absolutely no pressure. You'll let me know when you're ready."

"Yes, well." She clears her throat, bashful.

It's so fucking cute I can hardly stand it.

"If that happens—"

My eyes narrow at the word *if*, causing her to bite back a grin.

"Okay, *when* that happens," she amends, smoothing a hand over the damp cotton covering my chest, "I'm afraid the invitation will not be for *my* bed. Since, you know, it's at my parents' house."

"Hmm." Her rosy lips beckon me, distracting me, so I take advantage of their proximity and brush mine against them again. And once more for good measure.

Though I'm a man who finds simple joy in most moments, few things in life give me more pleasure than kissing this woman until we're both out of breath.

I want more of this. And I've got an entire sunny Sunday afternoon free. "I want to take you for a ride today."

"Sir." She scowls, swatting my arm. "You just said no pressure."

I tip my head back and bark out a laugh. "Not that kind of ride." Though her comment does bring with it an enticing mental image. "A ride on my bike."

Her cheeks are flushed again, her expression one of wonder. "On your motorcycle?"

"Yes, my Honda. Not the ten-speed I almost mowed you down with."

"I've never ridden on a motorcycle before." She fists my shirt and bounces on her toes, her eyes twinkling.

Though the excitement only lasts a moment. Just as quickly, she deflates, her button nose scrunching adorably.

"I don't have a helmet, though."

"Nat." I smooth the crease between her brows with my thumb. "I got you."

Her shoulders relax. "Right. I'm sure you have extras."

"I do, sweetheart." I kiss her forehead, and when she melts in response to my impromptu use of that pet name, my nerve endings light up. "I have an extra. I bought it just for you."

"Tuck..." Her body is practically boneless against mine as she peers up at me, trusting me to keep her from sinking.

I'll do it for the rest of our lives if she'll let me.

When she pulls away, her lashes are damp. "Thank you for thinking of me. I'd love to go for a ride with you."

"Awesome. Why don't you finish up what you've got to do here, and I'll run home and shower. Text me when you're ready to go."

"Perfect."

Since she's so agreeable this morning, I go for broke. "And we need to tell Cam. Today."

She hangs her head with a heavy sigh.

I hook a finger under her chin and duck so we're eye to eye. "He's off at seven. After our ride, I'll make dinner and we can tell him then. Together."

"Okay." Her voice is full of defeat.

"Nat," I plead, with her and with my suddenly nervous stomach, "it's the right thing to do. It'll be fine."

Lips pressed together, she nods. "You're right."

After a steamy goodbye kiss, I head home, my thoughts zigzagging like thunderbolts. In the shower, I rehearse a dozen ways to break the news to Cam and dwell on all the ways the conversation could go, preparing for every possible reaction.

I cruise back downtown three hours later. The sun is high, but the breeze has kept the temperature in the mid-eighties.

I steer my bike to the back of the studio to ensure Cam won't see it from the fire station on the opposite side of the square. The photography studio can be seen clearly from the station parking lot, where a basketball hoop was installed for the guys to use to pass the time between calls, and on a day like today, I can guarantee they'll be out, soaking up the unseasonably cool weather.

When Natalie emerges, wearing a pair of jeans that show off her perfect curves, a vintage Fleetwood Mac T-shirt, and a smile brighter than the sun, all worries about Cam dissipate. We'll figure it out. Together.

"Think there's room for this?" She holds up a small silver digital camera that looks like it's been around a hell of a lot longer than the large, expensive one she used at the gym and the wedding. "Looks a little worse for wear," she says with a shrug, "but it still shoots like a dream. It was my first digital camera. My dad gave it to me as a graduation present."

I open one of the integrated saddlebags and she nestles the camera in the folds of the extra jacket I keep there.

"I start shooting for the tourism campaign soon, so I thought I'd bring this one along today. See what we can capture."

With a glance around to ensure we're alone, I peck her lips. Then I pull out the spray-on sunscreen I keep on hand for long rides on sunny days and do a quick pass over her arms, then mine.

When I hand over her sleek modular helmet, her eyes light up and her smile stretches wide. She brushes a thumb over the silver, black, and teal designs, a perfect match to mine. "This must've cost a fortune. I can send you—"

"Stop." I take the helmet from her. "I like buying things for you." I settle it on her head and buckle it. Then I show her how to flip up the built-in sun visor and chin guard, exposing her face so I can steal a quick kiss.

I give her a quick rundown of my bike and its features, and all the while, she's enthralled, nodding and asking questions.

Before I slip on my helmet, I tell her, "I don't have a communication system installed on yours yet, so we'll have to communicate by touch for now."

With a nod, she blinks at me. The genuine trust in her expression causes an ache to bloom behind my ribs.

I spin, putting my back to her the way we'll sit on the bike. "You'll hold on to me here." I pat my waist.

She places her hands there, her touch tentative, like I knew it would be.

I take her right hand in mine and tap it against my flank. "If you need me to stop immediately, you tap me here."

She repeats the motion without my assistance.

I do the same with her left hand. "This means you want me to pull over at the next convenient spot, but it's not an emergency."

We go over a few more signals—the left-knee squeeze I'll give to warn her I'm going to speed up and she should hold me tighter, as well as the right-knee squeeze that signals she can relax.

Now that I've had her hands all over me, I consider waiting to install an intercom in her helmet.

Helmet secure, I straddle the bike and hold it steady so she can slip on behind me. Once she's close, it takes every ounce of willpower I have to keep my blood from rushing straight to my groin. After lusting for her the way I've been for the past couple of weeks, just the warmth of her luscious thighs gripping mine is enough to get me hard.

When I start the bike, she grips my waist with trembling hands. Though she's left a gap between our torsos. Hoping the tremors are from excitement and not fear, I grasp her wrists gently and ease her hands to my sternum, the move bringing her chest flush against my back.

Best backpack I've ever worn.

"You good?" I shout over the rumble of the engine.

She doesn't shout back, but her helmet bobs against my shoulder blade.

With a pat to her hands, I take up the grips, and when I ease forward, her arms tighten around me, making me smile.

The town of Holly Holler has a total of five stoplights, and we hit three as we head north out of town. At each red light, I hold her right leg, my fingers molding to her curves through the denim.

She keeps her hands tight to my chest as we pick up speed on the outskirts of town and as we cruise down the two-lane highway that bisects the farm. The fields on either side are packed with bright green soybean plants in their vegetative state. The sight of the neat, uniform rows cutting through the dark, fertile soil makes my chest swell with pride. I may not be part of the day-to-day operations of Lacey Farms, but this place is in my blood. My brothers and I invested plenty of sweat equity into it during our adolescence and early adulthood. Even in his early off-seasons as a pro, Griff would come home and help with spring planting.

As we pass the turn-offs to my parents' place, to Shaw's cabin, and to the newly graveled lane that cuts to the clearing where Griff and Brynn's new house will be, I can't help but imagine having a plot of my own, complete with a cozy home out here one day. Sharing the land that built me with a special someone, building a legacy of our own.

I've never spent much time dwelling on the future, choosing instead to focus on the present. It's always been my intent to enjoy the hell out of now. But the more time I spend with the woman clinging to me, the more my mind wanders and the more frequently scenes of domestic bliss flit in and out of the frame.

The wooded patch on our left opens to reveal the last stretch of Lacey acres planted for this season. I take a winding left, curving toward the highway, and when Nat squeezes my left thigh, I instinctively place my hand on hers. When she squeezes again, I understand the message. A squeeze to her left knee is a warning that I'm about to speed up. So, if she's squeezing my left leg...

I twist the right grip, opening up the throttle, and that weightless, stomach-dropping thrill I've only ever associated with speeding down an open road rushes in, exhilarating all five senses.

Over the past month, I've experienced this same swoop-to-the-gut sensation while standing perfectly still, too. Every time the woman wrapped around me smiles.

Twenty miles later, I pull off the highway and slow, cruising along back roads until we come to a lone roadside haven. I ease into the gravel lot carefully, then cut engine and pat Natalie's leg, signaling for her to dismount first.

The second I tug my helmet off, her hands are on my cheeks and her mouth is on mine.

The kiss, although very welcome, takes me by surprise. My helmet drops to the pebbles with a plop as I lock my knees to keep the bike balanced between my legs. Weaving my hands into her hair to tilt her head, I kiss her back with the same ferocity. Lips bruising, tongues caressing.

When we separate, breathless, she touches her forehead to mine and toys with the hair at my nape. "That was incredible."

"Hmm." I roll my head so that our noses brush. "And the ride wasn't too shabby, either."

She tips her head back, laughing, and I press a line of kisses down her neck.

Arms still resting on my shoulders, she peers at our surroundings for the first time and quirks a brow. When the unmistakable scent of fried food hits her, her nostrils flare. "Corn dogs, huh?"

"Footlong corn dogs. And the best funnel cakes this side of a county fair."

Cam and I discovered this tiny roadside stand a few years back. It's little more than a cinder-block hut with a walk-up counter on one side and three metal picnic tables on the edge of the property, which is where we head after ordering our corn dogs and a large soda and funnel cake to share.

Once Natalie is settled on a metal bench, I straddle it and scoot in close to her. Even after having her suctioned to my back for the past half hour, I can't stand the idea of putting even a foot of space between us.

She snorts a laugh. "Wait, are we one of those obnoxious couples who sit on the same side of the booth?"

I open my mouth to affirm this, but before I can, she drops her head and huffs a bitter laugh.

"Oh, sorry," she says, her face blanching as she stares at the bitten end of her corn dog. "I shouldn't have called us a couple."

Alarm bells sound in my brain. "Why the hell not?" The words come out more harshly than I intend. Frustration and fear wrestle for dominance as I contemplate how we're still *here.* Still stuck in this damn limbo.

What more do I have to do to convince her that I'm all in when it comes to her? And why the fuck is this still an issue after every truth we've given each other?

Her throat bobs in a nervous swallow, but she tries to play off her discomfort by rolling her eyes. "Tucker. I'm not under any delusions that this makes it past August."

A dull ache blossoms in my chest. "The fuck it won't."

Her hazel eyes, flashing with anger, slice my way. "And how exactly would that work, pray tell? We live nine hours apart. My life is in Austin—"

"It doesn't have to be."

The second the words are out, my stomach sinks. Getting Natalie to consider moving back to Holly Holler was not on my agenda for today. I figured I'd let Cam do the heavy lifting, then sprinkle in my own persuasive hints when opportunities arose.

Fuck it.

She hangs her head, lids closed, but I won't let her shut down on me.

I gently grasp her chin and force her gaze to mine. "When I held you in my kitchen last weekend and told you that I was grateful for the chance to make you mine, that didn't mean just for the summer."

Her lips wobble and tears pool, but she doesn't look away.

Heart cracking, I swallow thickly. "We agreed to talk to your brother. Today."

Jerking her chin from my hold, she scoots down the bench. "Right. We're telling my brother that we're fooling around this summer. Not that we're an actual couple." Her words sting with bitterness, but they're laced with sadness, too.

I rake a hand through my hair, an attempt to tamp down my exasperation, and focus on taking a calming breath. As I exhale, I slide a couple of inches closer, determined to get through to her. To rid, for good, any of her lingering doubts. "I want to be an actual couple, Nat."

"You don't—"

"I abso-fucking-lutely do."

She stands in a blink, crossing her arms, closing herself off again. "You don't, though, Tucker. You don't—" She raises her chin. "You don't really want this."

I open my mouth, prepared to argue, but she plows ahead.

"You have your whole life ahead of you. You don't want a long-term commitment to a forty-year-old woman who can't have children."

CHAPTER SEVENTEEN

NATALIE

The words spill from my lips like the foulest acid, dripping onto the gravel between us, sizzling and solidifying into spiky lumps of truth I can't take back.

The bewildered expression on Tucker's face matches the chaotic thoughts in my mind.

Minutes ago, I was enjoying a thrilling motorcycle ride with a gorgeous, kindhearted man—an experience limited to my wildest dreams. Yet here I am, sparking an absolute dumpster fire of an argument.

My tendency for self-sabotage knows no bounds, apparently.

Was I triggered by my inadvertent *couple* label? Maybe. Though it could be that unnameable emotion finally overwhelming me. The one that's crept up on me over the past month. The one I refuse to acknowledge, ignoring it in the hope that I can figure out how to deal with it before it becomes a problem.

Clearly, it's too late for that.

Why the fuck did I ruin one of the best afternoons of my life by pulling this thread? And now that I've tugged on it, will I be forced to witness everything unravel?

The happy, bright June sunshine above belies my inner anguish. My thoughts coalesce into a swirling vortex that threatens to undo me, but one irrefutable truth glares brighter than the rest: I've never been anyone's first choice, and that makes it difficult to trust that someone would *ever* choose me. The idea that someone would genuinely want me when a long, long line of others have said *no thanks*? That feels impossible to believe.

Yet Tucker Lacey claims he wants me. And not just for the summer.

Maybe it's a good thing that I've dropped this truth bomb now, before either of us is in too deep.

I activate my full body armor, even as I worry it won't be enough to protect me from what comes next.

The perplexed man before me braces his elbows on his knees, his dark brows knitted. "You can't—"

"Likely can't," I amend, my tone clinical. I choke back even the smallest hints of emotion threatening to leak into my explanation. "I have a condition called polycystic ovary syndrome. It can cause infertility. It's common for women who have it to require medical intervention to get pregnant. And at my age, the chances of conceiving, even with help, aren't great."

He studies the ground at his feet, his exhale a slow leak through pursed lips.

Fidgeting, I clamp my mouth shut, giving him time to process while telling myself not to count his blinks or panic when he rubs his day-old stubble. In a matter of seconds, he nods. Then he does it again, as if he's making up his mind about how to proceed.

When he aims those blue-gray irises my way, my heart trips over itself. And as he assesses me silently, I make myself a promise: I'll handle his rejection with grace. It wouldn't be right to make him feel guilty about wanting a future I can't give him.

Finally, he speaks, and his words nearly bowl me over.

"I'm sorry you've had to deal with that," he says. "That's shitty. But it's not a dealbreaker. Not for me."

I rear back, shock giving way to disbelief. "Why isn't it?"

He pops a shoulder. "Maybe I'll want kids someday, maybe I won't. I try not to stress about the future. Even so, there are many ways to build a family. I won't let a what-if ruin a good thing now."

My fragile self-esteem screams at me to confirm that I'm the *good thing* he speaks of, but I mentally throat punch that bitch.

Can't wait to share that breakthrough with Regina.

As we stare at each other, I tuck a wayward strand of hair behind an ear. Is this man real? Or have I been stuck in a coma for the past month? Surely he's a gift my unconscious mind has conjured.

He stands and approaches me, kicking up dust as he goes. Gently, he grasps my wrists and pries my arms loose, lowering the shield I've created with them. Then he tugs me closer. With every inch he gains, a piece of my mental armor disintegrates.

"Let the record show that I don't scare easily, shutterbug. You can pick fights—"

I inhale sharply, ready to argue, but he presses a finger to my lips to silence me.

"Lob all the excuses at me you want. I'll smash every damn one. I'm not running from this. From you." He brushes his thumb over my bottom lip, then cuffs the back of my neck, his hold both reverent and possessive. Using that same thumb to notch my chin higher, he leans closer, so close our noses almost touch. "If I have to remind you every damn day that you're the woman I want, I'll do it. I'll do it until you believe it."

I swallow a groan. God, I don't want to be a woman who needs constant reassurance from a partner, but here I am, needy as fuck. He's saying all this now, but there's no way he won't get tired of my constant questions and never-ending doubt.

"Mm-hmm." He places a soft kiss on my cheek. "Wheels are spinning in this beautiful brain." Another kiss, this one to the corner of my mouth. "It's okay if you don't believe it yet." Now a kiss to my left brow. "I'll believe it for the both of us." When his lips find mine, his final target, he keeps them pressed there like he's imprinting a promise.

I want to believe it. More than anything.

Maybe I've been alone all this time because he was out there. Maybe I've been waiting for him, giving him time to grow and mature into *this* man. The man who takes me for motorcycle joy rides and kisses oaths into my skin.

He releases my neck and trails his hand down my shoulder and arm. As he twines his fingers with mine, he steps back toward the table and tilts his head, smiling. "You still need a bit of proof?"

I could never get enough, but I don't tell him that. Instead, I let him pull me back to the picnic table and guide me into my seat.

When he joins me, straddling the bench with his knee pressed to my thigh, he squares his posture. "Let me tell you a little story."

I take a tentative bite of my lukewarm corn dog as he launches into his tale.

"Once upon a time, in a hella quaint Arkansas town, there was a devastatingly handsome and fit guy who was working hard to build his business and just all-around doing his best to enjoy life."

My lips twitch, but I take another bite and nod for him to continue.

"Needing photos of said business, he set up an appointment with the town photographer. The day of the appointment, Handsome Guy expected to meet up with a seventy-year-old gentleman with gray hair—"

"He's sixty-eight," I whisper.

Tucker winks. "Instead, on that fateful Saturday morning, the universe sent the guy none other than his first crush, all grown up and gorgeous."

I lower my lashes as my face heats.

"When he discovered that she'd be in town for the entire summer, Handsome Guy vowed to shoot his shot. He manifested opportunities to see her around town so he could charm her socks off."

I stretch out my leg and gesture to my non-sock-wearing foot snug in my favorite Adidas. "Mission accomplished."

With a smug grin, he cocks his head. "One of those opportunities presented itself when he noticed that she visited the town coffee shop for her morning caffeine fix." He tucks a wave of hair behind my ear. "So he showed up every morning, too. But here's the twist: Handsome Guy doesn't drink coffee."

My breath escapes me in a whoosh. "But you order a black coffee every single day."

He shrugs, twisting his lips in a sheepish smirk. "It's the simplest thing on the menu."

Brows furrowed, I scan his face. I don't get it. "Why would you pay for something you don't want? Every day?"

"Nat." His voice is a gentle rumble. "I'd pay triple that for the chance to see your smile every morning and give you a hug to start your day."

My vision goes blurry, distorting his frame. Blinking back tears, I blurt the first thing that comes to mind. "I'm sorry I ruined our afternoon."

"Ah, sweetheart." He runs his knuckles over the curve of my cheek. "You didn't ruin anything."

Eh, debatable. "Well, sorry for springing that heavy personal info on you like that."

"I'm glad you shared that part of yourself with me." He wads up our corn dog wrappers, his eyes still locked on mine. He only looks away to shoot the ball at the metal trash can a few feet from the table. When it lands easily, he wipes his hands and scoots a fraction closer. "I want to know everything about you, Nat. The good parts and the hard parts."

Oof. A heaviness settles in my chest. My hard parts are messy and cumbersome. But rather than warn him off, I offer him an all-encompassing apology. "Okay, I'm sorry for…I don't know, for *me*, I guess." I wave a hand at myself and sigh. "There's a lot of baggage here, Tucker."

The lines on his face soften. "Then let me help you carry it."

The words escape him so casually, but the devotion in his gaze is as clear as the endless blue above us. With that simple phrase, spoken straight from his heart—*then let me help you carry it*—our connection strengthens.

That unnameable emotion I've sensed but denied over the past month is no longer a quiet whisper. It's no longer easy to ignore. It's a passionate roar from the depths of my soul: *You are falling in love with this man, Natalie.*

And it's time for me to get out of my own damn way. To let it happen. To embrace it.

But it's not time for me to confess it, so I stick to cupping his stubbled cheek and kissing him. With my lips, I make a promise of my own.

When I pull away, Tucker licks his lips and makes a satisfied *hmm* sound that vibrates through me, from my heart to that spot between my thighs.

Unaware of how viscerally he affects me, he rubs his hands together and pulls the paper plate holding our dessert closer. "One of my personal mottos is *leave no morsel of funnel cake behind*. Let's finish this plate of fried dough and head home. We'll take the scenic route back so you can take pictures."

We devour the fried treat, laughing when occasional gusts of wind carry powdered sugar into my hair or across Tucker's black T-shirt. And when my final bite leaves a trace of it on my lips? He uses his mouth to clean it off.

He stops several times on our way home, never once complaining about my frequent taps to his ribs. I capture several images along Tucker's scenic route, including a few sneaky shots of a gorgeous man straddling a Gold Wing.

Just after six, he drops me off at Wayne's so I can drive my car over to his place for dinner. My brother's truck is still parked along the side of the fire station when I drive away from the square, but as long as they don't get called to a fire, he'll be home in about an hour.

From there, Tucker and I will deal with the fallout. Together.

When I pull into the guys' driveway, he's waiting for me, propped up against the side of his Jeep, scrolling on his phone.

Once I've exited my SUV, he straightens.

"How does homemade pizza sound? Figured we could soften the blow with one of Cam's favorites."

"Mmm, yummy. Are you making the dough?"

He takes my hand and leads me up the front porch steps.

"Nah, we'll used the canned stuff tonight." He hauls me into an embrace, his hands finding their way to my ass and giving it a rough squeeze. "But I can think of something else I'd like to knead."

I tip my head back and let out a cackle. In response, he buries his face in my neck and sucks on the sensitive skin below my ear.

That shuts me up real quick. Tilting my neck to give him better access, I grip his shoulder and delve my free hand into his thick hair. "Tuck." My voice is breathy, sultry.

His stubble tickles and chafes as he teases me, and when he seals his mouth to mine and kisses me, I swear he's on a mission to weaken my knees and steal my breath. Controlling the pace with his lips and tongue, tasting me, drinking from my mouth like he's thirsty for me. His grip on my ass tightens. It's not quite bruising, but enough to force me up on the balls of my feet. Our hips align like puzzle pieces, slotted together so there's no mistaking the ever-growing hardness behind the fly of his jeans.

Then, like a scene straight out of one of the many rom-coms I spent hours watching as a teenager and young adult, he swings me around and dips me, all without breaking the kiss.

Panic zings through my belly instantly—let's face facts: this body I've come to love and appreciate is not thin or dainty—but Tucker's strong muscles don't quiver a bit as he holds up my size-fourteen frame.

I force myself to imagine his deep voice reminding me that he's got me like he does often, and once I relax into the moment, remembering to savor it, I can't help but wish there was someone with a camera here to capture it. I've always been most at home behind the lens, but Tucker makes me feel like I'm worthy of being in front of it, too.

We're both laughing as he steadies me. Then he angles in for another kiss, this one languid and soft. It stretches on, pulling satisfied little moans from both of us as the world melts away.

I brush my thumb along his laugh lines, mesmerized by him. "Am I dreaming?"

With a wicked smirk, he smacks my ass and squeezes. "Nope."

A sudden crackle and a disembodied voice interrupt our magical moment. A voice I'd recognize anywhere, and one that makes my heart plummet.

My brother's. And he sounds pissed. "Why the *fuck* do you have your hands on my sister's ass?"

Chapter Eighteen

Natalie

Tucker mutters a curse, his eyes snapping shut. "The damn doorbell."

I swivel, surveying the front door a couple feet to my right. Sure enough, there's a black and silver rectangle attached to the white casing around it. One that wasn't there the last time I was here.

"I forgot he ordered one. He must've installed it after his shift last night."

"*He* can still hear you." Cam's irritated voice blares through the tiny speaker, and from the slam of a door and start of an ignition on his end, he's on the move.

"Shit," Tucker whispers.

"I'm heading home. Don't leave." With that, all noise from the intercom stops.

My heart races as my corn dog threatens to reappear. "God, I didn't want him to find out like this."

"Yeah." Tucker scrubs a hand over his face. "You should go. I'll deal with him."

"What? No." I jerk back. "We'll handle it together. That was the plan."

"Okay." He exhales a sigh I feel in my bones, one that's half defeat and half relief. "I'm sorry it's going down this way, but I'm not sorry about you. I need you to know that." He smooths his hand down my hair and plants a quick kiss on my forehead.

"I feel the same." I slip my hand into his.

We plop down on the top step of the porch, hands clasped on Tucker's knee, and wait for my brother in silence.

When Cam parks his truck in the driveway five minutes later, he doesn't storm out of the cab like I expect. Instead, he sits inside for a solid three minutes, staring at us through the windshield. Eventually, his shoulders slump and he shoves the door open.

He stalks across the yard and stops at the bottom of the steps, hands on hips, eyes narrowed. When his attention lingers on our joined hands, a muscle in his jaw ticks.

I don't think I've ever witnessed Cam this angry. My brother is usually unflappable. But right now? He's a coiled spring seething with anger, hurt, and frustration.

Feeling like a kid awaiting punishment, I open my mouth to explain.

Before I can get a single word out, though, Cam barrels ahead. "*Maybe* I know her, huh?" He zeroes in on his best friend. "What the *fuck*, man?"

My heart lurches. Damn it. There's no way I'll let this ruin or damage their friendship. "Cam, maybe we should—"

He slices a hand through the air. "Just a minute, Nat."

Tucker's on his feet in a flash, his hands fisted. "Don't dismiss her like that."

Instantly, Cam's features are shadowed with remorse. "I'm sorry," he says, his focus fixed on me. "I just..." He closes his eyes and inhales. "This is a lot to process."

Pulse thumping wildly, I rise from the step and join him on the sidewalk. "It is, and I'm so sorry you found out like this. For what it's worth, we were going to tell you tonight. That's why I'm here."

"Not the only reason you're here, apparently." He can't disguise his snark, nor his contempt.

"Cam," Tucker warns, stepping up beside me. "I get that you're pissed, and I'm not saying you shouldn't be. But hear us out. If you're still big mad after we explain, then direct that shit toward me, not your sister."

I gape at the gorgeous man at my side, a riot of fluttery butterflies taking flight in my gut. I've never been defended by a man like this. It causes a gooey warmth to coat my insides, sweet and golden like honey.

At the scuff of footsteps several feet away, the three of us turn to the street, where a petite redhead strolls our way, her arm shoved into a can of Pringles. When she reaches us, she pulls it out, one chip in her hand, and waves in a *carry on* sort of way. "Don't mind me." She crunches on a chip, engrossed in the scene.

Cam huffs a sigh. "Goddamn it, Trix. Not now." Despite the curse, his tone holds no vitriol, only weariness.

Trixie wipes her hand on her purple denim cutoffs and plants it on her hip. "Yeah, no way am I missing this. It's about damn time it was out in the open." She winks at me. "Totally approve, by the way."

Tucker's brows climb his forehead. "You knew?"

She scoffs. "Natalie's car has been parked here nearly every night for the past week. Yes, I knew. Plus, I saw the way you were eyeing her that night at the Hoot." She gives him a triumphant grin. "Who says I can't keep a secret?"

"Everyone." Cam rubs his eyes. "Because it's a fact. Yet *this* is the one time you keep your mouth shut?"

She pops a shoulder, unbothered, and grabs my hand. With a tug, she guides me up the steps. When she plops down on the warm concrete of the top step, she pats the spot next to her and settles in to enjoy the show.

Trusting that Trixie's unexpected arrival has defused enough of the tension, I give in and join her.

Tucker cuts right to the chase, leaving no room for doubt. "Natalie and I are in a relationship, and we don't care about the age difference or the zip code difference. We're going to keep seeing each other while she's here. We'll deal with the rest when we have to." He lifts his chin. "No, we won't be sharing private details. And yes, we're blissfully happy and we firmly believe that's all that matters. I think that about covers it?" He peers over at me, his eyes deep pools of devotion that make me swoon.

Trixie fixes a hand over her heart and pivots to me. "Blissfully happy?"

I give her a shy nod, and she taps her feet and squeals. As she settles, she plucks another chip from its canister, then tilts the whole thing my way.

I decline her offer and study my brother. Cam's posture is still guarded, and I don't think he's unclenched his jaw since this showdown began. But he remains quiet, giving his friend the opportunity to explain.

"While we won't apologize for having feelings for each other, we do apologize for keeping it from you. I should've been upfront with you from the moment I decided to pursue her."

"You lied to me yesterday," my brother grits out. "More than once."

Tucker winces. "I did. And I'm sorry. It ate at me to do it, but I wasn't okay with opening up to you without checking with Nat first."

Cam's hazel eyes find me, the hurt swimming there causing my heart to crack.

"Cam—" Emotion chokes me, making it difficult to say more.

Trixie links her arm through mine, offering silent support.

I clear my throat and try again. This time my voice is a little steadier. "I'm so sorry we hurt you. You're the last person on this planet I'd ever want to deceive. I understand if you need time to accept this. But I *need* you two to be okay with each other."

Holding my breath, I look from him to Tucker and back again. Cam's shoulders are tense, his arms crossed over the navy polo he's already untucked from his utility pants. Tucker's posture is less rigid, though he keeps his hands fisted on his hips, primed for his friend's reaction, no matter what it is.

Clearly not adept at reading the room, Trixie blurts, "You could offer to let him punch you, Tuck. One shot. Let him knock you on your ass, then we can put all this to rest."

I stiffen. Though my brother doesn't have a violent bone in his body, his demeanor since he showed up indicates that he might be capable of socking his best friend over this.

Before I can scold Trixie for suggesting such a thing, Cam's whole body relaxes and he runs a hand through his hair, giving her a deadpan stare.

"Really?" He huffs a breath. "I'm gonna knock this guy on his ass? A former MMA champion?"

She shrugs and chomps down on another chip.

Tucker drops his hands. "If that'll help you, dude, go for it. I won't hit back."

Cam scoffs. "I'm not punching you, dumbass."

"Why not?" the woman at my side goads. "Imagine the street cred you'll gain once people hear you unleashed a haymaker on Tucker Lacey and lived to tell the tale."

Cam's lips twitch. "Not gonna happen, silly rabbit." He kicks at the sidewalk, his shoe scuffing against the concrete, and tucks a hand in his pocket. "Not today." When he looks up at his best friend, his expression is set in a glare again. "But if he hurts her, I'll knock his fucking lights out."

"If I hurt her," Tucker concedes, "I'll let you do that and worse."

Cam weighs Tucker's words, considering him, then me, the moment stretching on. Finally, he focuses on me, the look full of brotherly concern. "You're happy?"

Tucker watches me, too, giving me just a hint of a smile.

"Yeah," I say without breaking eye contact with Tucker. "I am."

Trixie squeals again, this time kicking her feet in the air.

When Tucker holds out a hand, I take it without hesitation, and when he pulls me into his side, I go eagerly.

We face Camden, a united front. Whether or not Cam accepts our relationship won't change how we feel about each other.

But God, I really don't want them to drift apart because of it.

Cam releases a drawn-out sigh. "It's gonna take me a minute to get used to the idea of..." He waves at us. "This. But you're both important to me." Another huff. "So this is me, getting on board."

"The Green Crayon Brotherhood remains intact," Trixie cheers with a waggle of her brows. "Now kiss and make up."

Cam sneers, but Tucker follows his cousin's directions.

Well, sorta.

When he presses his lips to mine, Cam groans. Trixie, on the other hand, lets out a wolf whistle that rings through the air.

My face flames after, but once Tucker releases me, there's no hiding my happy smile.

Trixie reclines on her elbows, a satisfied smirk on her face. "Looks like another Lacey brother is down for the count."

The first day of July blooms bright and hot, so I slip on my favorite pair of linen shorts and a white tank. My hair's too short for much more than a low ponytail, so I pull it back in preparation for the helmet I'll wear on the plane.

Cam switched shifts with a buddy, so he's free today, and I'm meeting him at the hangar in an hour.

It's exciting, the idea of being in the sky, but the prospect of flying with my brother isn't what has my tummy in a nervous uproar this morning. No, my evening plans with Tucker are what have me in a tizzy.

He's taking me to Memphis to get my first tattoo.

When I mentioned wanting to get one before my forty-first birthday—which is four days away—he reached out to his tattoo-artist friend, then made dinner reservations.

Over the years, I've become so hyper-independent that letting him make the plans for me was a challenge. In the end, though, it was freeing to let someone else manage the details for once.

As I drive out to the hangar, I replay the conversation Tucker and I had at Loblolly two nights ago—our first outing as a couple—unable to wipe the smile from my face.

"Your birthday's next Sunday," he says between bites of pot roast and mashed potatoes. "What do you want to do for your big day?"

I swallow the bite of burger I've been working on and follow it with a gulp of sweet tea. "Mom mentioned having a pool day. Grilling burgers and hot dogs like we used to. You're invited, of course."

His eyes flash teasingly. "Ah, but in what capacity am I invited? As Cam's friend, or as your man?"

Your man. *The words make my heart rate kick up.*

Face aflame, I covertly glance around the diner. It's not super busy, but several of the booths and tables are occupied. I'm not ashamed to be seen with Tucker like this, but this is a small town, and news spreads faster than wildfire.

Good thing I brought the topic up with Mom and James before work this morning. They were surprised, and they were worried about the details Tucker and I have chosen to postpone dealing with—like my eventual return to Austin—but ultimately, they were supportive. They've known him all his life, so they know he's a top-notch guy.

"How about you come as both?"

When he lifts his brows, I tell him about my conversation with Mom and James.

He breaks into a sincere smile. "I'm proud of you, shutterbug."

His praise makes me float.

"Any other big birthday plans?"

Lips pressed together, I dip a fry into ketchup. This ask is nerve-racking, but day after day, Tucker's affection has emboldened me more, so the words come out more easily than I anticipated. "I know it's short notice, but I want to get a tattoo. Before I turn forty-one."

"Hell yes. Let's do it." His eyes shine with pride.

"I'm sure your friend is booked, but maybe he'd recommend someone? Will you share his number with me so I can call and find out?"

Tucker sets his fork on his plate and pulls his phone from his back pocket. "I'll text him right now, get it all set up for you. Send over a picture of the design you want, and I'll forward that, too."

He taps at his phone, his expression one of pure excitement.

I, on the other hand, am frozen in stunned silence.

When I don't respond, he looks up, and when he finds me gaping like a fish, he leans forward, concerned. "What's wrong?"

I shake my head to clear my disbelief. "You're going to take care of it, just like that?" I snap my fingers.

He puts his phone down and sits back, regarding me. "Natalie. I see you. All of you. I listen when you talk. You're tired of always handling your shit by yourself. You've done it your whole adult life, and it's weighed you down."

The now-familiar incredulity that comes with being in this guy's orbit washes over me. Without thinking, I murmur, "Who are you?"

Tucker breaks into a devastatingly hot smirk. "I'm the man who's going to handle your shit."

"You're going to handle my shit," I repeat.

He nods, picking up his phone again.

Hello, self-doubt, my old friend. *"Hmm, doesn't seem like a good deal."* I fidget with my silverware. *"What do you get out of it?"*

His lips twitch. "You."

Now, two days later, the memory of him speaking that solitary word gives me chills.

When I arrive at Little Aviation, a handful of vehicles gleam in the sun in the gravel lot, including James's SUV and Cam's truck.

I park, then skirt around the office to the back of the property where the large metal hangar opens to the private airstrip used for takeoffs and landings. A couple guys on the ground crew wave hello as I make my way to where Cam waits next to a small yellow plane.

When he sees me, he turns my way. "Guess you do trust me, then."

"Of course I trust you." I slide the strap of my camera bag higher on my shoulder.

One side of his mouth lifts, but it's not his full smile.

We've communicated via text since Sunday's accidental reveal, but we haven't spoken until now. According to Tucker, things have been kind of awkward between the two of them, but I'm clinging to the hope that the three of us can figure out how to navigate this eventually.

"Thank you for taking me up."

He shrugs and turns. "It's nothing. I'm sure you have plans later, so we should get going."

"Hey." I grab his forearm and circle around so I'm standing in front of him. "It's not nothing. It means a lot to me. *You* mean a lot to me."

His eyes shine with moisture, and mine reciprocate and then some. Before I can stop it, a rogue tear rolls down my cheek. "I love you, Camden James Little," I say, swiping at my now damp cheek. "And that's not going to change. Ever. You are the best present Santa ever brought me."

He rolls his eyes, but he sniffles and swallows thickly before he speaks. "Love you, too, Natalie Elena Torres." He pulls me in for a hug. "Now let's get you some kickass photos of northeast Arkansas's greatest hits."

Cam steadies me as I climb the wing of the only two-seater here. James owns three planes, but the other two are for solo flights only. Once I'm settled in the small seat directly behind the pilot's, he hands me a helmet with built-in comms so we can talk while we're in the air.

While he conducts his final pre-flight checks, I unpack my camera and stuff the bag between my feet.

Excitement zips through me as I do my own checks, ensuring my camera is ready. When I applied for the grant that would allow me to capture the state's best features, I did so on a whim, thinking I'd never get selected since I currently live in Texas. When I opened the acceptance email, I nearly fell out of my chair.

For the next four weeks, I'll juggle Wayne's bookings along with mini road trips around the state for content for this project. At the end of the month, I'll submit my top ten pictures to the tourism board for use on their website and in print ads.

Cam and I breeze over the northeast corner of our home state for the next two hours, taking in the landscape. He expertly maneuvers to places where I can shoot cool pictures of the Mississippi River, the delta, and Crowley's Ridge.

The most precious part of the adventure, though, is the time spent with my brother. We laugh and reminisce about growing up in this corner of the world while making more memories.

Back at the hangar, I check my phone while Cam finishes his post-flight routine. Mom texted while we were in the air. Liv did as well. Nancy sent me a reminder about a photo session for a high school senior. The last message I check is from Tucker, and its contents are enough to make my blood heat.

Tucker:

> **Can't wait to have you on the back of my bike for a couple hours tonight. Pick you up at six.**

I check the time, discovering then that I have to endure four hours before I see him. I suppose I should be grateful. It'll allow me enough time for an "everything" shower and to agonize about what to wear, knowing full well I'll end up in jeans since we're taking the motorcycle.

After I give my brother one more hug, I leave the hangar without bothering to hide the bounce in my step.

A flight with one of my favorite guys and a bike ride with the other? This day is shaping up to be picture perfect.

Chapter Nineteen

Tucker

Looks like another Lacey brother is down for the count.

Trixie's statement has echoed through my mind since Sunday.

It's 100 percent accurate.

I'm down bad for Natalie Torres.

Sucker punched. Knocked out. On the mat.

Honestly, my heart's been on the ropes since the moment she walked into my gym.

I swipe the steam off the mirror and smirk at my reflection, racking my brain for more cheesy boxing metaphors.

Nat and I have come so far in the past few days. It's a physical relief, knowing she's accepted that this isn't just a summer fling.

I've never been a *fling* kind of guy. With the exception of two hookups, I've only ever been intimate with women I've had an emotional connection with. Though I thought I was in love with my college girlfriend and the girl I dated seriously in my mid-twenties, it's clear as day now that I'm with Nat that I wasn't anywhere close.

She is *it* for me.

Her confession about her likely inability to have kids threw me, though I think I succeeded in keeping it to myself.

That admission was clearly difficult, and I'm thankful as hell that she felt comfortable enough to share it with me.

Despite my shock, I wasn't lying when I told her that I haven't given much thought to being a dad. I guess I've always assumed I would be, but it's always been an abstract idea, an item on an adult checklist that I'd get around to eventually.

And my reassurance that it's not a dealbreaker was genuine. If we decide that we want a family in the future, then we'll cross that bridge when we come to it.

A little voice pipes up in the back of my head, reminding me that we've built a lot of bridges to span, but I squash that doubt before it has a chance to grow.

As I'm buttoning my jeans, my phone lights up on my dresser, and the name of a man I've tried to avoid for the past couple years flashes on the screen.

Tim Sutton, a fight promoter in Memphis, has reached out every six months or so since I stepped away from fighting, begging me to come back for special one-night-only bouts, promising huge payouts if I'll step into the cage again. The last time he called, he even pitched a harebrained idea that included convincing Griffin to go up against me in a "brotherly brawl."

With a groan, I press the decline button. He'll no doubt leave a lengthy voice mail, but I'll deal with that later.

For now, I check the time, refusing to let thoughts of him dampen my mood. I get to spend the next several hours with my girl, and that has me walking on air.

My girl. She's all woman, but her curiosity and sweetness are pure innocence in a way that draws me in and makes it impossible to get enough of her.

After pocketing my wallet and phone, I stride out in search of my boots. Cam stands in the kitchen, warming up leftover stir-fry, having come in while I was in the shower, I guess.

"Hey." I lift my chin in greeting. "How was the flight with Nat?"

He gives me a quick look over his shoulder, then turns back to the microwave. "It was good."

Three-word sentences have become the norm for him since Sunday. Our dynamic has been awkward as fuck, but I have the patience to wait it out. It won't be like this forever.

I hope.

He retrieves his plate from the microwave and wanders to the table. "She mentioned y'all are going to Memphis tonight."

I don't really have time for a chat, but this is the most he's talked to me since Sunday, so I quell the temptation to dart for the door. "Yeah. Did she tell you why?"

"Tattoo." He lifts his chin and eyes the ink on my arms. "Are you getting more?"

I press my lips together. "Nah, not this time."

"I didn't know she wanted one." He stirs his food, thoughtful. "Didn't know a lot of things, apparently."

I let the comment slide. He's got to work through this at his own pace. Constant suggestions that he get over it won't help.

Instead, I say, "It's good that the two of you are hanging out while she's here."

"Yeah." He nods at his plate, then at me. "Guess I've got an ally to help me convince her to move back, huh?"

I prop a shoulder against the fridge. "Operation Get Natalie Back to the Holler commences."

"It's got to be subtle, though," he urges. "I want her to come back because *she* wants to."

"I can be subtle."

He breaks into a smirk I haven't seen in days. "Subtlety is not your specialty." He huffs a laugh. "'Go big or go home' should be your middle name."

Head bowed, I chuckle. He's not wrong. And damn, does it feel great to joke with him again. "Fine, fine. You're right. But I can be subtle when it's important. And this is important. For both of us."

"Yeah, I reckon it is." He pierces me with a look. "You're taking the bike tonight?" I dip my head, and he points his fork at me. "Precious cargo."

"Always."

With a nod, he goes back to his dinner, stabbing a broccoli floret.

As I turn to leave, a question springs to mind. "Hey," I say, spinning around again, "what's Nat's favorite movie?"

Brows bunched, Cam surveys me. Then, suddenly, he straightens and snaps his fingers. "*Grease 2*. Not the one with Travolta. The sequel. She's got it memorized. Used to act it out, the whole nine. Named her dog after one of the characters."

Satisfaction blooms in my chest. *Got you, shutterbug.* I'll be watching that movie as soon as possible, though I'll keep my discovery of Goose's name origin a secret for now.

"Good to know." I smack the doorjamb. "If I don't see you in the morning, *Semper Paratus*."

"You, too, bro." This time, his smile is more genuine, more Cam, and the relief it brings is palpable.

I pull up to the Littles' ten minutes late, and Nat's mom and stepdad both venture outside to send us off with waves and reminders to be careful and have fun. When we park in downtown Memphis an hour later, a little sweaty and wind-blown, I'm rethinking the decision to bring the bike, but Natalie doesn't seem to mind.

Thinking she'd love the vibe, I made reservations at a restaurant on Main that was once a movie theater. An old black-and-white movie plays on a huge screen in the main dining area as we're seated at a booth and given menus to peruse.

Over a shared appetizer and pasta dishes, we discuss our favorite teachers while growing up, several of which we have in common, our college years, Goose's adoption, favorite dishes and desserts, and places at the top of our bucket lists (New Zealand for me, Scotland for her).

After dinner, we cruise down South Main. Griff bought a historic three-story building here when he signed with the Blues last September and lives with Brynn in the apartment that makes up the top two floors. The ground floor's commercial space is where Lux's shop, Blue Note Ink, is located.

When we park in front of the studio, the sky is a hazy swirl of dusky pinks and oranges painted with cloudy grays.

I help Nat remove her helmet, and as we step inside the shop and are welcomed by bright neon signs, I squeeze her hand. "Nervous?"

"A little." She shrugs. "But determined, too."

"You're gonna love it. You'll probably wonder why it took you so long."

Her hazel eyes sparkle. "I've been wondering that about a lot of things."

With a wink, I lead her farther into the shop. The midnight blue walls feature an eclectic mix of art including electric guitars and macrame and actual mannequin legs. The decor is just as funky. The velvet-upholstered settees and chairs contrast with the industrial chrome benches and tables in a way that makes the space feel a little chaotic but welcoming. The glass display case that serves as the cashier counter is filled with a row of large apothecary jars stuffed with Matchbox cars, LEGOs, and Barbie heads. Beside the computer monitor, the shop's resident pet, a sapphire blue betta fish, swishes his fins proudly in a hexagonal tank. The plants tucked in corners and on shelves bring a bit of nature indoors. The artists' stations are all visible from here, though there are private rooms for piercings down the hall.

I wave at a couple of the artists I know as we wait for Lux to put the finishing touches on the shoulder tat he's inking onto a woman with purple hair. Then I slip in behind Natalie and pull her body flush to mine. With one arm around her shoulders and the other around her waist, I rest my chin on her crown. "Your turn to wear me like a backpack."

"Hmm," she muses, smoothing her hands up and down my inked arms. "Way hotter than the purple JanSport I carried around in high school." She eases her head to the side, resting it on the arm I've got wrapped over her collarbone.

When Lux is finished, he swaggers over, a charming smile on his face and his hand extended. "Tuck, good to see you." He turns his dark eyes to my woman next. "You must be Natalie." The fucker extends his hand to her, too, but rather than give hers a shake, he brings it to his lips and kisses her knuckles.

I release her, though I tilt my head, my mouth near her ear. "Yes, he has a hot accent, but you're not allowed to fall in love with him."

Her body shakes with silent laughter. "I'll do my best."

"Few can resist, I'm afraid." He tucks her hand into the crook of his arm like the suave flirt he is and leads her back to his station.

I roll an extra stool over as Lux shows her the design he's already printed on the transfer paper. He asks her about sizing and placement, then transfers the design to her inner left forearm and starts his gun.

As the familiar high-pitched buzz fills the air, I hold Natalie's right hand.

The dandelion design she's selected is delicate, with fine lines and tiny star-shaped seeds floating from the head of the flower. She's opted for only black ink, so the process doesn't take long.

When Lux is finished, he sits back and admires his work. "And there it is. A beautiful dandelion for a beautiful woman."

Natalie stares at the design, a riot of emotions crossing her face. "I absolutely love it."

"That's what I like to hear. I'm sure this guy's warned you that this can become addictive." He gestures to the grayscale sleeves on his arms.

She laughs. "He has."

As Lux wraps a clear Saniderm bandage around her arm, he reviews the aftercare steps with her, then guides us to the counter. "Promise you'll come see me when the craving strikes again."

Her cheeks go pink. "I promise."

When we exit the shop, the wind's picked up and the temperature is significantly cooler.

"Shit." Standing on the sidewalk, I peer up at the sky. "I think it's about to rain."

Griff and Brynn are still in Holly Holler, meaning I could get the spare key from Lux and we could wait in their apartment for the storm to pass. Or we could chance it and head home on the bike anyway.

As a low rumble sounds in the distance, my mind is made up. I turn to Natalie to tell her not to bother putting her helmet back on, but before I can get the words out, she grabs my arm. "Let's get a hotel room."

My heart stutters in my chest. "What?"

Despite the way my hopes soar, I tamp down on my excitement. Checking into a hotel won't automatically lead to what I hope it will, but...I'm a dude. My brain and my dick are on the same page.

Head ducked and lashes lowered, she tucks a chunk of hair behind her ear. Though when she looks up at me, her eyes shine with the same determination they held when we walked into the tattoo studio.

When she repeats her request, the sultry tone of her voice makes me flush. "Let's get a hotel room."

My pulse thunders in my ears. "You're sure?"

"Yes, Tucker. I'm sure."

Fuck, yes.

I scan the street, heart pumping wildly. "Hang on." With a squeeze of her hip, I rush back into Lux's shop. Inside, he's propped on the corner of the desk in his private office, scrolling on his phone.

"Emergency stash?" I croak out, unashamed of how breathless and desperate the words are.

Smirking, he drags his desk drawer open.

As he holds out a strip of five condoms, I raise a brow. "Last time, you only gave me one."

He huffs a laugh. "Last time I only had two on me, and I was saving the other for that tall redhead who kept buying me pints. I'm gifting you more tonight because that one," he points his phone toward the front of the shop, "is different from the last."

Understatement of the century. The last—and only—time I've ever needed to hit a buddy up for an emergency condom was a couple of years ago, and that one-night stand was a tipsy mistake I'll never make again.

Natalie *is* different from any woman I've been with before. And my friend's acknowledgment of the distinction only confirms what I've known for weeks.

I am unequivocally, unabashedly in love with her.

And tonight, I just might get the privilege of worshipping her body.

Chapter Twenty

Tucker

With the strip of condoms secure in my back pocket, I find Natalie waiting on the sidewalk next to my bike, helmet on and ready to go.

The sky hasn't opened up yet, but we're living on borrowed time.

Along with the foil-wrapped treasures, Lux gave me the name and address of a hotel downtown, so with the information plugged into my GPS, I head in that direction.

Two blocks from our destination, the deluge pummels us.

Natalie squeals and tightens her grip on my torso as fat, heavy drops soak our skin and clothing.

The hotel's parking garage isn't attached, so as we reach the exit, I grasp Natalie's hand, and we make a run for the front doors. When we step inside the lobby and take our helmets off, we're drenched from the neck down, leaving a trail of droplets on the marble floors as we slink to the front desk.

The lobby is eclectic and modern, just like Lux's shop, and the clerk at the front desk is immediately friendly and helpful. When she notices our water-logged state, she darts through a door with an "oh," and returns quickly with two fluffy white towels.

I hand over a credit card, and while she taps away at her keyboard, Nat and I do our best to dry ourselves off.

"I'm sorry. We should've caught a cab or a ride share. I thought we'd beat the rain."

She squeezes the hem of her shirt with her towel and gives me a flirty grin. "It's fine. This is much more interesting, don't you think?"

My pulse spikes in response to the innuendo dripping from her words.

Soon, shutterbug, you're all mine.

"Okay, we have you all set Mr...." She eyes the name printed on my card. "Lacey." Eyes wide, she looks from me to the piece of plastic and back again.

Griff and I look enough alike for me to predict her next words.

"Lacey?" she breathes. "Are you by any chance related to—"

"Yeah, he's my brother."

Cheeks turning pink, she flashes me a smile. "That's awesome. I'm a big fan."

Natalie sidles up and gently grasps my bicep, her warmth seeping into me. "Are we all set?"

She's asking me, but the proprietary message to the flirtatious clerk is clear, and I fucking love it.

"Of course." She gives us a bright but more professional smile. "Here's your key card. The elevators are down that way. Enjoy your stay."

We follow her directions to the bank of elevators, and when the stainless-steel doors close behind us, I take Natalie's helmet and set it and mine on the floor.

She watches me, her face full of confusion, until I guide her back against the wall.

"Feeling territorial, shutterbug?"

She lifts her chin, petulant. "She was flirting with you." She crosses her arms between us, forcing me back a couple of inches. The action pushes her breasts higher. Her shirt is gray, though the outline of a dark bra is visible through the wet fabric.

Her possessiveness is my undoing. As need coils through me, I take her mouth in a searing kiss. I'm so lost in her that the ding of the elevator doesn't even register.

"Tuck," she says into my mouth, "this is our floor."

"Busy," I groan, diving in to nip her neck.

She grips my nape and fists my shirt. "Mmm, well unless you want to revisit your friend in the lobby, we need to get off."

The heat building inside me spikes. "Oh, we're definitely getting off. Multiple times."

Face flushed and lips parted, she pulls back and lifts her brows. "Ambitious."

"Motivated." I swipe up both helmets and step away, using my body to keep the door open.

The room is dark and cool when we enter, the lights of downtown Memphis glowing through the bay window. As I place our helmets on the desk near the door and toss the wet towels into the bathroom, Nat pulls the striped curtains closed, sealing out the rest of the world.

Tonight is for us only.

When I flick on the bedside lamps, I find that she hasn't moved from the window, though she's watching me with her arms wrapped around her torso.

"Need to get you out of those wet clothes."

She shivers in response to the gravel in my voice. That's what I tell myself, at least, though it could be from the chill.

She bites her bottom lip, fidgeting with the hem of her shirt. "It's been a really long time since I've done this." Peering up at me through her lashes, she forces a nervous laugh. "Like, really long."

"That's okay. You set the pace, Nat. And if you're not ready—"

"I am." Her words are bold, her chin lifted in defiance, though her skin flushes pink. "I am ready. I just..." She takes a deep breath and presses a hand to her chest. "God, my heart is pounding."

Another moment, another inhale, and then she smiles softly. "I am ready. I want this."

"I want this, too." Slowly, cautiously, I move toward her. "I want *you*. Tell me what you like, because I want to learn what makes you feel good."

She cocks her head, her eyes dark and brazen. "I like kissing."

Cupping her cheeks, I give her a slow peck. "Kissing—check. But kissing here only?" Another press of my lips to hers. "Or kissing in other places, too?"

Her breath hitches. "Oth-other places are good."

"Hmm. Noted." I tilt her head and nudge her mouth open with my lips. When she grants me access, I stroke her tongue with mine, a kiss so filthy it has my dick hard in seconds.

When we're both breathless, I pull back and sweep my thumb over her kiss-swollen bottom lip the way I long to brush against the stiff peaks that poke through her shirt and bra.

"What else do you like?"

She trails her fingers up my arms and over my damp T-shirt, then traces my collarbone before moving down to my pecs, where she rakes her nails over my nipples. "I like touching," she responds as she presses her hands to my chest firmly.

That's all the invitation I need.

I want to memorize her every curve, catalog each detail with my fingertips, and that means these wet clothes have got to go.

With her hand in mine, I lead her to the king-size bed. I pat the end, signaling that she should sit, and when she does, I drop to my knees and pull one of her feet into my lap. Slowly, I unzip and remove her tan bootie. I strip the wet sock off her chilled foot next and massage it to warm her skin. Then, eyes locked on hers, I lift her foot and place a soft kiss to her ankle.

Lips parted, she runs her fingers through my hair, her touch so intimate it knocks the breath out of me.

Once I've removed her other boot and sock, I drag my hands up her wet black jeans and bunch the hem of her shirt in my fists. "Okay?"

At her nod, I peel the soggy fabric from her body and toss it aside. I don't let my attention linger for long. I'm too eager to get all the wet material out of my way. When I place my hands at the button of her jeans and make eye contact again, she bobs her head and pushes off the bed.

I scoot back, giving her room to stand, then pop the button and peel the damp denim to her knees. Gently, I guide her to sit again, and with a few more tugs, she's free and my heart is racing.

My mouth goes dry as I take her in. She's clad in only a black lace bra and panties, the swells of her breasts peeking over the top of the lace and the dip of her waist flowing into shapely hips I can't wait to get my hands on. Her thighs are luscious. The perfect shape to hug my hips just right. If only I could see her delectable ass in this position. Though it doesn't matter. I've known from the moment she got out of her car in the gym parking lot weeks ago that I'd do just about anything to sink my teeth into it.

She's my perfect Rubenesque masterpiece, in the flesh.

I breathe her in, then leave a trail of scorching kisses from her knee to her upper thigh. "Kissing," I remind her as I drag my lips up to her stomach, then to the tops of her breasts. She smells divine, her usually floral spice mingling with the scent of fresh rain tonight. I cup the lace-covered globes and knead them gently, then use my thumbs to strum her nipples. "Touching. Tell me more."

She takes my face between her hands and pulls me in for another sizzling kiss, parting her thighs to make room for me to get closer.

When we part, she lets out a soft whimper. "Tasting. I like tasting."

I slide my hands to her back and pause at the clasp, arching my brows in silent question. Her hazel eyes are molten as she nods, and when I undo it, pulling the bra off to reveal her glorious, full tits, I swear my vision goes hazy. Cupping them, I relish their weight and the heat emanating from her. "I knew they'd be perfect." With a smirk, I tweak her nipples. "Now I get to taste them."

When I latch my mouth on to one stiff peak and lave it with my tongue, she moans and threads her hands through my hair to hold me in place. As I suck deeply, hollowing my cheeks, she tightens her grip and pulls at the strands, moaning louder. I release her with a pop and relish the sight of her reddened skin. "Yep, they're delicious."

She huffs a laugh, though it's quickly followed by a contented sigh. "You're still in your wet clothes."

I've been so caught up in her, in her pleasure, I've completely forgotten about my water-logged clothing. "Right." Standing, I strip off my T-shirt and bunch it into a ball. Then I toss it on top of Nat's pile. "You're the only one who needs to be wet."

Even in the dim light, her blush is unmistakable and the hunger in her hungry eyes as she catalogs every muscle and tattoo on my upper half is blatant.

My next words escape in a semi-growl. "Are you? Wet?"

Instead of answering, she boldly teases the silky material between her lush thighs. Her panties are soaked, and not from the rain.

Angling over her, I dip my fingers beneath the fabric and relish her warmth. Then I bring them to my mouth, my eyes locked on hers, and savor her arousal. Though my goal is to taunt and tease her, I'm the one who nearly comes in my pants.

Right—pants. *Focus, Tucker.*

I arch back and reach for my fly, but she stills my hand. "It's my turn to taste."

Heart rate accelerating, I hold up my hands. "Fuck. Yes. Okay."

She laughs at my eagerness as she unbuttons my fly and shoves my jeans down my thighs. "Well, this is unexpected."

At the humor in her tone, I duck, and what I discover makes me groan.

I shuck my jeans to my ankles and kick them off. "Clearly I didn't expect tonight to end like this."

She traces one of the bright yellow rubber ducks that cover my teal boxer briefs, her eyes dancing.

"If I had known, I would've worn sexy black ones like yours."

"Hmm, are yours lace, too?" She drags a finger along the rock-hard bulge in front, causing goose bumps to coat my skin.

"Maybe you'll find out next time."

Smirking, she hooks the elastic waistband and tugs.

My cock springs free eagerly, and in the space of a single heartbeat, she wraps her fingers around it and gives it a tentative stroke. Head tipped back, focus fixed on my face, she asks, "Good? I want to know what you like, too."

The tension coiling at the base of my spine tightens. Hell, she could get me off like this, softly pumping from root to tip, her tits bare and swaying with the motion. But I cover her hand with mine, urging her to tighten her grip and stroke a little rougher. Instantly, a bead of precum forms, and when she laps at it and wraps her lips around my tip, I almost blow again.

"Shit, baby, yes." I spear my hands into her hair and let her work me over like that until my spine tingles.

The first time I come, I want to be inside her, so I gather her hair at her nape and ease her head back. Then I hide my disgruntled dick behind the cotton ducks and drop to my knees and plant a kiss on her lips. "My turn."

She lifts her hips so I can peel her panties down. And then she's bared to me.

Natalie Torres, the girl of my boyhood dreams, lies naked before me.

As I survey her, my blood scorches me from within and my heart gallops wildly. She's all lush curves and smooth tan skin.

I place both hands on her shoulders and skim them down her body, wanting to commit every inch to memory—breasts, waist, hips, thighs, knees—and delight in the goose bumps that follow in my wake. And in the pink that stains her skin when I tell her, "You're magnificent."

With her lip caught between her teeth, she gives me a coy smile. Fuck, she's sexy. And all mine.

I guide her onto her back, then prop her feet on the edge of the bed and ease her knees apart. And when I use my thumbs to part the dark, neatly trimmed curls and nudge her with the tip of my nose to inhale the scent of her arousal, she gasps my name.

"You're so pretty down here. Pink, wet petals, blooming just for me. My very own O'Keeffe come to life."

She giggles, though the sound is cut off when I trace her clit and opening with a fingertip and is replaced with an exhaled "fuck."

I hum. "I'm going to fuck it so good, sweetheart. Take my time claiming it."

Trading fingers for tongue, I paint swirls around her clit. When I finally lick it in earnest, she bucks her hips. I alternate between licking and sucking, and when she thrashes her head and clenches the duvet with both fists, I pause to watch. And when I slide two fingers into her tight, slick pussy, she babbles softly.

"Ahi, no pares."

Fuck, the mumbled words in Spanish, in that breathy voice, are so damn hot. If I'm not careful, the encouragement alone will set me off. Though I don't slow, I mentally beg the ducks on my boxers to calm my dick the hell down.

When I've got myself under control, I flick and suck her clit one final time, then rise to my full height, leaving her a wet, writhing mess on the bed.

"Tucker," she whines, drawing out the two syllables.

"Oh, I'm not done, shutterbug." I pluck my jeans from the floor and pull out the strip of condoms.

Her eyes flash. "That's why you went back into Lux's."

"Mmm." I toss the condoms on the bedside table, then guide her up the bed. As I shuck off my ducky friends, I catch her watching, so I give her a show, sliding my hand up and down my erection. "Kissing. Touching. Tasting. What's next?"

Her lustful eyes penetrate mine. "Fucking."

God, I love her like this: brazen and confident, asking for what she wants, what she deserves.

"Yes, ma'am." Desperate to touch her again, I fondle her breast with my free hand. "And how do you want it?"

Brows furrowed, she looks past me, her focus fixed on something over my shoulder. "I'm not sure. I mean, I—"

Refusing to let her retreat into her mind and overthink this, I duck, catching her attention. "I got you, baby."

As I tear one of the foil packets, I bend to give her a deep, languid kiss. She watches me roll the condom on, and when I climb onto the bed, she bends her knees, inviting me in.

I brace my weight on my elbows as I settle between her thighs. "We'll take this as slow as we need to," I tell her, dipping my head for a kiss.

With a hum of agreement, she wraps her arms around me.

I give her a little more of my weight "Too heavy?"

She shakes her head. "Just right."

Length in hand, I notch myself at her entrance and push forward an inch or two.

When her tight, wet heat coats the tip of my cock, my vision goes dark around the edges. Fuck. Already, this is the most incredible sensation I've ever experienced. With a deep breath in, I remind myself to take it slow and rest my forehead against hers. "Good?"

She nods, and I push an inch deeper. Her pussy clenches around me, pulling a groan from deep within my chest. Holding myself back from surging to the hilt, I kiss her, finding a rhythm for our hips to mimic.

"Tuck." She whimpers as I slide in another inch.

"Fucking love it when you call me that, sweetheart." I rock my hips in tiny thrusts, grunting as I gain access to more of her, my skin coated in a sheen of sweat.

Natalie sucks in a breath, her body tensing slightly. "I don't think—"

I bring my mouth to her ear and make a soothing shushing sound. "I'm gonna fit, baby. You were made for me."

A few more thrusts, and I'm fully seated inside her. For several seconds, I hold still, focusing on murmuring praises in her ear, overwhelmed with how perfect this moment is. "Feels amazing, Nat. You're doing so good."

"Yeah?" Her voice wobbles, the tiny note of doubt there making my heart clench.

I lock my elbows and catch her eye. "Are you okay?"

A slow smile curves her lips, her expression full of passion and adoration. "Yeah, I'm good." She lifts her head and brings her mouth to mine, her hands drifting up my back and gripping my shoulders.

With a nip to her lip, I say, "Let me know when you're ready."

"You can move, Tuck."

Thank fuck.

Heart bursting and need coiling tight in my groin, I roll my hips. I stick to retreating a couple inches only before gliding back in, setting a rhythm. With every forward pump, my pubic bone makes contact with her clit. In moments, she's bucking her hips in sync with mine, though I keep my thrusts shallow, needing her to reach that peak before I do.

Her soft whimpers turn into moans, and when those stretch into "oh, fuck, yes," I increase my tempo. She digs her blunt nails into my back as her internal walls quiver around me. As the sensation builds, she tosses her head back on the pillow, her thighs squeezing my hips like a vise.

"Eyes here," I grit out. "I want all of you when you come."

Those gorgeous hazel orbs hold mine as we share panted breaths. Three more thrusts, and her lids flutter closed.

"Tuck!" she cries out.

I keep up the rhythm, sending her hurtling over the edge. "That's it. Come for me, baby."

Her inner muscles spasm in a rhythm that pushes me dangerously close to my own release. My control slips and my thrusts grow erratic as my heart rate speeds, that telltale tightening of my balls an unmistakable signal of the pleasure that awaits. Like I'm cresting the highest point of a roller coaster, I tip over the edge, groaning with pleasure.

I bury my face in Natalie's neck and let go, giving my body permission to melt in blissful satisfaction.

As we come down from the high of lovemaking, our breathing still ragged, she peppers my shoulder with sweet kisses.

"Good?" I mumble against her skin.

"Amazing." She sighs, the sound one of pure contentedness.

I'd puff my chest if I wasn't flattened against her.

Smiling, I press a kiss to her neck. Then I push up and ease out of her. When I stand from the bed to deal with the condom, she grabs my hand, though her focus drifts from me just a little. "Thank you," she says timidly, "for knowing exactly what I need, when I need it, and for giving it to me."

My heart stutters, my ribcage suddenly tight.

I'm so fucking in love with this woman, and it's so fucking overwhelming.

Transcendent.

Permanent.

I trace her cheek and tip her chin up so I can press a soft kiss to her lips. "Remember when I told you that I couldn't wait to show you what I'm best at?"

She frowns, though the expression quickly smooths out again, like she's recalling the text I sent after she agreed to let me cook dinner for her.

"This is what I'm best at—taking care of you. From the moment you reappeared in my life, Nat, it's all I've wanted to do."

Her bottom lip wobbles, but I dip to kiss it before she gets too emotional. One of us deepens the kiss immediately, I'm not sure who, but with a growl, I force myself to pull away.

"Let me go deal with this." I wave a hand at my dick. "Then we'll cuddle for a bit before round two."

She smirks and quirks her brow. "Round two, huh?"

I snatch the remaining four condoms from the nightstand and hold them between us. "Oh, sweetheart. We're just getting started."

CHAPTER TWENTY-ONE

NATALIE

On the morning of my forty-first birthday, I wake up tangled up with Tucker, locked in an embrace, our legs entwined like the strands of a rope and his head tucked under my chin.

The soft rise and fall of his chest tells me he's still asleep, so I lie still, content to luxuriate in the moment. This level of intimacy is one I wasn't sure I'd ever get to have again, so I soak in every second of it I can.

Eventually, Tucker stirs, arching his back and letting out a long groan. As he props himself up on one elbow, he blinks several times and gives me a sleepy smile. It's so boyish and cute it hurts. Like a pang in my heart.

Until now, I've been going through the motions, living my life convinced that my chance at love has passed me by. Certain that I'm not worthy of an epic love story. And then someone's thirty-two-year-old son with a slutty little earring comes along and demolishes all those beliefs.

"Happy birthday, Nat." He presses his lips to mine in a birthday kiss that makes my toes curl.

As he pulls back, I sigh, content and happy. Pre-Tucker Natalie would've been freaking out about morning breath, or she'd be racing to the bathroom to pluck the annoying trio of stray chin hairs I've not so lovingly nicknamed Alvin, Simon, and Theodore.

But after our first night together, this man made it clear that he doesn't give one fuck about any of that.

In fact, those were his exact words three mornings ago when I tried to sneak out of the hotel bed as the sun came up. "Nat," he'd groaned. "I don't give one fuck about any of that stuff. Come here so I can eat my breakfast."

The memory makes me smile. And clench my thighs.

He touches the corner of my mouth. "What's this smile for?"

"You."

He beams, all shiny white teeth and kissable lips.

Since I've found myself waking beside him regularly, I've discovered that his dark hair starts each day in a wild, unruly arrangement, like it spends the daytime hours playing by the rules and lets loose in the dark.

As he hovers beside me, I drag my fingers through the rebellious locks in an attempt to tame them into submission.

Another sigh escapes me as I do, though this one is laced with regret. "I should get up." Already, sunlight is filtering through the slats of the blinds. I've spent every night since Memphis in Tucker's bed, but I've successfully avoided awkward morning-after meetups with my brother by sneaking out with the first rays of dawn.

"Nat." He hauls my body into his, locking his arms around me to prevent my escape. "He's gonna have to get comfortable being around us together. We're not doing him or ourselves any favors by dodging him. You're not a sordid secret for me to hide."

I give him a dubious look, my lips tugged down.

He's undeterred. "Sure, it's gonna be hella awkward at first. But the only way past that stage is through it."

He tugs the soft sheet over our heads, cocooning us in the gray cotton that smells like his masculine scent mixed with lingering notes of our joining last night.

"Plus, it's your special day." He squeezes my butt cheek and pecks my face cheek. "And I want to give you your presents this morning." With a grin, he lowers his head and suckles at my collarbone.

"Mmm." I whimper. "But my party is this afternoon."

"The first present isn't suitable for family gatherings." He flexes his hips, making his meaning clear, and kisses his way over my chest. When he takes a nipple in his mouth, desire floods my core.

"Tucker." I grab his head, considering whether I want to push him away before this becomes too heated to stop or let it happen.

Every cell in my body is screaming for me to give into the need, even as my brain fights to stay in control. One thing my gynecologist didn't cover at my last yearly appointment was how fucking horny I'd be in my forties. Until Tucker, my only outlet for all this pent-up desire was my trusty bullet vibrator. But now? I have an insatiable stud to satisfy my cravings.

God, dating a younger man has serious perks.

He releases my breast, pulling a soft moan from me, and gently rolls me to my back and gives me puppy-dog eyes. "C'mon, Nat. Birthday sex."

I rake my fingers through his hair. "What if we save the birthday sex for tonight?"

With his chin on my chest, he squints at me. "How about birthday cuddling?"

I arch a brow, unconvinced.

"We'll just cuddle...and if it slips in, it slips in."

Amusement threads through me, but I manage to keep a straight face. "Tempting..." I press my lips together, pretending to mull it over, but my resolve wanes. My libido is a demanding bitch these days. I'll deal with the probable awkward encounter with my brother when it happens.

Holy shit, I'm starting to *think* like Tucker, too. Though I should embrace the instinct.

"Very tempting." He slips his hand between my thighs and uses two fingers to tease me with the wetness his attention has caused. "Mmm, feels like she's on board for birthday sex."

Even as I sputter a laugh, I open my legs wider like the wanton hussy I am. "*She* is, huh?"

"*She* is always ready for me." He rubs tight circles over my clit, making my breath hitch. "Never makes me wait." Now he traces my opening. "Doesn't talk back."

As I arch my back, I mentally give thanks for the bathroom between Tucker's and Cam's bedrooms.

"She's a goddess, really. But—" He takes his hand away.

My body protests, my nerve endings sparking and desperate for more.

"If you need to go…" He twists his delectable lips in a smug smirk that makes me want to slug him in the arm.

Chuckling, he presses those same two fingers to my chin and eases my mouth closed to keep me from protesting.

For that, I smack his bicep, causing him to laugh harder.

I poke out my bottom lip in a pretend pout. "We can table that particular gift for now. But you said *presents*, plural. If the other is really good, maybe I'll consider the birthday sex."

He barks a laugh. "Maybe you'll consider it?" He tickles my ribs and bites my shoulder playfully.

As I unsuccessfully ward off his attack, we both fall into laughter. He pins both of my arms to my sides, but instead of unleashing another tickle strike, he kisses me, invading my mouth with his lips and tongue and teeth. I'm powerless to resist, so I match his intensity, kissing him like we're in a race against time.

You kind of are, a tiny voice in the back of my mind taunts.

I shove the doubt down, way down deep into a locked chest at the bottom of the vast ocean of my mind. I refuse to let my expiration date worries taint any moment we're together.

When Tucker finally breaks away, I'm soaked and he's hard. He takes me in like he's staring into my soul before he breaks into a smile and pecks my lips once more. "Present time."

Before I can protest, he swipes the sheet away, exposing us to the real world and his semi-messy bedroom. He scrambles off the bed and strides to the dresser, the hard globes of his delectable ass on full display. While he rummages in the top drawer, he peeks over his shoulder and catches me blatantly ogling him.

If pre-Tucker Natalie had been caught doing this, she would duck her head in shame. But this sexually satisfied and brazen version straightens her shoulders and tracks his every step back to the bed, pausing on the proud jut of his semi-hard cock.

He folds his knees on the mattress and sits back on his heels, holding out a small wrapped cube.

I scoot closer, crisscross my legs, and hold out my hand.

The box, wrapped in shiny silver paper patterned with bright birthday streamers, is light in my open palm. I rip the paper off in a flash and inspect the plain white box. When I lift the lid and discover the black velvet box inside, my heart rate kicks up.

I zero in on Tucker, worrying my bottom lip with my teeth. He's watching me intently, anticipation alight on his handsome face.

Tipping the cardboard box on its side, I let the velvet one slide into my palm. I swallow and inhale a brave breath, then I thumb it open. Immediately, pure joy zooms through my body and a million questions flood my mind.

"Tucker..."

His smile is wide and proud. "Took some finesse to make that happen."

I finger the pendant that rests against black velvet. "How'd you find out?"

"Cam."

I roll my lips to ward off the burn in my throat. "I love it. So much." The words are inadequate, but they're all I can get out.

He tilts his head, irises sparkling. "Let me help you put it on." He takes the box and gently removes the necklace, then twirls a finger.

Obediently, I shift closer and turn so he can clasp it around my neck.

When he's done, he kisses my shoulder, and I spin back, dragging a finger along the chain.

"Perfect," he muses.

It's a small gold motorcycle. Just like Stephanie wears in *Grease 2*.

"When did he tell you?"

"Wednesday. Before we went to Memphis."

"When did you watch it?" He's been with me every night since, and our nighttime activities certainly haven't included movie watching. "I'm assuming you did, if you know about the necklace."

His smile turns sheepish. "At work on Thursday afternoon." Straightening, he breaks into a typical confident smirk. "Goose, huh?"

I sigh, a little sad that his guessing game has come to an end. "Yep. The moment I saw his scruffy face, the name popped into my brain. He's my doofy sidekick. But he's way more intelligent than movie Goose."

"Of course he is." He brushes a finger over the pendant. "When I ran this idea by Cam, he was certain you'd love it. Said something about you acting out that ladder scene?"

Groaning, I hide my face with my hands.

"Gotta say, shutterbug, I'd pay good money to see that."

"Not gonna happen." I hold in my laugh. "He was a toddler when that went down, by the way. But it's family lore now. That story's been retold so many times, he probably thinks his memory is real."

He takes my hand, caresses it. "I love learning these things about you. I want to know all of your family lore." He ghosts his lips along my knuckles, then gives the back of my wrist the same attention. Then my forearm. My elbow. With every kiss up my arm, he draws us closer together, like I'm a prize catch and he's reeling me in.

When he gets to my shoulder, he scoops me up and settles back against the headboard, positioning me so I'm straddling his thighs, sandwiching his erection between us.

"Ready for your other present?" He palms my ass and kneads. "Birthday sex with your Cool Rider, wearing nothing but this necklace?"

"Mmm," I purr as I rise to my knees and position myself over his shaft. "Best birthday ever."

"I kid you not, she hauled that ten-foot ladder out of the shed all by herself." James holds court at the grill as titters of laughter break out around us. He flips one last hamburger and faces the crowd, waving a pair of tongs. "Set it up right over there. Climbed all the way to the top, swung a leg over, and froze in fear."

Tucker playfully pinches my upper thigh through my shorts, though he keeps his attention on my stepfather.

Mom winks at me over her wineglass and picks up the retelling. "James was mowing the front lawn. I was in the middle of giving Cam a bath." She quirks a brow at my brother. "I was as wet as he was. You'll remember that bathing a one-year-old boy is not for the faint of heart," she directs to Tucker's mom.

"Front-row seat to the splash zone," Mrs. Lacey confirms fondly from the love seat she shares with Trixie.

"The blood-curdling scream and the 'help!' from the back-yard made my blood run cold. I snatched Cam out of the bath and ran, dripping water and suds all through the house."

James chimes in again. "I took off from the front. Left the damn mower running in the middle of the yard. Just as I came around the side of the house, Isabel crashed through the back door, Cam naked and squalling in her arms."

"My favorite part of this story," my brother grouses.

His cheeks are tinged pink from our time in the pool this afternoon, but when Trixie chortles, that shade deepens.

Mabel leans forward, trying to placate him. "Everyone has naked baby stories, Cam."

"Nat was perched up on the top of the ladder, hysterical because she couldn't get down. I had no idea what she was trying to do up there, but Isabel knew immediately."

"It's from her favorite movie," Mom explains to the group. "She was recreating a scene where the leading lady climbs a ladder backstage in the school auditorium—"

"*Grease 2!*" Trixie proclaims.

She peers around Mrs. Lacey to where I'm propped on Tucker's lap.

While everyone was busy finding seats on the back patio, he clutched my hips and tugged me to his rock-hard thighs. When I protested, he pinned me in place with his dumb strong muscles. And when I voiced my displeasure (not because I didn't want to sit here, but because it felt as though there was a flashing neon arrow above us), he shrugged and brought his mouth to my ear, whispering, "There won't be enough seats, shutterbug. You're fine here."

A simple headcount revealed that he—with his freakishly fast math skills—was correct.

"I love *Grease 2*." Trixie tips her head back and belts out the opening lines from "Girl for all Seasons," sounding better than the soundtrack.

Her voice sends goose bumps prickling along my arms. Damn. She's amazing. According to Cam, she performs with the house band at the Hoot most weekends, but I had no idea she had pipes like this. I survey the group, finding that no one but Cam seems affected by her angelic voice. My brother, though, is watching her like every move she makes fascinates him.

When James announces that the hamburgers are ready, we shuffle over to the outdoor bar where hamburgers, buns, and all the fixings have been lined up, buffet style.

When our plates are full, Tucker insists I sit in the chair while he plops down on the concrete next to me. As I settle in and pick up my burger, I regard the crew at the bar with a smile. What was supposed to be a small family gathering became a larger celebration when Trixie found out about my birthday. When she traipsed into the backyard with Mrs. Lacey and Mabel hot on her heels this afternoon, a bolt of surprise worked its way through me, followed by one of pure appreciation.

Tucker runs his hand up the back of my calf, causing a shiver to race up my spine, then digs into his own meal.

Goose, who's soaked up every bit of attention Trixie and Mabel lavished on him this afternoon, sits next to him with a paw on his leg, begging. The sucker falls for it, sneaking my dog a potato chip when he thinks I won't notice.

"Donna, where's the rest of your brood tonight?" Mom asks between bites of baked beans.

Mrs. Lacey dabs her mouth with a napkin. "Griff and Brynn left for Florida this morning, and Fred needed to go over some business with Shaw, so he picked up a pizza and took it over to his cabin. Texted that he was staying to watch a game."

For several seconds, we're quiet, chowing down. The silence is interrupted shortly, though, when Mabel perks up. "Had a Lisa Marie sighting in the square earlier."

"Fur or hair?" Cam blurts as James asks, "Biped or quadruped?"

Mabel laughs so hard she nearly spills her plastic cup of sweet tea. She sets it on the coffee table, grinning. "Fur and quad."

Mrs. Lacey groans. "That damn goat."

"Saw her eating on the honeysuckle bushes next to Dr. Putnam's office a couple days ago," James interjects.

Mom sighs. "Poor Randall. That man tries so hard to keep that little escape artist penned."

"Rumor has it that when Dr. Putnam retires, his hot nephew from Texas is going to take over his practice." Mabel wags her brows at Trixie.

Trixie, on the other hand, rolls her eyes, then quickly concentrates on her potato salad.

We spend the rest of the meal discussing the town's Fourth of July fireworks display ("Best one in years," James declares) and Holly Holler gossip ("She's gatekeeping that pound cake recipe, and everyone knows it," Mrs. Lacey huffs). After dinner, we all pitch in to clean up, and as the sun dips below the horizon, Mom sneaks into the house and returns with a candlelit birthday cake.

As the group warbles "Happy Birthday," Mom places the cake on the coffee table in front of me and pecks my cheek.

I survey the berry-laden Chantilly cake—my favorite—and smile at the lit forty-one in the corner.

Forty-one is going to be a good year.

As I'm sucking in a deep breath, ready to blow out the candles, Tucker leans close. "Don't forget to make a wish, Nat."

Contentment rolls through me as I take in all the faces beaming at me, celebrating me. Without a doubt, this birthday will be hard to top.

So many of my wishes have already come true.

Chapter Twenty-Two

Tucker

"Good work today," I tell Luca as I swipe a towel over my face.

Chest heaving, he nods. He tilts his head back and guzzles a bottle of water, then wipes his mouth with the back of his hand. "Thanks for switching up your schedule to spar with me."

"Happy to do it." I strip off my gloves and tuck them into the waistband of my compression shorts. "Have you reached out to Sutton yet?"

The fight promoter has left two additional voice mails on my phone over the last couple of weeks. I deleted them without listening. I'm not interested in any scheme he could come up with to get me back in the ring, but I did pass his contact info along to Luca. With any luck, bringing him fresh, young fighter blood will get him off my back, and Luca deserves a shot at an undercard bout.

He exits the cage ahead of me and tosses his empty bottle in the blue recycling can by the door. "Yeah," he chuffs. "He's not big on texting, is he?"

I shake my head, the move causing a bead of sweat to roll down my forehead. "I don't think I've gotten a text from him in the ten years I've known him. He'll talk your damn ear off, though."

He smirks as he strolls out into the hall. "Yeah, I've noticed." Just outside the locker room, he stops, suddenly more timid than I thought possible for him, and stares at my feet. "If I can get on a card, you think you could come?"

Pride spreads through my chest, warm and gratifying, in a way I hope Shaw and Griff feel when I accomplish something great.

"I wouldn't miss it."

He ducks his head, his cheeks going pink. "Cool. Thanks."

I get cleaned up quickly, then spend the hours until lunchtime finishing up paperwork, helping Bethany at the front desk, reviewing Chris's training schedule, and supervising the main floor. I've invested so much of myself into this place, and fuck if I don't love that days spent here never feel like work. The stress that came with opening and the worry that plagued me early on, while I fought to grow this place into a viable business, are finally in my rearview. Now I can relish its existence and its steady growth.

Over the last couple of months, I've hired more staff, which has allowed me to cut my hours a bit. These days, I work half days on Fridays and leave the weekend hours to Chris and an assistant manager.

Which means I'm free to meet Mom for lunch at Loblolly today.

On my way out, I pull a ball cap on and wave at Chris and Bethany. The sun is shining and the air is already hot, steamy, and heavy. Going outside in summer in Holly Holler never fails to feel like stepping into a sauna wearing a weighted vest.

I hustle to where I parked my Jeep, eager to get the AC going, and when I spot a flash of bright yellow on the driver's side handle, I quicken my pace.

A huge, goofy grin overtakes my face when I get close enough to make out the details of the duck.

Yeah, this ducking was definitely deliberate.

Duck in hand, I sneak a futile peek around the parking lot. If the warmth of the yellow rubber is any indication, it's been out here for a while. Nat probably placed it here on her way out of town this morning. This afternoon, she's meeting with the tourism board in Little Rock to update her project's progress. Then she's shooting a rehearsal dinner and wedding for Wayne in Conway. Instead of driving back late after tomorrow's reception, she's reserved a hotel room, which means she won't be sharing my bed for two damn nights.

The thought makes me inwardly groan, but I take comfort in nestling the photographer duck in with the rest in my duck pond.

The parking spots in front of the diner are filled when I get downtown, so I ease into a spot around the corner. When I step inside, engulfed in the aroma of coffee and greasy food, nearly every table and stool is occupied. Mom waits in one of the booths along the front windows, stirring a cup of coffee.

"There's my baby boy," she crows as I slide across from her.

"Hey, Mama."

She pats my hand and beams at me. "Thanks for inviting an old lady on a lunch date."

I flip my hand over and give hers a squeeze. "You're timeless."

She preens as she sips her coffee, smoothing a hand down her bleach-blond bob. "How was the gym today?"

"Good." I fidget with the wrapped silverware, spinning it on the tabletop. "Friday is one of our slower days, but we saw a good amount of traffic this morning."

She peers at me over the rim of her mug. "Pauline Jenkins went on and on about the jazzercise classes at our potluck last week." As she sets the coffee on the table, she quirks a brow. "And Francine says that Bethany likes working for you. Said she called you a 'cool boss.'"

Grinning, I give my head a shake. That's high praise coming from the perpetually unimpressed Bethany.

"You've worked so hard to get that gym up and running," she says, her hands clasped in front of her. "Now most of this town wants to be a part of it. Doesn't that feel good?"

Pride and satisfaction coalesce in my chest. "Yeah, Mom. It does."

While my family has always supported and encouraged me, most of my past accomplishments have been met with an undercurrent of surprise that frustrated me. Like their natural instinct is to assume I'll fuck things up, so when I don't, there's no avoiding the disbelief.

But lately there's been less of that incredulity. Now, when a family member expresses pride in me, in my business, it fills me with undeniable confidence. When the people who love me and know me best notice my growth, it quiets my self-doubts.

At the sound of a small commotion in the back corner, Mom and I both turn. Two preteens stand at the *Pac-Man* machine that collected most of the Lacey brothers' life savings when we were boys.

Mom focuses on me again, a fond smile on her face. "Now that takes me back. Wonder if they beat your scores."

Nostalgia washes over me as I recall the summer I begged Granny to bring me here every Saturday so I could attempt to beat Shaw and Griff's scores and type my initials into the top spot.

I spent most of my childhood chasing my brothers' accolades, desperate to be as good as they were. My drive wasn't motivated by a need to show them up or prove that I was superior; it was simply a younger brother desiring a place in the bond they'd already established with each other.

I couldn't ask for better role models, and I worked hard to follow their examples during my youth. But after I started college—at Griff's alma mater—I felt a push to blaze my own path.

When our favorite harried waitress arrives at our table, I wink at Mom. Lisa Marie Hobson (human, not caprine, obviously) works at the diner several days a week and serves as one of Aunt Dottie's bartenders on the weekends.

"Well, if it isn't my favorite Laceys," she says, voice raspy. Her smirk reminds me that she says the same thing when any member of my family dines here. "What are y'all having today?" She pulls the pencil from its usual spot above her ear as she chomps on the nicotine gum she's been addicted to since she quit smoking fifteen years ago.

Mom orders her usual, a BLT with extra tomatoes, and I opt for an egg white omelet and turkey bacon.

After Lisa Marie disappears, my mother smiles serenely, a knowing glint shining behind her lenses. I've seen this expression enough to know she's about to go full Donna Lacey on my ass.

"Tucker Myles," she begins.

I inwardly cringe at the double name, already racking my brain for the reason behind my impending lecture.

Mom pushes up her glasses. "When you first told us about you and Cam's sister..."

My breath catches. Oh, hell. My folks' reaction when I told them about Nat a few weeks ago was subdued, but they didn't voice any concerns or objections. So I assumed they were fine with it, or at the very least passively accepting of it.

"At first, I thought this was one last hurrah before you pursued a serious relationship, a final sowing of your wild oats."

Instantly, my pulse thrums in my veins. It takes real strength to bite back the defensiveness crawling up my throat.

She reads the cues of my body language like only a mother can and huffs. "Now don't get into a lather."

Lisa Marie approaches, and as she sets our plates in front of us, we're silent.

When she flounces off, Mom wastes no time getting back to it. "I didn't think you were serious about her. The age difference and the connection to Cam? I figured it was a carefree fling that appealed to your rebellious side."

I open my mouth to object, but she holds up a hand, stopping me.

"But I was wrong." She opens up her napkin and puts it in her lap. "I was very wrong, and I'm sorry."

I blink at her, my defensiveness leaking out in a steady drip.

She pulls a toothpick out of her sandwich and takes a bite, giving me time to process.

Still feeling prickly, I chug my water. The icy trickle, blessedly, brings me back down to earth. "It's never been like that with Natalie."

She nods, swallows. "I get that now. It was clear to me last weekend that this relationship isn't just about sex or rebellion, and it isn't just convenient fun either. What you two share is real, and it's special. I'm so sorry I doubted it to begin with."

Though I flush at my mother's use of the word *sex*, I exhale a breath of relief.

"I want to caution you, though," she says, swatting that relief away quickly. "When she was young, Natalie was an overthinker. Maybe that's changed, but maybe it hasn't. Either way, when you tell her you love her, mean it. Show her. She needs words and actions."

All I can do is gape as a flood of far too knowing advice spills from her.

With a purse of her lips, she waves off my astonished expression. "I know a smitten Lacey boy when I see one, Tuck. I've witnessed it twice." For a moment, she looks out the window toward the gazebo and the Heart Path, a wistfulness in her blue-gray eyes. But she shakes off the sensation quickly and pivots back, smiling. "And now I'm privileged to see it for a third time. Fourth if you count your father. That man was smitten from the jump."

My mother's uncanny perceptiveness never fails to amaze me. She's spent mere hours with Natalie and me, and already she's figured out that I'm harboring deep feelings for my woman. The kind of feelings forever is made of.

She leans forward in the booth and gives my hand a squeeze. "Though she's probably thought of every conceivable reason not to fall for you, I'm certain she has. So when she finally confesses that she loves *you*, believe it."

⸺◦⸺

"You and that photographer are still a thing?"

I power through five more reps, only answering after Chris has helped me rack the bar. "Yep."

"That's cool." He steps back, hands on his hips. "How's that going?"

I sit up, sweat dripping down my temples. "Good." One-word answers seem to be my standard today.

With a grin, he shakes his head. "Small-town dating is like finding a needle in a haystack. If you find one, you better lock it down."

As I wipe my face with the hem of my shirt, I fight back a scowl. I haven't forgotten how he looked at Natalie when she photographed the gym.

"Could you check the towels in the training room?" I ask, working to keep my tone easy. "Looked kind of low earlier."

"Sure thing, boss." He taps the barbell and ambles away.

I huff a breath and try like hell not to check my phone for the hundredth time.

Truth is, things between Nat and me have been better than good. We get along great and we love spending time together. We make each other laugh and have a genuine interest in getting to know each other. And the sex? The sex is so good it feels illegal.

No, we haven't used the L-word yet, but I don't feel a need to rush that, even after my talk with Mom on Friday. And I refuse to dwell on her upcoming departure, either. We've got another month before she's supposed to head back to Austin.

Despite all that, I'm an easily irritated one-word grump today. Why?

Because something's up with Natalie.

We usually meet up after work to hang out and have dinner, but yesterday, she sent me a text mid-afternoon that said she was tired and wanted an early night. Cool, no big deal. Cam and I ordered pizza and spent the evening playing *Resident Evil.*

I'm not a Velcro-type of boyfriend. Spending time alone when it's needed is healthy. And she's here to spend time with her family, too. I certainly don't expect her to give me all of her free time.

It wasn't until a couple of hours ago, when I got a cryptic text from her, that my mood changed.

Nat:

Not working today. Not available tonight either.

My heart lodged itself in my throat as I responded.

Is everything okay? Are you sick?

She's yet to respond, and she didn't answer when I called her.

Before I step into the shower, I give in and send her another check-in message, then I shoot a text to Cam. Asking if he's talked to his sister today will no doubt put him on alert enough to call or text her, and when he does, maybe she'll answer him.

While I clean up and change, I work to convince myself that everything is fine. But there's a nugget of worry in my gut that I can't ignore.

Cam's text comes through as I'm slipping on my shoes.

Cam:

No. Why? Calling her now!

Two minutes later, my phone vibrates with another message.

Cam:

She didn't answer! What's going on? Is she at a shoot or at Wayne's?

That nugget grows into a lump as I grab my keys and jog to the front of the gym.

"I've gotta take care of something," I call to Bethany. "Tell Chris that if I don't make it back this afternoon, he's in charge of closing."

Once in my Jeep, I shoot Cam one more text.

I'm on it. I'll text when I know something.

I make a lap around the square, thinking that maybe she went to work after all and got so caught up in editing that she's not paying attention to her phone.

Gann Photography is closed and dark, her car nowhere to be found, so I make the turn that leads to the highway and out to the Littles'.

When I turn up the lengthy driveway and find Nat's SUV parked outside the garage, my breath comes a little easier.

I knock several times, and when the house remains quiet, I step back from the front stoop and eye the fence to the backyard, considering whether it'll hold my weight if I scale it. Maybe I should break a window instead. As I flip through my options, my heart beats so hard it hurts, striking up a frantic rhythm that screams at me to *find her, find her, find her.*

Fortunately, my brain comes through in the clutch, and I'm hit with a memory of standing with Cam on this very stoop on a dark night back in high school. Of watching him shimmy behind a shrub in the flowerbed and come out holding one of those fake rock hide-a-keys. I send up a prayer that the Littles haven't gotten rid of it and crouch beside the bush. I feel around blindly, and sure enough, my fingers come in contact with a rock much larger than the others surrounding it.

I send one final text before barging into the house unannounced:

> I'm outside with the spare key. If I don't hear back in two minutes, I'm coming in.

After I've waited the appropriate amount of time, I extract the spare key and unlock the front door. As I step inside, the house is dark, the gentle whir of the air conditioner the only sound.

"Nat?" I call softly.

I'm greeted by a soft jangle down the hall, and a moment later, Goose emerges, tail wagging happily.

I crouch to scratch behind his ears. "Hey, bud. Where's your mom?"

Like he understands perfectly, he leads me down the hall to where Natalie's bedroom door is open enough for a Goose-sized body to slip through. I nudge it, and as it creaks, I squint, surveying the dark space. The heavy, dark curtains are drawn, shutting out all but a thin sliver of sunlight that barely illuminates a lump curled up under the fluffy comforter.

"Nat?" I call quietly.

She lifts her head. "Tucker?" Her voice is rough, unused.

I take a step into the room. "Are you sick, sweetheart?"

She's silent for a long moment. "No."

Goose jumps onto the bed, sits at the end of the lump, and waits.

My back pocket vibrates, and when I pull my phone out and unlock the screen, it illuminates the room. Quickly, I send a reply to Cam to let him know I'm with his sister, promising that I'll call him later, then perch on the edge. I place my hand on the lump where I imagine her hip is and angle closer. In the dimness, I can tell her eyes are open, but she doesn't look at me.

Fear and worry lodge themselves in my chest, but I squash the sensations and focus on her. On giving her what she needs right now. If she wants to be left alone, I'll go hang in the living room until Isabel or James or Cam can get here. But I really hope I don't have to.

"Nat," I whisper. "Tell me what you need."

For a moment, she's still and silent. Then she shakes her head, her eyes empty and sad.

"Okay. Can I sit here with you for a while?"

Nothing, then she shrugs, which I take as a yes.

I keep my hand on her hip, remaining physically tethered to her, and wait, giving her space until she's ready to talk.

Never in my life have I remained this still for this length of time. For her, I do it, even though every cell in my body screams at me to move, to talk, to help, to fix, even if I don't have the first clue what's going on.

Finally, she whispers, "You didn't have to come over."

I marinate on that, but it doesn't sit right with me. "I'll always come for you."

Sniffles rent the air, cracking my heart.

"Please tell me what you need." Needing more contact, I brush a strand of hair off her forehead.

"I just want—" She stops there, swiping tears from her cheeks.

I don't push, considering that maybe she's unable to vocalize what she needs. Instead, I offer, "Would you be okay with me just holding you for a while?"

Another long pause. But then she nods.

Standing, I toe off my sneakers.

As I round the bed, she lets out a little huff. "Um, I haven't, uh, showered since Sunday."

I lift the comforter and slip in behind her. "You know I don't give a fuck about that."

With a sigh, she snuggles deeper into my embrace.

Goose's collar jingles as he moves to the vacant spot behind me and stretches his body next to mine like he's trying to be the biggest spoon.

Can't deny that being the center of a Natalie and Goose sandwich is a very good place to be.

After ten minutes of comfortable silence, Nat clears her throat. "Remember that condition I told you I have? PCOS?"

I hum in acknowledgment. I googled it the morning after she mentioned it, venturing down a rabbit hole of symptoms and causes and treatments.

"Some women with PCOS experience depression," she says quietly. "I call it my gray cloud. It's a constant presence in my life."

This isn't a surprise. I sensed a sadness in her the first time she came to the gym.

Plus, I'm not a stranger to supporting loved ones with depression. Shaw is, well...Shaw. And even life-of-the-party Griffin experienced a bout with the blues when his first team let him go after he suffered an injury.

She absently strokes my forearm. "It's bad the week before I start my period. More intense. The hormones get all out of whack, I guess. I'll cry more than my usual, which is already a lot."

I smile into her hair. She's made plenty of self-deprecating jokes about how emotional she can be. The heightened emotions and her willingness to show when she's feeling them are yet more pieces of the Natalie puzzle I love.

"But some months..." She releases a shuddering breath. "Some months, the days before I start are so heavy, so cloudy, that I don't have the energy to get out of bed. My typical loneliness and sadness are magnified. All I want is to hide from the world."

"And that's what this is?" I hold her a little tighter. "One of the bad episodes?"

"It is." Her voice is small and soft. "I haven't had one like this since January, so I guess I'm overdue."

I nuzzle her hair. "You're still seeing Regina, right?" Nat mentioned that she's continued sessions with her therapist while she's been here. "Are you comfortable sharing other ways you manage it?"

She heaves out a sigh. "I've taken antidepressants before. I'm an advocate for those who need them, but for me, being on them long term is a challenge. While I'm taking them, I struggle tapping into *any* emotion at all, and I don't like the way that feels. My doctor has prescribed several over the years, but the results were the same. So I check in with her regularly, and I do talk therapy with Regina at least twice a month. I deal with it one day at a time. And when these harder episodes hit, I take mental health days until they pass."

My heart clenches at the despondency in her voice. "Please tell me you let someone know when a bad episode starts."

"I told Mom when I felt this one coming on. And Liv knows."

"Good." Not being included in this small circle of trust until now causes a niggle of jealousy to work its way through me, but then my conscience reminds me that this isn't about me or what I want. "Thank you for telling me," I whisper into her ear.

"I'm glad you're here. Thank you for checking on me." She halts her mindless passes up and down my forearm. "I'm thankful for what we've got going on. And for you. I've been lonely for a long time. I'm sorry if I don't handle relationship things the right way sometimes."

I tighten my embrace. "There's nothing to apologize for."

She twists, finally looking at me for the first time. "As happy as I am with you, bad days will still happen. This won't go away because I'm in a relationship, regardless of how wonderful you are. Please know that I don't expect you to fix me."

"There's nothing to fix, Nat. I want *you*, just as you are." I kiss the corner of her mouth. "I'm here for the happy days and the sad days and all the days in between."

She rests her head against the pillow again. She's quiet for so long I think maybe she's drifting off. But then she whispers, "You're the best surprise of my life, Tucker Lacey." She snuggles deeper into my arms, letting me hold her as she fights her way through the sadness.

There's nowhere else I'd rather be.

Chapter Twenty-Three

Natalie

"**H**old still."

When Tucker mumbles something that sounds like "yes, ma'am," I can't help but giggle.

"And no talking," I playfully scold, tapping his lips.

They're the only parts of his lower face not covered in shaving cream. He bites at my fingertip and misses, so I pinch his side in retaliation. When he tickles my ribs and tries to rub his foamy face on mine, I dodge and weave, cackling.

Our laughter draws Goose from his warm spot on the bed. Now he sits in the doorway to the bathroom, tilting his head at our silly human antics.

"Goose, bud, your mom is a terror."

A dollop of shaving cream slides off Tucker's face and lands on my bare thigh. In one quick move, he swipes it up and dabs it on the tip of my nose.

"Ugh." I pluck a spare washcloth from the basket on the counter. "Maybe you should avoid tickling the woman who's holding a razor to your throat, mister." I lock my ankles behind his thighs to hold him in place. "Be. Still."

"Yes, ma'am." Lips twitching, he settles his hands on my hips and acquiesces.

I shift closer, the cold quartz countertop under my thighs doing little to cool my heated skin. Especially with Tucker's bedroom eyes following my every move as I tilt his chin and slide the razor along his skin. His bare chest and arms are on display, close enough to lick or bite, and with every passing minute, my resistance wanes.

Doesn't matter that we got each other off in the shower fifteen minutes ago. We simply can't get enough, and our first little getaway as a couple has provided us with ample alone time. Though this is supposed to be a work trip for me, and though I've taken several great shots this weekend, our time away has morphed into more of a sexcation than we intended.

Not that I'm complaining.

After three days of brutal cramps, my period peaced out early (ah, the joys of being a perimenopausal woman with PCOS—every month is a surprise) so I asked Tucker to accompany me and Goose on a quick jaunt through northern Arkansas.

We set out from Holly Holler on Saturday morning and stopped in Little Rock for a grueling hike up Pinnacle Mountain. Grueling for me, at least. The only reason Tucker broke a sweat was the ninety-degree weather.

Rather than make me feel like I was holding him back, he was upbeat and encouraging every step of the way, and he didn't once complain about my frequent need to stop. He, of course, insisted on lugging my heavy camera and equipment the entire way.

In the end, the views from the top of the trail were worth every out-of-breath moment and pint of sweat it took to get there. The nearly cloudless blue sky provided the perfect backdrop for several beautiful shots. I can't wait to edit them and select my favorites.

After Little Rock, we headed northwest to the Ozark Mountains and the Buffalo River. This little cabin tucked beside a creek has been the perfect home away from home, and we've spent our time floating and canoeing the river and hiking a couple of the easier trails during the day. And, naturally, we've made good use of the hot tub at night.

Sadly, today is the final full day of our mini vacay. Tucker needs to get back to the gym, and I have a full slate of senior portraits to shoot the rest of this week, so we'll head back in the morning.

But first, we have plans to hike to a couple of the picturesque waterfalls in the vicinity. The trails to both are labeled "easy," but there's a gorgeous one at the end of a harder hike that I'd love to shoot, too. When I mentioned this to Tucker last night, he narrowed his eyes and insisted that we could do the harder one. I reminded him that sticking to the easier trails meant we could bring Goose, and he relented. Way too easily, if I'm honest.

When I'm finished shaving Tucker's cheeks, I surrender the razor so he can handle the more challenging angles around his mouth and chin. He assesses his reflection over my shoulder, giving me free rein to admire him.

"You keep staring at me like that, shutterbug," he teases, his voice all gravel, "and we're not making it to any waterfall today."

Heat rushes through me, but I pop a shoulder like I'm unaffected and trace the outline of the wing that curves over his shoulder. The rest of the bird, along with two others, is inked on his shoulder blade and upper back. "Why three swallows?" I've gotten the backstory for nearly every embellishment, but not this one.

He studies me, then focuses on the mirror to finish his upper lip. "Swallows return to the same place to nest, year after year," he says between swipes. "They represent my family, my connection to them, and where we're from. Our loyalty to each other. Our home. I wanted three of them to represent Shaw and Griff and me."

"That's beautiful." I crouch and press my lips to his left pec.

"You're beautiful." He brushes my lips with a sweet kiss, then angles to one side to rinse the razor in the sink. After wiping his face with the hand towel, he juts his chin and tilts his head from side to side. "How's it look?"

I cup his baby-soft cheeks. "Gorgeous. I'm a natural."

Smirking, he slips his hands beneath the Memphis Blues T-shirt I swiped from his belongings after drying off. "Goose." He directs his words to my dog but keeps his focus on me. "We're gonna have to leave you alone for a while today, buddy."

A harsh exhale escapes me. "What? He's allowed on the trails we're taking."

Head shaking, he tuts. "We're not taking those trails."

"But the app said the other trail is challenging. I believe it was described as *strenuous*." I can't keep the whine out of my voice. I've never been an outdoorsy girl, and this weekend has pushed my limits.

"You can do challenging and strenuous, sweetheart. Your face lit up when you showed me that waterfall last night. You'll get there, even if I have to carry you on my back most of the way." Jaw set, he pins me with a look, daring me to argue. "And if we want good light, we need to get a move on." He swats the part of my ass he can reach and retreats from the counter. "Get dressed and let's do this."

I cross my arms, pouting, mostly because I hate the idea of him carrying me if I can't make it all the way.

Ducking, he crooks a finger under my chin. "I promise to reward you handsomely when we get back tonight."

Without another second's hesitation, I hop off the counter and spring for my suitcase, his laugh ringing through the air as I go.

Twenty minutes later, we're ready to tackle the hike. On the drive to the trailhead, I found facts about the area using my phone and read them aloud.

"Glory Hole," he snickers, rotating the steering wheel with one broad palm in a way that makes me clench my thighs. "I'd forgotten about that one."

I snort. "If my reward involves a glory hole, you can turn this Jeep right around."

Grinning, he reaches over the console to grip my thigh. "Nah, baby, your other holes keep me plenty occupied."

My whole body is a vessel of dread when we park at the trailhead, but one glance at Tucker's excited face encourages me to dig deep to find hidden fonts of enthusiasm. It's early on a Monday morning, so the parking lot is empty, save for a pickup and Tucker's Wrangler.

After double- and triple-checking that our packs hold all the necessary supplies, we begin the two-and-a-half-mile trek to the waterfall. Tucker sets a moderate pace and pauses often so I can chug water along the way. He distracts me by asking random questions like *What's your favorite Monopoly token to play?* and *Would you rather look like a fish or smell like a fish?* Before I even realize I'm hangry, he yanks out a granola bar and gently demands I eat it. When the laces of the hiking boots I bought in Little Rock loosen, he crouches to retie them, and he happily retrieves my camera from his backpack every time I pause at a photogenic lookout on the trail.

With every act of service, I imagine him saying his now-familiar "I got you." I've never felt more taken care of in my forty-one years. This man checks every box on the list of qualities I want in a partner.

Three little unspoken words bubble up inside me, desperate to burst forth from my lips. By now, I'm surprised they're not printed on every rock face and trail marker along the path.

Finally, after crossing a creek and stopping at two smaller waterfalls to snap photos, we reach the main attraction. My inner gray cloud pessimist tries to horn in on the glory of the moment by reminding me of what a bitch the hike back will be, but the intrusive thoughts are drowned out by the beauty of the two-hundred-foot-tall stream of water that empties into a small rocky canyon.

"You did it, shutterbug." Beaming, Tucker ducks to kiss me.

I refrain from admitting that I thought I would die four separate times on that torturous trek.

We're the only souls here at the moment, so we take advantage of the solitude and soak our feet in the cool, shallow pools at the bottom of the falls. Proving again that he's the most thoughtful caretaker, he leads me to a dry slab and guides me to sit, then produces two breakfast burritos and sports drinks from his backpack.

After we eat, I shove my tired, achy feet back into my socks and boots, then take pictures from every angle I can squeeze into. We take a couple selfies on his phone, and by the time I've photographed every inch of the area, the sun is near its crest.

Tucker's not as vocal on our return hike, probably sensing I need every puff of air to power through the rise in elevation. About a mile in, I regret every single decision I've made today, especially letting him convince me to try this. Jolting to a stop, I jerk the straps of my backpack off and drop it to the ground at my feet.

He spins at the sound, finding me standing with my arms crossed and my lower lip trembling.

Stalking closer, he takes me in. "Hey."

The gentleness of his voice only makes me more petulant.

"I can't do it," I whine. "I'm hot and tired and my feet are on fire. Every muscle hurts. I'm just going to stay here and rot, become one with the earth."

He puts his hands on my shoulders. "You can do it."

I shimmy to buck them off, but they stay firm. Ignoring how good his touch feels, I shake my head vehemently.

Natalie, you're acting like a five-year-old.

"You can and you will." He flips his cap backward, giving me a clear shot of his handsome, determined face. "I'm not leaving you here to rot."

Fat, angry tears spill over my cheeks.

He crouches and pulls my water bottle from the side pocket of my backpack. Rather than hand it over when he stands, he flips off the lid, presses it to my mouth, and tips it so I can greedily suck down the cool liquid. Then he rummages in my pack for the spare hand towel we borrowed from the cabin. After splashing it with water from my bottle, he gently uses it to wipe my heated face. When he presses it to the back of my neck, I can't hold back a sigh.

He stoops, zeroing in on me. "I'm not leaving the woman I love on some damn trail in the middle of Arkansas. I planned to give you a ride later tonight, but I'll give you one now, too." He wags his brows in an effort to lighten my mood.

It's pointless, since my brain gets stuck on the first half of his rant.

Oblivious, he unlatches his pack and drops it at our feet, then gives me his back. "Hop on, sweetheart."

Oh God. My heart thunders in my ears, even louder than it has been on our journey back.

Did he just say that he *loves* me?

In light of our current situation, I decide to revisit that statement later.

"Tucker." I take a step back. "You can't carry me and two backpacks on a steep, rocky trail for a mile and a half."

Brow knitted, he squares his shoulders. "The fuck I can't."

His righteous indignation breaks me. I sputter a laugh that quickly grows into hysterical guffaws that split my side and steal my breath.

The corners of his mouth curl in clear delight.

Eventually, I regain my senses and sigh out a final laugh as I bend to retrieve my backpack. "I'm sorry. You're not piggy-backing me out of here. I'll keep going."

He nods, satisfied. "Atta girl."

I poke his chest with a finger. "But I expect full princess treatment when we get back to that cabin."

He breaks into a heart-stopping grin as he grabs my finger and kisses its knuckle. "You got it, shutterbug."

After securing his pack, he takes mine from me and wears it on his chest, ignoring my protests. Then we begin the last leg of the journey, together.

Tucker's mid-trail love confession plays in a mental loop all the way back to the cabin. Part of me wants to mention it and even make my own proclamation, but my more sensible side questions whether I even heard him correctly. Maybe it was a figment of my fatigue-induced haze.

We stop at a barbecue place on the way to the cabin to pick up dinner, then swing into the liquor store across the street to grab a bottle of wine.

I'm so sore when we get out that I seriously consider taking Tucker up on that piggyback ride. My muscles scream in protest with every move I make.

I let him handle Goose's walk and bathroom needs as I shuffle to the bedroom, where it takes eighty-four years to peel off my dirty, sweaty shorts and tank. When I'm finally free of them, I'm tempted to toss them into the firepit out back, a sacrifice to Mother Nature. *You almost bested me today, you gorgeous, unforgiving bitch.*

I slip Tucker's T-shirt back on, not bothering with shorts, then force my aching body to the kitchen, where he's spread our takeout on the square table.

"Dinner first, then hot tub, then shower." He ticks off the agenda for the night.

I don't have the energy to agree or argue. I simply sink onto a chair and stab a bite of brisket.

When he joins me at the wooden table, he's smiling at his phone. "Griff sent Shaw and me a picture of Brynn taking a nap with her engagement ring on her head."

He passes his phone over so I can get a better look. Sure enough, a sleeping Brynn is curled up on a cozy sofa with a sparkling stunner of a diamond resting on her brown locks.

Grinning, I peer up at Tucker. "He leaves for training camp this week, right?"

He scoffs. "Yeah, I'm two days away from being two hundred bucks poorer."

As I hand his phone back, it buzzes with an incoming call, and an unknown number with a 901 area code flashes on the screen.

Frowning at it, he says, "Let me see who this is."

He steps onto the back deck to take the call and readies the hot tub with his phone tucked between his shoulder and ear. Then he paces the deck for a couple more minutes, his frame tense. And when he steps back into the cabin, his face is blanched and worried.

"What's up?"

He startles, like my presence is a surprise. "Sorry. Uh, it's nothing. Just, um, an old acquaintance reaching out."

Seeing him this out of sorts makes me want to push him for more, but I don't want to be a naggy, nosy girlfriend, either. If he had news to share with me, he would.

After a moment, he relaxes and sits. When he digs into his food with his typical gusto, relief washes over me.

After dinner, he insists I unwind in the hot tub while he cleans up our mess. Our cabin is secluded, so I strip down quickly and sink into the water, only stopping when it's up to my chin, the deliciously hot bubbles soothing my body. Resting my head on the ledge, I close my eyes and sigh.

When the water rises noticeably, I crack one eye open and find Tucker climbing in. I can't help but pout about the navy boxer briefs covering his goods, not only for not being a fun pattern, but for existing at all right now.

He settles on the bench across from me, his slate-colored eyes piercing my soul.

"I'm proud of you," he says. "For today. It took real grit to push through like you did."

I grip the edge of the bench and let my body float to the surface, buoyed by his words and the jets. When my nipples breach the water, he grabs my ankles and tugs until I release my hold and allow him to pull me closer.

With my arms around his neck, I straddle him. The feel of his hard body under me is a spark that lights every cell in my body. My exhaustion and soreness from today take a back seat as my desire slinks behind the wheel.

I hover my mouth over his. "I believe I was promised a handsome reward."

He fuses his lips to mine, lazily kissing me. "Mmm, I've got your reward right here, baby." He lifts his hips, pressing his hardness against my bare pussy. "But if you're too sore after that hike—"

I grasp his damp hair and tilt his head, kissing him deeply and rolling my hips. When he tips his head back and groans, I lick his Adam's apple.

He puts his hands to work, one gripping my ass to aid my movements and the other cupping my breast, strumming my nipple with the pad of his thumb.

I rock harder, whimpering as I chase the high.

"Don't you come," he growls against my lips.

I moan, ignoring him, and buck harder. So close. So fucking close...

He seizes my hips, halting my movements. "Don't."

I growl in frustration, but he only smiles, the smug ass.

"Tuck." I try to restart my rhythm, but the effort is in vain. He's too damn strong. "Please." I roll my forehead on his shoulder, my breath leaving me in pants.

He slides a hand to my center, teasing my clit with circular strokes. "I'll always give you what you need."

"Debatable at the moment," I mumble.

He drags his thumb over the place I need it most, and when I shiver in response, he chuffs a laugh.

I tug on the hair at his nape, and the pain spurs him on. His eyes flash, and he takes my mouth in a bruising kiss that stretches on, ratcheting up my desire until I'm slick and needy again.

When we finally come up for air, he grates out, "You're coming on this cock, Natalie."

I'm still reeling from the intensity of that kiss when he shoves down his boxers and lifts me up so I can notch his dick at my entrance. When I do so, he rolls his hips, and with one swift thrust, he's inside, his thickness stretching me. A glorious, irresistible pleasure-pain overtakes me as we find the rhythm we've perfected in the weeks we've been together.

We never last long like this, with me riding him into oblivion and him keeping time with his thrusts. This isn't slow, languid lovemaking with tender touches and deep, intense eye contact. No, this is fast, primal, and coarse, but no less passionate. Every time we join, our connection strengthens, each encounter weaving our threads tighter.

"Give it to me." He latches on to my neck and sucks. "God, you're close."

His grunts in my ear and his thumb on my clit tip me over the edge. As the intense pulses drum through my core and euphoric weightlessness floods my body, I cry out.

Tucker follows a few seconds later, cursing and calling my name as he empties inside me.

As we come down, I place my hand on his chest, delighting in the frenetic pace of his heart. His strong, loyal, kind heart.

As though he can sense the direction of my thoughts, he places his hand over mine. "It's yours, Nat."

I press his other hand to my chest, right above my left breast. "Yours."

He dips his chin and kisses me, sealing our promise.

Just as my bare feet hit the wooden planks of the deck, he smacks my ass and drapes a towel around me.

"Go shower," he says, securing his own towel around his waist. "I'll be in as soon as I close this up."

Inside, I hustle to the bedroom to keep from leaving too many puddles on the floors. As I pass by the luxurious bed, I smooth a hand over the soft comforter. I'd love nothing more than to sink into the plush mattress, but we need to wash the chlorine and sweat from our bodies first.

I toss the towel into a corner in the bathroom and step into the shower stall. As warm water pelts my skin, I close my eyes and let out a groan.

The shower door opens, snagging my attention, and when I zero in on Tucker, my mouth waters.

"I'm gonna get spoiled starting and ending the day like this." His touch is gentle as he runs his fingers through my wet hair.

"What's happening?" My voice sounds as drowsy as I feel.

With a hum, he grasps my upper arms and rotates me so I'm facing the spray. "Princess treatment, remember?" His hands find my hair again, this time massaging shampoo into the strands.

Once he's conditioned my hair and rinsed it, he runs a soapy washcloth over my body, his touches efficient rather than sexual. Then, with a final pat on my bottom, he ushers me out of the stall so he can finish his shower.

I towel my body and my hair, then wrap the terry cloth around my head so my wet hair won't soak the pillow and slip on a clean T-shirt and sleep shorts.

Though the sun hasn't quite set yet, the bed beckons me, and the instant my head sinks into the downy softness of the pillow, my lids grow heavy. As I drift off to dreamland, Tucker presses his lips to my brow. "Love you, Nat."

Chapter Twenty-Four

Tucker

There's no way to prepare for unexpected, momentous plot twists.

Or for out-of-the-blue phone calls that have the potential to blow up a man's life.

The second I answered Marissa's phone call, I regretted it. How many times have I ignored calls from unknown origins? Hundreds. Yet I idiotically chose to answer one during my getaway with Natalie.

I blame the multiple orgasms and loved-up hormones for that lapse in judgment.

The moment the woman on the other end of the line explained who she was, a regrettable blast from my past, I considered ending the call. But the desperation in her tone gave me pause. I've replayed that conversation dozens of times since Monday afternoon.

"Tucker?"

"Who's this?"

"Um, hey. It's Marissa. Uh, Marissa Willis." A pause. Then a muttered "Not that you'd even know my last name."

It only takes a few seconds to retrieve the memories of that night:

The cheering and jeering of the audience at the end of the last fight.

A crowded downtown bar with Lux.

Flirting with a sandy-haired blonde while my friend set his sights on a busty redhead.

Several beers and a tequila shot.

The blonde's confession. How she'd just broken up with her long-time boyfriend and she was looking for a rebound.

Lux slipping a foil wrapper into my sweaty palm.

Flashes of tossed clothing, bare skin, and white sheets.

An impersonal fuck in a shadowed hotel room that lasted a grand total of twenty minutes.

She bawled the second I pulled out, wailing about how her boyfriend would never forgive her for screwing a stranger. Only when I panicked and sought confirmation that she was indeed single did she elaborate on just how recently the breakup had happened. Two days. She'd been single for a whopping two days. I half-heartedly attempted to console her but then got the hell out of there and vowed to forget the whole encounter.

"Yeah, yeah. I remember you."

She sighs, the line between us crackling. "Okay, that's good. Um, listen, I'm sorry to bother you, but...well, I really need to meet with you."

Unease swirls in my gut. "You need to meet with me?"

"Yeah."

I double-check the hot tub's temperature, then scan the dense forest surrounding the cabin. "Why would you need to meet with a guy you slept with over two years ago?" My brain is a flurry of thoughts, unable to grab hold of one long enough to make it stick.

"I really..." Her voice wobbles. "I really don't want to do this over the phone. I promise I wouldn't reach out unless it was important."

Finally, a cohesive idea latches on. "How'd you even get my number?"

There's a long silence. Finally, she clears her throat. "I did some research and found the promoter for the fight. You mentioned that you used to work for him. That night."

Damn. That explains Tim Sutton's recent phone calls.

I remember virtually nothing of the short conversation we had that night, but I'll take her word for it. While I wouldn't classify our encounter as a drunken mistake, it was definitely a tipsy one.

As I consider that fact, my brain powers into overdrive, panic taking root deep in my gut.

"Marissa, it's been years, and I admittedly don't have the clearest recollection of what went down, but please tell me I didn't...I mean, I didn't, um—"

Fuck, I might puke on this cabin's nice deck.

"No, Tucker. It wasn't...I mean, I definitely gave you consent. More than once, if I recall."

I heave a relieved breath, though panic clutches at me again almost instantly. "More than once? Wait. Did we...multiple times?" Fuck, I'm damn fucking sure I only had the one condom.

She barks a soft laugh. "No. No, I meant that I gave you consent more than once. At the bar. In the lobby. In the elevator. Lots of consent, I promise."

I rub my forehead, a headache brewing behind my eyes. "Are you in Memphis? I assume you live there."

"Yeah, I do."

I peer in the window and watch Natalie give Goose a bite of her bread, one thought playing on repeat in my mind.

Please, please, don't let the reason for this phone call affect what I have with that woman.

After a couple more minutes of confusing back-and-forth, I agreed to meet with Marissa at my gym and hung up. She shot down my offer to drive to Memphis, insisting that she wanted to come to me but not providing the reason for it.

Which is why I'm sitting in my office on a Friday morning, focused solely on the damn clock.

Over the past three days, I've gone over every possible reason for her visit. All of them suck.

The first and most plausible possibility: Marissa has a sexually transmitted disease, so she's contacting all former partners to disclose it.

That one doesn't frighten me much since I've recently gotten a clear blood workup.

Weeks ago, after Natalie and I used up the condoms Lux so generously handed over, we decided not to purchase a new box. So I made an early morning lab appointment and resorted to giving Nat orgasms with my hands and mouth until we got the results. Since the labs she had done at her last physical were also clear and she's not worried about an unplanned pregnancy because of her PCOS, we've been foregoing condoms.

Which brings me to possibility number two: my out-of-character one-night stand resulted in a kid. The thought makes me break out in a cold sweat. But the timing doesn't line up, either. We hooked up over two years ago. If she ended up pregnant, wouldn't she have come to me shortly after that?

A third, admittedly egotistical, take? Marissa's been holding a torch for me since our midnight tryst and she wants to shoot her shot. Yeah, this one's the most unlikely given how she acted in the minutes following said tryst.

When Bethany pokes her head in my office at five minutes to ten and says, "Hey, there's, uh, some lady here for an appointment," I regret choking down my usual morning smoothie.

"Yeah." I clear my throat. "Send her back, please."

In the seconds it takes Marissa to get to my office, my heart pounds so hard I swear it's going to crack a rib.

When a blond head shyly peeks around the doorframe, I scramble to my feet, clutching the desk to steady myself. My breaths coming in near gasps, I wipe my palm on my gym shorts and wave her inside.

She enters, looking as terrified as I feel, but hovers just inside the doorway, one hand fidgeting with the hem of her shirt. The column of her throat bobs, and she licks her lips. "Tucker? Hi."

All my saliva suddenly disappears. I force a swallow and extend my hand, unsure of what greeting is appropriate in this situation. "Marissa."

Her hand trembles when she places it in mine. We share a quick, perfunctory shake, then I gesture to the chairs in front of my desk.

My nausea doubles when she closes my office door before she sits.

As she perches across from me, as if already preparing for escape, I take a quick survey of the woman I spent a couple of hours with over two years ago.

She's pretty, with wide icy blue eyes and heart-shaped lips. Her ivory complexion indicates that she likely keeps sunscreen within arm's reach. Her hair straddles the line between blond and light brown and hangs in a straight sheet to just past her shoulders, and a curtain of thick bangs covers her forehead.

When we finally find the courage to start, our words collide:

Me: "Do you want something to drink?"

Her: "I should've just told you on the phone."

She gives me a wobbly smile, then presses her lips together.

"Sorry," she says. "No thanks." She closes her eyes, inhales, opens them again. "I'm a nervous wreck."

"That makes two of us."

"Right." She wrings her hands, stalling.

"Marissa." I want to shout at her to spit it out, but I keep my tone soft. "What did you need to tell me?"

She nods and blinks up at the ceiling, then levels me with a watery gaze. "I discovered I was pregnant a couple months after our night together."

Instantly, spots dance in my vision and my office spins. Certain I'm on the verge of passing out, I rest my elbows on the desk and cover my face.

She launches into an explanation, her words coming fast, pelting me like tiny daggers. "You probably don't remember, but when we met, my college sweetheart had just broken up with me."

I want to lash out with a snarl. Of course I remember. Some details remain fuzzy, but it would be hard to forget a woman bursting into hysterical tears seconds after climax.

"Um, Jason," she says. "He was my boyfriend. He, uh, called me in tears the next day, claiming that our breakup was a mistake. He wanted to get back together. We'd dated since freshman year, and I thought he was the love of my life." Head bowed, she sniffles. "I hated myself for being so careless and irresponsible, but I couldn't move forward with Jason with that night hanging over my head."

I scrub a hand down my face and lean back in my chair, speechless.

"So I told him about it," she admits. "About sleeping with a guy I'd met at a bar as a way to get over him, to punish him for breaking us apart. He was mad, and hurt, of course." She wipes beneath one eye, then the other. "But in the end, he told me that he didn't want to throw away our years together because of the stupid mistakes we'd made. We moved in together two weeks before I found out I was pregnant."

Heart racing, I push up from my chair and pace behind my desk, hands on my head like I can block out the next part of her story. Because I'm certain I know what's coming.

The action doesn't deter her. "At first, we were happy, and we were positive that the baby was Jason's. He and I were together days before and after that night. Plus, you and I used a condom." She swallows thickly, her throat bobbing. "I asked once during the pregnancy if he worried about the possibility that the baby wasn't his, and what he would do if that came to be. He downplayed my concerns and assured me that he'd love the baby no matter what."

I force my feet to stop and face her. Rage and devastation course through me in waves, but I need her to cut to the fucking chase. "Are you saying this kid is *mine?*"

Her face crumples. "I'm so sorry."

When I close my eyes, Natalie's smiling face is the first image that appears.

God fucking damn it. I can't lose her over this.

I drop into my chair, exhausted and nauseous and wrecked.

But Donna Lacey didn't raise a jerk, so I drag a box of tissues across the desk and set it in front of Marissa.

She mops up her tears. "We were happy-adjacent for a little while, but after he was born..."

I don't hear what she says next. I'm too fixated on the way she just unintentionally revealed my kid's gender.

But after he *was born.*

He.

I have a *son.*

Possibly. I suck in a harsh breath and remind myself that I don't have any confirmation. A part of me doesn't trust this curveball yet anyway.

A knot forms in my throat as a million questions run laps in my mind.

Marissa studies me, shredding the damp tissue in her lap. "His name is Boden. I call him Bo sometimes, too. He's perfect."

Boden.

"Wh-why..." I pinch the bridge of my nose, wrangle my anger into manageable pieces. "Why are you certain this kid isn't your ex's?"

Swallowing visibly, she reaches for another tissue. "After Boden was born, my relationship with Jason was strained. We fought...a lot." A sob works its way out of her, but she chokes it back quickly.

"He was distant with Boden. Never wanted to hold him or help out. But I was overwhelmed and..." She pops a shoulder, her focus drifting to one side. "I loved him. I thought it would get better once Boden got a little older."

"It didn't." Damn it. I want to pummel the asshole.

She shakes her head. "No. He really pulled away around Boden's first birthday. Started sleeping at his office, claiming he needed to work late. But I hung on to the relationship because of my son. My parents were in their early forties when I was born, and they've already retired. They recently moved into a senior neighborhood. My brother is fifteen years older than me, but we aren't close, plus he lives in Seattle." She swipes at her nose with her tissue. "Jason's from a large family, with lots of aunts and uncles and cousins. I was desperate for Boden to have that."

Maybe I'm an asshole, but as she speaks, all I can focus on is the thought that if this kid is mine, I've missed his first birthday.

My stomach rolls, and once again, my smoothie threatens to make a reappearance.

"A month ago, Jason demanded a paternity test. That's when I decided we were done, no matter the results. He agreed to raise Boden with me regardless of paternity, yet it clearly mattered to him when it came down to it." Shoulders straightening, she lifts her chin a fraction. "My son deserves the world, so walking away was what's best for him. And for me." She shudders a breath, as if her burden has finally been unloaded.

The answer may seem obvious, but I have to ask. "So he isn't your ex's?" I can't even say the fucker's name. "Why are you certain that he's mine?"

She nods, like she's been expecting me to ask. "There's no other possibility. You're the only man I've been with other than Jason since before college."

She could be lying. But my gut tells me she's not.

My gut, churning with panic and fear, prompts me to make one thing clear.

"I have a girlfriend," I blurt. I want to add more—*I have a girlfriend; I'm madly in love with her; I can't let this break us*—but I keep those truths to myself.

Marissa tilts her head. "I'm not looking..." She quirks her lips, takes a breath. "I'm here for Boden. You deserve to know about him. My hope is that you'll want to be a part of his life, but I'm not here to ask you for anything. There's no ulterior motive. If or when you're ready, I'd love for you to meet him."

My already racing heart pounds faster, making it hard to breathe. Holy fucking shit balls.

She leans forward and places a palm on my desk. "If you'd like to request your own paternity test, we can do that, too. It's just a quick swab inside your cheek."

"Yeah." I nod woodenly. "Let's do that. ASAP."

Rather than flinch at my clipped tone, she nods and picks up her purse from the floor at her feet. With both arms wrapped around it, she hugs it to her body like she's waiting to be dismissed.

My whirling brain struggles to process all my thoughts and questions and the emotions bombarding me. Fear, anger, sadness, shock, desperation, doubt, and confusion all battle for supremacy in my brain and in my body.

What the fuck am I supposed to do now? How do I explain this to Natalie? To my family?

The only thought I can clearly put into words is a simple one. "Do you have a picture?"

She smiles, the first real one since she walked in here. After a few taps to her phone, she passes it to me.

As I study the dark-haired toddler, my heart lodges itself in my throat. He's cheesing at the camera, pudgy cheeks stretched into a happy grin as he holds out a toy truck, gray-blue eyes so much like mine alight with joy.

He's fucking adorable.

An image flashes in my mind. One of a framed picture on my parents' mantel. In it, we three boys stand together at the first ever Memphis Blues home game. I was about the age of the little guy in this photo, and I'm relatively certain that if I placed this picture beside it, we could pass as twins. Same dark hair and brows. Same eyes and wide smile.

I consider telling Marissa that a paternity test won't be necessary but decide that a monumental discovery like this requires definitive proof. The people who love and care about me will want it.

Swallowing past the lump in my throat, I pass the phone back, my hand trembling. "Can you—do you mind sending that to me?"

"Of course." She taps a couple times, and my phone lights up where it sits on top of a messy stack of papers. "I'll send you more, too, if you'd like. Newborn pictures, his birthday. I have videos, too." She waves a hand. "No pressure. Only if you want."

"Yeah," I whisper. "Please send me anything. Everything."

She bobs her head, her eyes rimmed with moisture. "Tucker, I...I don't have words for any of this. I'm sorry to spring this on you, to drop this bomb in your life this way. I agonized over it for weeks." She tugs another tissue from the box and dabs her eyes. "But he's the best little boy. He's so happy and curious. I know we don't know one another at all, but in the little time we spent together that night..." She heaves a breath. "I got the impression that you were a stand-up guy. I wish I could rewind time and go back eighteen months so you could have been involved from the very beginning." She inhales, the breath choppy. "But I can't. I'm so sorry."

Her tears and my swirling tornado of emotions wreak havoc on me. My nerves are shot, and there's no tempering the way my knee bounces beneath my desk.

"I need some time to process everything," I say. "Tell my family. My girlfriend."

She blinks, nodding. "Of course. You have my number now. Feel free to reach out. About anything."

When she stands to leave, my chest tightens and sweat coats my skin.

"I do want to meet him. Just…" I rough a hand down my face. "Just give me a minute to catch my breath."

Her lips curl in a soft smile. "I understand. We'll take it one step at a time, okay?"

I've run out of words, so I dip my chin.

"Okay. Bye, Tucker." After a small wave, she's gone.

I sit, overwhelmed, and urge my mind to clear so I can formulate a plan. The longer I'm stationary, the tighter the pain in my chest gets until my breaths come quick and shallow, making it impossible to get enough oxygen. All of my people flash through my mind, a highlight reel of the disappointment and shock on their faces when I tell them this news. Will this serve as proof to my family that I remain an absolute fuck-up? And Natalie…Fuck. Sweet, beautiful Natalie. Will she see this as a betrayal? Or as a reason to break things off?

My vision swims as I reach for my phone.

Cam answers in two rings, but before he has a chance to speak, I'm forcing out mostly incoherent words. "Where are you?"

"Hey, I'm at the station. We just sat down to lunch." A pause. "Everything all right?"

Guilt slashes through me. Natalie should be my first call. But I can't face her yet, and I don't want to see or hear her reaction until I have a better grasp on my own.

Yes, Natalie has become my person.

But Cam has been my go-to for a lifetime.

I need my best friend's cool, collected steadiness. He's the calm in the storm, and this is a storm unlike any I've ever experienced.

"I need you to get to the gym. Right fucking now."

Chapter Twenty-Five

Tucker

When Cam bounds into my office seven minutes after I end our call, my head and my breakfast smoothie are in the trash can. "Whoa, what's up?"

He immediately switches to first responder mode, fingers on my wrist to check my pulse.

"Your skin is clammy, your heart's racing, and you're pale as a ghost." He sticks his head into the hallway and calls Bethany's name, ordering her to bring wet washcloths or paper towels and the spare medic bag he keeps in his truck.

When he returns, he slides the trash can away and kneels by my side, taking my wrist again. "Tuck, open your eyes."

The room will spin if I do, so I keep them closed and clutch my chest. "Can't. Breathe."

"You're okay, man." His words are muffled and far away as he places his hand over mine. "Breathe in."

I huff in a ragged breath.

"And out. Good. Now in…" He repeats the pattern a few more times, his tone remaining calm, until I no longer feel like I'm breathing through a coffee stirrer.

Bethany appears, her wide eyes and bunched mouth swimming in my vision as she hands over the items Cam asked for. He tells her to intervene if anyone comes looking for me, then ushers her out of the office and closes the door.

Wrung out, I fold my arms on my desk and rest my forehead against them. The cool, wet cloth Cam places on the back of my neck brings a fraction of relief, though at the sharp sound of two pieces of Velcro being pulled apart, I startle.

Cam loops the blood pressure cuff around my upper arm and instructs me to sit up. Then he hooks a pulse oximeter on my finger. The squeeze of the cuff and the press of a stethoscope to my chest ground me further and give me hope that maybe I'll survive this after all.

"BP is a little high," he says as he wrenches the cuff open. "But your heart rate has slowed and you're getting some color back. Pulse ox is normal." He shoves his supplies into his kit. "Looks like I won't need to call the boys for backup. Nothing like a good, old-fashioned panic attack to make your day more interesting."

He pulls two sports drinks from the minifridge in the corner and twists the cap off one before handing it to me. The other he keeps for himself, only sipping from it after he's settled in the chair across from mine.

I force myself to swallow the electric-blue liquid, praying it doesn't come back up.

My best friend studies me with watchful hazel eyes. "Wanna talk about it?"

I exhale, grateful I've regained full capacity of my lungs, and grapple with how to tell Cam about Marissa's visit. About Boden.

Instead of meandering through the lengthy explanation, I navigate to the picture Marissa texted me less than half an hour ago and rip the Band-Aid off.

After sliding it across the desk, I sit back and wait.

Cam picks up the phone and examines the picture. "Cute kid." With an ease I don't know that I'll ever experience again, he slides the phone back.

"He's mine."

He does a double take and snatches the device up again. His eyes dart from me to the phone, then back to me. His mouth drops open as the gravity of my claim takes hold.

"What the hell?"

"I know," I gasp, my throat and eyes stinging. I lick my lips, knee bouncing again as I flail around for the right words. But there aren't any *right* words. There's only the truth. "God, I know." Tears spring free, and I don't even try to hold them back. "I'm freaking the fuck out here, Camden."

Eyes widening, he scoots forward and grasps my forearm. "Okay, let's breathe, slow and steady. It's going to be okay," he urges. *This* is why he was my first call. "This is big; it's huge. But it's not so huge that you can't handle it."

I clench my jaw and nod, willing his message to sink in and soothe me.

"Tucker." He angles closer, waiting until he has my full attention. "You can handle this."

I dig the heels of my hands into my eyes. I have to handle this. There's no other option.

A few silent minutes pass as we both grapple with the weight of this situation.

Eventually, I roll my shoulders back and guzzle a fourth of the sports drink. Then, with an incredulous laugh, I screw the cap back on. "I've had two." I hold up my fingers for emphasis. "*Two* one-night stands in my life."

Cam smirks and raises a brow. "Sexy nurse?"

I point at him. My brain is too muddled to conjure memories of that wild college Halloween party, but they're nothing but fond. "Sexy nurse. And this Marissa chick. What are the fucking odds that one out of two results in a baby?"

He holds up his hands. "You're the math whiz. Safe to assume you wrapped it up?"

"Of course."

With a long sigh, he tips his drink my way. "Yeah, those odds are slim. That sperm was motivated."

My best friend is ridiculous, but his attempt to lighten the mood successfully saps some of the tension from my shoulders.

So, sitting back, I give him the whole story, beginning with my encounter with Marissa at the bar two years ago and ending with our meetup this morning.

When I've finished, he whistles. "I'd say that panic attack was warranted. And the paternity test is definitely smart, even if that kid has Lacey written all over him." Expression softening, he shifts in his seat. "You can do this, Tuck. You're gonna be an amazing dad."

Fuck. I rub my eyes again, fighting back another wave of tears. Having Cam Little in my corner has always meant the world to me, but knowing his belief in me hasn't wavered because of this floods me with gratitude.

Though just as I'm consumed by it, his encouraging best friend demeanor morphs into brotherly protectiveness.

He reclines in his chair and laces his fingers on his stomach, jerking his chin. "Now. When the fuck are you going to tell my sister about this, and how the hell are you going to do it?"

"Nat, baby, please say something."

Hours after my whole world was upended, I squeeze my eyes shut and silently beg every deity I can think of to let me keep Natalie. Forever. To one day allow us to look back on this chapter as a speedbump we navigated together rather than a trainwreck that derailed us.

When I asked her to come over after her last session, I could barely get the words out. But the second she walked in the front door, I pulled her to the couch and let the story pour out like a flood.

"You're a dad."

Her smile is forced, but she keeps her hand firmly nestled in mine, so I take that as a win.

She blows out a breath. "I'm just...Wow." Her lips curl further, this time into a more genuine expression, and the vise on my sternum loosens. "You're a dad."

"Yeah. It's...unbelievable."

Cam sat with me for another thirty minutes to make sure I wasn't going to lose my shit again before he headed back to the station. I spent another thirty minutes after that examining the picture of Boden, hunting for more similarities and memorizing his little cherub face. I haven't even met him yet, haven't gotten undeniable proof that he's really mine, yet I already know I'll be devastated if he's not.

How's that for a complete one-eighty?

Since Marissa left my office, she's sent a couple more photos, along with a message that read:

> **Starting at the beginning. Don't want to overwhelm you, so please let me know when you're ready for more.**

The first picture is a grainy black-and-white blob. An ultrasound picture. The shapes of a head and four limbs are barely discernible. The next picture is of a red-faced newborn swaddled in a soft blue blanket, wisps of dark hair poking out from a pink-and-baby-blue-striped cap.

I place my phone on Nat's knee so she can scroll through the images with the hand I'm not clinging to like a life raft. As she studies them, I study her, bracing myself for the emotions her expression will reveal. Will I find sadness? Or detachment? Or anger?

But as she peers at my phone, taking her time to consider the tiny human in each frame, I swear longing flashes in her eyes, though it quickly morphs into a softer look. She tips her head, lingering on the first picture Marissa texted—the most recent one. And her lips curve into a happy smile.

"Tuck, he's precious."

I exhale a gust of relief. "He is, isn't he?"

"He has your eyes." She touches a finger to the corner of my eye, then traces a featherlight path across my cheekbone to my mouth. "And your smile."

Heart still thundering in my ears—that hasn't stopped all day—and overflowing with love and affection for her, I press a hard kiss to her lips. Now that I've explained the situation, the need to reassure her overwhelms me.

"Please tell me what you're thinking, sweetheart."

She tips her head side to side, her lips pursed in consideration. "I'm thinking that this is a hell of a surprise. One that will probably have some messy moments. But," she adds, "I think you're handling it maturely and as well as a person could. I think you'll be an incredible father. I think your folks will be head over heels once they get over the shock."

Shit. The reminder that I still have to explain all of this to my family makes my gut roil.

"I think this is big and scary and wonderful. And..." She trails off, blinking back tears. "And I'm wondering if there's room for me in all of this."

Ducking in close, I cup her cheeks. "Hear every word of this, Natalie Torres: This does not change how I feel about you. It doesn't diminish how much I want you or need you in my life." Though that lump has returned to my throat, my words are steady and vehement. "A better man might bow out, tell you that he understands if it's too much to handle, and let you walk out the door. I am not that man."

Her lips twitch, but the uncertainty still lingers in her eyes.

I give her head a tiny jostle to drive home my message. "I am committed to you, to our relationship, no matter what obstacles get in our way. We'll face them together. If that little boy is mine, I will love him with everything I have. But my heart is big. I have plenty of love to go around, and it already belongs to you. I love you, Nat."

She presses her forehead to mine and breathes the words I've been waiting for into my lips. "I love you. And I'm so proud of you."

Our kiss is a soft promise. A punctuation mark to our shared declaration.

When we part, she flips through the photos on my phone again. She swipes too far back, finding a picture of Brynn, open-mouthed, with her head on a fluffy white pillow, her engagement ring glinting from where it's perched on her temple.

Natalie snorts. "He's still at it, huh?"

"Yeah." With a relieved breath, I take advantage of the happy distraction and swipe back through the handful of similar pictures Griff's sent Shaw and me over the past week. "He reported to training camp yesterday. I'm saving them to make a slideshow to surprise them when he finally pops the question."

"You're a good brother, Tucker Lacey."

I soak up every drop of her praise. It's a balm to my soul after the roller coaster of today.

"How about we get started on dinner?" I ask as I pocket my phone. "I think my stomach has settled enough to allow food, and I promised Cam I'd make fajitas tonight. Wanna be my sous chef?"

As I prepare the homemade salsa she loves and Natalie unloads the dishwasher, we discuss what comes next. I've already sent a message in the group chat, requesting everyone's attendance at Mom and Dad's in the morning. An announcement this life-changing warrants an official Lacey family meeting.

Every individual in my family sent a nosy side text after receiving my original group message, sniffing for clues about why I want to meet. I'm sure rampant speculations are being passed along via text groups I'm not part of. Trixie and Shaw probably have a side bet going already.

From there, I'm driving over to Memphis to meet Marissa to have my cheek swabbed for the paternity test and to meet Boden. She ensured me that it would be okay if I wanted to wait for official results before meeting him, but the more I sit with the possibility that he's my son, the more I'm sure it's true. From my perspective, the paternity test is a necessary formality, especially since my brother is a famous NFL player and he'll want the proof for his own peace of mind.

Nat and I work in silence for a while, her with a cutting board, slicing bell peppers and onions, and me working on the steak and chicken. It isn't until I'm done slicing the meat that I work up the courage to ask her what's been on my mind since I made my Saturday plans.

"Hey." I swallow past the knot in my throat. "Will you come with me tomorrow? When I tell my family?"

Natalie sets her knife down and turns my way, brows furrowed. "You want me to be there?"

I wash my hands, then prop myself up against the counter to give her my full attention. I have every intention of making her a permanent part of the Lacey fam, so of course she'd be included in family meetings. But I'll keep that secret for now. We've suffered enough emotional whiplash today.

"I might need backup when Donna and Dottie try to stow away in my Jeep so they can come with me when I meet this kid." I shift my smirk into a soft smile. "Of course I want you there, shutterbug."

She smiles back. "Then I'll be there."

Chapter Twenty-Six

Natalie

The vibrant sizzle and the savory scent of the meat Tucker is searing should overwhelm my senses. They should anchor me to the present.

Yet as I slice through the last bell pepper, concentrating on keeping my fingers attached, I'm still fixated on his huge news.

The man I've fallen in love with is a father.

And honestly, I don't know how to feel about that.

Regina would remind me that all feelings are valid and that I don't have to give myself permission to experience any of them.

But right now? I kinda wish someone would take the reins and tell me exactly how to handle this revelation. Provide a roadmap to help me navigate the big emotions scrambling my brain. Do I take a left at Happy Highway or skirt past it for Anger Avenue? Merge onto the Feel-Sorry-For-Myself Freeway or exit at Supportive Street?

I'm genuinely happy for Tucker, and I'm definitely not mad at him. Or at the woman who turned his life upside down. I can't imagine there's an easy way to break the kind of news she did today, but from what Tuck has told me, it seems she considered his feelings and reaction before doing it.

What I'm angry about is the timing. I finally, *finally*, meet a man who's perfect for me, who loves me despite my flaws, only for the universe to step in and blindside us.

What the fuck, Universe?

The moment the words "I found out that I have a son" spilled from his lips, I activated the full power of my mental armor. I'm talking state-of-the-art Tony Stark–level technology, bulletproof and impenetrable. But one peek at that sweet round face on Tucker's phone, and my defenses disintegrated like one of the Vanished after Thanos's fateful snap.

The child is a carbon copy of the man who's stolen my heart. How could I be anything but supportive when Tucker needs it the most?

And yet Jealousy Junction beckons. Pinpricks of envy and maybe discontent stab at my heart. It's been a matter of weeks since I told the man of my dreams that the chances of me giving him a baby are slim to none, and I walked in today to discover that she's already had the privilege.

With every tiny jab that stings my soul, guilt follows. How can I be jealous of such a precious miracle?

In response to that thought, Regina's voice echoes in my mind: *You're allowed to feel how you feel.*

We finish prepping the fajitas, weaving behind and around each other in the kitchen, lost in our own thoughts. I've assisted him with cooking dinner often enough that we've nearly perfected the choreography the small space demands.

The ding of his phone from the countertop ceases my ruminating.

He grins at the screen and quickly holds it out for me to see. "She sent another one."

In this photo, a tiny baby Boden is spread-eagle on one of those monthly milestone blankets. It's light blue, with his name printed on it, along with a grid of numbers from one to twelve. He's dressed in a plain white onesie, and a small empty picture frame surrounds the number one.

If I had to guess, the next eleven photos will arrive in consecutive order.

As I study the image, I can't help but think about how Tucker missed out on all the days between those numbers. My heart aches, making my breaths stall, but I keep my smile bright as I hand back his phone.

"He's a natural," I tell him. "I can't wait to take father-son pictures."

"Ooh, yes." He tilts in for a kiss. "Professional photographer girlfriend perk."

The lightness in his tone eases the tension in my shoulders, making it easier to pull the plates out of the cabinet. I take them, along with the silverware and napkins, to the table while Tucker prepares our drinks.

"Eighteen months," I muse as I pull up memories of Liv's oldest when she was that age. "If he's got half your energy, I'm sure he keeps his mama on her toes." I arrange the three dinner plates on the table. "He can feed himself by now, I bet. Oh, make sure you ask Marissa if he has any allergies and what his favorite snacks are." I fold three napkins in half and drop one by each plate. "I wonder how many words he's saying. Chloe was calling me Nat by then, I think." As I rest the final utensil on the third napkin, I realize I've been babbling.

When I twist to help Tucker with the drinks, my heart plummets to my feet.

He's standing with his head down, his arms braced against the counter, his body quivering as he's racked with silent tears.

Fuck. My stream-of-consciousness attempt at being an excited and supportive girlfriend has backfired. Tremendously.

I grab his waist, and he engulfs me in a hug instantly. He buries his head in my neck, releasing huge shuddering sobs that soak my shirt and break my heart.

"I've missed so damn much, Nat."

I hold him tighter and rub his back. For weeks and weeks, he's reassured me with three tiny words; I use them, hoping they bring him the same kind of comfort they bring me. "I got you."

"I've missed all those things." His voice is broken, inconsolable. "His first word. His first steps."

His legs crumple under the enormity of his anguish. I'm not strong enough to take all of his weight, so we slide to the floor, still embracing.

My strong, carefree man is a wreck. My first instinct is to get swept away in the sorrow right along with him. To drown in the deluge by his side.

Tucker's been my rock all summer. His support and belief in me never waver. They're as constant as sunrise and sunset.

He's the sunshine to my gray cloud.

This is my opportunity to be the light for him, to help him through this dark night.

I hold him tight, murmuring reassurances and breathing soft *shh* sounds into his skin. I soothe him with my hands, every tender touch suffused with my love for him.

When his heavy sobs taper into quiet shudders, I lean back against the cabinets, my legs in a V on the tile floor. As if his body knows innately how to fit with mine, he slots between my legs, resting the back of his head against my chest and his elbows on my thighs. I bend my knees, hooking my legs around his body and curve an arm over his shoulder to rub his chest.

"I'm sorry that you've missed some of Boden's firsts." I rake my fingers gently through his hair. "It's not fucking fair, but it isn't your fault. The good news is he's too young to remember that you weren't there for those things." With my face pressed to his crown,

I inhale his scent and kiss him. "Yes, it will probably always weigh on you. But you get to love him from here on out. Rather than dwell on the eighteen months you've missed, try to focus on the eighteen-plus *years* you'll get with him."

His breathing has evened out, though his tears haven't dried yet. Here and there, he sniffles, and stray drops land on my arm as I consider the best words to comfort him.

"You know what firsts you *will* get to experience?"

In answer, he squeezes my knee.

"His first full sentence. The first time he calls you Daddy—or whatever name y'all decide on. The first time he catches a ball. Potty training." I wrinkle my nose, though he can't see it. "When he learns to write his name. You'll get to teach him how to ride a bike. Take him on his first camping trip. To his first Blues game. And you'll get all the first days of school: preschool and kindergarten, hormonal middle school and high school."

A silent chuckle vibrates through him and into me.

"First crush," I continue. "First kiss, first love. His high school graduation. His first job. You'll be there for all of them."

He inhales deeply, his chest expanding beneath my hand. "Thank you."

I kiss his head again and wrap him tighter, as if my limbs can shield him from further hurt.

The two of us remain on the kitchen floor, locked together as light breaks through the clouds.

That's how my brother finds us after his shift.

Wordlessly, Cam drops his bag on a chair and joins us on the floor, settling against the cabinet next to me. He gives Tucker's shoulder a comforting squeeze and hugs me to his side, a silent support to his sister and his best friend.

I've been added to a group text with Trixie and Brynn.

I discover this the morning after Tucker's kitchen meltdown, while he's in the shower, likely psyching himself up for another emotional day.

After our kitchen sit-in, the three of us warmed up the fajitas and choked down a few bites, though we quickly surrendered to emotional exhaustion and early bedtimes. Tucker didn't say much as we got ready for bed, but there were no more tears, either. As soon as we crawled under the covers and got comfortable (and I got to be the big spoon for once), he drifted off.

When my phone vibrates a second time, I steal Tucker's pillow and prop it against the headboard with mine, then scroll back to the beginning.

Trixie:

I officially christen this the LFUF group text. Now, Natalie, please spill the beans on this family meeting Tucker scheduled. I hate surprises.

Brynn:

I can't believe Griff and I are missing this. My first Lacey Fam meeting. [whiny face emoji]

Trixie:

No worries, ma'am. My mom's already charged her iPad to FaceTime y'all.

Brynn:

Yay! Does Griff know?

Trixie:

That was Dottie's responsibility. [shrugging shoulders emoji]

Brynn:

He just texted! Aunt Dot told him to sneak away at ten-thirty.

Trixie:

Perfect.

Brynn:

Drills break for lunch at eleven, so he'll only have to hide for a half hour.

BTW, what in the world does LFUF mean?

Trixie:

Lacey Females Under Fifty.

Being included in this group gives me the warm fuzzies, though I can't help but smirk, since no one in it has the last name Lacey.

Trixie:

Back to business...Nat, I need to know if this announcement of Tucker's is ring-shaped.

Brynn:

Trix, don't pressure them. They just started dating.

Trixie:

Pfft. I don't care if it's too soon. I want to sing at a wedding, damn it! And a certain middle Lacey Bro is dragging his effing feet.

Brynn:

AMEN, SISTER!

This time a laugh escapes me. If only she knew about all the sleeping-Brynn pictures saved in Tucker's phone.

Me:

Sorry, girls. My lips are sealed. [zipper face emoji]

I pinch my bottom lip, a niggle of worry working its way through me. They'll no doubt be shocked. Though I can't imagine them not welcoming that little boy—and his mom—into the fold immediately. That's the kind of family they are: inclusive and unfailingly kind.

The little guy is going to be so blessed.

After dinner last night, Tucker, knee bouncing, asked if I'd accompany him to Memphis this afternoon.

Though I hated the idea of telling him no, it's important that his focus be solely on meeting his son. The last thing I want is for him to worry about me. I want that moment for him and for Boden. So I gently declined and reminded him that there will be plenty of opportunities for me to meet his little boy.

Plus, Regina and I have a video session scheduled for this afternoon. When I sent her a frantic text after we'd cleaned up the kitchen, she agreed that an emergency Saturday session was a smart idea.

One final text from Trixie pings:

Ugh, fine. See y'all at ten-thirty. Nat, tell your dog I said hi.

We don't have to leave for the Laceys' farm for another hour, so I snuggle deeper into the bedding and scroll on my phone until Tucker shuts off the shower.

He enters the bedroom with a gray towel tied around his waist, his glorious chest and colorful tats on full display.

"Hey." I put my phone on the nightstand. "You okay?"

He rounds the bed and eases his body on top of mine, keeping the comforter between us.

When he rests his head on my chest, I grip the damp hair at his nape.

"Too heavy?" he mumbles against the blanket.

"Nope. Just right."

He props his chin on my breast, his blue-gray eyes fixed on my face. "I'm obsessed with you."

I trace one dark eyebrow over to his ear, then gently tug on the tiny gold hoop there. "I'm obsessed with you...and this earring."

He smiles, but it fades quickly. "I'm sorry that all this is happening right when you and I—"

"Stop," I say, my tone gentle. "Maybe the timing sucks, but you have nothing to be sorry about."

He sighs. "I wanted to spend every available minute of your time here with you. Just the two of us. But now..." His shoulders bunch, the muscles rippling in a way that would normally distract me.

In this moment, that kind of distraction is impossible. Instead I'm burdened by more than his physical weight on top of me.

If denial and avoidance were Olympic sports, we'd be gold medalists. We've avoided discussing what happens with our relationship when I return to Austin next month like a couple of champs.

And now an adorable baby-shaped obstacle has popped up.

"We'll figure it out," I say. "We still have time."

See? If I'd said that in front of a panel of judges, they would award me perfect tens.

"Hmm." He peers at the clock. "We also have time for breakfast. Can I make you pancakes?"

I sigh and hold him a little tighter. "Yes, please."

Over pancakes and bacon, we predict which Lacey will be the first to cry when they find out about Boden, and when Tucker clears his plate, I offer him my last slice of bacon, happy that his appetite has returned.

If Cam were here, he'd riot. Over the years, the Torres-Little kitchen witnessed many last slice battles.

Tucker's nerves reappear while he's getting dressed. For more than a full minute, he stands in the doorway of his closet, holding two hangers. "Which one says 'I want to make a good impression because I'm meeting my kid for the first time, but I'm still a badass'?"

Eventually, he settles on a pair of black shorts paired with a chambray shirt with the sleeves rolled up and half buttoned over a white tee. On his head, his weathered Lacey Farms ball cap, and on his feet, white and black Adidas.

When he shows off his final choice, I snap a quick picture with my phone. "Perfect. Definitely gives hip dad vibes."

He's quiet on the drive to the farm, but he holds my hand the entire trip.

When we enter the two-story farmhouse, it's filled with nervous anticipation. All the family members in attendance, minus Shaw, are situated on the cozy, lived-in plaid sofas and leather recliners in the spacious living room. The oldest Lacey boy is standing, his arms crossed and a shoulder propped against the cased opening that leads to the kitchen.

Dottie is perched on one of the recliners, holding up an iPad. In one box on the screen, Griff stands under a tree, the grass behind him lush and green, his face drenched in sweat. In a second box, Brynn's fresh as a daisy on a balcony with the ocean visible over her left shoulder.

Before Tucker and I settle on the empty love seat, Mrs. Lacey leans forward, her hands clasped and her eyes misty behind her glasses. "Why does this feel like bad news? Oh God, Tucker, please don't tell me one of you is sick."

Tucker tilts my way as we lower onto the cushions. "Told ya."

I bow my head and, out of the corner of my mouth, respond. "She doesn't even know yet. That doesn't count."

The smile he hits me with brings with it relief. It's his usual big, easy grin. The one I've missed over the last twenty-four hours.

I thread my fingers with his and squeeze his hand.

With our joined hands planted on his thigh, he pulls in a deep breath. "Yeah, so I have some big news."

As he launches into a play-by-play of yesterday's events, I observe his family's reactions, my chest tight with a protectiveness I wasn't expecting. I'm certain they'll accept the news with grace, but if anyone makes a single negative comment, I'm ready to come to his defense.

When he gets to the big reveal, all the women gasp and the men's jaws drop. Then the room erupts, comments and questions flying at lightning speed.

"My baby has a baby?" is followed by a tearful, happy shriek.

"Why didn't you bring him? Show us a picture."

"Son" is paired with an incredulous head shake and chuckle.

"Wait, what? Eighteen months?"

"I'm so sad I'm not there to hug you, Tuck. Congratulations."

"Dottie, don't you think we need to be with Tuck the first time he meets this precious angel?" (That causes Tucker to lean in close with another "Told ya.")

"Oh em gee, I can't wait to squish him. Please, please, please let us meet him soon." followed by another happy shriek.

"Whoa, whoa, whoa," Griffin shouts from the iPad, interrupting the bedlam. "Let's calm down."

Once the room is quiet, Shaw steps forward. "You gotta make sure, Tuck. We all love your big ole heart and your ability to see the best in everyone, but...you gotta make sure."

"I second this," Griffin says. "We're here for you 100 percent, bro, whatever you need. And we'll be stoked to be uncles, but..." He sighs and roughs a hand down his face. "I hate to say it, but my job being what it is—"

"I get it." Tucker's tone is calm and reassuring. "And that's the first order of business when I get to the city this afternoon. We'll get definitive proof that Boden is mine." He releases my hand, stands, and strides to the fireplace.

Dottie follows every movement with her device.

Tuck plucks a framed picture off the mantel and pulls out his phone, then he makes his way to his oldest brother.

Shaw rubs his short beard as he studies the image in the frame, then the one on Tuck's phone.

The rest of us wait with bated breath. By the time he looks up, an expression of wonder on his face, my chest aches.

"Well, I'll be damned."

The crowd erupts once more.

Chapter Twenty-Seven

Tucker

When I park at the curb in front of the sage bungalow in Memphis's Cooper-Young neighborhood, Marissa is waiting on the front porch with a dark-haired toddler on her hip.

I cut the ignition and take a moment to breathe. A few seconds to calm the storm in my gut and quiet the ringing in my ears.

God, I wish Nat had come with me. I understand and respect her decision to remain behind the scenes today, but damn, I miss her. I need her hand in mine and one of her no-nonsense pep talks.

I was so fucking grateful to have her by my side when I shared the news with my family. She's been a rock for me these last two days. I don't think I'd be handling this so well if it weren't for her.

While I didn't doubt that my family would be supportive, I worried that they'd label this another irresponsible mistake. But on the drive to the farm, I reminded myself over and over that though their opinions will always be important, what they believe about me isn't nearly as important as what I believe about myself.

Yet they met the surprise with enthusiasm and unwavering faith that I can do this, and that bolstered me the whole drive to Memphis.

Marissa speaks to Boden and waves, as if encouraging him to do the same, so I close my eyes and take one final centering breath before exiting the Jeep. I almost forget to grab the scruffy white and brown stuffed dog Nat helped me pick out. As we left Mom and Dad's, she suggested that I bring Boden a gift, so we stopped by the only spot in the Holler that sells toys—the Dusty Britches Mercantile—before I dropped her off at Wayne's studio on my way out of town.

Stuffed version of Goose in hand, I stride up the front walk on shaky legs.

Marissa descends the front steps, murmuring to Boden the whole way.

"Hey." I give her a cursory glance, but my attention is quickly drawn to the little guy in her arms.

"Bo," Marissa croons. "This is the new friend I told you about. This is Tuck."

He hides his face in his mom's neck, then gives me a bashful peek and a toothy grin.

Fuck, I'm a goner.

That look is like a sucker punch. I blink up at the sky and swallow the knot in my throat. "Hi, Boden," I rasp. "It's nice to meet you."

"Can you say hi?" she prompts.

When he squeaks out "hi" in a tiny voice and follows it with a giggle? My heart melts. I'm a gooey puddle smack dab in the middle of a Memphis sidewalk, and it has nothing to do with the ninety-degree day.

As Marissa sets him on the ground in front of her, he keeps curious eyes on me. He sticks close to her, and when I squat down to his level, he wraps his arm around one of her legs.

"Hey, bud. I've got a prize for you." I hold out the stuffed dog. "This is Goose. He has a bird name, but he's a dog."

His eyes dart from me to the dog, but he doesn't reach for it.

Marissa crouches next to him and sweeps his dark hair off his forehead. "You love dogs, baby. Can you say Goose?"

He studies my face, his gray-blue eyes full of curiosity and apprehension. "Goo." With another look at the dog, he tentatively reaches for the toy. As soon as he locks his pudgy fingers around the fur, he clutches the dog to his body.

"Good job, dude." I hold up a hand. "High five?"

Grinning now, he smacks his little hand to my palm.

As Marissa and I share a smile over his head, I suck in the first full breath I've taken in over twenty-four hours.

Yeah, this'll all work out.

I spread my arms wide. Maybe it's too soon, but if there's a chance he'll let me hug or hold him, I'll take it. He wavers for a second, glancing at his mom for assurance, and when she gives him an encouraging nod, he toddles into my embrace.

I rise and instinctively press my lips to his head, breathing in my son's clean, powdery scent for the first time. With Nat's advice in the forefront of my mind, I close my eyes and soak in the moment. I don't let myself wallow in what I've missed; instead, I imagine our future adventures and am overwhelmed with gratitude.

When I open my eyes, Marissa's are shining with tears.

"Would you like to come inside?"

"Yeah, thanks."

I prop Boden in the crook of my arm and follow her up the steps. "You're moving?" I ask, tilting my head to the *For Sale* sign in the front yard.

She opens the front door and gestures me inside. "Downsizing."

The layout of the house is similar to the one Cam and I share. The front door opens directly into the living room, where honey stained wood floors and soft blue walls provide a calm backdrop for the upholstered khaki couch and matching love seat. A cartoon plays on the muted flat-screen mounted on the wall, the animated dogs wearing uniforms. The space is tidy, but the handful of trucks parked haphazardly on the floral rug make it obvious a young child lives here. So do the set of blocks and the toy telephone. Along the wall under the picture window are two push toys and a mini basketball hoop.

Marissa closes the door and tickles Boden's belly. "Things have been tight since, um, since my ex moved out. I can't afford the place on my own."

Shit. I haven't even considered the child support aspect of this situation. I'd be glad to help her out and ensure Boden has everything he needs, but we've got other logistics to iron out first.

Cheeks heating, she peers up at me. "Shoot. I wasn't—I mean that wasn't...ugh." She presses her hand to her stomach, flustered. "I didn't say that to guilt you into anything. Please believe that." She wrings her hands. "We're fine. But Boden and I can make do with something smaller."

Boden kicks his legs and babbles unintelligibly, snagging our attention.

"He's asking to be let down so he can show you his ball."

Sure enough, as soon as his feet touch the floor, he waddles over to a squishy soccer ball. Holding it high, he jabbers. "Baw. Baw. Sah baw." He wanders back and offers it to me.

I chuckle. "Your Uncle Griff's gonna riot."

Marissa sweeps Boden into her arms and tilts her head. "Are you okay with getting the cheek swabs done first? Then we can visit and Boden can show you his room."

"Yeah, let's do it."

Her kitchen is spacious, with oak cabinets and earth-toned granite countertops, and on the island, she's already laid out the items we'll need for the paternity test.

"I'm in the business of mouths," she says as she swabs my cheek. When I furrow my brows, she explains. "Sorry. Dental hygienist humor."

Boden, thankfully, lets me hold him again when it's his turn. She's careful with the samples, double checking the directions so that they're packaged the correct way for the lab.

"My coworker has a cousin who works at the testing lab. I'll drop this off first thing Monday morning, and we should have the results in a couple days."

Since Boden isn't squirming to get down again, I take the opportunity to study his features up close. The shape and color of his eyes and his smile may come from the Lacey side, but there are shades of Marissa there, too. He has her nose and her full cheeks.

When he grabs the brim of my cap, I flip it around and distract him with a tummy tickle. "This is a cool shirt, my man. What's this?" I ask, pointing to the cartoon dinosaur printed on the material.

"Rah."

"Yep, dinosaurs say 'roar.'"

He smiles and pokes at my mouth with a chubby finger.

"Mouth," I say as I tap his with my knuckle.

With a giggle, he squirms. "Moww."

I look at Marissa and grin. "This kid is a genius."

⋅⋅◆⋅⋅

Adrenaline still courses through my veins and a thousand thoughts sprint through my brain when I climb into the Jeep and dial Natalie.

She answers on the second ring. "Hey! How'd it go?"

"It was...it was perfect." Warmth unfurls inside my chest. "He's the cutest kid, Nat. I can't wait for you to meet him."

"Aw, me too."

"Good, because...I kind of invited us back tomorrow."

She inhales sharply. "You what? Back to Marissa's?"

"Yeah."

"And she's...comfortable with me coming?"

"God," I breathe. "I want to kiss your face so bad right now."

Her surprised laughter fills the Jeep. "I'm serious, Tucker."

"Me too." I toss my ball cap into the passenger seat and massage the back of my neck. "And yes. She wanted to know how serious we are before she agreed. I told her very, and that was enough."

She's quiet for a moment. Before my nerves can get the best of me, though, she lets out a soft "oh."

"You're worrying me, shutterbug. Was that the wrong thing to tell her?"

"No." The conviction in her tone eases my anxiety. "I just want you to be sure. This is a big deal, and things are happening very quickly."

She's not wrong. We've been bombarded with a shit ton of changes over the past two days. But I have zero doubts about our relationship, and I want to erase any concerns she has about me or the unconventional situation we're in.

"I just..." A heavy sigh crackles over the line. "I just want you to be sure," she repeats.

"Let me tell you what I'm *sure* about, Nat." I stop at a red light and eye the photographer duck on my dash. "I'm sure about you and me. I'm sure that I've never felt for anyone the way I do for you. I know this summer's been a whirlwind and clearly life isn't going to settle down anytime soon, but there's no one I'd rather have along for the ride than you."

"You always know the right things to say." Another sigh. "But—"

"The only *but* I'm okay with is yours, sweetheart."

"Tucker."

I sigh, a mix of frustration and exhaustion. "Let's hear it."

"We've totally ignored that I'm going back to Austin in a couple weeks. Doesn't that concern you?"

Yeah, we've avoided this discussion like Lisa Marie (the goat) avoids captivity. Here and there, we've dropped hints about it, but for the most part, we've kept our blinders in place.

Now, though, the bridge looms large.

"All right. Let's discuss it."

"Now?" she squawks.

I wish like hell we weren't doing this over the phone. I'd give anything to hold her and look her in the eye the way Griff handles important discussions with Brynn, but I can't dodge the topic any longer.

"Yep, now."

I change lanes, passing a slow Mini Cooper, willing my heart to settle before I figuratively lay it at her feet.

"One of the reasons I've avoided talking about this is because I never wanted you to feel pressured. But fuck it. Here's the truth: I want you to stay in Holly Holler. I understand that would mean uprooting your whole life, but I'm selfish when it comes to you." When she doesn't immediately shoot me down, I suck in a breath and go on. "I want you to stay and figure out this big, messy, beautiful life with me. But—"

"Hey." She sniffles. Her voice wavers, but I swear she's smiling. "I thought you said my *but* was the only one."

I chuckle. "It's definitely the only one. Let me rephrase. *However*, if you decide you'd be happier in Austin, I'll support that. And I'll apply for a credit card that'll earn frequent flier miles, because there's no way I'm letting you go for good. If we have to be long-distance, we'll make it work."

"Sounds like you're making me the boss of this relationship."

My grin is so wide it makes my cheeks hurt. "You're the boss everywhere but our bed, baby."

Goose barks, keeping my thoughts from drifting to those moments when I'm in charge.

"Boden loved the toy dog," I tell her. "I told him its name is Goose."

She snorts. "Hope he's not confused when he meets the real deal."

The ease with which she casually mentions introducing her dog to Boden fills me with warmth.

"Same. Let me double-check that it's okay with Marissa, but I think we should bring him with us tomorrow."

As I recount more details of my visit with Boden, I merge onto the highway that'll take me home, to the place where the majority of my heart waits for me.

But a quick glimpse in the rearview reminds me I'm leaving a piece of it behind, too.

CHAPTER TWENTY-EIGHT

NATALIE

I trace the path of a water droplet with my finger, then bring the glass to my lips. The sweet, tart flavor of the lemonade is the perfect match for my mood.

In the chair next to mine on the back deck, Marissa shields her eyes with a hand, fending off the brutal early August sun.

This is our second visit with her and Boden in Memphis. The temperature is a scorching ninety-eight, so Tuck, his son, and Goose are playing in an inflatable pool and splash pad out in the yard.

His son.

Tucker received confirmation four days ago that Boden is indeed a Lacey.

Two hours after his family got word, his front yard was decorated with giant baby blue letters spelling out *It's a Boy!*

And two hours after that, Trixie texted a dozen photos of Donna and Dottie raiding the baby section at the Target in Jonesboro, their carts overflowing with toys and clothes and boxes of furniture.

This kid is already loved beyond measure.

Still, the whole crew is navigating this carefully, not wanting to overwhelm Boden or Marissa. Tucker has introduced his family in stages. Boden met his grandparents on Friday afternoon when they accompanied Tucker for a visit. Trixie and Dottie came over with him yesterday while I photographed a wedding in Wilson. Shaw and Cam have to wait, though. Donna's planned a big family dinner at the farm two weeks from now, and that Sunday, we're all headed to Memphis for the Blues' first preseason game.

I met the little guy a week ago, and I haven't ever felt the word *bittersweet* as deeply as I did that day. But the first time I witnessed Boden reach for his father, its meaning sank all the way to my bone marrow.

It was a moment I'll carry until my memories fade.

Beautiful and devastating.

Joyous and traumatic.

Since I learned about the little boy's existence, long-buried hurts regarding motherhood have come back to haunt me, including the what-could-have-beens and the hundreds of tiny cuts left in their absence.

I think part of me will always grieve the unfulfilled dream of being a mother.

But when I met Boden, when I held him in my arms, when he gave me a toothy smile and when he broke into a sweet belly laugh, a great many of those tiny cuts were healed.

I'd never, *ever* horn in on Marissa's role in his life. I'd sooner cut out my heart than try to take her place or step into shoes meant only for her.

However, being in Tucker's life means being in his son's, too.

A high-pitched baby shriek interrupts my thoughts.

I snatch my phone to capture a video of the heartwarming scene.

Boden cackles, his head tipped back in utter joy, as Goose shakes, sending water droplets flying. Tucker, full of merriment, takes a knee beside them and ruffles my dog's wet body.

"Goo!" Boden points at the wet mop of fur and holds out his hand for Goose to lick.

When Tucker stands, I shift my gaze to Marissa's unguarded face, inspecting her from behind my dark sunglasses. He stripped off his shirt as soon as we exited the house, draping it over the deck railing, then got to work setting up the water toys. Rather than longing, or even appreciation for Tucker's shirtless physique, her smiling expression is full of serenity.

My inner possessive girlfriend is on high alert. She's been pacing the bars of her mental enclosure for over a week, ready to lash out at the first sign of attraction on Marissa's part. Typically, I can placate my internal cavewoman by reminding her that although Marissa is the mother of his child, I'm the one sharing his bed. The woman who gets his sleepy love declarations when we turn off the lights. The one he eagerly brought to orgasm this morning. Twice.

Though I try to stay vigilant, and though neither Tucker nor Marissa deserves it, those tiny sparks of jealousy flare up here and there.

Tucker Lacey is a dream man, so my claws are primed. Just in case.

Clearly more intuitive than I realized, Marissa leans over the small wicker table between our chairs and says, "I feel the need to reassure you that my only interest in Tucker is as a co-parent and friend." She checks over her shoulder quickly, then continues. "I don't have any romantic notions about this situation. None. In fact, I'm done with men. At least for a good long while."

I slide my motorcycle pendant back and forth along its chain.

"Sure, anyone with eyeballs can see he's a good-looking guy. But that night was more about his kindness than his looks." She lifts one shoulder. "Tucker was nice and flirty and nothing like my ex. In a desperate attempt to move on from Jason, I went into self-destruct mode and threw caution to the wind. Not my finest hour, that's for sure."

In the yard, Tucker swings a happy Boden through the splash pad's waist-high spray.

"How could anyone look at those two and not see the resemblance?"

Marissa goes still beside me.

Only now realizing that I muttered the words aloud rather than inside my brain, I adjust my sunglasses. "I'm sorry. That was…"

"No, that's a fair question. To be honest, I wouldn't let myself consider the possibility that Tucker could be his father. Jason and I are blond, but even when Boden was born with a head full of dark hair, I didn't worry. My dad and brother both have dark hair." She surveys the father and son in front of us. "I feel awful about that now. I wanted him to be Jason's so badly that I squashed any tiny doubt that crept up. Unless Boden had a medical emergency or something like that, I probably would've kept living in denial. And I hate that. I'll regret it for the rest of my life."

The remorse in her tone is genuine and undeniable. Her answer hurts, but it's honest. If her ex hadn't turned out to be a jackass, Tucker might not have ever known about his son. It should infuriate me. Instead, I'm filled with a mix of heartache and gratitude.

She gives me a wistful smile. "Now, despite the pain and heartache, I'm glad he's not Jason's."

For a long moment, we watch Tucker and Boden in silence.

Before long, though, Marissa is eyeing me again. "Tucker mentioned that your brother is his best friend?"

I nod once. "Yeah. Cam and Tuck have been best friends since kindergarten." Fond memories wash over me. "Their personalities aren't quite night and day…more like sunrise and sunset. Similar enough, but still altogether different. I love their friendship."

"I'm looking forward to seeing more of y'all's hometown when we visit. From what I saw when I stopped in to talk to Tucker a few weeks ago, it's darling. And Tucker's family is precious."

"They're an amazing bunch," I agree. "They'll love and cherish Boden with everything they've got."

Lacey Love, Trixie calls it.

Marissa clears her throat. "I'm so grateful he'll have them. And that he'll have you, too."

The honesty in her voice brings tears to my eyes, making me thankful for my dark lenses.

"When Tucker told me about you," she goes on, "my only concern—other than you worrying about me making a move on your man—was Boden meeting a woman who may not be around in the long run. My little guy's resilient, but he's been through a lot of changes." She smooths a hand over her blond ponytail. "But when Tucker described you as vital to him, that concern disappeared."

Vital. The word thrills me and terrifies me at the same time.

"I consider it a blessing," she says, "having another person in Boden's life who will love him and help him learn and grow. I'm a firm believer that child-rearing takes a village. And I couldn't be more grateful for the one we've found. I'm not so naive enough to think that the road we're on will always be smooth. But building this solid foundation now will help us iron out the rough patches later."

I can't help but smile at her. Damn, I really like her. I already had a healthy respect for her as Boden's mother, but now? Maybe it's wishful thinking, but I can envision an easy friendship blossoming between us.

She twists her ponytail up off her neck and purses her lips. "*Pfft.* I don't know about you, but I'm sweatin' buckets. What do you say we leave them to their water time and go inside and break open the salsa y'all brought? I'm dying to hear how your brother reacted when he found out you were dating his best friend."

I release a satisfied sigh. "Sounds perfect."

The back door to the studio creaks open, and Nancy calls out. "Yoo-hoo. Nat, are you in here?"

Goose trots out into the hallway to check out our visitor.

Without looking away from the computer, I respond. "In the office."

When a deep voice rumbles down the hall, I roll back from the desk, leaving the Kennedy twins' birthday portraits pulled up on my laptop, and shuffle out into the hall.

"Hey." I grin at Nancy, then Wayne. "Fancy seeing you here, mister."

He grimaces as he adjusts his crutches. He's only been to the studio once since his surgery, right after his hard cast was removed three weeks ago. Today, he's in a full leg brace, but he's not been given the go-ahead to put full weight on it yet.

"I'm running to the DB to pick up a couple things, then I'll come back for you, hon." Nancy briskly kisses her husband's cheek, then does the same to mine. She brackets her mouth with a hand, her eyes twinkling. "This one is going stir-crazy. Trips to the physical therapist aren't cutting it anymore. We're going to grab dinner at the diner so he can catch up on the town gossip."

Her husband rolls his eyes, but the corner of his mouth lifts.

After a couple pats to Wayne's chest, she bustles out the back door.

"Come sit." I lead him into his office. "Let me find something for you to prop your leg on."

He waves me off and drops into one of the chairs in front of the desk, using the spare seat for his leg, leaving me no choice but to take his usual spot.

I've never once sat in his chair while he's present. It feels downright disrespectful. This is his office and his studio. The place that's served as the home base for his life's work.

He studies me, his brown eyes twinkling behind his dark-rimmed glasses. The same pair he slides up on his head like a pair of shades when he's in his photography zone. I bet those frames have spent as many hours perched on his head as they have on his nose.

With his hands laced on the plaid button-down covering his slight paunch, he regards me. "You look good in that chair, Nat."

My heart pounds and nerves course through me. "Thank you?" I don't intend for it to sound like a question, but there's a definite inflection at the end.

He rubs his salt-and-pepper beard, scrutinizing me in a way that makes me twitchy. I've known him for most of my life. I've spent hours upon hours upon hours with him, but suddenly, I can't figure him out.

"Sally Peterson called me last week, raving about the engagement pictures you took of Sarah and her fiancé. Bragged about how creative and unique your poses are. Said they're leagues better than the ones I took of her and Joe many moons ago."

Forearms resting on the desk, I angle forward and sputter. "Sally Peterson is a conceited trophy wife."

His brows hit his hairline. "Conceited trophy wives need photographers. And they're willing to pay handsomely. She dropped hints about wanting you to shoot the Witches' Ride in October. Offered to double my event sitting fee if I could guarantee you'd do it."

"I won't be here in October." The moment the words leave my lips, the probable truth of them floors me.

Even after Tucker's phone declaration, I haven't made up my mind. Maybe the decision should be a no-brainer. I'm in a solid, loving relationship with an incredible man. Half of my family lives here. And it's a familiar, comfortable community.

Yet something is holding me back from committing to Holly Holler.

"You could be here. In October." Wayne sticks out his chin.

"You'll be back in action in a couple weeks," I remind him.

He expels a put-upon sigh. "I've been thinking it might be time for me to step back."

My stomach drops. He may be in his late sixties, but it's hard to believe this injury could be the thing that forces him to hang up his camera. A Holly Holler without Wayne Gann documenting every birth announcement, kindergarten graduation, capped-and-gowned senior, engagement, and wedding? It's unfathomable. He's as evergreen to this community as the town square or the multiple Lisa Maries.

"So you cut back on your sessions. Maybe pass on the out-of-town weddings. Stick closer to home."

He clears his throat and shifts, careful of his leg. "What I'm trying to say, though apparently not so well, is that I want it to be yours, Nat. I'm ready to pass the baton."

My heart lurches. "*What?*"

"C'mon, kid, this shouldn't be shocking. I'm not a spring chicken anymore, and I'm not selling my baby to some yahoo from off the street who doesn't know this town or its people. Nance and I weren't blessed with progeny to carry on my legacy..." He swallows thickly. "But you're as good as. It should be yours."

"Wayne." Tears blur my vision, but I swipe at them quickly. "I don't know what to say."

"Say yes." He shrugs. "You and that Lacey boy have a good thing going. Your mama would be over the moon to have you home again. Nancy and I would be, too."

"But my business. Austin..." I trail off, my dumbfounded brain struggling to formulate coherent sentences.

"So you buy me out. I'll give you a good deal." He winks. "You can transform Wayne Gann Photography into Shutterbug. Give the studio an update. God knows it needs it." He turns his head, eyeing the place. It's far neater than it was when I took over a few months ago. "I'll still be around to help out if you need manpower or an extra lens."

Mentally, I berate myself. How could I not be screeching *yes* at the top of my lungs? I should be rounding the desk to hug him and thank him profusely for the opportunity. I should be reaching for my phone to call Tucker.

What the hell is wrong with you, Natalie?

My lungs constrict, and suddenly, I feel like I'm trapped in a locked room with no way out.

Wayne peers at me like I'm holding his future happiness for ransom.

Maybe that's accurate. But I'm not ready to give him an answer yet. My overthinking brain needs to do its thing and weigh every possibility. I need to talk to Tucker. To Liv. To Mom. To Regina.

I need space and time to figure out how to keep everyone happy without sacrificing the safe life I've built for myself.

Fortunately, Nancy returns, rescuing me. When the back door opens, I fix my eyes on her husband and tell him the truth. "I'm immensely flattered that you want me to do this, but it's a huge decision. I need a couple days to think about it."

Chapter Twenty-Nine

Natalie

"We're engaged!"

Every head swivels to where Griffin and Brynn—holding up her hand where a diamond sparkles as brilliantly as her smile—stand in the entryway.

A split-second later, the crowd gathered in the living room descends on them, cheering and yelling. Donna, Fred, Trixie, Dottie, and Tucker surround Griffin and Brynn, sharing hugs and back slaps and handshakes.

I remain near the kitchen entry with Marissa, who hefts a wary Boden in her arms. "Lacey love," I murmur to her as the tearful, excited reunion continues.

Shaw's close but not quite in the middle of the bedlam, a pleased, nearly full smile on his face.

I add to the mental tally of almost-smiles I've witnessed on the man today, delighted and shocked when I realize the total is nearing double digits. The biggest came when Tucker passed his son to his oldest brother and said, "This is your Uncle Shaw." I may have teared up then, witnessing Shaw's icy defenses thaw a little.

As Griff and Brynn hug a teary Donna, Tucker slaps cash into a smug Shaw's upturned palm.

Once the initial shock and giddiness dissipate, Tucker gives Brynn a second hug. "Welcome to the family, sis. Officially."

"Tuck, you're a dad!" Brynn hastily wipes under her eyes and scans the room. When she finds Boden, she lights up.

"Yeah, come meet him."

Tucker proudly introduces Boden to his brother and soon-to-be sister-in-law. "Bo, meet your Aunt Brynn and Uncle Griff."

Brynn extends her arms, patiently waiting for Boden. He deliberates for a moment before deciding she's safe and reaching for her. She hugs him to her body, one hand on the back of his head. "Oh, I'm in love," she croons as Griffin puts his hands on her shoulders and makes a silly face that gets Boden grinning.

"Putting in my request for more from you two," Donna chirps as she and Dottie pass on their way to the kitchen. "Dot and I've gotta finish gettin' this dinner ready, and then I want to hear every proposal detail."

I've attended family dinner at the Laceys a couple of times this summer, but it's never been this crowded. It's so crowded, in fact, that Mr. Lacey arranged a spare folding table at the end of the dining table to accommodate the extra bodies. Shortly after Griffin and Brynn's arrival, Mabel shows up with a bottle of wine. The only person missing is Cam, but he plans to join us when his shift ends at seven.

Once the seating arrangement is decided, Mrs. Lacey settles Boden's new highchair between her spot at the head of the table and Marissa. I end up sandwiched between Tucker and Shaw, across from Brynn.

"Mom, Aunt Dottie, this looks amazing." Griffin rubs his abdomen as he inspects the dishes.

The table's laden with platters of smoked sausage and grilled chicken along with serving bowls filled with freshly sliced tomatoes and cucumbers from the garden and baskets of steaming rolls.

Donna smiles, proud. "I have to give your father and his grill credit for the meat."

Mr. Lacey, as taciturn as ever, simply nods and reaches for the bowl of purple hull peas.

"Now, when did this happen?" Mrs. Lacey shifts her focus to Brynn.

Brynn's face goes pink as she flutters her lashes up at her fiancé. "This morning."

"Start from the beginning. I want every last detail."

Griff smirks in response while Brynn's blush deepens.

Damn, it looks like in present company, a few details will be left out

We all load our plates as the happy pair launch into the retelling of their proposal story.

Dinner is a sometimes loud, always happy event; Boden charms the whole group, and we're all eager to hear the newly engaged couple's wedding plans. The Laceys do a great job including their guests in the conversations, effortlessly weaving in questions for Marissa and Mabel and me.

"Natalie." Dottie interjects as she scoops up a forkful of seasoned potatoes. "How'd the tourism board like your final submissions?"

I take a sip of sweet tea to wash down a bite of chicken and clear my throat. "They were very impressed. I was worried about going in a somewhat unconventional direction, but they were enthusiastic that I chose to think outside the box."

The ten photos I submitted at the end of July are ones I'll forever be proud of. As I pored over the hundreds of options, narrowing down my choices seemed impossible. But a couple nights before the deadline, as I sat bleary-eyed at my laptop in James's home office, I noticed a pattern, and an idea took root.

My favorites weren't beautiful shots of well-known landforms or buildings. Sure, they were elements within the frames. But every one of my favorite pictures had one thing in common: people. Not portraits of people. In fact, none of them feature anything identifiable to the individuals I memorialized. Instead, they show-case artistic glimpses or hints at one of this state's best resources: its citizens. A close-up of weathered, hard-working hands. A boot print in the rich delta soil. An out-of-focus shot of a pilot's helmet as he glides his ag plane over the river. The shadow of a motorcycle rider on his bike.

With that part of my homecoming mission complete, all that's left are the handful of photography appointments I'll cover until Wayne returns to work in a few days.

It's been more than a week since he told me he wants to turn the business over to me, but I haven't given him an answer yet.

Also haven't even mentioned the suggestion to the man beside me.

Yeah, I have to be the worst girlfriend ever.

I've tried a dozen times to tell him, but without fail, I have a last-second change of heart.

I know he'll be thrilled, so this procrastination is all on me.

The reason for my reticence remains a mystery. A future in Holly Holler would be akin to an amazing puzzle where every tab—Tucker, Mom and James, Cam, the Laceys, Wayne and Nancy, the studio—slots perfectly into place. The knobs fit seamlessly into the blanks, creating a beautiful, colorful mosaic. Except...it's not complete. There's a gaping hole, a missing piece, ruining the whole image.

This missing piece continues to elude me. I've lain awake for hours, racking my brain for the cause. Why am I holding back when it seems everything has fallen into place?

Tucker didn't outright ask me to stay, but he made it clear he wants me to. Cam's hinted at it several times; last week, he sent a Zillow listing for a house a block from his. Even Mom and James have given me subtle nudges.

Saying goodbye to the life I've built in Austin would be hard. I'd miss Liv, Jordan, and their girls. The thought of not having a front-row seat for their future milestones makes me sad. And I'd definitely miss Dad and the rest of my family there. But like Tucker reminded me, direct flights from Memphis to Austin are relatively plentiful.

Yes, leaving Austin would hurt. But would that hurt outweigh the love and family I'd have in Holly Holler?

Reluctance to move from Austin isn't what's stalling my decision. No, it's bigger than that.

Tucker smooths a hand down my thigh, drawing me back to the present. Only then do I realize that all eyes are on me, as if I've been asked a question.

"I-I'm sorry," I stammer, face heating. "What was that?"

Tucker bumps my shoulder with his. "Trixie asked if the photos have been added to the tourism website yet."

"Oh." I give Trix an apologetic smile. "No, they said the link should be live by the end of this month."

"I can't wait to see them." Donna beams. "Mabel, your co-op should display prints of Nat's pictures in the gallery."

"Ooh, that's a great idea. I'll ask," the table's resident artist confirms.

"They're amazing." Tucker squeezes my thigh, then pecks my cheek.

I duck my head and spear my last bite of sausage with my fork, but not before catching the subtle, friendly wink Brynn gives me in the wake of Tucker's PDA.

As dinner goes on, I catch Mabel's gaze wandering to our end of the table several times. At first, I figure she's watching Boden feed himself. He's covered in food, and it is pretty damn cute. But the third or fourth time it happens, I discover that Marissa's eyes stray Mabel's way periodically, too.

Hmm, interesting.

I make a mental note to ask Tuck if he noticed.

A little after seven, Marissa excuses herself to rock a fussy Boden in the downstairs guest room where Donna set up a pack-and-play.

"I'll have to wake him up to drive home, but he should go back to sleep quickly in the car," she explains.

"Do you mind if I join you so I can see how you handle his bedtime?" Tucker asks, his expression serious. "Or do you think he'll be too distracted with me there?"

Smiling, she lifts the baby from his highchair. "I think it'll be fine. Let's try it."

By the time Cam bursts through the side door, it's a quarter to eight, little Boden is asleep in the playpen, and the adults are still at the table enjoying Dottie's blueberry cobbler with vanilla ice cream.

"Sorry I'm late."

He bends to peck Donna's cheek, looking haggard. His hair, face, and navy HHFD T-shirt are sweat-soaked, and his eyes are red rimmed.

Trixie straightens in her seat, her lips turned down. "Cam, you okay?"

My brother rubs a hand over his tired, damp face and sighs. "Yeah. Had to wrap up a call. Took longer than we thought." His eyes, full of sorrow, cut to Shaw. "It was, uh, it was out at the Donovan place."

The entire room stills, and the only sound is the "fuck" Griffin mutters under his breath.

For a long, silent moment, no one moves or speaks. A quick survey of the table reveals that everyone—save for Brynn, Marissa, and me—sits with heads bowed and somber expressions.

I catch Brynn's eye, and she simply gives me a tiny, confused shrug.

Finally, Trixie breaks the spell. "Do you know if anyone's called M—"

The harsh, grating sound of Shaw's chair scraping the floor makes everyone flinch. He stands, head down, and says, "Don't." Then he's gone, storming out of the house.

A minute later, his truck's engine revs, and Donna raises her chin to look at her middle son with teary, pleading eyes.

Griffin sighs and stands. "I'm on it." He presses a kiss to Brynn's temple. "I'll be back in a little while." He gives his mom's shoulder a squeeze as he passes her, and then he disappears, too.

Brynn hugs herself, as unsure about what just transpired as I am.

Mabel angles her head toward Trixie. "Want me to follow you home?"

The redhead, fighting tears, nods. "I'm sorry, Aunt Donna."

The older woman waves her off. "We're fine, sweetheart. Call you tomorrow."

Trixie fist bumps her Uncle Fred and gives her mother a long hug, then she and Mabel quietly leave.

Once Cam has loaded a plate and parked himself on one of the stools at the island, the rest of us help clear the table. Donna and Dottie load the dishwasher and put away leftovers while Mr. Lacey breaks down the extra table and carries it outside.

After the kitchen's neat and tidy, Dottie gathers her dishes and her purse. She doles out goodbyes, and when it's Marissa's turn, she places her hands on the blonde's shoulders. "I'm sorry your first Lacey dinner ended on such a somber note."

Marissa doesn't bat an eye. "It was still a lovely time. Thank you for welcoming us."

Dottie laughs lightly. "You're stuck with us now." She pushes up on her toes to pinch Tucker's cheek next. "Be good."

He pulls me into his side. "Always."

"Mm-hmm." She narrows her eyes at him playfully. "Natalie, wonderful to see you as always. Get this hunk to bring you to the Hoot for a dance."

"Soon," I promise.

Her gray-streaked cinnamon hair tickles my cheek when she hugs me. She whispers into my ear, low enough that Tucker can't hear. "That boy's wild about you. Don't ever doubt it."

"Thanks, Dottie."

A wail sounds from the extra bedroom, startling all of us, and both Marissa and Tucker spring into action.

I join Cam and Brynn in the kitchen while Mrs. Lacey ventures outside to help her husband secure the barn for the night. Brynn does her best to clear the awkwardness by telling us about the book she's nearly finished writing.

Marissa emerges from the hall with a sleepy, whimpering Boden in her arms. Tucker follows them, harried and concerned.

She peers around the kitchen. "I want to tell your parents good night before we go."

Tucker steps close and rubs soothing circles on Boden's back. "They should be in soon." He checks his smartwatch, his face a mask of concern. "I wish y'all didn't have to drive back so late. It's over an hour."

Her lips curve in a soft smile as she switches Boden to her other hip. "It's not so bad."

He frowns. "Still..."

The two of them continue speaking in low voices off to the side, consoling their son and reassuring each other.

That's when it hits me. Like a surprise uppercut Tuck has used to win countless fights.

They deserve a chance to be a family. The three of them. A family that lives together. Has breakfast at the same table. Develops a familiar bedtime routine.

Tucker and Marissa may claim they have zero romantic interest in each other now, but that could change. Friends evolve into lovers all the damn time. Who's to say it won't happen for them?

Of course, it might not work out. But don't they deserve a shot?

If I remain in the picture, they'll never have a chance to explore a deeper connection.

Marissa's young and obviously fertile. She can give Tucker what I never can: more children. Boden could have siblings.

God, the realization hurts like a bitch, but I can't shake it. The noble thing for me to do is step away.

Society loves to spout advice about how to make relationships work. Though I haven't been in many, I've heard my fair share of wisdom regarding them. The one bit that's stuck with me over the years? *Love is a choice.*

Yes, I love Tucker. Love him with a passion and a devotion I didn't think I'd ever get to experience.

But maybe I'm supposed to love him this way, with this choice. Maybe I should let him go. Give him the freedom to explore a deeper connection with the mother of his child.

I agonize over these thoughts through our goodbyes to Marissa, Boden, and the Laceys. And after that, when Tucker asks Cam to drive me to their house so he can stop by Shaw's.

My brother and I are quiet on the ride back into town. I want to be nosy and ask about the Donovans and their connection to Tucker's family, but I refrain. I've heard stories about the family through the years, of course. Their tragedy became a cautionary tale discussed in hushed whispers, especially by parents of young children, in town.

For now, I'm too busy plotting my own personal tragedy to stick my nose into that of others.

After my nighttime routine, I change into my pajamas and slip into Tucker's bed. As I close my eyes, my decision weighs on me, but I remind myself of the numerous special moments I could give Tucker and Marissa.

They could have beach photo shoots where little copies of them cheese at the camera with pink cheeks and noses. Family Halloween costumes. Matching Christmas pajama mornings beside a tree decorated with ornaments handmade by small, clumsy fingers.

And so many more small, huge, meaningful, beautiful, wonderful moments.

It'll mean breaking my own heart. And probably Tucker's, too, for a little while. But with his live-in-the-moment, go-with-the-flow personality, he'll bounce back.

And it'll mean returning to the life I built in Austin. To the routine I've developed to weather my cloudy days. Loneliness will welcome me back like an old friend, but I'll weather that, too.

By the time the mattress dips under Tucker's weight, my tears have dried. As he wraps me in his arms, that final puzzle piece slots into place. And I know what I have to do.

Chapter Thirty

Tucker

The morning Wayne Gann's scheduled to return to his studio, I wake with my hand cupping Nat's breast and my face buried in her hair.

Has the woman beside me mentioned that tomorrow's the day she originally planned to leave town? Nope.

Has this made me cautiously optimistic that she's really going to stay? For sure.

Am I a delusional idiot in love who's avoided broaching the topic with her because I'm afraid her answer will break both of our hearts? Undoubtedly.

Life has been a whirlwind for the past month, starting with finding out about Boden and rolling into meeting him, bonding with him, and introducing him to my—our—family. Juggling all that along with work and love has me feeling like a plate spinner at the circus. If I slow down to take a breath, one or all of the dishes I'm twirling will fall, shattering to pieces. I've been going full throttle, trying to establish a work-life balance that doesn't leave anyone or anything short-changed.

I'm fucking exhausted.

So yeah, I've avoided that conversation minefield. When we discussed it over the phone at the end of July, I left no room for doubt: I want her to stay. But it's her decision. She'd have to give up a lot to move back home, but I think the payoff would be worth it. And if she'd really rather stay in Austin, then like I told her, we'll figure it out.

But fuck, I don't want that to happen.

She stirs next to me, waking with a yawn and a stretch, arching her back. The move instantly has my cock primed. Sleepy, slow morning sex might be my favorite.

"Good morning." I sweep her hair to the side and press soft kisses to her neck and shoulder.

She sighs and grasps my length, lazily pumping. Her words are a breathy whisper. "Mmm...I need you."

"You got me."

I tease her nipple into a firm peak, then slip my hand down to the juncture of her thighs and slide my fingers through her folds to get her wet and ready.

She opens her legs wider, resting one on top of mine, giving me better access.

"You like it like this, don't you?" I grate the words into her ear. When she whimpers in response, my cock twitches. "Slow and easy, on our sides. It's the best part of waking up, baby."

"Yes. God, yes."

I swirl her wetness around her clit, and when she moans in response, satisfaction blooms in my chest. I continue working her like that as I ease into her from behind. Her tight, wet heat envelops me, the sensation as perfect as it always is.

I start with shallow thrusts, rocking my hips in a steady rhythm that draws out our pleasure and makes Nat gasp my name. Before long, I increase the tempo, each thrust driving her higher. When her pussy starts to pulse, I use more pressure on her clit. And when she digs her nails into my forearm in ecstasy, I don't let up.

I fuck her through her climax, stroking deeper as she comes, grunting when she spasms around my cock. A few more erratic pumps of my hips, and I tip over the edge and empty inside her.

Damn, I want to wake up like this for the rest of my life.

Nat's quiet as we bask in the afterglow, letting our bodies and passion cool, but she grips my hand and presses it above her breasts, right over her heart.

"I love you, Tucker."

The words are hushed, but they're powerful all the same.

"Love you, too, sweetheart."

We snuggle, burrowing under the covers for way longer than we should, neither of us ready to start the day. This lazy snuggling is not a luxury we usually get on a weekday morning, but clearly, we could both use the time together, shielding ourselves from the world outside my bedroom door.

Eventually, though, the real world forces us from our cocoons.

It starts with a phone call from Griff. He and Brynn drove back to Memphis late Saturday night, and he's back to the grind, preparing for what is probably his final season.

"What's up?"

Natalie slips out of bed silently and drags on a T-shirt, then plucks her overnight bag off the floor. With a soft smile, she pads from the room.

"You talk to him today?" Based on the muffled sound of Griff's voice, he's in his truck, probably on his way to the stadium for practice.

"It's seven a.m. No, I haven't."

"You gotta be vigilant about this, Tuck. I can't be there to tag-team this with you. I hate that it's falling on your shoulders, but if she comes back to town—"

"I know." I scrub a hand down my face.

Our oldest brother's gone full hermit since Cam showed up at dinner on Saturday night.

"I'll handle it." Even as I assure him, my chest tightens. That promise is like adding another plate to the ones I'm already spinning.

"All right, keep me posted. I'll call when I can. We'll see y'all in two weeks."

While Natalie showers, I pull on a pair of shorts and shuffle to the kitchen. Cam, who's back on night shifts this week, comes in through the back door as I'm slicing a banana over the blender.

"Hey." He toes off his shoes and bends to give Goose scratches. "Took Shaw a bag of bagels from Hollow Haven this morning. When I knocked on his door, he yelled about being left the fuck alone." He shakes his head. "But the bag wasn't on the doormat when I backed down the driveway."

I assess my best friend, overwhelmed by the care he shows my family and by how often he steps up for me without even being asked.

Cam smirks as he steps around the table. "You good?"

Emotion clogs my throat, but I cough it away. "Yeah, I'm good. And I'm so fucking glad I let you convince me to stick that green crayon nub up my nose."

He barks a laugh. "Ah, the Green Crayon Incident." With a hip propped against the counter, he peels a banana. "I know you've got a lot going on right now. Learning how to be a dad, the gym, my sister..." He rolls his eyes at the last part. "And Griff is back in game mode, so I don't mind stepping up."

I silently beg Cupid to get off his ass and pelt Trixie with an arrow for the man in front of me. My cousin's a knucklehead for not seeing what's so obvious to the rest of us, and this guy deserves a big love I know Trixie is capable of.

When Cam finishes his breakfast, he shuts himself in his bedroom to get some shut-eye, and I trade spots with Nat, hopping in the shower while she stands at the sink to apply her makeup.

Outside, I load Goose into her SUV, then pull his mom in for a steamy goodbye kiss.

"Have a good day, shutterbug."

I release her and pivot for my Jeep, but Natalie clutches my shirt and tugs me back, her mouth on mine again, this kiss deeper and longer. Our goodbyes are always passionate, but this one makes the rest seem like chaste interactions. The connection is fierce yet tender, like she's an artist sculpting a beautiful masterpiece with each caress of her tongue and press of her lips. Like she's pouring every ounce of her love into it.

When we part, my legs are Jell-O. "Wow."

Her mouth curves, but it's not a full smile. "I love you."

"And I love you." I press my lips to the tip of her nose and grab her ass, pulling her in. "Now get in this car before I drag you back inside to take care of this." I press the evidence of how much that kiss affected me into her hips, then swat her rear. "See you tonight."

With another half smile, she gets behind the wheel.

And after she's reversed down the driveway, I follow and spend the entire drive to the gym hot and bothered.

It's a typical Wednesday at Club Lacey Fitness.

Mr. Abernathy walks his mile on the treadmill; Mrs. Abernathy picks him up in their Town Car.

Chris flirts with three women—two of the town's single moms, and Mabel, who's having none of it.

Bethany rolls her eyes seventeen times before lunch.

I forget it's my turn to empty the trash can in the break room and have to race to the dumpster out back as the garbage truck rolls slowly by.

The dentist Marissa works for in Memphis takes half days on Wednesdays, so she's started FaceTiming me as soon as she gets home from picking Boden up from daycare. Today, he grins and says "Tuh" as soon as he sees me.

That single syllable makes my heart thunk, but I'm holding out for the day he calls me Daddy.

I miss him like crazy during the week, and I hate that our time together is limited to weekends right now, but I truly believe in letting our relationship unfold naturally.

By four o'clock, I'm counting down the minutes until I can meet Natalie at home and finish what that goodbye kiss started.

When she sends me a text just after four, asking me to meet her in front of the gym, a thrill shoots down my spine. It's probably wishful thinking, but there's a chance she's visiting for a little afternoon tumble in the back seat of her car.

That buzz becomes an unpleasant chill when I stroll out to the parking lot and find her waiting beside her SUV with tears rolling down her cheeks.

"What's wrong?" I hold my arms out and step in close, but she waves me off. Red flag number one.

Red flag number two? Goose barks at me from the car, and when I peek through her open window to greet him, I notice the dog bed that's been in my living room for over a month on the back seat next to where he's strapped in.

And on the passenger seat, the hefty toiletry bag she brought on our weekend getaway sits beside her purse. Red flag number three.

I panic, but I dig deep and force my voice to remain even as I prop my hands on my hips. "Going somewhere?"

While she inhales, like she's finding her bearings, I pray I'm wrong. Fuck, I've never wanted to be wrong more than I do right now.

"Yeah. I'm going back to Austin." She lets the tears course down her cheeks, her hazel eyes squinted against the afternoon sun.

"This a brief visit? Or an extended stay?" My voice trembles despite my best effort.

"Tucker, let me get this out. Please."

I cross my arms and ignore the beads of sweat that roll down my back. I'd invite her inside to have this chat in my office, but something tells me she'd refuse.

Instead, I'm getting crushed in hell-level weather, with heat radiating off the asphalt around me.

Fitting, I suppose, given that mentally, I'm already in hell.

She presses her lips together, lips I tasted mere hours ago, then sucks in a shuddering breath. "I'm going back to Austin, and I need you to let me go. I need you to give me space. I loved spending the summer with you, and you will always be special to me. But I need to move on, and I can't do that here. I don't think a long-distance situation will work, so I need to end this. Now. But I also need you to promise me that you'll move on, too."

Every word out of her mouth sounds rehearsed. Her phrasing is too intentional. Damn it. How many times did she run through it on her way here? It isn't lost on me that each statement centers around her *needs*, because I've promised to always give them to her.

I chuff a humorless laugh. "Move on? You want me to move on? Please enlighten me; how I'm supposed to *move on* from the love of my life?"

She shutters her eyes, causing more tears to spill. "You can't say things like that. This is already hard enough."

"Too fucking bad, Nat." My throat closes up, but I force the words out anyway. "I'm not about to go easy on you when you want to break us apart. For no fucking reason, it seems."

"It's not—"

A patron exits the gym, his presence making her snap her mouth shut.

When he's shut inside his vehicle, she pulls her shoulders back. "It's not for no reason, damn it. You have a precious son, and you deserve the chance to build a family for him."

"I thought that's what *we* were doing—together." I tug at my hair until it hurts. "Before I even knew about Boden, I told you there are many ways to make a family. Sure, this isn't the conventional way to do it, but who gives a fuck about conventions?"

"But maybe you and Marissa—" She clamps her mouth closed.

Ah, now I see. She's bowing out because she thinks Marissa and I should trial run a romance, see if we're compatible. Like falling in love is as simple as trying on an article of clothing.

I clench my jaw, grinding my teeth until it hurts.

The pain is nothing compared to the ache in my chest.

"So this is about Marissa? Even though I've repeatedly assured you that I have *zero* interest in her, you've unilaterally decided that we should be together? With no regard for what I want?"

She puffs out her chest, but her bottom lip trembles. "You—you said I was the boss, remember?"

Fuck, I want to throttle her as badly as I want to kiss her. *Natalie, you beautiful fool, what are you doing?*

I step closer. "Yeah, well guess what? You can't *boss* me into falling out of love with you."

Her lips part, but no sound comes out. That's what I thought. She has no counter for that one.

As my anger boils over, my brain urges me to spew vitriol her way. My heart pipes up, whispering that if I do, I'll regret it.

Unfortunately, my brain wins this round.

"When we fucked this morning, did you know then it was the last time?"

"Tucker—" She sobs.

"Answer the question, Natalie." I can't keep the bitterness out of my tone. "Did you wake up this morning knowing you were going to break my heart today, then fuck me anyway? Or was this a spontaneous decision?" I glance at my watch. "It's kinda late to be getting on the road. You planning on driving all night?"

She sniffles. "I reserved a hotel in Texarkana."

"Oh, so this isn't spontaneous, then." My fucking heart cracks in two. "How long have you been planning on leaving me?"

Her already blotchy face turns red. "You make it sound like I concocted some nefarious plan to hurt you—"

"What about Cam?" I bite out. "Have you told your brother you're leaving town?"

She nods once. "I stopped by your house on my way here."

The fuck? And he didn't warn me, didn't text with a head's-up that my world was minutes from shattering?

As quickly as my anger at him rises, it washes back out again. She would've begged him not to tell me, and his loyalty will always belong to her first. As it should.

I don't have the energy to stay mad at him anyway. He's losing her, too.

Just like I know I won't stay angry with Natalie. I love her too damn much, and she loves me. She believes she's sacrificing her happiness for me, but she doesn't get that her martyrdom is futile.

I can't have true happiness without her. As much as I love Boden and my family, if I don't have her, I'll never be complete.

Grasping at straws, I move closer. "How long do you expect this twisted experiment of yours to last, huh?"

She bunches her brows, parting her lips, but she doesn't reply.

So I rephrase. "How long do you expect me to stay away from you, shutterbug?"

"I-I'm not negotiating a timeline with you."

I take another step, but this time she halts my progress with her hand.

"Please." The pain in her voice rips my heart to shreds. "Don't. You have to let me go."

Frustration bubbles up inside me. "No."

"Tucker." Her face crumples in agony, a fresh wave of tears spilling over. "I won't take your future away from you."

Now it's my turn for tears. Hot, angry drops scorch my skin. I clasp the sides of her neck. "Don't you see that's exactly what you're doing? You're the only future I want."

No words, just a resigned shake of her head.

Fuck, she's breaking both of our goddamn hearts.

I swipe her tears away with my thumbs, but more fall in their place. "Will you at least text when you get there, let me know you're safe?"

"I'll text Cam."

My gut plummets to the searing-hot parking lot. Breaking off communication? Shit, she's being ruthless. She probably thinks it will be better this way, to make a clean break.

What she doesn't realize? A Lacey goes down swinging. I'll concede this round to her, let her have some distance, give her time to miss me. It's gonna fucking hurt to be apart, but I'm not giving up.

Knowing I'll have the opportunity to fight another day, I press my lips to her forehead and retreat. For now.

She quickly slides into her seat and fastens her seat belt. Before she pulls away, she gives me a sad wave.

I watch her car until it's out of sight. Watch her drive away with my shattered heart.

On shaky legs, I make my way back to my office and snag my keys from my desk. I start the ignition, and though cold air blasts from the vents, I can't feel it. I sit in numb disbelief, my mind a jumbled mess. How'd we get here? How could something wonderful and right turn into *this*?

I survey the lineup of ducks on my dash, stopping first at the yellow photographer duck and then at the newest edition beside it. The tiny baby blue rubber duckling I found perched on the door handle last week.

The short trip home is a blur, one of those out-of-body drives that feels like a fever dream.

When I turn into the driveway, Cam is sitting on the front porch steps, elbows on his thighs and a beer bottle dangling between his knees.

"Thought you were on tonight." I lower to the concrete step beside him.

He twists the lid off a second beer and hands it over. "Heidecker traded shifts with me."

"Hmm." I take a pull of the hoppy liquid and relish the way it burns down my throat.

"Shitty day."

Understatement. How can a day that began as perfectly as this one end so terribly?

"Yep."

What else is there to say? The most precious of people walked out of our lives today. At least he'll still get to talk to her. Me? I'll be out of my mind until I can hear her voice again.

We sit in silence, neither willing to move to the coolness of the indoors. Like remaining in this horrendous heat is our penance.

I've downed half of my beer when Cam finally speaks. "So." He stretches out his legs. "How are we getting her back?"

I tip my bottle toward him, and when he clinks his against it, I start laying out my plan.

Chapter Thirty-One

Natalie

I tap the X, closing out of the streaming site on my laptop, then burrow deeper into the heap of pillows I've piled against the headboard.

Not even Stephanie Zinone and the Pink Ladies can rescue me from this pit of despair.

With a whine, Goose rests his head on my leg. My dog is tired of my moping.

"I know, boy." I brush his fur out of his eyes. "This sucks."

If I created a pie chart to organize how I've spent my time since I've been back in Austin, its title would be *Natalie's Month of Misery*. One-third would be labeled with *Pretending to Be Fine at Work*. Another third would represent *Becoming One with Her Bed*. The final third would be split between *Pretending to Be Fine Around Friends and Family* and *Actual Adulting*, like grocery shopping, laundry, and caring for Goose. And in the corner would be a tiny asterisk with a footnote that reads *Cries Nonstop*.

I've replayed that parking lot scene with Tucker a thousand times since that deceptively sunny afternoon. His shock, anger, and heartbreak haunt me every time I close my eyes. It's a miracle I found the strength to drive away. I was so distraught that it didn't hit me until the last chorus of "Heartache Tonight" that my music app had chosen *that* song's bouncy riffs as the soundtrack for my escape. Tears flowed like unrelenting rain until Little Rock, then became intermittent as I drove to the lonely hotel room awaiting me in Texarkana.

Over and over, I've agonized over every decision I made that day. Did I wake up that morning knowing that was the day I'd say goodbye to Tucker? Not completely. I knew I had to leave, and I figured the least painful way would be to have all my things packed and ready to go when I broke the news.

Like an excruciating final task on the world's most depressing to-do list.

But that morning, when I woke in his arms and he made love to me, a little voice warned that if I didn't do it that day, I'd lose my nerve. And at the time, I was totally convinced that taking myself out of the equation was the right thing to do.

Now, though?

"You did the right thing" has become a constant refrain in my mind, a never-ending torturous reminder I recite in weak moments, when I almost break down and call to beg him to forgive me.

But it feels more and more like a lie every day I'm not with him.

I drag my fingertip over the trackpad and hover the cursor on the desktop folder I haven't allowed myself to open since I returned to Austin. I should close my laptop and resume my rotting. But self-loathing creeps in and takes over, and before I can stop myself, I click to open it.

The folder contains the hundreds of photos I took of Tucker this summer. From that first consultation at the gym all the way through our last night together, I captured the magic of the man I fell in love with, all versions of him.

There's professional Tucker, in the cage with Luca, talking to members, and joking with his employees. There's friendly Tucker, who's the star of the shots from our private session at the studio, when I asked him to tell his story, and in pictures from the wedding where he served as a groomsman, when my gaze was drawn to him all night. Carefree Tucker appears in dozens of candids I snapped with my camera or phone when he wasn't looking: close-ups of his colorful tattoos, random shots of him hard at work in the kitchen, several of him tussling with Goose in the backyard or on his bike or with Cam on the couch, laughing. Family Tucker is documented through shots of him with the Laceys at the farmhouse or around town, as well as in the more recent pictures of him and Boden, with their matching happy smiles.

I don't let myself linger too long on the ones that exhibit in-love Tucker, the many selfies we took over the months. When I suggested a photo, he never once refused or rolled his eyes. He was always willing to indulge my need to preserve our memories. God, I miss him so much it hurts to breathe.

As raw as an exposed nerve, I drag my cursor to the X in the corner. But before I can close the folder, a thumbnail near the bottom catches my eye. I click to enlarge the image and am transported to the instant it happened.

We were saying goodbye to Marissa and Boden after the backyard splash day. Tucker had just passed his son back to his mother, and the little guy waved to his father, and without prompting, said, "Bye-bye, Tuh." In the frame, Marissa's head is tipped back in delight, half hidden by her son, whose eyes are riveted on his dad. But Tucker? His eyes, wide and full of wonder, are only for me, his amazement evident in his broad, shocked grin and raised brows.

It was the first time Tucker's son had called him by his name, and the man's foremost instinct was to look at *me*. To beam at me with a did-you-just-hear-that expression of utter joy on his face.

Every single photo of Tucker in this folder could fall into the "Tucker In Love" category, I realize. Because he gives his whole heart to everything, to every person, he holds dear: his gym, his friends, his family, his son. And to me. He gave that wonderful, beautiful heart to me, and I fucking walked away.

I snap my laptop closed with a huff and hide under the bed-sheet.

Somewhere in the downy mass of pillows, blankets, and com-forters, my cell buzzes. I waffle between hunting for it or letting it go to voice mail, but curiosity trumps apathy, so I dig it out from between the folds of my comforter. At the name on the screen, a smidgen of comfort works its way through me. His timing is impeccable.

I accept the call and switch it to speakerphone. "Hey."

My brother and I have talked nearly every day since I left. He checks on me, asks about Goose, and keeps me up to date on Mom, James, and daily life in the Holler. The one topic he's forbidden from mentioning? The six-two tattooed gym owner I left behind.

Tucker's texted me here and there since I left. Just short mes-sages sent at random times. Notes like:

I'm thinking of you.

Have a good day.

I miss you.

Tell Goose I miss him.

I haven't responded to any, but damn, have I been tempted.

I'm starving for any scrap of information about him, though. Have he and Boden gotten more comfortable with each other? What new, cute mannerisms has his son developed since I've been gone? How are the Laceys doing? Have Griff and Brynn settled on a wedding date? How's Shaw? Have Tucker and Marissa grown closer in the past month?

Scratch that last one from the record. I couldn't handle know-ing they have, even if my suspicion that they might was the sole reason I left.

"Hey." His voice is a little distant and muffled, like he's speaking through his truck's Bluetooth. It's just after seven on a Sunday morning, so he must be on his way home from the station. "How's your weekend?"

I chew on my cheek. "Same as all the others." He knows I'm sad, but I haven't given him a true peek behind the curtain. The last thing I want is for him to know that if I didn't have a job and a dog that depends on me, I'd morph into a sloth.

"Yeah? What are Liv and the girls up to?"

This is Cam-speak for *Have you left your house recently or spent time with people who care about you?*

"Chloe started four-year preschool. She'll be in kindergarten next year."

There. A generic update should suffice. The truth is, I haven't seen Liv and her family in a couple weeks. I've made excuses each time she's invited me to dinner or asked if I could hang out.

"Yeah, you mentioned that the last time I asked about them."

"Oh."

He sighs. "And your dad?"

I perk up a bit. "He's good. Saw him Friday night."

What I don't tell him? That I saw my father for a total of ten minutes when he dropped off the grocery order I didn't have the energy to pick up.

But at least there's food in my kitchen.

"Mm-hmm. Did you know he called Mom yesterday?"

Fuck. Alarms bells clang in my mind. *Abort! Abort now!*

Instead of cooking up an excuse to end the call unscathed, my brain joins forces with my mouth in a moment of absolute weakness, and I spew the one question I've refused to ask over the past four weeks.

"How is he?"

For a moment, he's silent, like he's weighing his answer. It's pure agony.

Finally, he says, "How do you think he is? He's miserable."

I cover my eyes, like the action will keep the tears at bay, and breathe through my nausea. Might as well dig this hole deeper, right? "So have he and, um, have he and Marissa—"

Cam snorts, the sound harsh. "Have he and Marissa started dating and fallen madly in love and started working on baby number two? No, Natalie. Not even close."

His uncharacteristic pulse of anger cuts, but I've been expecting it for weeks now.

He sighs, causing the line to crackle. "I'm sorry. That wasn't fair."

"It was." I sniffle, unable to hide my emotions any longer. "It was fair. God, I really fucked up, didn't I?" Before he can respond, I make a confession so vulnerable it comes out in a whisper. "I miss him."

"Nat," he chides, "this isn't unfixable. Call him."

"I can't. He'll never forgive me."

"You know that isn't true."

When I don't respond, he goes on.

"I get why you thought you had to end things with him, even though it was a wild swing. And I know he's done his damnedest to reassure you of this, but I'll repeat it anyway: There is nothing romantic between Tucker and Marissa, and there never will be. They share a kid, so yeah, they'll always be in each other's lives. But you belong in his life, too. He's juggling a lot right now, but if you reached out, I'm convinced it would fix 99 percent of his problems."

My heart plummets. Oh God, I've *really* fucked up. I knew Tucker had a lot on his plate. A surprise kid, his brother's sudden departure at dinner last month, keeping his business going. I stupidly thought removing myself would help, not hinder.

"You left thinking you were doing what's best for him," Cam says, "but I've known the guy almost all my life. I'd say that makes me an authority on what's best for him. And that's *you*, Nat."

Air wheezes from my lungs. "You really think so?"

He chuckles, the sound making me homesick. "Wouldn't say it if I didn't believe it." His ignition cuts off. "I just got home, but I can call you later if you need to talk more."

I wipe at my eyes and sit a little straighter. "Thank you for checking on me."

"Always. I love you."

"Love you, Cam."

It takes me fourteen hours to work up the nerve to send a tiny, three-word text in response to the dozen or so Tucker's sent over the past month. I may stew over it and consider deleting it a hundred times, but when I finally do press Send, a weight lifts and I breathe easier than I have in weeks.

I miss you.

Four seconds after the message is marked as delivered, he calls. "Hey."

His relieved exhale is palpable from seven hundred miles away.

"Hey, Nat."

—◆—

"I can't believe I let you talk me into this." I give my best friend the stink eye as I wipe sweat from my brow.

We're on a bench in a neighborhood park a couple blocks from my condo. When I texted her last night and asked her to come over, I didn't expect that she'd show up this morning and demand that we come here instead of chatting in my air-conditioned home.

"It's eight a.m. I figured we'd beat the heat. Guess I was wrong." Liv adjusts the bill of her cap and slurps her iced coffee. "Chloe, that's far enough."

We watch her oldest daughter help her fourteen-month-old sister jump through the faint spray of water that shoots from the mouth of a concrete fish.

Damn, kids have got it made with these splash pads. Adult-sized attractions like this would be fabulous to combat these brutal temperatures. Mid-September is as hot as mid-July in Texas. Sometimes hotter.

Goose stretches out under the bench Liv and I share, panting. He'd love to be in the mix with Chloe and Sophie, but I can't let him off his leash here. I'll let him splash around before we leave if I can stand the direct sun for that long.

The memory of Goose and Boden in the water hits me like a bittersweet slap to the face.

Soon, I remind myself.

"So..." Liv drags out. "Catch me up, please."

"We talked yesterday morning while he drove to Memphis to see Boden."

She shifts my way, raising her brows.

"I told him I think I'm ready to start the process of moving back."

Liv squeals, though the sound is cut off abruptly. "Wait. Start the process? Girl, load up your car and get your hiney to that one-goat town *today*. What are you waiting for?"

With a light laugh, I shake my head. "There's a lot to consider. I can't just leave today."

Even if I'm itching to pack up Goose and anything that will fit in my SUV and lead-foot it back to Tucker today.

I'm dying to get back to the man who's called me every night since we first talked one week ago. He's been as patient and kind and loving as he's always been, urging me to stop apologizing and reassuring me that I'm forgiven a million times over. He's ended every call with "I'll talk to you tomorrow. I love you."

Not once has he asked me to move back, though. He's let me come to the decision on my own. And yesterday, I finally told him I'm ready to go home.

What he doesn't know is I took the first step in this process a week ago. The day after I texted Tucker last week, I called Wayne to see if he was still interested in turning his business over to me. Two nights ago, I had dinner with my dad and informed him of my decision. He's sad that I'm leaving, but more than that, he's proud of me for following my heart.

That's all I've ever wanted for you, mija.

My next visit was with Regina, who assured me that I could continue seeing her virtually. She's probably ready for a reprieve from me and my tears; over the past month I've seen her once or twice a week, needing her help coping with my moronic decision to leave Tucker.

I've already talked to Mom, James, and Cam, but I swore them to secrecy. I want to be the one who tells Tucker. Needless to say, they're ecstatic.

"Everything that needs doing here can be handled from there. You might have to come back and clean out your studio, but you've got to be tired of being away from that man. You love him; he loves you. Go love each other...repeatedly. Makeup *smex* is the best."

Liv's deliberate mispronunciation backfires when her four-year-old asks, "Mommy, what's *smex* mean?"

We brave the heat for another hour, but when the kids start whining and Goose's fur has dried from his dashes through the sprinklers, we make the short walk back to my condo. By the time we round the corner onto my street, my tank and shorts are plastered to my body and I'm grievously regretting not bringing a hair tie.

Four steps past the corner, I notice that my front door is open and grab Liv's arm in panic.

"*Wait*," I whisper-shout. "I think I'm being robbed."

She brings the girls' wagon to a halt and whips her head toward my condo. "What?"

I throw out an arm. "My front door is wide open. I know I didn't leave it like that." With Goose's leash wrapped around my wrist, I dig my phone from my back pocket. "Should we hide while I call the police?"

Liv takes off, pulling her daughters with her down the sidewalk as if she's not the least bit concerned that there could be armed assailants lying in wait inside my home.

"Liv!"

She ignores me, so I have no choice but to follow. Only when I reach my neighbor's driveway do I register the U-Haul truck parked at the curb in front of my unit.

"*Liv*," I sputter. "They brought a truck to haul off my stolen goods. Get back here."

When a man carrying a box exits my front door and my best friend *waves* at him, I'm certain I'm in the middle of a nightmare. The kind that feels like reality until something so wacky happens that the subconscious finally gets the memo that it's a dream.

Wacky incident number one? The thief looks an awful lot like my cousin Diego...

"Hey, Nat," he calls as he trundles up the truck's ramp.

I freeze, wavering between dialing 911 and letting the dream play out. When my dad passes through the doorway with a box a moment later, I spring into action, meeting him at the end of my driveway.

"Morning, Natalia." He pauses to kiss my forehead before continuing to the ramp.

Liv grins like the cat that got the cream.

Next through the door, carrying two suitcases that look suspiciously like my mom's, is James. My stepfather winks at me as he passes.

"What the hell is going on?" I ask.

Liv simply shrugs, still grinning, as Chloe cheers from the wagon.

My garage door rolls open with a familiar grinding sound, making me jolt, and when two ball cap-wearing figures emerge, hefting a mattress between them, my heart kicks into overdrive, thumping against my ribs so fast I'm glad one of them has medical training. I may need it. Unbidden, tears pool in my eyes.

The two men pause in the driveway, holding the queen-size mattress like it weighs nothing, my watery vision making them blurry. The man facing me, with a navy blue HHFD cap covering his dark blond locks, smiles and tilts his head. Then the man in the backward Lacey Farms cap twists his neck and locks his eyes on mine.

After a month of free-floating, my world spins back into orbit.

CHAPTER THIRTY-TWO

NATALIE

"What's happening?" A teary, happy, incredulous laugh bursts out of me.

Tucker moves, and as if the moment were choreographed, Diego swoops in and keeps the mattress from falling.

The man I've missed like a limb strides over and doesn't stop until the toes of his sneakers brush the toes of my flip-flops. He searches my face, and I do the same to his, checking for differences a month apart might have caused. Other than the bruise-colored half-moons beneath his eyes, he's as excessively handsome as ever.

I'm as besotted as ever, too.

Though the two of us are motionless, the rest of the bandits carry on with their thievery.

Finally, I find my voice again. "What's happening?"

"I'm bringing you home, shutterbug."

With a sob, I loop my arms around his torso and hold on for dear life. He lifts me off the ground, and I hook my legs around his hips and bury my face in his neck, inhaling his scent and his goodness.

Goose's leash slips from my hold, but a quick "got it" keeps me from panicking.

"Oh my God, I've missed you," I whisper into his skin.

"I've missed you, too." He adjusts his hold and hugs me tighter. "I need you to promise that I'll get 100 percent of my daily dosage of these for the rest of our lives."

"Done."

He cranes back, and I do the same, taking in his gorgeous face. One dip of my eyes to his lips, and he surges forward, kissing me with abandon, uncaring that four members of my family and my best friend are in the vicinity.

When he squeezes my hip, I lower my legs and slide down his body.

The moment my feet hit the ground, baffled questions spew from my lips. "What? How? When did you—why are you stealing my mattress?"

He smirks. "It's way better than mine, so it made the cut." He pops a shoulder. "As for the rest, you told me you were ready to come home. That's the only green light I needed."

"But the truck…" I glance over my shoulder at the vehicle my family members continue to fill.

"The minute we hung up yesterday, I called in reinforcements. After my visit with Boden, Cam and James met me in Little Rock, and we got on the road. Got here late last night and found a hotel near the truck rental place. It killed me to be so close to you and not rush straight here, by the way." He tucks a strand of hair behind my ear. "After we picked up the truck this morning, we met your dad and cousin at a coffee shop nearby. Liv's job was to get you out of the house so we could pack."

Happy tears splash my sweaty tank top as overwhelming love and gratitude for these people swamp me.

"Why were the rental truck and moving necessary *today*?" I wag my head. "This couldn't have waited?"

"Fuck no, it couldn't wait." He brushes a thumb over my cheek. "You tell me you want to come home, I'm making it happen. Immediately. I wasn't about to give you a chance to change your mind. Like I told you—I'm the man who's gonna handle your shit. This is me handling it."

With every assurance he makes, my heart stitches itself back together a little more. It's been like this all week. I don't deserve him, but I'm keeping him.

"Thank you for handling it." I smooth a hand over his chest. "Even though it's kinda abrupt."

"Abrupt, huh? I saw that realtor's business card and the notepad with the list of moving companies on your counter. When were you planning on putting it on the market?"

I pin him with a look, though I give him the truth. "I have an appointment with the realtor tomorrow morning."

"So we're moving the timeline up a bit, then. And that appointment can be virtual." He kisses my cheek, then pulls back. "We started packing up the essentials. Books, photo albums, artwork. Clothes, toiletries. Now that you're here, you can decide what furniture goes and what stays. Then we can head to your studio space and pack up what you want from there."

"But—" I sputter. "Where the hell will we put all this stuff once we get home?"

His lips curve, like he noticed the way I used the word *home*, then in true Tucker fashion, he ducks his head and angles closer. "We'll figure it out when we get there. I just want you near me, sweetheart."

Never thought I'd wing a long-distance move, but here we are. Shockingly, the not knowing doesn't stress me as much as I would've thought. It feels...right.

"I love you." I cup his cheek, running the pads of my fingers over his stubble.

"Love you, too."

When we kiss again, Cam hollers, "All right, lovebirds. Save it for later. We've got work to do."

I spin and pad to my brother, who's standing in the shade next to the garage. "Thank you," I whisper as I hug him tight.

"Anything for my favorite sister."

After I've doled out grateful hugs to Dad, James, and Diego, the men get back to work and give me a minute of privacy with Liv. My best friend's not a chronic crier like I am, but she dashes away a stray tear as I approach.

"I should get these hooligans home, let y'all finish up."

I plant kisses on Chloe's and Sophie's sweet heads, then grab their mom in a crushing hug. "I'm going to miss you like crazy, Livvie."

"You're my ride or die, Natalie Torres." She places her hands on my shoulders, her expression serious. "Never forget that you're a badass with a good ass. Go write the next part of your story with that gorgeous man. I'm so effing proud of you."

I help her load her girls into their car seats, and after one final hug, she waves and drives away.

I watch until her minivan turns the corner, hugging my torso. When a pair of strong, warm hands curve over my shoulders, I lean back into the solid frame behind me.

"You'll still see each other," he promises.

"Mmm."

He presses a kiss to my temple and smacks my ass. "C'mon, shutterbug. Let's get you home."

⸎

It's just before midnight when Tucker steers his Jeep into the Holly Holler town square. When he parks alongside the sidewalk at the intersection where he almost crashed his bike into me all those weeks ago, I roll down the window and inhale a deep breath of the fresh night air.

Home, my soul sings.

Its song is not only for the ground beneath us and the buildings that surround us. It's for the faces who share this zip code, for their generous spirits and unwavering optimism. It's for the man who sits beside me, most of all.

The town's tucked away for the night, the businesses shuttered and in dreamland, all except for the Hoot 'n' Holler. Its neon sign glows, a bright contrast to the darkness that's settled over the town like a blanket. In the square, the gazebo stands in the moon's ethereal spotlight, a beacon to all who call the Holler home.

Tucker sweeps a hand over my hair. "Want to walk for a bit?"

Tomorrow, there will be adulting to do. Calls to realtors and banks, business discussions with Wayne, and a search for a place to live. Not to mention dealing with the U-Haul that Cam and James parked at my parents' house when they got into town a half hour ago.

But all of those affairs will keep until the light of day.

Right now, I'm saying yes to a midnight stroll through my hometown with the man I love.

We leave the windows half down for Goose, who's snoozing in the back seat after a long, eventful day. As I push the door open, my muscles ache from overuse, but I relish the slight bite of pain, welcome it because it signifies a new beginning.

Tucker rounds the Jeep and laces his fingers through mine, then guides me down the sidewalk. The day's heat has surrendered, giving the night air a slight nip that makes me glad I grabbed Tucker's Club Lacey Fitness sweatshirt from the back seat.

We stop at the corner across the street from Wayne's studio, catty-corner from where I stood with Mom and James to watch the Founders' Day parade four months ago, oblivious to how tremendously the ensuing weeks would change my life.

"I want to get a new awning." I point to the hunter green one that's held court over the studio for as long as I can remember. "Maybe black-and-white polka dots? Or stripes?"

Tucker hums. "Either of those would be fun and playful."

"And artwork on the window." I wave my hand, envisioning my Shutterbug logo painted on the glass. "That'll be my first priority. I want to update the foyer area and front desk. And the walls definitely need a new coat of paint."

He kisses my head. "It's going to look amazing. I'm excited for you to breathe new life into that space."

A symphony of crickets keeps us company as we amble down the perimeter of the square. My mind is a kaleidoscope of possibilities for the studio, so I don't realize Tucker's steered us down the Heart Path until we're a couple of segments in and he stops and points to the bushes near the playground section of the square.

"Look," he says. "There's Lisa Marie."

Sure enough, that wily escape artist is grazing on the grass next to the swings.

When I turn back to comment about her, Tucker is no longer standing behind me. Instead, he's got one knee on the Heart Path, the other bent in front of him. And he's holding a small square box.

Inside it, a stunning oval diamond glints in the moonlight.

I cover my open mouth with a palm as goose bumps erupt all over.

"I need you to take one more leap with me today, shutterbug." Eyes shining, he takes my hand in his. "When I explained to you how today happened, I left one detail out." He raises the ring higher. "What I didn't tell you is that after you said you were ready to come home, I drove straight to a jeweler in Memphis. I don't want to wait another day to lock you down."

Laughing, I wipe my tear-soaked hand on my shorts.

"I know this is fast, but I don't care. We've got a lot to figure out, but I don't doubt that we will. I believe in us, in you. And the people who love us believe in us, too. Cam and James gave their blessings on the drive down, and I got your father's this morning.

So I'm not waiting, sweetheart." He squeezes my hand gently. "You fit in my life like you were always meant to be in it. You're beautiful, and funny, and loyal, and I want to spend the rest of my life handling your shit."

I huff a chuckle, and he laughs in response.

"You've become my purpose," he says, sobering. "You and Boden. Your heart was meant to find a home here, with us. I love you with every ounce of my soul."

Tears spill from my eyes unchecked as I full on ugly cry, but my grin is so wide it makes my cheeks ache.

Twin drops crest Tucker's dark lashes as he gazes up at me. "Marry me, Natalie Torres."

It's the easiest yes of my life.

Epilogue

Tucker

"They say it's good luck if it rains on your wedding day." Griff eyes the ominous clouds that have been hovering over the farm all damn morning and early afternoon.

With a glare, I pull one of his navy suspenders and let it go with a snap. "Go tell that to my bride, you fucker."

He rubs his pec. "Shit, that hurt."

"Wuss." I smirk.

He retaliates with a quick jab to my bicep.

"Cut it out, assholes." Shaw adjusts the sprigs of greenery that Trixie pinned to his white button-down.

She peers over her shoulder as she works on Cam's. "Don't you touch that."

My brother raises his hands and takes a step back. "You got it, Trix."

When it's my turn, my cousin smooths the fabric of my vest and deftly pins the boutonniere in place. "Natalie is the most beautiful bride, Tuck. I'm so happy for y'all."

Her words should comfort me, but they only make me more anxious to get this show on the road. The impending rain has made me tense, and it's only amplified by the number of hours my soon-to-be wife and I have been separated.

Aunt Dottie hustles from the giant white tent in my parents' backyard, her narrowed eyes fixed on the sky. "Everything's good to go for the after-party," she says as she approaches. "Caterers will be set up by the time the ceremony's over. Trix and the band are all set up, too. This is going to go off without a hitch," she promises with a pinch to my cheek.

"Who needs a wedding planner when we've got Dorothea?" Trixie jokes as her mother hoofs it to the back deck. "Now," she says, smoothing the ruffles of her pale pink dress, "I'm going to pass out the girls' bouquets and get everyone lined up." She blows me a kiss and follows her mother's path to the house.

My oldest brother smacks my shoulder. "Nervous?"

"Nah. Just ready to get to the good part."

Griff wags his brows, and Cam wallops his arm in the same place I just hit him. "Watch it, that's my sister."

As if any of us need the reminder.

"Why am I being abused on my little brother's wedding day?" Griff pouts. "And everyone knows he was talking about the *cake*, Camden."

In my most solemn tone, I say, "I was definitely talking about the cake. Lisa Marie makes a mean buttercream."

Griff pouts. "Can't believe I'm going to be the last Lacey brother standing. Brynn and I were engaged first."

Shaw and I share a look, the hint of a smile twitching his lips.

It seems two-thirds of the Lacey brothers prefer brief engagements.

The next fifteen minutes pass in a blur.

While my brothers and I stand behind the rows of white folding chairs that have been arranged to form a makeshift aisle, greeting the guests as they arrive, Wayne buzzes around, snapping photos of the scenery and the people, pride shining in his eyes.

Five and a half months ago—two weeks after I brought Nat home for good—Wayne Gann Photography officially became Shutterbug Photography, and almost the entire town showed up for a joint retirement-slash-grand opening celebration. The community's embraced its new photographer, keeping her calendar booked and her favorite Adidas well worn.

At three sharp, Dottie starts the music on the speaker she brought from the Hoot, signaling for my brothers and Cam—my best man, naturally—and I to take our spots to the right of the rustic square arch Shaw built for the ceremony's backdrop.

Emotions clog my throat as Dad escorts Mom down the aisle and again when James walks Isabel. Both moms beam from their seats in the front row.

The bridesmaids take their turns down the grassy aisle, each of them beautiful in long, flowy dresses in various cuts and styles, ranging in color from pale pink to dusty rose.

Marissa's stroll is slowed by the two-year-old ring bearer who clasps two of her fingers as he toddles beside her. When he spies me a few rows into his procession, he releases her to run as fast as his tiny legs allow.

"Dada!"

I swing him up into my arms to the sound of a collective "Aw" from the crowd.

I kiss his round cheek and pass him to his Uncle Cam.

Marissa collects herself and winks as she passes Mabel, who's seated behind my parents. When she slips into her spot in the bridesmaid lineup, she mouths "Sorry."

I'm all smiles in return. Nat and I promised each other we'd go with the flow on our special day, and nothing my little guy could do could negatively affect any of this.

Liv starts up the aisle with a freshly groomed Goose, who's sporting a pink bow tie and a sparkly leash, eliciting more *aws* from the guests. She takes her matron-of-honor position as her oldest daughter, Chloe, fulfills her flower girl duty perfectly, enthusiastically dropping pale pink rose petals as she practically floats toward us.

When she's in place in front of her mom, all eyes swivel to my parents' back deck.

I squint, only getting a glimpse of a full white skirt and Luis's navy dress slacks through the French doors that lead to the dining room.

My limbs tingle as excitement and nerves battle for dominance in my body. For weeks, we debated about whether we wanted a traditional first look during the ceremony or to have a private moment together before. But as I stand here waiting, I reconsider our final decision.

I haven't seen her or heard her voice since we kissed goodbye outside of the Hoot last night after our rehearsal dinner, and the anticipation is wreaking havoc on me.

As the guests stand, I'm so eager to see my bride that I throw tradition and protocol to the wind and barrel up the aisle. All the way to the end, I ignore the shocked gasps and chuckles that fill the air. Even my mother's astonished "Tucker Myles."

When I reach the wooden steps, Griffin shouts, "Tuck, that's supposed to happen *after*!"

Laughter and whistles erupt behind me as I cover my eyes with one hand and wrench the doors open.

"*Tucker*." Natalie's surprised tone soothes my nerves instantly. "What the hell?"

I grab the bouquet from her hand, keeping my eyes downcast and mostly covered so I can't see her face or more than the hem of her dress. "I just need a minute with your daughter, sir."

Luis takes the flowers with an amused chuckle. "Sure, sure. Don't keep the folks waiting, though."

"Yes, sir," I call as I drag Natalie to the kitchen.

I head straight for the pantry, and after a brisk knock on the door, I step inside and tug my bride in behind me.

I yank on the string dangling from the bulb overhead and face her, still shielding my eyes.

"So many questions, Tucker." Natalie takes my other hand. "First of all, did you just *knock* on the door to this pantry?"

"I used to take chances opening doors willy-nilly, but I've seen more of my future sister-in-law than is acceptable, so yeah. I knocked."

"Okay," she drags out the word. "We'll save that story for when we don't have sixty guests waiting for us. Next question: Why in the world did you stop our wedding and pull me in here?"

"I needed to see you. I know we agreed to a traditional first look, but I got so amped up while I was waiting, and I thought, fuck it, we're doing it now. In private. I want this moment to be just the two of us."

"Tucker." She pulls my hand from my face, but I keep my lids closed. "Look at me."

I obey, and the vision I'm met with takes my breath away. She's always beautiful, but today? She's glowing, so gorgeous and all mine.

"Nat." Words fail me. She's a masterpiece.

"Look at my handsome groom." She cups my cheek. But then her happy smile twists into a scowl, and my lovely bride stomps her foot. "Tuck," she whines. "Now Wayne can't get an authentic first look shot."

Shit. I didn't even consider that when I went all rogue bride-groom.

I quickly dig my phone from the back pocket of my pants. "Here." I smash my face to hers and half extend my arm in the confined space. "Selfie."

We both grin like loons as I push the button, capturing dozens of shots, including some of me kissing her cheek as she beams at the camera.

As I slide my phone back into my pocket, I finally take in her dress. "Fuck," I groan, swiping a hand down my face.

She cinches the skirt and pulls it to the side. "You like?"

"I love." I study every detail from the bodice down to the hem. "It's phenomenal. You're absolutely stunning." The dress is simple, yet classic. As I slide a hand over the band of fabric cinched at her waist, I can't help but zero in on the deep V of the neckline. "Holy shit, your tits look amazing."

She snort-laughs, and it's the sweetest music.

The pantry door flies open, and a bemused Trixie appears. "I looked in every damn room in this house. Thought you two had made a run for it."

"Sorry, Trix."

Natalie's father still waits patiently by the back doors, holding her bouquet.

"Out," my cousin bosses in her best teacher voice. "Let's get y'all hitched. I'm starving."

Beaming, my almost-wife tilts her head. "Give us a sec, Trix."

With a good-natured roll of her eyes, she spins away.

Once the door is closed again, I take Natalie's hands and kiss both sets of knuckles. "We're about to be *married*."

Her deliriously happy grin matches my own.

"Love you, shutterbug."

"Love you, Tuck." She clasps my forearms. "But if you interrupt our wedding again, I will spend the night snuggled up with Goose instead of my new husband."

"Yes, ma'am." I brush a kiss to her lips, then rush back to my spot at the altar to thunderous applause and whistles from the guests.

The ceremony is sweet and poignant. We recite the vows we wrote together, promising to be each other's home and adventure, lover and best friend. After exchanging rings and a kiss that makes my bride blush, we're pronounced husband and wife.

I raise a fist in the air, and the crowd cheers wildly.

Nat and I have just made it to the end of the aisle when the skies open. Guests shriek, scrambling and running to the cover of the tent a few feet away.

But me and my wife?

We stand in the downpour, laughing. I frame her joyful face and kiss her deeply, unbothered by the heavy drops that thoroughly soak us.

Gray clouds or sunshine, we'll face them together.

And then, hand in hand, we race to our reception, where we spend the next three hours kissing and eating and dancing, surrounded by those who love us best.

Read Griffin and Brynn's love story in
THE CHECK DOWN

He's the superstar tight end staging a comeback. She's the hit he never saw coming.

For ten-year NFL veteran Griffin Lacey, football is life. Months after being released from his team due to a season-ending injury, he's given an unexpected opportunity—a one-year contract to play for his hometown team. His game plan is clear: play to win, no distractions. But a fender bender on the way to the first home game changes everything.

College literature instructor Brynn Nelson is thirty and *not* thriving. Trapped in a dead-end relationship and stuck in a city that has never felt like hers, every day seems to blur into the next. When she accidentally rear ends a sports superstar, the chance encounter makes her long to break free from the rut she's in. He offers to show her the magic of her adopted city, and through their adventures, she reclaims her spark.

As Griffin and Brynn's connection deepens, they discover magic of a different sort—that love happens when you least expect it.

A sexy, swoony football romance and a love letter to one of America's most iconic cities, *The Check Down* is the first book in the Lacey Bros series.

ACKNOWLEDGEMENTS

I've often called my debut novel, *Between the Lines*, the book of my heart. But *Down for the Count* is the book of my soul. It's deeply personal, the most personal thing I've ever written, and I'm immensely proud of it. However, this book wouldn't exist without my village.

Mel, as always, your thorough insights and advice helped me make this story the best it can be. So happy you're part of my process! (Let's reunite that grumpy farmer with the love of his life, shall we?)

Beth, best editor in all the land, hard to believe this is our fourth book together. Thank you so much for polishing my words until they shine. As I've said before, you're stuck with me. *To whatever end.* I'm grateful for your work ethic, expertise, and friendship, and I swear I'm gonna get to Michigan soonish.

For my beautiful Guatemalan friend Maggie, thank you for sharing pieces of your culture and language with me for this story, and for reading it early to ensure that I got Natalie's character just right.

Beta readers Kayla, Emily, Jenah, and Mel: thank y'all for reading this one early and providing much-needed feedback and encouragement. I'm so happy y'all loved Tucker and Natalie's story.

To my friend Leigh, who morbidly requests for me to unalive characters for emotional depth: sorry I didn't kill Wayne in this one. Maybe you'll get your wish in the next book? Thank you for being unapologetically you, and for keeping me flush with pep talks and dream analysis. Oh, and for taking me on murdery Facebook Marketplace adventures. Imma keep l-i-v-i-n', just like my characters! (And if you didn't read that in a Matthew McConaughey voice...well, I'm disappointed.)

Jocelynn, my real-life Liv (minus the *smexy* advice, cause we know that makes you roll your eyes), thanks for being my ride-or-die. I'm so damn happy you moved into that classroom across the hall from me many moons ago. (Cue the forced proximity friendship trope!) Thank you for helping me workshop the hell out of every fictional scenario that pops into my brain, for saving me a seat at your family's table, and for believing in me on the days when I feel like I can't.

Page 349 Girlies-your enthusiasm for my work is unmatched. Thank you for coming in clutch right when I was having serious doubts about *that* storyline. Your exuberance gave me the confidence to see it through, and I'm so proud of the results.

Friends and family cheerleaders—I love you. Thank you for your encouragement, for buying my books, and for telling others about them. For helping me film silly reels and for being helpers at signing events. For Sonic gift cards and celebration dinners and book club invites and all the other ways y'all support this dream of mine.

To romance author Elliot Fletcher: you have no idea who the heck I am, but my eager anticipation for your book's release was a major motivator for me to finish writing this one. *Scotch on the Rocks* released two days after my deadline, a bookish carrot dangling just ahead, pushing me to reach Tucker and Natalie's finish line. I loved Callum and Juniper (and Shakespeare) so much.

My fellow indie romance authors—look at us, doing the damn thing. I'm endlessly proud of you and every milestone you reach, the big ones and the small ones. Thanks for your willingness to be open and answer questions from this no-name whenever I slide into your DMs.

For the many Bookstagram friends who continue to show up even when the algo's wonky, thank you for including my books in your posts, reels, and stories. For signing up for ARCs and my newsletter. For your genuine excitement every time I share something new. This journey wouldn't be possible (or nearly as fun) without y'all.

To my Lacey Bros Fan Club, thank you for being a safe place for me to share unhinged ideas and thirst trap reels. What a fun corner of the Internet we've carved for ourselves. Here's to one day meeting IRL and gushing about book boyfriends over skillet queso at Chili's.

Which leads me to *you*. As a reader of my words, I can't thank you enough for choosing this book and escaping into its pages for a while. As always, thank you for making this author's dreams come true.

ABOUT THE AUTHOR

Brandy Pelletier spends her days as a reading specialist and her nights and weekends reading anything she can get her hands on. She's wanted to become a published author ever since second grade, when her original story "How the Giraffe Got Its Long Neck" was published in her school district's annual writing anthology.

When she's not blasting Taylor Swift or attempting to tackle her ridiculously long TBR, she can be found collecting book boyfriends and dreaming of living in a witch cottage with her miniature schnauzer, Pippa.

Keep up with Brandy's writing journey by visiting her website www.brandypelletier.com, or say hi on social media.

instagram.com/thebrandyland

tiktok.com/thebrandyland